Sally Worboyes was born and grew up in Stepney with four brothers and a sister. She is married with three children and lives in Suffolk, running the highly successful Fen Farm residential writing courses. She has had several plays broadcast on Radio Four. Other work includes *Past Becomes the Present*, *Biding Time*, *Wishing Well*, *Where Bluebells Grow* (all for radio) and *The House Plant*, produced by Anglia TV.

Sally Worboyes' previous novels, *Wild Hops*, *Docker's Daughter* and *The Dinner Lady*, a trilogy of East End sagas, are all available from Headline.

Red Sequins

Sally Worboyes

HEADLINE

First published in 1996
by HEADLINE BOOK PUBLISHING

First published in paperback in 1997
by HEADLINE BOOK PUBLISHING

10 9 8 7 6 5 4 3 2 1

ISBN 0 7472 5519 9

Typeset by CBS, Felixstowe, Suffolk

Printed and bound in Great Britain by
Cox & Wyman Ltd, Reading, Berks

HEADLINE BOOK PUBLISHING
A division of Hodder Headline PLC
338 Euston Road
London NW1 3BH

This book is dedicated to Maurice Brody, who started with two sewing machines in the mid thirties and worked his way up to win the Queen's Export Award in the mid eighties. The East End rag trade would not have been the same without him.

My thanks to Olive and Rodney Brody for passing on their knowledge of the sequinned-fabric industry.

My thanks also to Kirsty Fowkes.

Chapter One

The train crash at Moorgate underground station in 1975 killed thirty-five people. Sandy Brent might have been one of the victims had she followed her normal daily routine. Even though she had not caught that ill-fated train, the 28th of February turned out to be the worst day of her life.

It was a glorious morning. The sun shone down through the thin mist and in at the car window, warming Sandy's face and highlighting her long copper hair. She usually travelled to work by tube, but today Roy had offered to give her a lift. There was something on his mind. It had been there since the night before. Soon he would say something – the signs were there: the clenching of his jaw, the hopeless sighs, the shifting in his seat and the old tell-tale restless moving of his head to left and right.

She thought about the clematis by the front door. It needed pruning. 'Do you think you might have thrown out the secateurs with the rose cuttings?' She hoped her subdued, nervous voice would not fail as she attempted to steer him away from making a damning confession. 'The dustmen are due tomorrow. I could go through the bin liner when I get

1

home . . . if you think they might be in there.'

Roy adjusted his glasses, let out a tiny sigh of boredom and indicated left. 'I knew I shouldn't have come in this way. Mile-long bloody queue.'

She was right. There was something on his mind and he didn't want her to talk domestic. With just ten minutes of the journey left she would have to keep talking if she hoped to fend off his rehearsed talk.

'I'm pleased with the new washing machine, even though it doesn't boil. Ninety degrees is fine. It can't just be the new washing powder. I bet you were impressed with the tea towels. Sparkling white.'

'Not really.' He made no effort to hide his rising anger.

'You have a look when you get home. The sheets as well.' She lit a cigarette, knowing he hated her to smoke in the car now that he had given up, but her needs right then were greater than his. 'Vi promised to give me her secret jam recipe today—'

'*Sandy*,' he broke in, 'we need to talk. About life, not jars of jam.'

''Course we need to talk. Nothing like a good rabbit to get you through the rush hour. Did I tell you I've seen the perfect wallpaper for our bedroom? William Morris – Honeysuckle?' She looked at him and smiled, painfully aware that she was behaving like an old married woman instead of her usual vibrant twenty-six-year-old self. It was an act she would much rather not be playing.

'Pink and green – just right.' She opened the window a fraction and blew smoke through the gap.

'You don't make it easy, do you, Sandy?' He changed

down into second gear and stopped at another red light. 'It's not working.' He spoke slowly to get the message across.

Sandy swallowed against the lump in her throat; she had heard this before, more than once. He might at least try to come up with something original. 'It was working last night, Roy, in bed, unless I was dreaming. I thought we did it twice. Was I dreaming?'

'Half an hour of screwing doesn't make a marriage. There are twenty-four hours in a day.' He tugged at his collar, loosening his tie. It was a waste of time. Beads of nervous sweat stood on his brow.

'You were timing us, then?' she said, unable to check the sarcasm, and then quickly sidetracking with, 'God I hate London traffic.'

'But the rest of us love it,' Roy muttered between clenched teeth. The queue was so long at the traffic lights that red, amber and green were going through a second sequence.

'There's not much, is there? Sex now and then, visits to the parents for Sunday lunch . . .' He let go of the steering wheel and splayed his hands. 'No joint hobbies. No joint interests. I love the theatre, you loathe it—'

'I don't loathe the theatre, Roy – just the boring plays. Now give me a lively musical and—'

'I don't like musicals! That's the point.'

'You used to . . . before the sudden change.' She raised her eyebrows and sighed. 'I wonder what the cause of that was?' Next he would be telling her that it was natural for people to change and have different interests. 'I expect you're moving on. That's what it'll be. It happens in films, doesn't it? He grows – she shrinks.' She pulled down the flap above

3

the window and checked in the mirror to see if her pale apricot lipstick had smudged. 'I hope ninety degrees won't shrink your pants . . . sorry . . . boxer shorts. Them being brand new . . .'

'Maybe you should move in with your mum and dad for a while to see—'

'No, that's OK thanks.' Remaining cool, she stubbornly refused to participate in his prepared colloquy. 'I'm happy in our place. And anyway, I'll need the plums from the tree to make jars of jam.' She carefully wiped away the lipstick from the corner of her mouth and wished she had the guts to tell *him* to move out, and then quietly cursed herself for still loving the bastard. She flickered her lashes, forced back her tears and peered more closely at her eyes. 'This new mascara's not as good as my old one.

'What's her name – Annabel? Theodora? Isabelle?'

'There isn't anyone else. We made a mistake. I'm not saying I don't love you . . . I'm not *in* love any more, that's all. And I should be. We should be—'

'You've been sneaking a peep at my Mills and Boon – you old romantic.'

He gritted his teeth. 'Bloody hell . . .'

'I know. I'm such a bitch. No wonder you want to leave me. No one'll blame you, not when you tell them what a bitch I am, behind closed doors.' She wasn't a bitch, and in a different mood he would say so, but in his search for reasons to leave her, he might dream up a worse scenario and she guarded her self-esteem jealously. Criticism was fine if it faded under praise.

She was not beautiful; but attractive and sexy had been

good enough for Roy in the past. All of that was forgotten now, waived.

She allowed herself to imagine what the other woman looked like. Soft white skin, nicely rounded, long blonde hair, full lips, sophisticated.

'All right, Sandy.' He inched his way forward, bumper to bumper, sandwiched between a Beetle and a lorry. 'All right. It's not your fault. It's me.' He meant it. Honesty at last.

'Well thanks for that, anyway.' She felt the lump in her throat again. 'What did I do wrong?'

'Nothing. I told you. It's not you.'

'There is someone else though?' She looked out of the window. 'This is better. Most of the traffic's heading for the West End. See – there is an advantage working in Aldgate. Once you've dropped me off you're gonna 'ave to weave your way back into that nightmare—'

He moved into third gear before he should have done. Commercial Street wasn't that clear. But then Roy was a bit like that. Impatient.

'If you moved in with your mum I'd send you a weekly cheque.'

He was trying to win her over but it wasn't going to work. She used her sing-song voice to get her message across. 'I ain't going nowhere. Try to accept it, babe.'

'I earn six times as much as you, Sandy. It's my salary that's been paying the mortgage.'

'I know. You've been very generous. I'll tell everyone.'

He jerked his head and glared into her face. 'Just because we're not working out it doesn't mean I shouldn't be happy with someone else.'

'Ah, so there *is* someone else. And I've made you miserable. Well . . . I'm happy, Roy. I still love you. You can stay as long as you like. You make living a little easier. I like having you around. When you can make it.'

'Self. All self.'

'Glasses.' She wiggled her finger at his nose.

'Cow.' He pushed them up and looked back at her. 'I love her. OK?'

More honesty. This was a turn-up for the books. Whoever the bitch was she had had an effect on him. Whitewashing the spots rather than changing them. Three years of good marriage down the drain. The past two months had been a nightmare, it was true, but before that they had been good together – or so she had believed.

'I'm no good for you.'

'Now you tell me.' Bridling at his lack of originality and his conceit, she deliberately cleared her throat, hoping he would stay quiet.

'It hasn't been easy . . .' He slowly shook his head, heavy with the burden of guilt. She let him ramble on, making excuses, drawing lines from songs, adding one cliché after another, throwing her a crumb now and then. This wasn't the Roy she knew. He was turning into a wimp. She had started with a strong macho truck driver and ended with a soft chauffeur who had no doubt been hooked by some spoilt brat he had been escorting to places which impressed him.

'What was it – the Harrods knickers, expensive perfume, nice furs? Or was it the labels? You always did like a good label, didn't you?'

'I was wrong!' His faced looked like thunder. 'I said I still loved you. I don't. You've changed. I don't even like you any more.'

She tried to laugh at him, but it wasn't easy when the knot inside was twisting tighter and tighter. She smiled instead and waited.

'I'm glad you find it amusing.'

'You mustn't lose your sense of humour, Roy,' she said, using one of his lines. 'Don't take yourself so seriously.'

'You're such a cow.' He slowly shook his head. 'You've changed, Christ knows—'

The queue of cars ahead moved on and Roy stabbed his foot on the accelerator.

'Don't blaspheme and pay attention. Traffic lights.'

'I was mad . . . a blind fool. Should never have married you. My own fault . . . should have listened—'

'Traffic lights!'

'I won't make the same mistake twice. I'll follow my instincts from now on.'

'*Roy!* Lights!'

'Keep the fucking house—'

'*They're red!* Brake you bastard, brake!'

Waking up to the sound of someone in the room, Sandy focused on the woman at the end of her bed. She looked familiar. 'My mouth's dry.' She hardly recognized her own voice; it was quiet, all confidence gone.

'Could I have a drink?' Why was she asking? Why wasn't she reaching for her glass of water on the shelf next to her bed? And who was that woman? Why was she there?

'Of course you can.' The voice was familiar too. Familiar and strange. 'Don't try to move, love. I'll get it for you.'

Don't try to move. The words fixed in her brain. *Why not?* An effort to lift her arms proved futile: they felt like lead. *Are you my dream?* Sandy raised her head another inch and flinched against the sharp pain. 'I know you.' Her head flopped back down on to the big welcoming pillow.

With the woman's arm supporting her shoulders, she sipped water from the clear plastic cup. Water had never tasted so good. The desert came to mind. The honeymoon. She and Roy in Israel. The sand mountains which had gone on for ever. They hadn't taken anything to drink. 'St Katherine's monastery,' she said.

'No dear. The London. You're in hospital.'

She closed her eyes. 'Is it night-time?'

'Uh-huh. Try to get some sleep. The morning will come soon enough.'

Staff Nurse Ella Murry put the cup on the side table and looked at Sandy's pale freckled face. The young woman's life had certainly been mapped out. Now her dreams and plans were smashed. She slipped the thermometer between her patient's lips and took her pulse. Normal. She would be fine. Her broken bones would mend. Cuts would heal. She glanced at the band of gold on her finger. *Don't let this break your spirit, child. Don't get bitter. The Lord has seen. He knows. He cares.*

Writing her notes on the clipboard at the foot of the bed, she raised her eyes as Sandy mumbled something in her sleep and made a feeble effort to raise herself. Ella Murry winced. Both the patient's arms were in plaster and three of her ribs were broken. The young woman was in pain but at least she was out of shock.

Sandy gazed in the nurse's direction. 'Roy?'

'Try to get some sleep, darlin'.' Forty years of nursing and Ella had not hardened the way the English nurses said she would. She still felt other people's aches and pains. Especially the aches. Her life was simple and uncomplicated. And for that she thanked the Lord Jesus Christ daily.

'The lights were red.'

The staff nurse sat on the chair beside the bed. 'So — we're wide awake and need to talk?'

'Am I dying?'

'No, sweetheart. You've fractured both arms and your ribs are a bit of a mess but they'll soon heal—'

'What about my husband?' She moved her eyes to meet the nurse's. 'He was driving.'

'He's upstairs, darlin' – in the men's ward.'

'And?'

'Doctor will be round in the morning. He'll explain everything to you.'

'You tell me.'

'If I could I would. Would you like a word with the house doctor—'

'Yes. Bleep him.'

'I can't do that. He's in theatre. An emergency. We've never had so many in at once.' She stopped there. This patient had enough to cope with – she didn't need to hear about the dreadful tragedy that had killed and maimed so many people. Like all the staff at the hospital, she too was still reeling from the shocking news of the disastrous train crash.

'I have to know. Please.' She wanted to see Roy, to say that she was sorry. To tell him she loved him. She imagined him lying in his bed feeling low – never mind his physical injuries. Guilt was worse than anything and she knew him well enough. He would be riddled with guilt for saying he wanted them to split up. She looked into the nurse's face. 'Please? I won't say you told me. I promise.'

The staff nurse sucked her teeth. 'Darlin' – I can't tell you what I don't know.' Ella wasn't lying, she was simply withholding information in the usual way.

'Fair enough.' She tried to ease the terrible pain in her chest. 'Pain killers?'

'In an hour's time. You've had your quota.' She stood up. 'Would you prefer an injection for the pain, or tablets?'

'Tablets.' Sandy closed her heavy eyelids and thought about Roy. About their good times together. They had been happy. Very happy. Until she had noticed the change in him. Maybe he had always been selfish and she had chosen not to see that side of him. His cruelty was the worst thing. Mental cruelty. He would go for days without talking to her and when he did speak, it would be to criticize. She could do nothing wrong when they first met, and recently she could do nothing right. When she dared mention this to him he simply smirked and told her to stop searching and give him some space.

She should have faced facts sooner. Taken stock. His obvious lack of interest in anything she did should have been questioned. She should have demanded answers. She should have cleared the air. Maybe if she hadn't been so busy at work, had spent more time trying to talk to him in the evenings instead of dropping into a relaxing bath and then bed, things might have been different. But all of that could be changed. Once they were out of hospital and on the mend she would make a real effort. Wear feminine underwear again instead of sensible cotton knickers from Marks and Spencer's.

Drifting in and out of pain and dreams, Sandy was comforted once more by the warm, velvet voice of Nurse Murry. 'I'm going off duty now, love. I'll see you tonight. Are you ready for a visitor?'

'What time is it?'

'Just gone seven a.m. Your sister wants to see you. She's been around quite a bit. You must be very close.' Ella walked to the door. 'Look at all these flowers! It's like a florist's in here.'

'How long have I been here?'

'You were admitted the day before yesterday. You won't remember much about it. Just snatches.'

'I remembered you. Last night.'

'I was the first one you saw when you came round from the anaesthetic. See you later, darlin'.' She showed a hand and left.

Sandy wondered if now was the right time to tell her sister about Roy, about his wanting to leave her. Maybe getting it off her chest would ease the pain. It had worked when they were small. When they would sit on one or the other's bed and whisper things they did not dare let their parents hear.

In their teens they had discussed other things; painful periods, fashion, boyfriends, betrayal. She couldn't remember when all that had changed, when they had stopped being so

11

intimate. Too busy getting on with our lives, she told herself; too wrapped up in getting the most out of it. If they could get back that intimacy it would be heaven. She was in dire need of a good close friend to talk to.

If Roy had truly meant that he wanted them to split up, once she was back home and living by herself, she would ask Ruth to move in with her. She might even sell the cottage in Woodford and buy a luxury flat in St Katherine's Wharf, once they had been completed. The thought of living in the East End again warmed her.

'How's tricks?' Ruth stepped into the room, looking as glamorous as ever. Her tanned face from the Canary Island sunshine made her eyes appear more turquoise than blue. Her long fair hair was streaked silvery white. 'You look all right. There's a tinge of colour back in your cheeks.'

'You've been crying, Ru.'

''Course I have – all night, on and off.'

That surprised her. Ruth had stopped crying a long time ago, when she had become chameleonic, when she would change her looks according to her mood. Now, wearing a fashionable cream trouser suit, she looked like a model.

'Is Roy OK?'

'He's as compos mentis as you are. He'll be fine. You were very lucky, Sandy – the car's a write-off.'

'Don't . . .' She turned her face away. 'The other driver?'

'Killed outright. There weren't any passengers. She didn't know a thing about it.' How could Ruth sound so matter-of-fact? As if she were talking about a cat instead of a person?

'How old was she?'

'You're better off not knowing.'

12

And so she was. The other car, a Beetle, had been reduced to a mass of twisted metal, and somewhere in the wreckage was the body of a thirty-year-old woman who had been in a hurry to visit her father in Bethnal Green Hospital where he was recovering from a heart attack.

'The guy in the lorry walked away with a few bruises.'

'And Roy? Don't keep it from me, Ruth. I want to know.'

Shamefaced, Ruth felt her cheeks beginning to glow. She had been hiding things from her sister for so long now it had become second nature.

'I'll walk up there myself if I have to. There's nothing wrong with my legs.' She saw the look on Ruth's face. A distant look of concern. 'Ruth? There isn't, is there? My legs?'

'No. Your legs are fine.' She ran her fingers through her long sun-bleached hair. 'Lay back and enjoy the rest. It could have been worse – for you, that is.'

'How can I just lie here, while Roy's up there. He'll want to see me. See that I'm all right.' The shooting pains in her chest reminded her that she would find it difficult to go anywhere. Frustrated, she sighed and closed her eyes. 'You go up then. But come straight back and give me a report.'

'Why did Roy give you a lift to work?' Ruth said, casually picking off a dead flower from one of the bouquets.

'Why not?' Sandy didn't want to go into that. Not yet. 'Nothing odd about that, is there?'

'As it turns out, yes. For you anyway. You catch the same tube every morning, don't you?'

'So I'm a strict timekeeper. What of it?'

'The train you would have been on crashed.'

13

Sandy opened her eyes wide. 'Say that again.'

'It crashed. More than thirty are believed dead – God knows how many injured. You should have been on that train.'

'Should 'ave been?'

'*Would* have been. Don't start jumping on my words.' She looked at her and raised an eyebrow. 'At least you weren't in that nightmare.' She pressed the dead flower between her finger and thumb and rolled it into a tiny ball. If Sandy had been on that train, Roy would not be in hospital with a broken back and pierced lung. 'Did you have a premonition?' There was a tinge of spite in her voice which went undetected. Sandy's thoughts were elsewhere – upstairs with her husband.

'Go up to Roy for me, Ru. Tell him I love 'im – regardless.'

'Regardless of what?'

'He'll know what I mean. Don't probe.'

'Wouldn't dream of it.' Ruth rose to her feet and pulled a packet of cigarettes from her pocket. 'Not supposed to smoke in here but . . .'

'Plead ignorance. I'm dying for a smoke. Light one up and we'll share it.' The jovial voice of an auxiliary and the sound of the food trolley drifted along the corridor outside the side ward.

'Breakfast is on its way,' Ruth said, turning away and gazing out of the window. Below she could see the busy Whitechapel Road, commuters making their way to work. 'How would you feel . . . if Roy had damaged his spine in the crash? If he had to spend the rest of his life in a wheelchair?'

Silence filled the room. Sandy waited, hoping that her

sister would say she was surmising, looking at the worst-case scenario, preparing Sandy so that she would accept a lesser injury. 'Don't say things like that.'

Don't say things like that. Ruth could feel her anger rising. She had spent her entire childhood being told by Sandy what she should and should not do. When would her sister accept that the two-year gap between them had now closed – as far as she was concerned? Ruth had realized long ago that although younger, she was smarter than Sandy. At sixteen she had sailed through her first job interview with flying colours and now, eight years on, she was due for a third promotion to property valuer at William Burns, the expanding estate agency where she worked.

'Do you think you would cope with something like that, Sandy?' She feigned interest in something outside.

'What are you talking about?' Ready for some more painkillers, Sandy closed her eyes and wished all her aches away.

'I'm just asking, that's all. Thinking of all those commuters on that train. Some of them might never walk again. Poor sods.'

'Stop it, Ruth.' She eased herself into a more comfortable position. 'I can see what you're trying to do – but it's not working.' Of course she wouldn't have wanted to be in the train crash, but that stroke of luck made no difference to the way she felt right then. 'I'd cope. I would have to. You'd be hopeless. You've got the looks – I've got the strength. Would that it had been reversed. I would have loved to have had your blue eyes and blonde hair.'

Ruth brushed her hand against a bouquet of flowers.

15

'These are nice,' she said, smiling inwardly. How little her sister knew her. Ruth might have lived in her shadow as a child but things were very different now. Sandy might think she was stronger in character but she was wrong, and that was fine by Ruth. She liked to give everyone plenty of rope – have them believe she was not too bright. *Act the lamb and play the fox*, was her motto.

'Who's it from?' Sandy glanced at the bouquet.

Ruth read the card as if she were bored. '*We're all thinking of you – love from everyone at Johnson's*. Very touching. Let's hope they don't replace you while you're out of action.'

'Johnson's aren't like that.' Sandy flinched again. 'Jesus – the pain . . .'

'You shouldn't try to move.'

'I know. How are Mum and Dad coping with this?'

'They've pestered the doctors . . . even after they were told you'd be able to go home in a day or so. Don't they just love to have something to worry over.'

'I think they might 'ave been in to see me. I vaguely remember them at the foot of the bed. It could 'ave been a dream.' She closed her eyes tight but the tears leaked through her lashes. If only it were all a dream, a nightmare that she would wake from to find herself in bed with Roy on the morning of the accident. She would have refused his offer of a lift and gone in by tube. Maybe *they* would both be out there, getting on with their lives. Maybe. She blocked the train crash from her mind.

'Of course they've been in. Dad took the week off. Once they get here, I'll go and see Roy . . . if that's what you want.'

'Thanks. Shouldn't you be at work?'

'I took the week off as well. I—'

'Well, well, well. Would you credit it? Don't she look well!' Her dad, Terry, slowly shook his head. 'I might 'ave known your sister'd fetch the colour back into your cheeks.' He tousled Ruth's hair and leaned over to kiss Sandy. 'Not in too much pain are you, babe?' He straightened, pulled back his broad shoulders and studied her face. 'Silly question, eh?'

'I'm fine, Dad.' She moved her head slightly and looked beyond him to her auburn-haired mother standing in the doorway. 'It only hurts when I move.' She wished Ruth and her dad away. All she wanted was to be cradled and rocked and soothed by her mother. She wanted to hear her say that everything would come up roses. She tried to lift her arms and reach out but it hurt. She looked at her arms in their plaster casts and struggled to stop herself from crying.

Maggie saw the look in her daughter's eyes. She stepped forward nodding and half-smiling. 'Never mind, love. Never mind. We'll soon have you up and about – don't fret.' She kissed her daughter on the cheek and winked at her, her warm brown eyes promising that everything would come out right.

Moving away from the bed, Ruth lowered her eyes. 'I'll get some tea from the vending machine.'

'Not on my account!' Maggie quickly softened her tone and relaxed her face for Sandy's benefit. 'We've been up all night drinking one pot after another.' She cupped Sandy's face and smiled. 'We'll soon have you well again,' she said, stroking her hair and sitting on the chair beside the bed.

'Been having a cry, eh? Well, that won't hurt. Better out than in.'

'Go and find another chair, will you, Ruthie?' Terry Brown said. 'One chair between the three of us! They'd soon create if we sat on the bed.' He flicked a piece of fluff from his navy serge suit.

'Dad . . .' Sandy breathed in slowly. 'Will you go and see how Roy is?' She loved her father dearly, but she wasn't up to coping with his usual act of putting on a brave face.

''Course – if that'll put your mind at rest.' He turned to Ruth. 'Ward E10 weren't it? Third floor?'

'Go with 'im, Ru. He'll be wandering around for ages otherwise. Take one of those vases of flowers with you . . . say they're from me – with love.'

Smiling benignly, Ruth reached for a vase of red roses.

'Not *those*,' Maggie snapped, throwing her a black look.

'Why not?' Sandy looked from her sister to her mother and wondered if there had been a row earlier on. They did tend to rub each other up the wrong way.

'Roy had them sent down to *you*, love. The card must have fallen off. Roy told the nurse to bring a bunch of his flowers down to you. She chose the red roses.'

'Sounds like musical flowers,' Terry laughed. 'You can 'ardly send 'em back up again.'

'No. I can hardly do that . . .' Sandy felt sick. The card hadn't been lost. There hadn't been one. It was obvious who had sent them. Roy's lover. How quickly bad news travels. Maybe she had even been in to see him. Seen him before his own wife had. Maybe she *should* send them up to him? Write a few cryptic words on a card. She looked at her fingers poking out from the plaster of Paris. They were bruised and swollen.

'I'll take these. They're from the blokes in Roy's office. They sent you flowers but not Roy. Chauvinism or what?' Ruth placed the vase of red roses back on a shelf and picked up a bunch of mixed carnations.

Alone with her mother, Sandy was relieved to offload some of the guilty feelings she was harbouring. She told Maggie about the row in the car, that she had been a cow, that she had caused Roy to lose concentration, that the crash had been her fault.

'I just couldn't stop myself from being bitchy.'

Maggie raised her eyebrows. 'With good reason?'

'You'll think so. Promise not to say anything to Dad.'

'Come on – get it off your chest.'

'Promise me?'

'You know better than to ask, Sandy. I know when you're telling me something you want kept between us.' She brushed wisps of ginger hair from her daughter's pale face. 'Go on.'

'The row we were having . . . just before we crashed.' She swallowed, breathed in and waited for the pain to subside. 'Roy said he wanted us to separate. I knew it was coming. He's tried to tell me a couple of times before but I changed the subject. I didn't want to hear it. That's why he told me in the car. I couldn't walk away. I *had* to listen—'

'Don't you *dare* blame yourself. I'm sorry for him, Sandy, but I can't sympathize or forgive. I knew something was wrong months ago.'

'You knew?' Sandy was stunned. 'Why didn't you tell me?'

'I thought it would blow over. And I was angry. Too angry. I felt like smacking him round the face too.'

She was angry? How did she think Sandy felt? She didn't want to hear her mother criticize Roy. That wasn't what she needed. She didn't want her to know more than she did. But then she and her mum were so close it hardly surprised her. They sometimes had the same thoughts at the same time. Her mother had been her eyes, she had seen and kept silent. If Maggie could bear the brunt of all of life's pains for her daughters, she would.

Her two girls were Maggie's life. And she had spent most of that life looking out for them, traipsing back and forth on the underground in the rush hour to spend the day on her feet serving customers in the lighting department of John Lewis's.

'It happens, Mum,' she murmured, 'all the time. You can't open a newspaper without reading about the rising divorce figures. Mind you . . . two blows in one go is a bit much . . .' Now there was the car crash to get over, on top of everything else. 'He's fallen out of love with me, I suppose . . . and she was there, available. You can't blame her, Mum, Roy is quite a catch. Good-looking, good sense of humour, high-flying—'

'It shouldn't have happened, Sandy, and I won't forgive either of them. Never. How could I?' Maggie looked away.

'Let's hope she'll feel guilty once she hears about the crash.' She raised her arms slightly. 'Once she hears about this . . . she'll have a change of heart.'

A change of heart? Maggie didn't think so. Something

like this was water off a duck's back to Ruth. She sometimes wondered what she had done wrong to make her younger daughter turn out so cold and calculating. She seemed more like an actress who could no longer tell the difference between a part to be played and her real self. She performed as if she was on stage most of the time – the heroine, of course.

'How could she do such a thing? It'll finish your father when it comes out. You know how close those two are.' Maggie shuddered at the thought of it; of what his reaction to her would be when he learned, as he no doubt would, that Maggie had known Ruth was having an affair with Sandy's husband. Terry would want to know why she had not said something to him about it.

'Roy and Dad, close?' Sandy was surprised to hear that. The two of them did get on well, but close? Hardly. They had always been in competition with each other with their smart suits, gold cuff links and polished shoes. If Roy had realized just how hard her father had to work to keep his small business in profit, things might be different. But her dad was both proud and a bit of a snob. He wanted to be a cut above the rest; prove that an East Ender could make it. He was an excellent electrician no doubt, but a good businessman? Not quite. 'Roy and Dad close?' she said, her voice full of doubt.

'No. Not Roy and Dad. Dad and *her*.' There was more than a touch of anger in Maggie's voice. She jerked her head at the open door. 'You wait till your dad knows the truth.'

There was a heavy silence as Sandy looked searchingly at her mother. What was she trying to tell her? What truth? 'Why are you linking Dad and Ruth with Roy's affair?'

Maggie raised her eyes to meet Sandy's and the look of fear she saw in them turned her stomach. She had foolishly assumed that Roy had told Sandy who his lover was. Her mind flashed from one thought to another as she tried to think of a way out of her predicament. Panic and guilt swept through her, and once again she was faced with the terrible dilemma of having to decide whether to expose the truth or lie.

'Mum?' Sandy's questing, pained expression caused Maggie to cover her face with her hands, ashamed and embarrassed. She knew, in that instant, that she had made a terrible mistake in keeping silent until then.

'You're not trying to tell me that Ruth and Roy . . . *Ruth*? My own sister?'

Maggie turned her head away, unable to look Sandy in the eye. 'Oh my God . . .' she murmured, 'what *have* I done?'

'*Ruth* and *Roy*?'

'The way you had been talking . . . I thought you knew.'

'My husband and my *sister*?' Sandy rested her head back on the pillow and closed her eyes. This was surely the worst nightmare of all. 'Why didn't you tell me?'

'I hoped it would burn itself out,' Maggie sighed, unable to think of anything else to say.

Smiling weakly at the irony of it, Sandy was floored. It was her marriage which had burned itself out, not their affair. And how clever Ruth had been at covering her tracks. She had been the one to persuade Roy to change his job. She had been the one who had asked him if he would give her a lift home each evening after work. And she had also been the one who turned up with unusual greenhouse plants, knowing

22

that was his only bit of horticultural interest; had given him a *Passiflora*. And he had smiled and said he couldn't wait for the passion fruit to grow. It seemed strange that she should remember that now. It certainly didn't strike any chords with her at the time. She knew that they were good friends but never, not in a million years, did she ever suspect that her sister and her husband were sleeping together.

Overwhelmed by the betrayal, she tried to clench her fingers and cried. Her mother had blown away the smokescreen. The smoke was slowly rising and Sandy did not like what she was seeing in her mind's eye: a picture of Ruth and Roy, hand in hand, smiling. Smiling at her gullibility. Laughing at her.

Anger simmered inside her, then abhorrence crept in and took over. She had been used – made a fool of. Ruth had used her to get to Roy and he had sucked it up.

'Judas!' Sandy raised her arms and brought them crashing down on to the bed. 'The cow! The bastard!' Piercing pain shot through her.

'*She* sent him red roses! I'm lying here with broken bones and she sent *my* husband flowers!' She lifted her arms again, but Mrs Brown pushed her hands under the plaster of Paris and used all her strength to stop her daughter from causing more damage to herself.

'Don't.' Maggie was crying now. 'He's not worth it. They deserve each other. Let's see how she copes now – with him in a wheelchair.'

Sandy's senses reeled under this new blow. Roy in a wheelchair. Her mother was talking about the man she loved – her husband. Telling her that he would be in a wheelchair as if she was telling her the time of day. What was it Ruth had said? *How would you feel . . . if Roy had damaged his spine in the crash? If he had to spend the rest of his life in a wheelchair?* So that was it. The only man she had ever loved was paralysed.

'His spine . . .?'

'I'm sorry, Sandy . . . but you had to know. At least it came from me and no one else.'

Sandy had never wanted to hold Roy as much as she did right then. The tears came like a fast-running stream, pouring down her face and neck. *Don't let it be real . . . please, dear God . . . not Roy . . . please . . .*

'Once they're out there in the real world she'll run a mile.'

'When *they're* in the real world?' Her voice sounded as if it were coming from somewhere else. 'Roy is *my* husband.' The anger was returning; she wanted to thump her chest. '*I'm* the one who should take care of him – not Ruth!'

Maggie cast her eyes down. 'We had a terrible row last night when her dad was out. She said she was gonna look for a ground-floor flat and—'

'Roy won't want *that*. He won't want her! He thinks she's shallow, stupid even. He's said so over and over. I had to stick up for her!'

'You might as well face it, Sandy, now you know this much. He does want her. God knows why.'

Sandy turned her face away. This had to be the ultimate insult. Roy didn't even want her to nurse him. He didn't want her. He had spelled it out in the car and she hadn't listened. *I was wrong! I said I still loved you. I don't. You've changed. I don't even like you any more. Keep the fucking house!* Those had been his words.

And what of Ruth? Her one and only sister – her one-time best friend. How could she ever trust her again? Those long intimate talks they used to have . . . telling each other things that they wouldn't dream of saying to anyone else. *You're my best friend, Sand.* That's what she used to say, ever since they were at infant school. And while Sandy held to that, always putting her sister before her schoolmates, Ruth had had many friends come and go and Sandy had never been invited to join them.

When they had gone to the fairground at Victoria Park, they had gone without her. Later, in their teens, Ruth and her small crowd would go clubbing – but was Sandy ever asked if she would like to join them? Not once. She had always believed it was because her sister was two years younger and she would have cramped her style. It was only when Ruth's friends had gone from her world, married or moved on, that she had started to tag along with Sandy and her friends when they went out on the town.

Out on the town. That's when she had met Roy. That's when her life had really begun . . . her dreams had started to become real . . . and now, in the space of a day or so, her world had been sucked hollow.

'Don't let her come in here . . .' Sandy was gazing at nothing, her eyes fixed in a stare. 'Stop her in the corridor. I don't ever want to see her again. My sister is dead.'

'I don't think so. Not quite. Not *yet*. But don't worry – neither of you will ever have to see me again.' Ruth was in the doorway. 'I'm out of your lives – so you won't have to whisper behind my back any more.' She dropped the bouquet of carnations on to the floor and flicked them with the toe of her shoe, sending them skimming across the polished floor. 'He's dead. Roy's dead. Five minutes ago!'

A high-pitched scream resounded through the first floor of the hospital. Then another and another. Sandy didn't want Roy to be dead. She didn't want to be lying there unable to jump up and punch her fist through a window. She didn't want nurses running to her aid or buses to be running outside. She wanted the world to stop and take notice. She wanted to open the window and shout his name at the top of her voice. But more than anything else she wanted to be by his side with his warm arms holding her. She wanted her Roy.

Ruth arrived home feeling very sorry for herself indeed, knowing that her parents would be comforting Sandy and not caring that she might well be grieving in solitude. After all, she and Roy had been seeing each other for over three months – they had been a couple who looked right together and could have had a future. No doubt they would be blaming her for the fact that Roy had stopped loving Sandy; that he had been smitten with Ruth. It had hardly been her fault that he had a wandering eye when it came to a pretty face; she hadn't set out to steal him away from her sister! She went into the kitchen and filled the kettle. *He* had done the chasing, not her.

This was quite untrue, and deep down she knew it. She had taken a shine to Roy from the moment she had set eyes on him in the West End nightclub, the Flamingo. Roy had spoken to her first. Her mistake had been to ask him and his friends to join her party. While Roy and Sandy had exchanged a few polite words, the DJ had placed an Abba record on the turntable and then pointed a finger at them, telling Roy to go for it. Once they had started to dance close together, neither Ruth nor the other two girls had got a look-in. He and Sandy had danced, talked, drunk and laughed into the wee hours.

As far as Ruth was concerned, her sister had not been the pick of the bunch, even with her big promising hazel eyes. It was that smile of hers which had captured him, that smile and clever sense of humour which seemed to attract the men.

They had seen each other on a casual basis after that, until Sandy had him turning up on the doorstep every night. Ruth remembered only too well the way she had gradually changed her appearance from then onwards. Not having been one for keeping up with the fashion, Sandy changed, becoming more trendy under Roy's influence. She had even started to grow her hair and had had the strong ginger toned down to a dark attractive red.

Unplugging the boiling kettle, Ruth cursed herself for introducing Roy to the girls at the nightclub that evening. If she hadn't, if she had kept him to herself, maybe she would have been the one to walk down the aisle with him and not Sandy.

'How's tricks?' Her flatmate, Helen, came into the kitchen, plaiting her long mouse-coloured hair. 'Is he any better?'

'No,' Ruth said flatly, 'he's dead.' She poured steaming water on to ground coffee beans. 'Maybe that *is* better than spending his life in a chair on wheels. Who knows?' She would have cried there and then, if only for the show of it, but her tears had dried up the moment she had seen the ward sister's look of sympathy when she stood in the doorway of

Roy's isolation ward. She had blocked her way; her expression had said it all; her voice had floated way above Ruth's head: *Such a young man.*

'That's terrible . . . ' Helen flopped on to a kitchen chair and stared at the floor. 'I don't know what to say.'

'I'd rather you didn't, Helen. I can't talk about it right now.'

'Do you want a drink? I've got a bottle of vodka in my room.'

'Later. We'll get pissed together . . . unless you've got better things to do.'

''Course not, silly. I'll phone Dave and tell him not to come round.'

'Thanks. I don't think I could face your boyfriend and his banal jokes.'

Helen winced. That hurt. But she was used to it. Ruth could be thoughtless. She was most of the time. But she had her good side. Underneath her layers of tough skin she really was quite sensitive. Not everyone saw the other side of her; not everyone could be bothered to peel away the layers and who could blame them? She looked as if she had everything going for her. Looks, independence, a good job, an excellent salary.

'I'll go out and get us a takeaway. A Chinese. Spicy ribs . . .'

'Helen, please . . . I'm not hungry.'

'You will be.' Helen stood up and left the room. In her present mood Ruth was best left to herself. She would read in her bedroom and wait for her to come in and pour out her heart. She wondered how Sandy was taking it; to ask would be to invite a torrent of abuse. She had asked her once if Sandy knew that Ruth was having an affair with her husband. She didn't ask twice. In fact she didn't mention Sandy again after that. Sharing a flat with Ruth was not easy, but Helen's part of the rent was lower than it should have been and even though she had the smallest bedroom, still Ruth was being generous. And that generosity set the house rules – Helen was the underdog.

'I don't think I want to live here any more.' Ruth came in and sat on the edge of Helen's bed and sipped her coffee. 'I've never really felt at home in this area. Islington's not my idea of a friendly place to live.'

Helen pretended to read her paperback. She had heard this before, several times. 'Where would you like to live then?'

'Back in the East End.'

This was a new one on Helen. Ruth was a social climber and had made no secret of it. She had had her sights set on Mayfair, no less.

Helen studied her flatmate's face. She meant what she said. This time she was not just airing ideas for the sake of it. 'What about me?'

'You?' Ruth slowly shook her head, smiling with contempt. 'That just about sums it up, doesn't it? No one cares about *my* needs, only their own. You, my mother, my father, Sandy . . . all wrapped up in yourselves.'

'Am I missing something here?' Helen asked. 'I mean . . . Sandy is in hospital . . . her husband *is* dead? She's not exactly on top of the world, is she?'

Choosing to ignore all of that, Ruth made for the door.

'Now that Roy's dead, I'm on my own. My family have turned their backs on me and all you can think about is what's going to become of you.' She reached the door and turned to face Helen. 'That's why I have to move back to Bethnal Green, to be close to my parents, to try and win back their affection.'

'Nice speech, Ruth, but I didn't think you cared that much for your family. You're always criticizing your parents—'

'I'm entitled to! I'm their daughter! And I intend to remind them of that inconvenient little fact! Sandy might think she has them all to herself . . . but I'll have no trouble winning them over once I put my mind to it. Once I show them what Miss Goody-Two-Shoes is really like!'

'Goody-two-shoes now, is she? That's a new one. I can't remember you saying that before.'

Ruth shook her head, all-knowing. 'You don't know Sandy the way I do.'

'No. And whose fault is that? I've only seen her a few times I'll admit, but from what I saw, she was OK. Normal.' Helen closed her paperback and pointed a finger at Ruth. 'You have got a problem. You're jealous of your own sister. Jealous if your mother buys her something new; if your father praises her . . . and look how you reacted when Roy asked you not to slag her off. You came back here and went berserk. She's your sister, for Christ's sake!'

Ruth stuck out her chin and sneered. 'I hope you can't find anyone to share this flat with you. I hope you have to move back with your self-righteous family!' She tossed back her long fair hair. 'I bet they miss you.'

Leaving Helen close to tears, Ruth stormed out and went into her own bedroom, slamming the door behind her. So much for sympathy! She opened her wardrobe and then shut it. She opened one drawer after another and banged them all shut. She pulled the covers off her bed and threw them across the room. She picked up a photograph of Roy and tore it to pieces. He had let her down. He had left her. He had crashed his car while Sandy was in it. He was giving her a lift to work! *Why*? Had the bastard been two-timing Ruth all along? Just pretending not to be on good terms with Sandy?

'I hate you!' she screamed, 'I'm glad you're dead!'

The slamming of the street door stopped her. Helen, the cow, had gone out. Gone out and left her to grieve alone. Ungrateful bitch! Well, let them all turn their backs on her – she would survive. She would come up smelling of roses! She lit a cigarette, sat on the edge of her bed, crossed her legs and began to make proper plans. She would not go to the funeral. She would not send flowers. Let the Brown family cry without her.

And as for the cocksure Helen, she was going to find out that her precious Dave Gerrard had not been as faithful as she might like to think! Ruth had been good so far, passing up an opportunity to hook a man once she had got him interested. That little show of charity was about to change.

Picking up her address book from the bedside table, she looked up the name Gerrard and dialled. 'Mr Gerrard please,' she said curtly.

'This is he. Is that you, Ruth?'

'Yes. Sorry, I didn't recognize your posh voice. Expecting to clinch a nice house deal, are you?'

'I live in expectation, sweetie.'

'Yeah, all right, Dave. It's me you're talking to now. Listen – I've been thinking . . .'

'About us, I hope.'

'What you said about us buying houses with sitting tenants . . .'

'Hey, babe!' He lowered his voice. 'Not now, chick; not here. Wise up, yeah?'

'Can you get away?'

'Of course, but . . . cool it, eh? What's the big hurry?'

'Catch me while I'm on the boil. I want to change direction.'

'Ri-ight. Sounds good. I'll be with you in an hour. I take it you're at the flat?'

'Yes, but I'll meet you in the pub. In the Bell. Wipe your brain nice and clean, right? Oh and Dave, clean of sex too. I'm not available . . . yet.' There was promise in her voice.

'Of course you're not,' he drooled. She could tell he was smiling hopefully. It was his confident attitude that turned her on. Other than that, he didn't have much else going for him – except for his terrific contacts with people in the property market.

'I mean it, Dave. This is strictly business. Let's get ourselves set up first, OK?'

'Bye-bye, Ruthie. See you in an hour.' He whispered the next line: 'Wear that sexy perfume for me.' His contagious laughter made her smile.

'Dave, listen. I don't think we should mention this to Helen.'

'Hardly.'

Smiling to herself, Ruth replaced the receiver, went into

Helen's room and picked up her bottle of vodka. 'New beginnings,' she murmured. 'Goodbye Roy, hello Dave. And as for you, Helen, my ex-flatmate, if you can't keep 'em – you don't deserve 'em.'

Curled up in an armchair with her vodka and tonic, Ruth imagined herself and Dave viewing large Victorian houses in the East End. Those which hadn't seen a lick of paint in years. Those which had sitting tenants who were on their last legs. She remembered Dave's words and smiled. 'Buy cheap with a sitting tenant – sell expensive without.'

Having worked for estate agents since leaving school, Ruth knew exactly what he had meant. She remembered the look in his eye and the smile on his lips. They had been on the same wavelength in an instant. Tenants were usually very old, parasites, who refused to leave the property and go into a home or die obligingly. She imagined the very loud parties she could organize once they had purchased the right property. Old people liked the quiet, usually. So noise was probably the one hindrance which would kill them off. Noise and constant aggravation from the landlords – Ruth and Dave. They were both perfectly placed to spy out the land and get in first when a gem of a property came on to the market. And Dave was in the prime position of being at the beginning – pricing properties according to what he saw. Ruth was about to catch herself a surveyor.

Excited by the prospect of becoming a property magnate, she went into the bathroom to take a quick shower. She would wear her sexiest underwear for Dave – the silk ivory – to show off her tan. She would go back to his flat and be what he wanted her to be. A perfumed, sexy woman. And little by little she would find out more about him, about his needs, his desires. She knew he liked Bob Marley, so that LP would go with her to the pub. She would offer it as a gift. Changing sides about political ideas would be the tricky bit. A Tory at heart, she had changed for Roy and became a Liberal, and now she would have to change again – Dave was a socialist, or so he liked people to think. In reality this guy was someone who didn't give a damn who ran the country, as long as his own personal interests were given priority. Well she could go along with that. Let him think he had taken her in too.

Tall and blonde, Helen's boyfriend was quite a looker. Maybe with time Ruth might not have to fake an orgasm. It would be the first time. She had allowed at least twenty men in and out of her life and each had believed themselves to be God's gift to her. She had flattered them, pandered and listened, seduced and smothered, stripped them bare, filled their raw spaces with love and healing until she had finally gained control – body and soul. Then, and only then, did she give them the boot.

Unlike the other men, Roy had slipped through her net before her goal had been achieved. She hadn't quite got him, not one hundred per cent. Yes, he had said he would leave Sandy for her, but he had got himself killed before carrying out his promise. She determined there and then that she would not allow another man to leave her cheated. She would have to work doubly hard on Dave. She would make them a team. Just the two of them, exploiting the sitting-tenant market. She would make him feel like a king until he was of no further use and it was time for her to drop him.

Chapter Two

Six weeks had passed since the accident. Now, in early spring, with the plaster casts removed from both arms, Sandy was ready to pay a visit to Johnson's Fabrics where she was employed as a pattern-cutter. She had been staying with her parents in their small back-to-back terraced house in Bethnal Green, and now it was time for her to rebuild her life. Terry and Maggie Brown had done everything they could to lighten their daughter's load and make her life bearable. Her friends had been welcomed and fed, visiting relatives tolerated. They had even driven her to see Roy's family. But it was time for her to go home, back to Woodford, to the cottage. They knew it, she knew it, but still the thought of her living there alone was painful. She had coped quite well up until the day of Roy's funeral, but once that was over and life around her continued, she had sunk lower than she imagined possible.

Pleased that she could now put on make-up and brush her hair, Sandy examined her face in the dressing-table mirror – she looked pale and drawn, dark around the eyes. She had lost weight and was now down to nine stone four. If she lost any more she would begin to look gawky – her height, five foot eight, didn't help matters.

She pushed her thumb inside the waistband of her skirt and pulled it away from her. There was a two-inch gap at least. She would have to go shopping soon to buy clothes that would fit. The life assurance company had been very prompt in paying out and Roy's firm had been excellent – her bank balance was healthy. It would take a few months before her own accident claim came through.

'You sure you don't want me to come with you?' Her mother appeared in the doorway.

'No. I'll be all right. The taxi should be here any minute.'

'Will you ask him to wait – fetch you home?' Maggie couldn't bear the thought of her daughter getting on a bus just yet.

'No need. Mrs Johnson'll insist her driver brings me home. No question.' She pulled the brush through her long hair and flicked the ends with her fingers. 'I look dreadful.'

'Tired, that's all. A good sunny break is what you need. A couple of weeks in Greece wouldn't go amiss. I'm sure Dad could cope without me for a fortnight.'

Sandy stood up and pulled on her jacket. 'It sounds perfect. But give me a bit more time, eh?' She kissed Maggie and walked out of her old bedroom. 'Don't rush me, Mum!' She called back over her shoulder: 'And don't use me as an excuse to take a break from Dad!' She went down the stairs – the taxi driver was tooting his horn impatiently.

Maggie looked around the spacious bedroom which her girls had shared as children and teenagers. It was full of memories. Old teddy bears and dolls on every surface – even on the twin beds. On the window sill was Sandy's toy sewing machine and Ruth's Meccano-built house. She closed her eyes and prayed. *Please come back, Ruth. Be a good girl. We need you. We need to feel like a family again.*

Seated in the back of the taxi, Sandy thought about her garden. She knew it would have been well cared for in her absence; the gardener had continued her work, going there fortnightly, and she was efficient. She imagined the flowering cherry tree in the far corner, at the back of the house. Soon it would be in blossom. The daffodils would be out, small clutches around the young willow tree where she and Roy had sunbathed and sometimes made love in the summer evenings when they first bought the cottage.

The sudden jolt as the cab driver slammed on his brakes caused her to stiffen. 'Woman driver!' The man pushed his head back and spoke to Sandy through the open sliding glass partition. 'No offence meant, love.'

'Pull over! Anywhere. Just pull in.' She felt sick and giddy. If she had been on her feet she would have collapsed.

'Wasn't *that* bad,' he chuckled, affronted at the request. 'We are on the edge of the City.' What did the silly cow expect?

'Pull over!'

Deliberately making a dangerous swerve around and in front of a bus, he pulled up sharply and looked at his meter. 'That'll be—'

'I don't want to get out.' She dropped her head back.

Narrowing his bright blue, piercing eyes the cabbie read her face. 'No need to be frightened.' His face softened and it touched her. It touched her so much that she unclenched her hands and allowed them to tremble. His look of concern made her cry.

'What's your name?' She surprised not only herself by her directness, but the driver too: he stopped smiling.

'Mr Dresden. D'yer want my number as well.'

'*First* name.'

The fifty-year-old shuffled in his seat. He looked embarrassed, shy even. 'Siddy.' He turned off his clock.

'I'm sorry about this, Siddy.' She leaned back and breathed in. 'I was in an accident not far from here.'

He nodded slowly. ''Ow long ago?'

'Six . . . seven weeks – I don't know. My husband . . . Roy . . . was killed.' She held out her arms. 'These are only just out of plaster.'

The bus driver gave a sharp toot of his horn and scowled at the cab driver. Siddy's face tightened as he pushed his head through the open window. 'Bollocks!' It was just as well that the bus was moving on in the slow, heavy traffic.

'Was a Beetle involved?' He tried to sound casual.

Sandy lowered her eyes. 'I think so.'

The world was a small place – the East End smaller. 'You're gonna 'ave to try and forget it.' He was reminded of his daughter; she would be about the same age as the young woman in his cab. He didn't want to think about that – didn't want to imagine the same tragedy befalling his girl. He peered in his mirror. She was breathing deeply again, trying to relax.

'I'm OK now. You can carry on.'

'Sure?'

'This is the first time I've been out . . . other than the local shops . . . And a walk in the park.'

'Sit back and relax! I've bin cabbing since you were born.'
He indicated and pushed his right arm through the window
to stop the traffic. Something he wouldn't usually do, but he
wanted her to feel safe; he was aware that her fear could
distract him. Once he had got her to her destination he could
go for a beer and forget about it. No doubt every fare he
picked up had problems of one kind or another.

'I s'pose you read about it in the *East London*?' For the
first time since the accident, Sandy felt a need to talk about
it.

'No.' It would have been easier for the cabbie to lie and
say yes. That would have been the end of it – but he had
strong principles about speaking the truth. The no-nonsense,
take-it-or-leave-it type.

'How did you know then?'

'Forget it, love. No point.' He carefully wove his way
through the traffic. 'Where you off to today then?' He resumed
his light-hearted tone.

'Did you know 'er? The woman who was killed?' She
couldn't leave it alone. Like it or not, this taxi driver *would*
tell her what he knew.

'Her mum and dad used to live in the same block of flats.'
She was making him feel uncomfortable. He didn't want to
talk about it. He had a job to do and didn't need all this
emotional stuff.

'Well then, you must 'ave known her. She was thirty.'

'Brushfield Street, wasn't it?' His tone and expression
told her to drop it.

'Johnson's Fabrics – it's an old red-brick—'

'Yeah all right . . . I know it.' He hated it when passengers spelled it out, as if he hadn't spent a year doing the knowledge.

'I did think I might try to find her family . . . say I was sorry.'

'Leave it alone. You'll only make it worse.'

'I can find out from the *East London Advertiser*. It shouldn't be too difficult . . . I just thought it would be easier, since you know 'em, if you could—'

'Leave off!' He laughed lightly. 'What d'yer take me for?' He pulled into Brushfield Street and slowed down. There was no need to turn off his meter – he hadn't turned it back on. 'Fare's on me.' He just wanted her to go.

'Just tell me the name of the buildings.'

'No.' He sighed deliberately. 'The family are still in mourning. They don't need you turning up at their door.'

She reached into her handbag for her notebook.

'Put your purse away! I told you—'

'Name of the flats?' She knew she was pushing it but her old determination was to the fore.

'Out you get.' He lit a cigarette.

'Thanks for the free ride.' She climbed out and shut the door. 'See you again, Siddy – whether you like it or not.' She smiled at him through the open window.

'Mind 'ow you go.' He pulled away without looking at her, but glanced in his rear mirror to see that she was writing down his cab number. The cabbie had done more for her than he realized – given her the grit to go in and face everyone.

Without thinking she turned and grasped the brass handle of the heavy entrance door to Johnson's, causing an excruciating pain to shoot through her arm. As she let go, the solid door swung back and hit her right thigh. Leaning on the door she counted to ten, willing her eyes not to water – the last thing she wanted was sympathy. She would weaken if anyone showed pity.

Easing the door open with her back, she entered the old-fashioned 1930s building, which was just as busy as the day before the accident. The clanking of the machines resounding down the stairwell was punctuated by footsteps on the granite steps.

'Sandy!' Louise Drake looked both surprised and pleased to see her. The spontaneous smile faded from her face as she held out her arms. 'Welcome back.'

Feeling a body against her own felt strange. So far she had managed to keep everyone at arm's length. She hadn't wanted to be held; she did not want to be held; she valued her space. 'I'm sorry,' the forty-year-old whispered in her ear.

As she pulled away, Sandy felt her confidence wane. 'I'm fine.' She tossed her hair back and smiled. 'Busy?'

'It's been murder,' Louise shook her head. 'Psychedelic material. Everyone wants it. We've had to reset all the machines. Coffee?'

'No thanks. You carry on. I can see you're meant to be somewhere else.'

'Embroidery department. It's bedlam in there too. We've hit the jackpot!' She gave a short wave of her hand and skipped down the stairs, heading for the basement. 'I'll catch you later!'

It wasn't going to be easy smiling through it all. She went up one flight of stairs and looked through the glass-panelled door into the machine room, which was full of activity.

Six die-stampers were in operation, punching out purple, bright pink, indigo blue, pearl, gold and silver sequins. Each puncher was serving six schlinging machines fixing the tiny spangles on to cotton. The finished schlung sequin thread was serving the knitting machines which were stitching them on to various backing fabrics. With the exception of one machine, all were turning out multicoloured fabric of various designs.

The atmosphere inside was electric – everyone was on the move, keeping the manpowered conveyor system going. Sequins were still enjoying a very high profile in the world of fashion – at both couture and street level. The boom was still on, and the staff looked happy in the knowledge that they were probably the highest-paid factory workers. They were all on a bonus system.

'Sandy.' The soft, quiet voice of Michael Johnson, MD of Johnson's Fabrics, came from behind. She turned slowly to face him. 'You look great.' His voice was full of compassion.

'No, I don't, Michael.' She could feel her hands trembling again.

'Let's go into my office. I'll have some tea sent up. Would you like something to eat?'

Mrs Johnson's only son was doing his best not to sound choked. He had met Roy more than once and had liked him. He and his wife Rosemary had attended their wedding. Sandy had worked at Johnson's since she left school at sixteen. Like other employees within the small business, she was like one of the family. The entire building, office staff and factory workers alike, had been stunned by the news of the tragedy.

As she followed Michael into his office Sandy knew, now that she was in these womb-like surroundings, that if she was to get back her equilibrium and her confidence she must not allow Johnson's to become her sanctuary. She must go out into the biting wind and make a fresh start. New beginnings. She would become a one-man band.

'Make yourself comfortable. I've just got one urgent query to deal with and I'll be back.' He pulled out his padded leather chair and offered it to her. 'Would you like me to ask my mother to sit with you for a few—'

Sandy raised one hand and shook her head. 'No offence, Mike, but this is difficult enough. Mrs Johnson'll have me blubbering in no time. I will go up to see your mother once you and I have had a chat.'

'Five minutes, OK?'

'Perfect. Just enough time for me to collect myself. What's happening with Korea, by the way?'

Michael smiled and shook his head. 'Don't tell me you've been lying awake at night worrying over that?'

'It comes and goes.'

'It's not a problem. Their fabric's cheaper but the quality of the sequins is dubious. Tests are being done now. Personally I don't think they'll stand up to dry-cleaning. You can smoke if you want to. I'll bend the rules today.' Michael went out, closing the door behind him.

Alone in the office, Sandy smiled. She knew that the Korean sequins would cope with dry-cleaning. She had had them tested a couple of months ago. She had typed up her report but it had sunk under the sea of orders and paperwork. At the time she had been annoyed that no one had taken the time to read it.

She was pleased now that she had made the effort to do something which at the time seemed irrelevant. The thriving family business did not fear competition from overseas. Johnson's was the only sequin-making factory in the UK, and their American counterparts were unable to match their quality.

Rising quickly, Sandy moved to the door and turned the key in the lock. If anyone were to question why she had shut herself in, she would shed a few tears and say she couldn't face sympathetic colleagues popping in to see her.

She smiled as she pulled open a drawer of the grey filing cabinet. The file almost jumped out at her. *Overseas Suppliers*. She carefully withdrew it, placed it on Michael's desk and pulled her notebook from her pocket. Using speed-writing she jotted down the names, contact addresses and phone numbers of the Korean suppliers. She had spoken to the rep at Yujan's several times and was on good terms. Other suppliers would be equally easy to handle. Korea couldn't wait to get into Britain.

She scanned the price lists. Nine pounds a yard of Johnson's stretch sequinned fabric could be obtained from Juyun's at £4.10 a yard. The quality would be inferior, but so long as it dry-cleaned it didn't matter. The high-street customers that she would appeal to were aged between sixteen and thirty – the throwaway age. If they only got three or four parties out of a dress but looked stunning, and it had been cheap, they were happy to go on buying. The rate at which paper knickers were selling was proof of the mood. Wear and tear – they didn't give a damn. There was a carefree, live-for-the-moment attitude on the high streets, and old traditions were disappearing fast. The rag trade had a lot to thank the revolutionary sixties for.

The file back in the cabinet, Sandy unlocked the door, sat in Michael's chair and composed herself. She would write to the Korean manufacturers telling them she had left Johnson's to go into business.

Knowing how difficult it was to get the manufacturers to supply small orders, she would ask for samples. Anything between two and five yards would be complimentary, but Sandy would ask for fifteen-yard samples. Let them think she was a potential prime customer. If she played her cards right, there would be no charge for any of the samples.

She had had personal contact with the main dealers and the smaller suppliers. One or two of them had offered her a position with accommodation. Koreans liked to headhunt in the UK. To them it made good business sense to have an English pattern-cutter join the company. Sandy remembered when she had mentioned it to Roy. When one offer had been tempting. He had said she could go if she wanted but she could kiss him goodbye. That was six months ago. She wondered how long he and Ruth had been being unfaithful to her.

When the door opened she expected to see Michael, not Louise. 'I've brought a couple of jam doughnuts – your favourite.' She tried to sound at ease but her words were tinged with compassion.

Admiring Louise's outfit – pink hot pants with purple

tights to match her skinny-rib top – Sandy visualized her posing on the front cover of a fashion journal.

'Michael's been nabbed I'm afraid. He's gonna be another five minutes or so. You'll have to make do with me.'

'Good. I want you to be my messenger. Sit down, Louise . . . I can't crane my neck for much longer. Your platforms have got platforms.'

Grinning, Louise sat down, crossed her long legs and passed a mug of tea to Sandy. 'Don't you love 'em?' She stretched a leg and admired her pink patent shoe. 'What's the message?'

Sandy lit a cigarette. 'I'm OK. All right? It's been bad . . . really bad, but I'm on the up. I've had lots of support and the doctor at the hospital assured me that Roy's pain had been dulled with injections. He didn't know much about it. His broken back proved fatal.'

Louise swallowed and widened her eyes, determined not to weep at her friend's matter-of-fact account. 'That's good,' she whispered and sipped her tea.

Of course Sandy was putting a brave face on it. It hadn't taken her long to realize that nothing and no one could shift the constant ache inside her. She was unhappy. She was lonely. Only she could pull herself through it. And pull herself through she would. The bottles of sleeping pills and aspirins were always out there. And out there they would stay.

'I think you should come back to work as soon as possible. Get back into the swing of it. So you won't have time to brood.' Louise was trying but she wasn't known for her diplomacy and tact. Her gift was design. Sandy held her in high esteem and could remember the creations she had sketched in a matter of minutes. She was as good as some of the top designers, but her ambitions did not match her skill. She was happy to be a big fish in a small pond. 'He's at peace now. I know you won't want to hear this but it was for the best – that he went like that. He wouldn't have wanted to be a burden—'

'It's all right, Lou. I've been all through that. I agree with you.' Like hell she did. Roy was better off *dead*? Maybe Sandy was better off with weak arms and ribs too.

'So . . .' Sandy leaned back in Michael's chair. 'What's hot?'

'Multi. The more colours the better. And boob tubes *again*. You must have seen them. They're in just about every frock shop.'

'Embroidery?'

'Can't turn it out quick enough. Denim is big. Embroidered denim, cotton, hessian . . . you name it. And now the studding department's going mad – thanks to punk.'

'You're not saying that the plain-coloured stock isn't being used?' Sandy's mind was still on sequins.

'It's not exactly dead but very slow. Which is just as well—'

'Because the machines have been set for multi-coloured?'

'All but one. Mr Michael's acting diplomat on the third floor right now. They need all the machines on multi. Black's always a reliable seller, sure, but it's not in demand,' she shrugged. 'Neither is red.'

'But Louise – we reordered sheets of red. Crimson and scarlet. Even though we had rolls of made-up fabric in stock.'

'You know it's all a guessing game, Sandy. We were wrong. And now it's taking up precious space in the stockroom.' She shook her head. 'Don't mention the dread red to Mr Michael, or Mrs Johnson.' She drew her finger across her throat.

'See that drum?' The girls focused on the cardboard container under the window. 'That and another two dozen boxes are going to children's homes for art play. What d'yer think's in it?'

Sandy stood up and pulled off the lid. She dipped her hand into the loose sequins, scooped some up and then let them slip through her open fingers, leaving just a few sticking to her sweaty palm like drops of blood. The crash came to mind. She hadn't wanted to think about broken glass and cut flesh. Blood on the windscreen was vivid in her mind. Drops of her blood, and Roy's. And that was the problem. Roy was still in her veins. She stared at the shimmering crimson.

'They didn't even make it to the schlinging machine. Mrs Johnson had the machine stopped when she saw the sheets of red PVC stacked next to a machine. You all right, Sandy?'

'Yep.' She flicked off the odd sequins and made a snap decision. She would ask Michael if she could buy the stock. She wanted to be surrounded by red until it no longer reminded her of that fatal morning.

'Sorry, Sandy!' Michael Johnson breezed into the office. 'Never a dull moment.' He smiled.

'I'll leave you to it then,' Louise said politely, relieved that her presence was no longer required. Grief had a strange way of enveloping anyone who came near. 'Come and say goodbye before you go.' She winked at Sandy and left.

Try as he might, Michael Johnson looked far from relaxed. Life at the top in this factory was demanding.

'I know you're busy—'

'Don't be silly. If we can't stop for ten minutes . . .'

'So I'll come to the point.' She could feel her old confidence returning. 'You've always said you would prefer it if your staff said what was on their minds.'

Michael sat down and looked at her studiously. 'Absolutely.'

'I don't want to carry on with my life as it was without Roy. It would be like a tapestry with the main pattern removed. So . . . regret it though I may, I'm going to have to leave Johnson's. Start again. Something new.'

'I can understand you feeling like this, Sandy, but—'

'I *have* to do it.' She raised her eyebrows, hoping he would see that she meant it.

'We'll be very sorry to lose you.' He lowered his eyes. 'Very sorry. What will you do?'

'Open a shop. A boutique – in the East End, in a market, maybe in the Lane, whatever.'

Michael shifted in his seat. His advice would be for her to stay put, where she was among friends, but he could see the sense in her making the break, going off in a new direction. 'Starting a business can be expensive.'

'I know, but I'll have enough, just. If I rent or buy a shop with accommodation above, then I shall sell our . . . my . . . cottage in Woodford, which will help. If I can't sell, well . . . Roy's policy will be enough to set me up. Just a small shop.' She smiled.

'A boutique?' He looked thoughtful.

'I'll make some of the clothes, shift dresses, mini-skirts, hot pants – and I'll buy in if the price and styles are right.'

'You'll always be welcome to come back, you know that. We'll give you all the help we can. You've obviously thought this through, so I'm not going to try to dissuade you—'

'You don't think it's a good idea then?'

'I think it's a great idea. But I would rather not be losing my best pattern-cutter. We're in for a busy season. There's Paris, Brussels, Milan . . .'

'I know. But I cut all the dress and jacket patterns before the accident. I presumed my replacement would have seen that they were made up as per my instructions. Has she?'

Michael shrugged. 'Sure, they're fine. But we're short on evening dresses. Could do with two or three more designs in gold, silver and black zig.'

'I could come in for a week . . .'

Michael laughed. 'Who are you kidding? Once you start up on your own you won't have a minute to spare.'

'That's why I have to do it, Michael. I don't want time to think.'

'Listen . . . I understand. OK? Do what you have to do.'

'Thanks. I appreciate that. Now then: will you be my first supplier? If the price is right I'll take the red sequins off your hands –' she waved a finger at the cardboard tub in the corner – 'not the loose ones, though.'

'Haven't you heard? Red is dead. At least that's what everyone around here keeps telling me.'

'I can't afford to go with what's in, Michael. I'll have to

take my chances. Make up plain shift dresses and turn them over quickly and cheaply.'

'OK. A guinea a yard. Take it or leave it.'

'A guinea?' She couldn't help laughing at him. 'You don't work in guineas any more.'

'I do with the old boys. They prefer it. And long may it last.'

'Listen – I know what you price it out at, don't forget. Your mother'll go spare.'

'Of course she won't. She'll nag me for charging you. And she'll flay me for letting you go.'

'Cash or cheque?'

'Cash. But not until you're up and running. I'll give you six months' credit to give you a chance to get on your feet.'

Delighted at his generosity, she offered her hand and then quickly withdrew. 'Nearly forgot. It's still painful.'

They talked for another ten minutes and he gave her some good solid advice on how to deal with people in the rag trade. He didn't mention Roy once; he didn't have to. Silence said far more than words could.

'Let me know when you've found somewhere. I'll arrange for those sewing machines in the basement to be delivered. They're taking up valuable space.'

She was by the door and smiling. 'Thanks Michael. I'm gonna need all the help I can get.'

'Mmm . . . as did my father when he started up in the thirties. Someone gave him his first sewing machines at a rock-bottom price.'

'I know – and look at the little empire he built. I'm gonna

take a leaf out of his book.' She smiled and winked at him.
'See you at the opening.'

'Opening?'

'My boutique.' She pushed her fingers through her hair.
'I'm gonna do it, Michael. The adrenaline's pumping!'

Chapter Three

Parking her ageing Mini on the waste ground behind the market, Sandy smiled, sighing with relief. She had finally confronted the fear of driving again. This was the first time she had driven her car since the accident. Reading through the particulars of number eleven Roman Road, she had a strong feeling that she had found just the right place: spacious shop with living accommodation above and a basement with natural light – price £11,000 freehold. Her cottage had been valued at £7,900, so it was within her reach. Why this particular one was more expensive than others in the area she had no idea, but typically it was the one which appealed most. She had seen three others and had four more to look at.

As she stood in front of the shuttered window, she knew why this property was overpriced. It was in a prime position just yards from where the market stalls began, and there were no vehicles parked on either side of the road – the yellow lines saw to that. Looking up, she felt a tingling inside: the two long sash windows on each floor of the flat above had narrow stained-glass panels on either side of them. As a child she had been to the market a thousand times and could not remember this shop. She moved in closer and read the fading green sign above the window – NOVA. Underneath, in smaller lettering, it said: *Spectacles to brighten your vision.*

'Mrs Brent?'

Taken by surprise, Sandy spun round to face a woman in her late forties wearing red metal-framed glasses which dwarfed her face. 'Mrs Goldstein?'

'It's so nice when people turn up on time.' She pulled a bunch of keys from her pocket and picked out one with a yellow tag. 'Spring's here at last.' She smiled broadly, showing a row of sparkling white teeth with a gap in the middle. Her bright red lipstick almost matched her dyed hair. Giving the door a good shove to open it, she withdrew the keys and put them back into the pocket of her orange and green check swing-back coat. 'Have you been here long?' The marcasite decoration on her glasses sparkled in the sunshine.

'About fifteen minutes. I wanted to get the feel of the market again.' Peering through the open doorway, Sandy couldn't wait to get inside. She had a positive feeling about the shop.

'Lovely property this. Beautiful. Such a nice man, too – when he was alive. Mr Cohen – beautiful frames.' She adjusted her glasses. 'I bought these here just before he passed away. His wife was a lovely woman.' She stood in the centre of the empty shop and shrugged. 'Things change . . . we must adapt . . .'

Pleased that Mrs Goldstein was caught up in the past, remembering the way it used to be, Sandy took the opportunity to soak up the atmosphere, feel the vibes.

'The family had been here for years. He was the last of

them. The youngsters didn't wanna know. He wasn't an optician, you know. Very clever man. The organ-grinder and not the monkey,' she laughed. 'Good luck to 'im.' She ran a finger along the dusty wooden counter. 'There are three other dry-cleaners in the market, you know.'

'Can we open the shutters?'

'Of course! Why not?' She pulled up the metal bar and folded back the wooden panels. 'Solid pine, you know. Look. See where the brown paint has chipped . . .'

'Why did you say that about the dry-cleaners?' Sandy peered at the flaked paint. There were at least six coats to be stripped off.

'Competition, darling. I just thought you should know. These hinges are brass. Tch. They don't make them like this any more.'

'I don't want to turn this into a dry-cleaner's.'

'You don't?' She pulled back her head, a puzzled expression on her face. 'What then?'

'A boutique.' The sun shining through the window caught the corner of the woman's spectacles again and reminded Sandy of silver sequins.

'A boutique with a difference,' she said. 'I want to sell clothes that can be worn during the day as well as in the evening.'

'You do?' Mrs Goldstein looked interested and bemused. 'How so?'

'Sequins, georgette, satin . . . simple styles – plain colours.'

The estate agent flicked Sandy's arm with the tip of her fingers. 'I like it. Make a wonderful change from all this hippy and punk rubbish. I've never known fashion to be so scruffy!' She slipped back in time again. 'Now when *I* went out dancing, the clothes were gorgeous. Of course I'm talking the late forties, early fifties . . .'

'So am I.' Sandy knew she was on to a winner. This woman would spread the word in no time. 'Can I see the basement, Mrs Goldstein?'

'Freda. Call me Freda. Everyone else does. It's in good order, you know.' She crossed the room and opened a green-painted door. 'I wouldn't lie. There's no point.' She waved a hand. 'People aren't fools. They can see. The bottom step is a little steeper than the rest . . .' She flicked on the lights. 'Mr Cohen used to make the frames down here, you know. I can still see him. Lovely man. Lovely.'

'It says natural light on the details.' Sandy said, stepping carefully down the wooden staircase.

'Sure. There's a window. You can't see it from the front. A window and a door leading into the back garden. Here – see for yourself.' Mrs Goldstein stood beside the grimy sash window. 'It's a nice garden. It's not so big, but does it matter? Look.' She pointed up to the lovely old walled garden. Sandy's eyes were on the red-brick steps leading up and the herringbone brickwork on the ground. No grass to cut, and the garden walls were covered in overgrown climbing roses and her other favourite climbers – clematis.

Turning around slowly, Sandy scanned the basement room. It was spacious, airy and dry – it was perfect. She squeezed her lips together, turned her back on the agent and attempted to fight back tears, doing her best to slow her heartbeat. But it was all proving too much for her. She felt such a fool. All she could hope was that her emotions would go unnoticed by the woman who seemed lost in her memories, gazing out at the back garden, carried away by nostalgia.

'Come on.' Sandy felt a hand on her shoulder. 'Let's get the worst of it over. The living accommodation.' Her voice was honest and sincere.

'I can't . . . not just now.'

'Yes you can, darling. The sooner the better.'

Sandy looked into the woman's face. Why was she in such a hurry? Surely she knew that investing in a property was an enormous step to take. She wasn't buying a piece of furniture that could be returned if it didn't fit in. But there was a look of compassion in her light brown eyes. She didn't seem the pushy type.

'You don't understand, I—'

'Yes I do. I know what you're going through. You're a widow.'

The penny dropped. When Sandy had filled in a form at the estate agent's office, there was one line which had caused her to freeze. *Are you single, married, divorced, widowed?*

Freda placed a hand on Sandy's shoulder. 'You can do it. You will have to, sooner or later. So why not let it be sooner? This place is perfect for what you want. Believe me, I know this market. It's crying out for another fashion shop. Why should I lie? It will go soon enough.'

Sandy nodded thoughtfully. She was right. Everything about the property so far fitted in with her ideas, but could she really go it alone? Could she take the plunge, having no one by her side to talk over the pros and cons with?

She felt the tears welling behind her eyes. 'I feel so . . .'

She swallowed and turned away.

'Lonely. Lonely is what you feel. Isolation. Fill the space, sweetheart. Fill it with worry, fill it with work, fill it with anything, but fill it. It worked for me – it can work for you. Come on. Come and see the flat.'

Following Freda Goldstein up the stairs, across the shop and through another doorway up to the first floor, Sandy felt the blues begin to slip away. Freda Goldstein *knew* what she was going through. A complete stranger had managed to give her comfort – a glow of hope.

The sitting room was perfect. The sun was shining through the stained glass, reflecting soft shades of pink, green and blue on to the wall. The wooden floorboards were bare, but a rug had been rolled up against another wall. In the alcoves beside the chimney breast were dusty mahogany cabinets with glass-panelled doors. The faded flowery wallpaper looked as if it had been there for a century, and the plain brass light fittings on two of the walls, originally gas, had been converted to electricity, along with the rest of the property.

There was a brass gas poker hooked on to the small, ornate iron fireplace which was surrounded by embossed pink and cream patterned tiles. In one corner of the room was an old armchair which had been discarded by the house clearance people.

'Do you think that gas poker works?' Sandy was trying to imagine warming herself by the fire on cold, lonely nights.

'I know it does. We used to play whist in this room.' She tapped her foot on the roll of carpet. 'This has been here since I was a child,' she waved a hand in the air, 'so it needs

58

a good clean!' She shrugged. 'Those removal people have no idea.' She pushed the roll back a few inches to reveal a very dirty red, blue and gold pattern. 'Look at the pile!'

'Does it go with the property?' Sandy was beginning to feel as if she had known Freda all her life.

'Of course. What you see is what you get.'

Sandy slowly circled the room, scanning each and every nook and cranny as if she were returning to a place where she had once lived. That's what it felt like: coming home. She didn't believe in ghosts, but was convinced that people did leave the spirit of their lives behind – happy or otherwise.

'This faces south, doesn't it?'

'Which means that you don't get the sun in the small back bedroom or in the kitchen-diner. The garden –' she shrugged – 'the sun is out there all day but in different areas. I don't think I've ever seen it in full sunshine, yet it's always sunny – if you see what I mean.'

'Suits me.' She followed Freda into the kitchenette which was small but compact; the dining area which came off it begged for some fresh primrose paint and wallpaper. There was a large picture window which, although out of character, somehow seemed to suit the room, and it did give a good view of the back-to-back gardens which were surprisingly well kept, apart from the house next door which was neglected and overgrown.

On the second floor there were two bedrooms, a spacious one at the front of the property and a smaller one at the back. Both bedrooms had panelled cupboards which had been purpose-built by the owner in 1945 and which also bore layers of paint which was quite badly chipped.

'Will they come down on the price?'

'How soon can you exchange?'

'I've got a cottage to sell but I can get a bridging loan. That won't be a problem. I've found a buyer who says he's ready to exchange on his own house, so . . .'

'I'll see what I can do. I can't promise, mind. We're dealing with a nephew who thinks we've underpriced it. But –' she looked over the top of her glasses and smiled – 'he can't wait to get his hands on the cheque. The young man's a compulsive gambler. He'll be broke again in a year.' She flicked Sandy again with her fingertips. 'Repeat that and I'm out of business. Word travels fast in this close-knit area.'

'I know. I was born just down the road in Cyprus Street.'

'So we're neighbours. I was born in Kirk Place. Listen – if I was in your position, I would snap this up. Shoes though, not frocks. I love shoes. I can't help it.' She held out one foot and admired her crocodile T-bars. 'My mother always said look after your feet and you'll go far. We were poor but we always had good shoes.'

Sandy looked into Freda's honest, heavily made-up face. 'I feel as if we've met before . . .'

'Maybe, maybe. Do you want to have another look at the basement?'

'No. But I would like to come back tomorrow, once I've had the night to think about it. It's a big step I'm taking.'

'Sure it is – but don't dawdle. There's another interested party. A young couple. I can't delay them for much longer.'

Sandy looked questioningly at her. Why should she want to delay them? She felt sure the woman was being honest and not giving her clichéd sales talk.

'I don't like them. Let's leave it at that.' Freda reached into her coat pocket and pulled out a small wad of business cards and wrote her home phone number on the back of one. 'Call me if you need to talk.' She offered Sandy the card.

'You don't just mean about business, do you?'

'No.'

'Thanks. I appreciate that. And I might just take you up on it.'

'I'm part of a group of people who have . . . well, let's just say we're friends. Nothing heavy. Just a bunch of people who like to get together occasionally.' She shrugged. 'Sometimes we go to see a show, maybe a meal out, but mostly we share a few hours together and enjoy a glass of wine. And no, darling, we're not all widows. Single, sure; single and in need of the right sort of company now and then.' She smiled broadly. 'You'd be surprised at the age range. They're not all oldies like me.'

They made arrangements for Sandy to have a second view the next day, but a handshake between the two women confirmed that the property would be held for her. Freda had taken an instant liking to Sandy, and she wanted her to have the property. She had seen a look in her eyes which she recognized – the desperate look of someone trying to go it alone after being one of a pair.

The East End of London was on the brink of becoming a fashionable place in which to invest or reside. Number ten Roman Road had been snapped up at a bargain price because there was a sitting tenant, Albert, an elderly gentleman who kept himself to himself.

The couple who had purchased number ten were prepared to pay the asking price for number eleven, and had insisted that they have first refusal if there were other interested parties. Freda Goldstein had been suspicious of their motives from then on. She abhorred the idea of Roman Road, her birthplace, changing, having seen the gradual mood swing over in Bow, where middle-class couples were coming into the area and buying the spacious old properties. She didn't want to see the same thing happening in Old Ford. It seemed bizarre that middle-class couples should be so eager to live in an area which up until recently had been seen as the pits. And they were bringing their politics with them – a different kind of liberalism to the one Freda had grown up with.

The Liberal Focus group was trying to enlighten the residents as to their rights, but old East Enders took umbrage at anyone trying to tell them how to think. Leaflets through letter boxes in this part of London did not go down well. As far as Freda was concerned, the new Liberals would do well to slow down a bit; wait until they were accepted and seen as part of the community before they tried to make changes.

The property business in the East End was on the up, but it had arrived too late for Freda's parents, who had started the small estate agent's in Old Ford in the mid-forties. Had Freda's young husband not gone AWOL during the war, when he was a young twenty-year-old, and disappeared from her life, she might now have children who could share her new prosperity and perhaps help run the business.

Locking the shop, Freda felt happier than when she had set out. She liked Sandy Brent, and she liked the idea of a new fashion shop. Boutique or not, it sounded right up her street. But more than that, she was pleased to think that she might be spending some time in the upstairs flat again, the way she used to – playing cards, perhaps? She felt as if she had found a new friend. Her instincts had not let her down in the past.

Pushing a key into the door of the flat above number ten, the shop next door, Freda was aware of Leo the tobacconist signalling to her through his shop window. She pretended not to have noticed. In his eightieth year, Albert, the tenant in the flat above the tobacconist's and once Freda's hairdresser, was more in need of someone to chat to than Leo was. Just as she was about to close the door behind her, Leo called out her name.

'Leo. I was going to come in after I had been up to see Albert. What's wrong?' His face showed worry.

'I phoned but I kept missing you. Listen . . . these people, the new landlords, they've reneged on our handshake.'

'*What* handshake?' Her frustration showed. How many times did she have to tell people to get everything in writing?

'The shop lease runs out in four months, right? Ms Brown gave me her word that should I want to renew the lease an increase, if any, would be a token amount.'

'Yes – and I told you to ask if they could put that in writing. You're telling me you ignored my advice?'

He hunched his shoulders, splayed his hands and his expression changed from despair to irritation. Then he casually swatted the air with the back of his hand. 'I believed her. She seemed such a nice girl.'

'How much?' She narrowed her eyes.

Leo rubbed the side of his nose and turned his head to

avoid seeing her reaction. 'She wants to double it.' He slowly turned to look into her face. 'They are *going* to double it – and this she did put in writing. The letter arrived this morning. So, in four months' time I shall be out of business. How can a tobacconist afford to double his outgoings? Ah – forget it!' He flicked the air again. 'It's my own fault. I shouldn't have so much faith in people.'

'You'll fight it, Leo – you know you will. But wait until you're not so angry; then go to the tribunal.'

'Freda – do me a favour. I'm too old for all that. Let them have the bloody shop. Good luck to them.' He turned away and went back inside, too choked to talk about it further.

Freda followed him into the small tobacconist's. 'Leo, have you heard a rumour that someone wants next door for a dry-cleaners?'

Serving a customer, a young skinhead, he rolled his eyes. 'Of course I've heard. Ms Brown again.' He pressed the keys on his till. 'You know what I think? I think she wants me out so they can knock through. For what they have in mind, you would need more floor space than what next door's got. That's what she wants.'

'Not Asian, are they?' The skinhead, with those few words, was offering his services.

'No, I don't want their heads kicked in, thank you.' Leo had no time for the National Front. 'As a matter of fact they're English,' he said, staring the young man out.

Grinning, the skinhead backed out of the shop. 'Get your knuckleduster out. Still under the counter, innit? I bet you polish it every day. You're still a fucking Teddy boy, Leo.' Sniggering, he swaggered out.

Freda shook her head despairingly. 'This couple, they haven't been worrying Albert, have they?'

'How should I know? He hardly steps out of his flat. They've been up there, sure . . .'

'I'll come back and see you later. I think we need to compare notes. If they come in – keep stum.'

She left Leo's and got into her car. She would call in on Albert later. She would go back to her office and make a couple of phone calls. Ms Brown would be first. She would tell her that number eleven had been sold. She would also, very casually, slip in a lie about Albert, just in case Ms Brown did have ulterior motives. She would give a glowing report on the old boy's new lease of life since he had become engaged to a younger woman, a lively sixty-year-old, who had him taking vitamin pills and drinking herbal tea. A small white lie could sometimes be invaluable. She smiled at the thought of it.

Pulling into her parking space, she felt sure that Leo was on the right track. When the couple had first viewed number ten, Ms Brown had said they were planning to be married in a couple of years and would be living with her grandmother in the country until the poor old gentleman, Albert, had passed away. Then they would redecorate the flat and move in.

A month later, when number eleven came on to the market, she had wasted no time in asking if they could view. Ms Brown had given a poor performance, telling Freda that she had fallen so much in love with the idea of living back in the East End, she couldn't wait to move into the Roman Road.

'Yes,' Freda murmured as she entered her office. 'Leo's right. He saw through them before I did. They're developers.'

'Talking to yourself again, Freda?' Her young and trusted assistant grinned. 'You'll be washing your 'ands every five minutes next.'

'What are you talking about now, Barbara?'

'S'wot mad people do, innit? Keep washing their 'ands.' She leaned back in her chair and grinned.

'Look . . . I've got a teeny-weeny man in my 'and, right? An' he's got a temprecha, yeah? So I'm gonna take some of 'is clothes off, right?'

Freda gazed down, bemused by the mind of the curly-haired blonde. If she didn't have her to brighten her days, maybe she would go mad. 'Go on.'

'Now you can imagine 'ow small 'is boots are. So I'm gonna ask you to 'old 'em for me – but don't drop 'em, OK?'

Freda nodded while Barbara mimed the pulling off of boots, then a hat, a jacket, trousers . . . 'I take it you've finished the typing I left?'

'Done ev'ryfing. Bin up the post office an' all.' She looked into her employer's face and narrowed her eyes. 'You do believe I've got a man in my hand, don't yer?'

Freda pushed her lips together and slowly shook her head. 'And you made the phone calls—'

'Everything's done. Stop worrying.' She leaned back again and looked sulky. 'You don't believe he's there, do you?'

'No, strangely enough, I don't.'

'Well why're you 'olding his blooming clothes then!' She clapped her hands, laughing out loud, enjoying her own joke.

Freda showed no sign of a smile. 'Make me a cup of tea. *I've* had a hectic day.'

'So've *I*.' Barbara stood up and took her dirty mug into the tiny kitchen. 'Just 'cos I don't rush about as soon as you come in, don't mean to say I've not bin busy!'

'I was joshing! Any phone calls?'

'Only about a dozen, that's all!'

'Anything urgent?'

'Nope! I've written notes in the black book.' She stood in the doorway. 'That young widow phoned – Mrs Brent. Wants you to call her today or tomorrow morning.'

'Did she now?' Freda liked the sound of it. 'She must have gone straight back to her parents to phone. Where is her file?'

'Where it should be! On top of the pile – all ready for ya!'

'Good girl.' She picked up the form Sandy had filled in, removed her glasses and dialled the number. She recognized Sandy's voice straight away.

'Hello my dear, it's Freda Goldstein. You phoned me.'

Seeing the expression on Freda's face, Barbara ignored the steaming kettle behind her. She hadn't seen her boss looking so chuffed before.

'I think we might be able to arrange that. I take it that's your final offer?'

Now Barbara *was* puzzled. The client obviously wasn't putting in a bid at the asking price, yet Freda looked like a cat with the cream. She returned to the kettle and poured water into the teapot.

'Looks like we've sold number eleven!' Freda could hardly contain herself.

'I thought that snooty cow, Muzz Brown, offered the asking price?'

'She did. But she pulled out.'

'No she never!'

'Yes she did.'

'When?'

'Never you mind. As far as you know she pulled out, OK? We're going to persuade young Cohen that he should take a drop of a thousand pounds and sell to Mrs Brent. I'll phone him this evening once the betting shops have closed. Tea?'

'It coming! It's coming!'

'You'll never guess what . . . old Albert is full of the joys of spring.' If anyone could spread a rumour with speed, Barbara could. 'He's in love and it's taken a decade off him – at least.' The news would go through the market like lightning, and into Ms Brown's ears, no doubt.

Barbara arrived carrying two mugs of tea. 'I didn't fink he was that way inclined?'

'Everyone says that about hairdressers.'

'He's still old. Too old. Shouldn't fink 'is winkle's seen the inside of—'

'Yes, all right Barbara!' She sipped her tea. 'Don't be coarse. Sex isn't everything, you know.'

'Yes it is, it's lovely. Better than a box of chocolates. Why're you doing it?'

She slowly raised her eyes to meet the girl's. 'I beg your pardon?'

Barbara laughed. 'Not *that*! I'm talking about number eleven. Why are ya manipulatin' fings? Up to your old tricks again, are yer?'

'I feel sorry for the girl.'

'She's not a girl, she's a married woman . . . well . . . you know.'

'Exactly. There's no need for me to tell you to hold your tongue.'

'Well, why *say* it then!'

A comfortable silence filled the room. Barbara had only been working there for six months but Freda had known her from as far back as she could remember, when her mother, a market trader, had first parked her in her pram next to Freda's agency – in front of the family fruit and veg stall.

'The thousand pound would only go to the betting shop,' Freda said, easing her conscience.

'If you say so.' Barbara wanted to know more. Freda was sidetracking.

'He's lucky to be getting that much. Lazy little bugger – always was. His uncle wasn't overfond of him. He's the only living relative, can you believe. They couldn't have children.' She leaned back in her chair and sipped her tea.

'Shame.'

'You would think an only nephew would have looked after his aunt and uncle in their old age but no . . . they saw nothing of him.'

'Mmm.'

'It's not working, Barbara. I can keep this up for days.'

'Good.'

'It's not right that I should have to tell you everything.'

'No.'

Silence again. 'I've discussed too much with you in the past, that's the problem. You expect.' She shrugged as if she wasn't bothered whether they conversed or not.

'Mmmm.'

Freda tried a different tack. 'I can't wait for her to start up. You'll be in there on the morning it opens. It'll be a different kind of shop to one this market's ever seen. The young people will love it.'

'Mmm.'

'Young ideas, fresh new designs . . . Didn't you mention once that you wanted something nice and dressy to wear for parties?'

'Might 'ave done. Can't remember.'

'I expect the window will be full of those hot pants everyone's wearing.'

'She's gonna open a dress shop – so what?'

'A boutique.'

'And that's why you're letting 'er 'ave the place at a rock-bottom price?'

'It's only worth ten in any case.'

'You *are* joking? We've bin offered eleven!'

'I told you – the other woman pulled out.'

'No she *never*!'

'Yes she did.'

'Never.'

'Did.'

'If this comes out, you're finished. And see if I care. It'll be your own fault! Who d'yer think you are – Joan of bleedin' Arc?'

Freda gazed up at the ceiling. 'Sequins, satins, lace . . . dresses, skirts, tops.' She looked at Barbara and raised an eyebrow. 'Or would you prefer another dry-cleaner's?'

'Is that what Ms Brown was gonna do wiv it?'

'Yes. She is going to squeeze Leo out of the tobacconist's, drive Albert into his grave . . . knock through to make one big laundry. The flats upstairs would no doubt be tarted up too and sold at a huge profit . . .'

Smiling, Barbara shook her head. 'You'll never be rich, you know.'

'I feel better than I could ever feel – even if I had a million pounds in the bank. You can't buy a clear conscience. It's priceless.'

'So all that about Albert was a trick? I knew he was queer anyway. You wanted me to spread it for you so's Ms Wotsaname got to 'ear? It's not enough you've robbed 'er of the property – you've gotta rub it in as well?'

'No. I don't want her to think he's without a friend, that's all. I don't trust that couple. I've met their type before. They buy cheap with a sitting tenant and then finish them off. Tormenting the life out of old people until they give up. One man who bought and moved into a house with a sitting tenant left every window open – even in the bitter winter. Stepladders and cans of paint without lids would be left on staircases . . . and it worked. The old woman finally tripped on something, fell down a long flight of stairs and smashed her head against a wall. Accidental death? Do me a favour. You think we should risk Albert coming to a similar end?'

'Yeah, 'course. I'm a wicked cow.'

'Leo we can do nothing about. His rent will be raised out of his reach. But Albert?' She slowly shook her head. 'Let her try, that's all – just let her try.' She smiled and slowly nodded her head. 'Do me a favour, Barbara – nip along to the fish stall before Ada packs up. I fancy a nice bit of rock salmon.'

'And collect your winnings?' Barbara grinned knowingly. 'It's in the envelope, top drawer. Ten pound. Not bad, eh? I told you *Lucky Cow* would come in first.' She pushed her thumbnail under the chipped pink varnish on her middle finger. ''Course, if you'd placed it earlier, when it was twelve to one . . .'

'You'd be getting six pounds instead of five.'

'You don't *have* to give me half! Just because I told you what to do.'

'No? You think that a fiver is worth me suffering your sulks?'

'I don't sulk. I just like to let people know wrong from right, that's all. I still reckon a silent mood beats all that 'ollering and shouting you do at times.'

Freda sniffed nonchalantly. The girl was right, and she was beginning to realize that there was something to be gained from listening to young people. If only the young would do the same – take a leaf out of their elders' books. Experience still counted for more as far as Freda was concerned.

When Maggie Brown got in from work, she found Sandy curled up in an armchair, crying. This should not have struck her as unusual since her daughter was still grieving, but she had not shed a single tear in front of her parents for at least a month. Her crying was done in her bedroom – Maggie frequently heard her sobbing in the small hours. She stood in the living-room doorway wishing her husband, Terry, had come home before her. He had enough will-power for them both.

'Oh Sandy . . .' She could think of nothing else to say as she flopped into an armchair and laid her head back. 'You don't have to go home to Woodford yet, you know. There aren't any medals for that kind of bravery.'

'That's not why I've been crying.' Sandy sat up and smiled, mopping the tears from her face. 'That's better. That's the best cry so far.'

'I can see that. Look at the state of your eyes! I've never seen them so red and puffy. What's brought this on – apart from the obvious?'

Sandy blew her nose and then sniffed the air. 'Nice perfume, what is it?'

'Worth. D'you want a drop of brandy?'

'Got any champagne?'

'As it happens, yes. It's been in the cupboard since Christmas – one of Dad's customers.'

'Can you put it in the fridge so it's cold for when Dad gets in?'

'What's there to celebrate?'

'I put an offer in on a place I saw today. I think it's been accepted –' she started to cry again – 'it's just right; it's perfect; and it's only up the road.' She was talking, smiling and crying at the same time. 'It's so right –' she splayed both hands – 'and it's gonna be mine!' She held her hand against her breast and slapped it. 'Mine, Mum! A shop of my own with space in the basement for a cutting table and six sewing machines. I can design, cut and make up my own garments! Make – up – my – own – designs!' Clenching her fists, she waved them in the air. '*At last!*'

Laughing, Maggie stood up. 'I'll chill the bottle then. Dad said he'd be in early tonight so—' She cocked her head to one side and listened. 'That's the van. I wonder why he's left the car at work?' She went in search of the champagne.

'All right, babe?' Terry Brown tossed a small bunch of keys at Sandy and then loosened his tie. 'Six pubs in one day and if I'm right, every bloody one of 'em will accept my estimate. I'm gonna have to take on another sparks at this rate. Make us a cup of tea, Sand.'

'These are your van keys.'

'Yep.'

'Why did you throw them at me?'

'Gonna need a van once you find a shop. It's yours. I've just 'ad it serviced – it's in good nick. Look after it.' He pointed a finger at her. 'And don't treat it rough just 'cos it's a van. It's only four years old.'

'I can't believe this. I should have read my stars this morning.'

'Load of rubbish. What about this tea, then?'

She was still grinning at the keys in her hand. 'This definitely calls for champers.' She threw her arms around him and kissed his cheek.

'What's the other bit of news then?' Terry squeezed her shoulder and sat down, pulling off his shoes and wiggling his toes. 'I'm ready for a good soak.' He leaned back in the armchair and closed his eyes. 'Come on then – cough it up.'

'I've found a shop. It's perfect. You should see the flat above. I fell in love with it the minute I walked through the front door. The position is just—'

'How much?'

'Eleven thousand.'

'Do what?' He sat forward. 'What is it – a supermarket! Eleven grand? Forget it.'

'But the estate agent thinks they'll accept ten!'

'Still too much. Don't run before you can walk.'

'I can do it! Nine thousand cash for my cottage and a thousand out of the insurance money.'

'The claim's not through yet though, is it?'

'No, but I'm getting a bridging loan anyway. I don't want to lose it!'

'Sandy – you're not telling me that you're gonna buy it before you sell the cottage? Because if you are – you *can* forget it!'

'One month, that's all – one month and the contracts will be exchanged.'

'Well then, you *wait*!'

'But what if I lose it? I want this shop. It's exactly right, and it's got a garden. Drive up there with me now.'

Terry creased his forehead, causing his dark eyebrows to meet in the middle. 'What d'yer mean – nine thousand cash? The cottage is mortgaged.'

'We took out a policy to cover it. If I had been killed and not Roy, he would have got it.'

'Well, that's news to me.' He gazed thoughtfully. 'We can't say he hasn't taken care of you . . .'

She didn't want to think about that. She didn't want to get all morbid again, not today, not when everything seemed to be turning out right. She wanted to move forward, not look back.

'Listen, babe.' He leaned forward and looked into her face. 'Running your own business is not easy, and you couldn't have picked a worse time. Inflation's at twenty-five per cent; unemployment's at its highest since 1940; electric's gone up by thirty-three per cent; the telly licence 'as gone up . . . and what did the miners get in the end – a *thirty-five* per cent pay rise! Now you'll see what this bloody government's done. You'll 'ave every trade in the country screaming for the same. Including machinists!'

'I *know* all that.' She tapped a finger on her temple. 'I'm not stupid. And as for unemployment, it'll keep on rising. With so many out of work, *begging* for work, I'll be able to employ cheaper labour. Good, hard-working people – Asians. You should see them once they get going, it's as if they're a part of the works – they don't stop. *If* they're on piecework and overtime, which they will be. I won't have to employ office staff – I can do the books. I've got a good brain.'

'Well then *use* it.' He stood up, agitated. 'You can cut your patterns on the table in our conservatory. No one uses the bloody thing. Waste of time 'aving it built on! You can cut out there and do your machining. A stall in the market is what you want. If that works out, *then* think about a shop!'

All that he said made sense, but she didn't want to be sensible. She wanted to take a risk – that was the whole point. 'I *want* a shop! And I don't wanna stop there neither. Export—'

'Sandy . . . come *on*! You're setting yourself up!'

'I know what I'm talking about. I don't mean straight away! Of course it'll take time, but time I've got.

'I can buy fabric from Korea, make up the dresses and

76

sell them on to Germany, Italy, Paris, you name it. All I have to do is make sure that the garments for export are tip-top: every edge perfect, not one piece of loose cotton, all joins to have French seams where possible. Cheap labour, good fabric, my own designs—'

'All right, all right . . . so you've thought it through.' He sighed and shook his head. 'International Women's Year, innit? No sex discrimination and equal pay? Next thing we know I'll be 'aving to take on a woman sparks!'

She grinned and pointed a finger at him. 'But don't advertise for a pretty one . . . discrimination.'

Terry rolled his eyes, wishing it was still the fifties. 'Christ knows what'll 'appen if Mrs Thatcher wins the leadership . . .'

'You can't *stand* Heath!'

'At least he's not a woman!'

'Which is *exactly* what this country needs!'

'Yeah? Next you'll be telling me you've changed colour.'

'If we can 'ave a woman prime minister I will change sides. It's about time!'

Maggie came into the room and sighed. 'Well that didn't take long, did it? Not in five minutes and you're at each others' throats.' She looked from Terry to Sandy; how similar their stubborn expressions were. 'I've put the champagne in the fridge. Let's jump in the car and take a look—'

'No. You go if you like. Encourage her to get in up to her eyebrows.' He unfolded his evening paper.

'Come on, don't be like that. You're sure to find things wrong with it. What do me and Sandy know about damp or subsidence?'

He reached down for his shoes. 'And that's the *only* reason I'm coming! Bloody daft ideas she gets. I s'pose it's bin tarted up?'

'I'm not saying a word. Just look at it – that's all I'm asking.' She brushed her hair back off her face. 'I wouldn't buy a property without your opinion.'

Straightening his tie, he mumbled under his breath about trudging all over the place and then coming home only to have to go out again. Sandy and Maggie kept quiet. One wrong word and he would be in his armchair again.

The rush hour and slow-moving traffic made things worse. Terry sat at the wheel quietly cursing. There was a train of buses crawling along in front of them.

When they finally pulled up outside eleven, Roman Road, the atmosphere in the van could be cut with a knife. 'Just a quick look, right?'

Slamming the van door shut, Terry stood with his arms folded and stared at the top of the property and then slowly moved his eyes down.

'Who's got the key?'

'The office is at the end of the market – only a ten-minute walk.'

'Ten minutes? That's out then.' He strode purposefully into the tobacconist's next door and asked Leo if he had a key.

'Sure . . . but I can't let you have it. I have to have a call from Freda first.'

'Well get on the blower then. My daughter's practically bought the place anyway. She wants a second look – and *I* want to see what she's letting herself in for.'

Leo ignored his waiting customer and went to the door to take a look at Sandy. 'Was she here earlier?'

'That's right. Sandy Brent. The agent showed her round.'

Leo shrugged and smiled, pleased to see that it wasn't Ms Brown. 'I needn't phone. Freda won't mind. She was quite taken with the girl.'

'Woman. She's twenty-six.' He took the key from Leo and winked at him. 'Thanks. Ten minutes, OK?'

'Take as long as you want. Makes no difference to me.' Leo turned back to his customer and Terry left the shop.

Unlocking the front door, he walked in and made for the door leading to the basement.

'Come upstairs, Mum – you'll love it.' Before they had reached the door leading up, Terry was back. 'Wait there – I'll go up first.'

'He can't wait to get out!' Sandy snapped.

No sooner had he gone than he was back. 'I'll nip next door and give Johnnie a bell. He only lives a turning away.' Once again he strode out as if he had a schedule to keep.

'Johnnie?' Sandy asked.

'Dad's mate. The builder. He'll be better than a surveyor.'

'What does he think he's *doing*? I don't need a sodding builder to tell me whether I should buy it or not! I'm not putting up with this. Come on – we're going. I should 'ave known not to fetch him! I'm not a five-year-old, for Christ's sake!' She marched to the doorway and was barred by Terry.

'Five minutes and Johnnie'll be round. We can trust him to tell us the truth. Leo's put the kettle on. At least someone's got my interests at heart. I'm parched.'

'You could have *asked* if I wanted your bloody builder

79

friend poking his nose in!' Sandy's face was crimson.

'The temper's back then. That's a good sign. Swear again and you'll feel the back of my hand.' He swaggered out in a more leisurely manner.

Maggie squeezed Sandy's arm. 'He's with you. He loves it. So do I.'

'I think you're right.' She could hardly believe his whirlwind behaviour. 'You can see what I mean about the place, can't you? It feels right. Wouldn't it be strange if one of our ancestors had run a business here once, way back? Way back in the nineteenth century?'

'Your great-great-grandfather did have a cobbler's down here somewhere. He was a shoemaker by trade. You could check it in the records office.'

'I didn't know that.'

Chanting from the market drew their attention. 'Sounds like a protest march,' Sandy said, walking towards the doorway.

'Not another strike?'

Making its way through the shoppers and stalls was an assortment of people following their leader, a schoolteacher, who had a mop of hair, tidy, which reached to his collar. He was wearing Hush Puppies, soft corduroy flares and a long college scarf over his tweed jacket.

'Teachers, nurses – empty purses! Teachers, nurses – empty purses!'

There were at least forty people on the march, teachers, students, nurses and a few hippies. A young punk was handing out leaflets while a group of skinheads leaned against a shopfront and jeered at him.

'Expect they're on their way to the town hall.' Maggie turned to Sandy. 'You sure this is what you want?'

'Yeah. This is where I belong.'

Chapter Four

The summer of '75 could not have been better as far as Sandy was concerned. The warm dry days had enabled her to work long hours – alongside her parents, Maggie and Terry. It had taken her three months to make the necessary changes to number eleven, and Terry had come up trumps, rewiring the property and replacing the old-fashioned heating system with night storage heaters. Once his work was finished he had arranged for his friend, Johnnie the builder and decorator, to go in. Johnnie was methodical, scraping away ancient layers of paint and wallpaper before he began to decorate the property from top to bottom.

The doors, now brilliant white, stood out against the stripped pine stairs, banisters and floors, which had been given a light coat of varnish. For the bedrooms, kitchen and sitting room, Sandy had chosen wallpaper selected from the Laura Ashley collection. In the basement, six sewing machines had been fixed on to two purpose-built tables; deep shelving covered one wall and hanging rails had been fixed along the other three – every bit of wall space had been utilized. It was clean, light and airy, with the stripped-pine beams giving off a feeling of warmth.

With just one week to go before the opening, Sandy was beginning to feel tired and nervous. Having interviewed many machinists, she had finally chosen six of the best and her choice had been excellent. She and the girls had been working flat out to get a collection together. The new designs, apart from a few teething problems, had proved successful, and the finish on each garment was superior to the clothes sold on the high street. Insisting on good workmanship had paid off and although it had taken a while, Sandy had finally managed to get it across to her girls that they were not to work as if they were on a conveyor belt.

There was no danger of upsetting the local trade, because the Nova boutique was unique in that there were no other clothes shops in the Roman Road market making up their own designs. Sandy's only real concern was the decision she had made, against the advice of her mother, her staff and Freda. Working on a low budget, there simply wasn't enough money for her to purchase a full colour range as yet. All her designs, dresses, miniskirts and tops, had been made up in red. Sequinned garments, plain satin and stretch velvet; all purchased from Johnson's, on credit.

Standing in the brilliant July sunshine on the pavement outside her shop, she wondered how she might dress the window, when the soft gold-leaf sign, *NOVA*, etched into the glass, caught her eye. It was glinting in the sunshine.

'If you *are* going for all red, then you must drape soft black fabric at the back of the window.'

Sandy smiled. There was no need for her to turn around; she recognized the voice. It was Freda Goldstein. 'I thought soft gold to match the sign.'

RED SEQUINS

'You wanna look as if you're selling Christmas crackers? I'm telling you, *black* – maybe that way you'll save face.'

That hit the mark. Leaning against the window, Sandy sighed. 'You really think I've made a mistake? Maybe I should get the girls to run up a few royal-blue dresses. I've just had a delivery from Korea – twenty yards. A free sample.'

'You wanna look like a football club? Or have people believe you've only got two colours in stock? That you're doing this on a shoestring?'

'I am, Freda.'

'Exactly. At least this way it will look as if you're doing it out of choice – as a gimmick.'

Sandy nodded thoughtfully. 'What if I sprinkled some gold sequins on the floor?'

'No. Too cheap. An afterthought. Stick to your guns now – but use black as a backing. Black, red and white with the soft gold sign – it'll look wonderful. It came to me in the night. And I'll tell you something else. The opening party . . . black cardboard plates, red paper napkins. If there's time for your girls to run up six shift dresses in pale gold, soft fabric . . . let them wear those. You must be the only one dressed in sequins. Red hot pants – red shoes. You've got good legs, so show them.'

She turned slowly to face her friend. 'You think it'll work?'

'Of course. You tell customers that the garments in the shop are samples. They can order any style in any colour or fabric from your range.'

'The idea is to *sell* them at the opening.'

'You will. But tease them into it. You only need one of each style on the rail. The rest you sell once they've pleaded with you. Keep them in the basement.'

Laughing, Sandy tossed back her flame-coloured hair. 'You're a genius, Freda. There's only one slight hitch – I can't wear red.'

'I beg your pardon?' She lowered her eyelids and squashed her shiny orange lips together. 'Say that again.'

Sandy lifted her long hair and let it fall. 'Ginger hair. I never wear red.'

'Tell me something – you know the expression blue and green should never be seen?'

'Yes.'

'And what did I see you in the other day . . . when I said how lovely you looked?' She raised an eyebrow. 'I think it was a blue and green midi-dress. Was I wrong? When it comes to red hair, everyone's the same. Do it and be damned. You're meant to be leading the trend, not trailing behind with old-fashioned ideas.

'Now then – priorities. My Boy is twenty to one and due for a break. You want me to put fifty pence on for you?'

'OK, why not? You seem in a positive mood today.'

Freda showed a hand and walked out, making her way to the betting shop just across the road.

'If there's a horse running with red in the name put fifty pence on that as well!' Sandy called after her.

'Sandy?' The quietly spoken Asian, Seema Patel, one of her machinists, stood in the doorway of the shop. 'Can you come downstairs for just one moment?'

'What's the matter, Seema?' The expression of worry was spoiling her lovely face.

'It's so hot down there. We have had the garden door

open all morning but there is no breeze. The fabrics are warm too – it makes it very difficult for us to work on them.'

'We need fans.'

'Yes, but all of the shops are sold out. Ask anyone.'

'Right . . . take the fan from the shop for now.'

'I don't think it will be enough. We have a suggestion to make.'

'OK Seema – lead the way.'

As she stepped down the stairs the heat from the basement hit her. 'Bloody hell! It's like an oven.'

'We just heard on the radio that it is thirty-two degrees centigrade in London – the hottest day for thirty-five years.'

The girls looked a sorry sight, draped over their machines, sweat pouring down their faces – but Sandy couldn't stop herself smiling. She started to laugh. 'I'm sorry, girls . . . turn your machines off.' They stared dismally at her as her laughter grew.

'It's not bloody funny, Sandy!' Maureen, a pale, thin girl with a hardened face pointed at her. 'You bloody try it! You wouldn't last two minutes!'

'I know, Maureen, I know.' She pressed two fingers to her lips. 'You should have seen your faces.' She started again, and this time it was contagious – they all started to laugh.

'Lock the back door, draw the curtain across and come up. We'll 'ave a nice cold beer in the pub.'

'Sandy! Three of the girls don't drink – religion! You can't fob us off with a ten-minute break!'

'I'm not fobbing you off. You're finished for the day. Go and take a dip in the York Hall swimming baths and cool off.'

87

'Well I like that! D'yer fink you could hear us out first? Before you sling us on to the street!'

Sandy pressed her lips together – Maureen was so stupid she was funny. 'Go on then.'

'There's another week, right? Before you open. An' this sodding 'eatwave's forecast to go on and on, right? *Right*?'

'Yes. Right.'

'Well we've come up with an idea. Why don't we work from five until ten in the mornings, and then come back and do another stint from seven till eleven at night.'

Sandy looked from one hopeful face to another. They all wanted it. They were all prepared to work unsociable hours to get the job done. She swallowed against the lump in her throat and cupped her hand over her mouth.

'We're not gonna demand double time, it's all right! We're just trying to make our lives a bit more comfortable!' Maureen again.

'And,' Seema added kindly, 'we want to help you out.'

Nodding, Sandy slowly paced the floor. She was getting emotional again and she was meant to be the leader, the one in charge, the one to make the decisions. With just a few kind words from the girls she was like jelly. When would it stop?

'Thanks.' She smiled at Seema and then at Maureen. 'I don't mind which hours you choose. I can't offer to pay you double time but I will make it up to you – I promise. Work something out for me, Maureen.' Sandy turned to the staircase. 'And thanks again. I'm sorry about the tears. I expect they'll dry up soon – in a month or so.'

'It was a good idea, wasn't it!' Maureen smiled, trying to

make amends for her sharp tongue. 'Bloody good idea, eh?'

'It was brilliant, Maureen.' She stood on the stairs and looked from one to the other again. 'Listen – we're a team, right? If you keep on pulling together like this, I'll make you shareholders when the time's right. As soon as we're on our feet I'll put that in writing. I don't want you or anyone else to slave for me. Yes, I can be a hard taskmaster and that won't change. I know this side of the rag trade, and I know we can make a go of it. But I can't do it without you – and you can't do it without me.

'If you like – and this is only an idea – we can shut up shop all day and do night shifts for the next week. So long as I get five hours' kip sometime in twenty-four I couldn't give a monkey's whether we work at night or by day. Think about it.'

She went upstairs with the renewed feeling that she had done the right thing in leaving Johnson's to start up on her own. The girls rallying round like that meant more to her than they realized.

When the opening day finally came round, Terry seemed more excited than his daughter. 'Are you sure a dozen bottles of wine's gonna be enough?'

'Yes. I know you've slipped in a couple of bottles of whisky. It's not an East End booze-up! And I don't want your labourers in and out all day, either!' Sandy unhooked four velvet dresses from a rail and placed them between some satin frocks and sequinned tops. 'If they mark any of the clothes . . .'

Rolling her eyes at Sandy's bossy mood, Maggie checked

the buffet table. 'I've brought some ice cubes . . . We'll put some in the orange and lemon juice last thing. I s'pose our Asian friends do drink juice?'

'Of *course* they do!'

'What time are the girls coming in?'

'They *are* in! In the basement, getting ready.'

'What time d'you expect people to arrive?'

'Any time after eleven. The Johnsons'll be here on the dot. They can't wait to see it. They'll be chuffed. Listen, can you do me a favour and go next door and tell Leo to come in for a drink? I forgot to ask him. I don't know where Freda's got to.' She checked her wristwatch for the umpteenth time. 'I should think the girls from the office and factory'll be late – *if* they come. Do you think they will?' She scanned the shop. 'It looks OK, doesn't it? I've put some chairs in the garden if anyone wants to—'

'Oh Sandy!' Maggie's voice drifted above her head. 'They look gorgeous.' She placed a hand on her daughter's shoulder and turned her to face the six machinists who had come up from the basement, dressed in short pale gold dresses with mandarin collars.

Sandy looked from Sharon's black face to Seema's brown, and then gazed at the sunburned face of Ivy, the senior machinist. Milly the twenty-year-old West Indian was smiling and giggling, showing off her perfect row of white teeth.

'I wish Freda could see you now. This is her idea, not mine.'

'Right. What d'yer want us to do first? Pour the wine . . .?' Maureen was not happy unless she was doing something. 'What time they coming?'

'Any minute now.' Sandy glanced outside at the busy street and market. No one seemed to be taking any notice of the *Opening Today* sign. Two women aged around thirty were peering in the window.

'Looks expensive . . .' One of them read the hand-painted sign aloud: 'Exclusively designed for *Nova*.' She pulled at her friend's arm. 'Come on, we'd best stick to the market stalls.'

Back inside the shop, Sandy felt embarrassed at her pretentious wording. 'I should have put price tags on!' Her freckled face was scarlet.

Arriving, Freda squeezed her shoulder. 'You don't put price tags on for an opening.'

Spinning around, Sandy glared at her. 'No one'll come in! They'll think we're too pricey!'

'You don't want them in. Not today. It'll be too packed.' She flopped on to a chair. 'I'm gasping.'

'Well, where *is* everyone then?'

'Caught up in the traffic, I expect. Does she always go on like this, Maggie? She's not too old to have her legs slapped, you know.'

Sandy stormed across the shop, heading for the basement and the garden. If there was a gate leading out she would go through it and run. It was all going to go wrong, she could sense it. Why should she expect people to turn out on a scorching hot day to look at her boutique? If they had any sense they would be heading out of town to the seaside or the open fields.

Lighting a cigarette, she leaned on the wall outside in the shade, full of regret. If she was still working for Johnson's she would be in Woodford, sunbathing in the garden, sipping an iced drink and entertaining a few friends.

The sudden noise of a dog growling as it ran out into the next-door garden sent ice-cold waves through her. The fence between the two gardens was broken in places and there were gaps. Pressing her back against the wall and praying the dog would not come through, she held her breath, conscious of the sudden loud beating of her heart. Spiders she could take, mice didn't bother her, bats and vampires were a joke . . . but dogs she feared. Dogs had snarling teeth, wet jaws, long tongues. Dogs could run and dogs could leap and dogs could growl and dogs could bite.

Once the barking had ceased, she opened her eyes and peered at the end of the garden where part of the fence was missing. Standing there snarling was the biggest, blackest hound she had ever seen.

'Don't move, Sandy. Just wait a few seconds and then very slowly come inside.' It was Freda, who'd followed her out.

'I . . . I can't move,' she whispered, too scared to twitch a muscle.

'Grip my hand. I'll stand with you. There's nothing to be afraid of. When you're ready we'll back slowly in and go upstairs. Your guests are arriving and asking for you.' Freda spoke very calmly, as if she were used to talking people out of situations like this, as if it were part of her everyday routine.

Squeezing Freda's fingers, Sandy would not take her eyes off the dog, and when its owner stepped through the broken fence and stood next to it, she felt herself go numb. She blinked once, twice, unable to believe what she was seeing.

There, looking just as threatening as the dog, dressed in a black T-shirt and tight black corduroys, her head held high and her long fair hair almost reaching to her waist, braced as if she were ready for battle, stood Ruth.

'That's my sister.' Sandy spoke in a monotone. 'What's she doing here? I'm terrified of dogs – she knows that. Yet she brings one here.'

'Sandy! Everyone's arriving! Come on!' Maggie called from inside. 'Come *on*!'

Blinking, Sandy shook her head as if coming out of a trance. 'Did *she* know? Did my mother know that Ruth was coming?' She looked into Freda's face. 'Did she?'

Freda could only shrug. She had no idea what was going on. It seemed impossible to her that Ms Brown could be Sandy's sister.

Ruth's intention that day had been to begin the reign of terror over Albert, who she imagined was on his last legs and just needed a bit of nudging towards heaven. Shadow was to play her part. She had trained her not to be friendly unless she received her special signal.

When Ruth had discovered there was to be a grand opening at the shop next door, she had put off her visit to Albert. She was curious to see who had pulled the rug from beneath her feet and purchased what she had already considered was her property. Seeing Sandy and both her parents at the centre of things had both shocked her and fuelled her anger.

'Sandy!' Maggie's shrill voice filled the basement.

'I'd better go up . . .' Sandy turned to Freda. 'You look as if you could do with a drink too.'

'Is she really your sister?'

'Yes, Freda, she really is.'

For three long hours Sandy put on a brave face while she talked to everyone, keeping an eye out for Ruth. Had she come in the proper way, through the front door, they might have been able to make amends.

With good wishes and goodbyes drifting around her head, Sandy prayed for the last of her guests to go. She was mentally, physically and emotionally exhausted. The opening had been a success, the best she could have wished for, and Maureen had been excellent. She had stopped serving drinks early on and begun taking orders for garments instead.

'Sandy – well done.' Michael Johnson hugged her. 'I'm sure you'll go from strength to strength. You deserve it.'

Feeling guilty that she had taken the names of suppliers from his files just after the accident, she felt like confessing but thought better of it. Knowing Michael, he would have been hurt but covered it up in his usual way. What he didn't know couldn't wound, she told herself.

Shaking first his hand and then his mother's, Sandy said she would like first refusal on old stock, any colour. It was obvious from their reactions that most people were attracted by the finished article rather than the colour, whether red was in vogue or not.

Later, once everyone had left and Sandy had locked up, she relaxed in a cool bath and tried to fathom Ruth's motives. Her sister had always been something of a rebel, but this latest trick was worrying. Had she not been so shocked at seeing her in the garden, Sandy would have given her a piece of her mind. A score was still to be settled. Anger surfaced once again when the vision of Ruth and Roy making love came into her mind.

She recalled the expression on Ruth's face – it had been full of spite as she stood there with the black dog. Maybe she blamed Sandy for Roy's death. Maybe she and Roy had not just made plans to make a life together but had actually set things up. She felt like slapping her sister's face, over and over.

Wrapping a big white towel around her, she went into the sitting room and lay on the sofa. The place was quiet, the street below empty, the market still. She wished she had someone to talk to. 'This is it, Sandy. This is how it's going to be.' She sighed and closed her eyes. Maybe she would doze off for an hour and then get dressed and call on her parents. The sudden shrill ring of the phone startled her.

She grabbed the receiver as if it were a lifeline. 'Hello?'

'Hello Sand, it's Johnnie. I'm sorry babe, I got held up. Did it go all right?' His friendly, caring voice was exactly what she needed to hear.

'It was great, Johnnie. Brilliant. Your ears must 'ave been burning. Compliments were flying about the way you've done the place up.'

'Yeah? That's nice. Listen, what're you doing?'

'Feeling a bit sorry for myself, Johnnie.'

'Can't 'ave that. Fancy coming out for a meal? Chinese?'

'Perfect. I'm starving. Haven't eaten a thing all day. We'll go Dutch.'

'What time d'yer want me to pick you up?'

Sandy glanced at her grandmother's chiming clock on the

mantelshelf. It had just turned seven o'clock. 'About eight?'

'You're on. See you then. Take it easy.' There was a click and then the dialling tone.

Smiling to herself, she wished everyone was as natural and easygoing as Johnnie. Nine years older than Sandy, he was like an older brother. If they were closer in age, she wondered, would they have been attracted to each other physically? Why his wife had run off and left him was beyond her; as far as she could tell he was the perfect husband: good-looking, hard-working and an altogether lovely man. 'Shame about your age, Johnnie,' she said, appreciating her solitude, able to say out loud what she wanted with no one to hear or comment.

She was pleased now that her dad, Terry, had called Johnnie in to do the decorating. He had been a godsend, working all-out to get everything shipshape in time, and he and Sandy had got on very well through it all. More than once his cheerful presence had snapped her out of her grief as nothing else could.

Feeling relaxed now, happy even, she looked out of the window at the street below. The refuse men were tossing squashed cardboard boxes into the cart while cats and dogs sniffed around discarded, bruised fruit and vegetables. Dogs, at a distance and with a closed door between herself and them, were fine. She thought about Ruth again and felt herself go cold. Why she had turned up like that in the back garden was a mystery. That she couldn't face Sandy after what she had done was understandable but out of character. Ruth was a tough boot when it came to sensitive areas. Not only had she been having an affair with her Roy, her husband, but in her own way had been the cause of the crash – and his death. But had she taken the trouble to write since he died? No. Not even a card.

Not that Sandy laid all the blame at Ruth's feet. Roy had always been a bit of a poser, lapping up female attention whenever it was on offer, and it often had been. Good looks were not always a blessing. In fact Roy's physique and handsome face had been his downfall, encouraging vanity. Sandy felt anger rise within her. Anger that she was a widow when she could have been planning to be the mother of Roy's children. Hate for both Ruth and Roy returned yet again.

Angry that so far she had not achieved her goal of rattling the old man above the tobacconist's, Ruth slammed about in the tiny kitchen at the rear of the small terraced house that she and Dave had purchased in Mile End Place. The cul-de-sac with its beautifully kept front gardens had been a real find. The end-of-terrace property was more like a cottage than a town house. It was in a good state of repair but in desperate need of redecorating and modernizing, which was exactly what she had been searching for. They had snapped it up at the bargain price of £4,500.

'I don't know why you're getting so het up about it.' Dave, his usual placid self, stood in the doorway drinking beer from a can.

'No?' Ruth said, doing her best to make him sound thick. 'You reckon the Roman Road property'll be worth just as much on its own then, do you?' She sprinkled Vim on to the white enamel sink.

'Of course not, but we can't win 'em all.'

'Sorry, but that is not a philosophy which *I* live by. I don't see any point in entering a race if I can't win.' She grinned arrogantly at him. 'You should think about that.'

'I'm beginning to.' His tone was equally elevated. 'How did the death threat go? The old man? Left shivering in his slippers, was he?'

Choosing not to answer him, Ruth pulled on her rubber gloves, ready to scrub the sink until it was spotless. There was little point discussing anything with Dave, she knew that now. He was good at spying out properties and securing excellent deals, but apart from that there was little else to celebrate. It was time for him to go. Between them they were now the owners of two properties and just about to sign the contract for a third, another terraced house in Morpeth Street, just off the Bethnal Green Road. Morpeth Street would be straightforward. She had found a buyer already – a back-to-back deal, the third so far, was in operation, and they stood to make two thousand pounds for doing very little.

'I don't know why you're doing that. It's one of Carol's cleaning days tomorrow—'

'I *want* to do it. I'm venting my anger. Or would you rather I smacked you in the face?'

'Well that rather depends on what you smack me in the face with.' He lowered his eyes to the crutch of her tight trousers and smiled.

'Don't be so vulgar.' She threw the scouring pad into the sink and peeled off her gloves. 'I'm going out for a walk. I'll be about an hour and a half. I don't want you to be here when I get back.'

'Fine.' He wondered if he should use the chains and ropes – she was begging for both.

Throwing her head forward she began to brush her hair. 'Once I've sold this house I'll send you a cheque for your half.'

'Uh-huh.' He slowly circled her, keeping his eyes fixed on her rump. The way in which she was bending over could be conveying a message. She might want him to take her in the kitchen. Pushing a cupped hand between her legs he grabbed her, and bringing his other hand around her body he squeezed her breast hard. Lifting her as if she were a child, he carried her through to the living room and spun her round. Laughing, she ordered him to put her down.

Once she was on the floor he playfully picked up the dog's heavy lead and ordered her to turn over. 'You're very naughty and deserve six of the best.'

'Promise you'll help me drive the ugly sister out of Roman Road and I'll let you fuck me.' She raised her knees, opening and closing her legs rhythmically. 'I want to own number eleven . . .' she pouted.

'And so you shall.'

'All dressed up, so you must have somewhere to go,' said Freda stepping into Sandy's living room. 'Who's the lucky man?'

'I was just gonna pour myself a drink; d'yer fancy one?'

'A drop of that amontillado would go down well.'

'We're going for a Chinese.' Sandy poured their drinks and joined her friend on the blue Habitat sofa. 'Johnnie's taking me out as a peace offering. He was held up: that's why he didn't make it to the opening.' She curled her legs under her and lit a cigarette. 'So – what do you think? Went well, didn't it?'

'It was wonderful.'

'I wouldn't have got through it without you.'

'Yes you would. What time is Johnnie coming to pick you up?'

Sandy looked at her wristwatch. 'In . . . twenty minutes. Why don't you come with us?'

'Don't be ridiculous. The man wants you to himself.'

'Freda, we're good friends and no more. He's a mate of my dad's, for Christ's sake!'

'Sure he is. So there's time for us to talk.' She looked at Sandy over the top of her glass. 'Your sister?'

'That would take longer than we've got. I've been racking my brains as to how she got into the back garden. I'm sure Leo wouldn't let her through with that dog.'

'I think you should finish that sherry and pour yourself another. I've got something to tell you.'

Taking her advice, Sandy poured another drink and rested her elbow on the pine mantelshelf. 'Go on then.'

'You remember I told you there was a couple who wanted this property? A young man and a Ms Brown?'

'*Ruth?*'

'And what's more, you're next-door neighbours. She owns number ten, though she doesn't live there. She's a very strange girl. I dread to think what growing up with *her* must have been like.'

With mixed feelings, Sandy sat down again. Her mind was spinning. She didn't want Freda to criticize Ruth – after all, she was her sister and she wasn't all bad. 'It was OK when we were small.'

'I'm pleased to hear it.'

Back in the past, caught up in an earlier life, Sandy gazed at a photograph of her and Ruth when they were seven and five. It had been taken at a Christmas party. Sandy remembered crying when it was her turn to go up to Father Christmas. With his long white beard and bushy eyebrows, he had scared her. She wouldn't sit on his lap or have a photograph taken with him. He was a kind man as it turned out and understood her fear. He had given her the pick of the tea sets. Cinderella. Each tin cup, saucer and small plate bore a different picture of the characters in the story. She adored it.

Ruth had been furious. She had wanted it. When they got home she had had her worst tantrum, stamping her feet and screaming that she didn't want the white plastic set with the stupid pink roses. When the Cinderella set was discovered one week later with pink nail varnish all over it, Sandy cried for a whole day.

The sound of the doorbell broke into her thoughts. She shook her head as if coming out of a dream. 'Johnnie's here already. Go down for me, Freed? Ask Johnnie to wait over the road in the Green King. No, wait a minute . . . don't do that. Tell him—'

'Stop worrying – I know what to say. I've got a brain.' She smiled as she pulled open the door. 'Freed – that's a new one. I think I like it.'

Sandy's mind switched back to Ruth's owning next door. It didn't seem possible. A weird coincidence. Hearing voices on the stairs, she quickly dabbed her eyes and checked her face in the oval mirror above the fireplace.

'Johnnie's invited me to join you for supper,' Freda said as she arrived with Johnnie.

'All been too much, 'as it?' He folded his arms and smiled warmly at Sandy. 'Bring a box of Kleenex with you if you're in a crying mood.'

'Stop for a drink first, Johnnie. I need a bit more time.' She looked at Freda. 'I want to know everything before we go out. Then I can put it out of my mind – for now.'

'Fine by me.' Freda shrugged. 'I suppose it's too much to ask that you do the same. Explain why the rift between you and Ms Brown, as she's known.'

'No, it's not too much. You up for it, John?'

'Up for what, babe?'

'Family feuds.'

He sucked in air and raised a hand. 'I'm your dad's mate, don't forget. Mustn't discuss family. Not on.'

'It's not a secret or anything . . . well, it won't be if you let me talk about it.' She showed him a half-empty bottle of whisky.

'Yeah, go on then. Any dry ginger?'

'In the fridge, in the kitchen. Help yourself. Freda?'

'Another sherry please, darling. I'm glad I called round now. I'm enjoying this.'

'Well,' Sandy said, pouring the drinks, 'you'd best be ready for this, Freed, I'm ready for a good cry – and I do mean cry. Brace yourself: it'll break your heart.'

'I doubt it. I haven't shed a tear since my Jack ran off and left me, the bastard. I should think my tear ducts closed up long ago.'

Johnnie arrived shaking his head. 'And I *can't* cry. Don't ask me why.'

'Why?' Freda was being her usual droll self.

'Very funny.' Johnnie sat in an armchair and crossed his legs. 'Right, come on then, out with it. Let's see if your 'ardships compete with mine.'

Having poured herself a third sherry, Sandy curled up on her beanbag and fixed her eyes on the leg of the coffee table. 'I was twenty-two when I met Roy. Apart from him, there hasn't been anyone serious. I liked him at first but then gradually fell in love.'

Freda and Johnnie glanced at each other. This was unexpected. The last thing they imagined Sandy would want to talk about was her late husband. Since the first time either of them had met her she had not mentioned Roy, not once. Raising an eyebrow at Freda, Johnnie sank back in his armchair and waited.

'I was a virgin,' she murmured, in a world of her own. 'Not that there 'adn't been other boyfriends, but I never let them go any further than . . . you know. That's probably why I never kept any of 'em. With Roy it was different. He was just as interested in what was between my ears as, well, you know . . . I felt as if he wanted me for me, for what I am, not for what he could get. When we did finally go all the way it felt right, natural. From that night to this day, Roy's been the only one. It's hard to describe love, but when it happens it's everything. We were very happy, but didn't need anyone else; we were looking forward to having children, little people who would grow from us. We used to talk about who they might look like. I said I hoped they wouldn't inherit my ginger hair; Roy said he hoped they would.

'Two years after we'd been married, he started to change. Just little things at first. Not bothering to shave when we went to bed; wearing expensive aftershave for work but not for me. Criticizing everything I did when I wasn't doing anything different from before. I tried everything to make him affectionate again, but it had gone. Sex turned into something we did because we were married and it was bedtime and that's what married couples were expected to do.

'If I had known it wasn't my fault, that my sister had moved in and was poaching his love, I would have packed my bags and gone. No one wants to be second-best.'

Sandy raised her eyes and looked at Freda. 'How could he make love to me after he'd been with my sister?'

Freda slowly shook her head and swallowed against the lump in her throat. Sandy with her questioning hazel eyes and freckled face looked so young. Too young to be hurting like this. It wasn't fair.

'So –' Sandy lowered her eyes again and focused on the floor – 'if Roy hadn't been killed I would still be on my own and my sister would still be my worst enemy.' The tears began to flow as if a tap was very slowly being turned on. 'I don't want her to be my enemy,' she said, her mouth crumpling, face distorted. 'I want us to be friends again. I *miss* her.

'I know I put everything into my marriage; spent every minute with Roy; when I wasn't with him, when I did go home to visit, I was talking about our plans or what we had bought for the cottage, how we'd decorated it.' Covering her face with her hands she began to cry more loudly, shaking her head and trying to speak.

'How *could* he smash what we had? We were good together. We were.' She lashed out at the air. 'I feel like *shaking* him! I want to hit him but I can't! I can't even ask *why*! There are a *million* words in here!' She slapped the side of her head. 'I'm like a prison. Everything's locked inside!'

She turned her back on them and screamed out his name, cursing Roy for leaving everything unsaid.

There wasn't anything Freda or Johnnie could say to help her, they were mature enough to see that. A comforting arm right then was not what Sandy wanted. All they could do was sit and wait until she calmed down.

Pointing to the bottle of whisky on the side table, Freda indicated to Johnnie that all three of them could do with a stiff drink. Choked and red around the eyes, he nodded and moved very slowly so as not to disturb her. This lamentation, this keening, was the best thing. She had not yet begun to grieve properly. This was her requiem, the beating of the breast, all inhibitions gone. Soon she wouldn't care that people rushed around her, getting on with their lives as if hers hadn't fallen apart.

'I'm sorry . . . I can't go to the Chinese . . .'

'Wouldn't expect you to, babe. I don't think me and Freda would much fancy going now. I'll go out and get us a takeaway . . . if that's what you want.'

'If you can manage to eat something . . .' Freda quietly offered.

'Manage to? I'm starving. I could eat a duck to myself.' She dabbed her eyes with her handkerchief, smudging her mascara. 'Couldn't go now, could you? I've not had a thing to eat all day.' She sounded as if she were talking through a funnel. 'Can I have some of those Chinese toffee apples for afters?' She broke into another short burst of sobbing when the doorbell rang.

'I don't want anyone to see me like this. Whoever it is, put them off. Say I had a migraine and I'm asleep. Say what you want, Freda, but don't let them come up!'

'What if it's your parents?'

She started to cry again. 'I don't know.' The bell went again. 'Tell them you're flat-sitting and that I've gone out. They mustn't see me like this! Please, Freda!'

'So where's the fire?' Freda lowered her eyelids at Sandy, to show she would not be rushed. Very slowly she left the room to answer the street door.

Albert from next door stood on the pavement, trembling. 'Freda love, I saw your car. I wouldn't trouble you but I'm so frightened. I don't know what to do.'

'I can see that. You're face is white. What's happened?'

'I just had a phone call from that young woman, my new landlady. She's going to renovate the flat. I don't want it renoviated. She's talking about taking the windows out and knocking down the partition between my kitchen and the store cupboard. I can't cope with all that! I'd sooner be sleeping in my grave!'

The eighty-year-old looked a pathetic sight in his over-large white shirt and baggy trousers. There were two days of white stubble on his chin, and his heavily greased black toupee was lopsided and looked as if it would slip off any minute.

'She can't do that to you, Albert. Don't worry, I'll—'

'She can do what she wants, love! That's the trouble. She sent a builder in last week to look over the place, poking about. He said that some of the work was urgent. That it wasn't safe for me to live there. I don't wanna live somewhere else while it's being done. Where would I go?

'Then there's the dog. I can't help it, Freda, I know I shouldn't say it but there's something menacing about it. It scared me half to death. I couldn't—'

'Whoa Albert!' Freda raised a hand. 'What about the dog?'

'She said that valuable materials and equipment would be arriving soon, so the dog has to stay in the backyard to guard it. I mean, have you seen it? It's so big and black . . . and the eyes, well . . .' He shuddered and drew his trembling fingers across his forehead. 'I don't like the dog.'

'I think you should come up. It's time you met your neighbour. And there's someone here I would also like you to meet.' She knew that Johnnie had contacts in the East End. Beefy dockers and market people who would sort out the likes of Ms Brown and her partner in crime.

'No.' He backed away, shaking his head. Albert wasn't up to meeting new people any more. He hardly saw anyone. The home help, a neighbour who collected his pension and did his shopping, and Freda. That was about it. That was all he wanted. He hardly ever went outside. 'No offence, Freda. Tell the young woman she's welcome to come up and see an old poofter like me when ever she likes but –' he waved a hand – 'I don't want to come up.'

'OK . . . OK. Go on home and I'll come in later, in an hour or so. And stop worrying – we'll sort something out.'

'The young woman said she might be calling round later tonight. I don't know what time. She never said.'

'Just go, Albert, and stop fussing. I'll sort her out. I'll come up and see you in an hour or so. OK?'

'Oh, I wish you would, love. I'm all at sixes and sevens over this.'

She waited until he was safely inside with his street door closed behind him, and went upstairs.

Pleased to see that Johnnie was making Sandy laugh with his hardships joke, she flopped into the armchair feeling drained. It had been quite a day, one way and another.

'Listen to this, Freda, it's hilarious—'

'I've heard it before.' She laid her head back on the big soft cushion. 'Don't bother to ask who it was, will you.'

'I looked out the window. It was the old boy from next door. You should have invited him up as well, he looked a scream.'

'Did he.' She glowered at Sandy. 'Well he's not feeling too secure at the moment.'

'He's not ill, is he?' Johnnie asked.

'No. Look, I don't want to bring you down, Sandy, now that you've cheered up a bit, but there's something I think you should know.'

'Can't it wait, Freda, till tomorrow? Or at least until we've had our takeaway?'

Freda nodded. Of course it could wait. What right had she to cry bad news? She would sit with Albert until eleven o'clock, and if Ms Brown hadn't turned up by then she would see him into bed and sort Sandy's dear sister out tomorrow. She closed her eyes and relaxed. Estate agent? She was more like a social worker. 'Go on then. Go and get this bloody food before we lose our appetites.'

Later that night, in bed, having relived the events of the day, Sandy began to drift off to sleep, happy that she had kind friends she could turn to. It had been a good evening, and she had learned a lot about the market traders and the people who lived in and around her. It was a close-knit community, and had been for generations. Freda and Johnnie had told stories which had made her laugh and sometimes want to cry. She hadn't realized how fascinating the East End, with all its changes, could be.

By one a.m. she was exhausted. When Freda got on to another of her favourite interests, fortune-telling, Sandy had to stop her. If she was to be up bright and early the next morning to open her shop, she would need her sleep. Promising she would let Freda look into her crystal ball the following evening, she thanked them both and turned them out.

Johnnie had been very sweet. When Freda had popped out for twenty minutes to see Albert next door, he had ordered her to put her feet up while he cleared away and washed up. No doubt he had promised her father he would keep an eye on his daughter and her welfare.

With the only light in her bedroom coming from the full moon, Sandy ignored the shadows it was creating. She didn't feel at home in this flat yet, and she still wasn't used to sleeping in a double bed by herself. She pulled Roy's pillow to her chest and curled up ready for sleep.

Just over three hours later, after a dreadful nightmare, Sandy woke up in a sweat. She had been dreaming about her teeth, that they were falling out one after another. The dentist had insisted that he drill into her jawbone and screw them back in. The large steel drill was entering her mouth and vibrating her skull when she woke up. Sipping water from her bedside glass, she imagined she could still hear the high-pitched whine of the surgical drill.

Knowing she wouldn't be able to get back to sleep straight away, she switched on her lamp and picked up a paperback. Again she thought she could hear the distant sound of drilling. She listened for a while and wondered if it was her imagination playing tricks. It seemed to be coming from next door, somewhere remote. She got out of bed and made her way to the kitchen. She was wide awake and wanting a cup of tea. While the water boiled she listened at the top of the stairs, but all was silent. The noise had stopped.

Back in her bed, sipping hot tea, she remembered the black order book which Maureen had been filling in. She had meant to see just how successful the day had been, which styles had proved to be the more popular. Wide awake now and looking forward to customers coming in for the first time, she decided to have a shower and slip on jeans and a vest. She could always catch up on sleep later. It was approaching five. The birds were already singing; pigeons perched on the chimney were cooing, making an eerie echoing sound.

Sandy hadn't seen many dawns before the accident, and

now as she opened the living-room curtains a few inches she was reminded of the few times she and Roy had been up and about early and how much she enjoyed that time of the day. Apart from the sounds of the occasional car in the distance and a milk cart going by, the streets were silent. She was pleased to be up and dressed without the worry of disturbing anyone. If she wanted she could switch on the radio or play her favourite piece of music – which Roy had found boring – *The Blue Danube*. It had captured her imagination when she was at senior school and her class had been taken to a concert at the Royal Albert Hall.

Opting for the quiet, she slipped her feet into her favourite old Egyptian sandals and went downstairs to the shop with a mixture of excitement and apprehension. What if there hadn't been that many orders? What if the apparent success of the day had simply been that her guests had enjoyed being there in the party atmosphere, sipping wine?

As she opened the door and switched on the shop lights she felt excited and elated. It was a wonderful sight. The soft black decorative drapes against the white walls and pine shutters made the sparkling deep reds of the different-textured fabrics look stunning. The sweet smell of fresh carnations filled the room.

Brushing the back of her hand against the satin and sequinned dresses, she swelled with pride. Up until this moment she had worked and worried non-stop, cutting the patterns single-handed to keep up with the six machinists. Each night she had dropped exhausted into her bed. Now, in her solitude, she could afford to congratulate herself. If nothing else, the shopfitting itself was a success.

Tucked inside the order book was a note from Maureen. *Congratulations boss – you're on the road. Thanks for everything. I've had the best day ever. Mo.* She opened the book and couldn't believe her eyes. The first three pages were filled with orders, and four of the customers were buyers from other shops.

As she studied each page it was plain to see that sequins were the most popular. She put her hands together and thanked God. In the basement there were 530 metres of sequinned fabric in the stock cupboard.

Glancing at the old-fashioned brass wall clock, she couldn't believe that an hour had slipped by – she had done little else other than study the orders and admire the dresses and shop decor. She picked up the order book and opened the door to the basement, in the mood for work. She would check and separate the orders and make a list of the designs the girls were to make up that day. She had a stock of patterns cut out and ready to go; with luck she had got it right, and the shift dresses in both satin and stretch sequin would prove to be the most popular. Her first analysis of the orders had looked promising.

Two thirds of the way down the stairs, the sound of gushing water stopped her. She gripped the handrail and stared. The basement floor was awash, and the base of the new wooden shelving was soaked. Her eyes darted everywhere – a large roll of red satin had been left on the floor and was taking up water like a sponge.

'My God!' was all she could say as she splashed through the water, which was still pouring out of a narrow pipe that ran along the adjoining wall between her shop and next door.

Lifting the heavy roll of satin, she felt pain in both arms. She took everything off the floor and placed it on the workbenches; rubbish bins, square scrap baskets, boxes of sewing cottons. They were all dripping wet.

Looking around at the disaster she wondered how to stop the water flowing from the broken pipe. 'Johnnie!' She rushed upstairs to phone him, her wet sandals squelching with every step.

'I'm sorry, John! Really sorry! I know it's early but—'

'Sandy?'

'I had to wake you! The basement . . . it's flooding!'

'Shit! Open the back door and bale out. No, wait. The stopcock – do you know where it is?'

'No! I'll do what I can; I don't know anything about plumbing! All I can see down there is a broken pipe with water pouring out.' She heard the receiver slam down and then the dialling tone.

'Bale out, Sandy! Right. A bucket. Bucket, bucket, bucket! I don't know where the fucking bucket *is*!' she screamed. 'Kitchen!' She darted upstairs and grabbed one from the broom cupboard. Halfway down the stairs a thought struck her. 'Broom!' She turned back and then stopped. 'Garden shed!' She ran on down the stairs, not caring that the enamel bucket was banging against the freshly painted walls.

Arriving in the basement, in her panic she forgot about the bottom step, the one Freda had warned her about, the one Sandy was always telling the girls to watch out for, the one which now sent her face first on to the floor, which was under an inch of water and rising! The enamel bucket went flying across the room and crashed against one of the sewing machines. Excruciating pains were shooting through her left arm and making her feel sick. Very sick. She grabbed the stair-rail with her right arm, pulled herself up and took deep breaths, hoping the strange sensation in her head would go. But the few white flashing stars multiplied to a million, and she felt her body go limp as everything went black.

With his finger on the bell, Johnnie stepped back and looked up at the living-room window, wondering why Sandy was taking so long to answer. He knew the bell could be heard from the basement because he had installed it himself. Searching in his pocket to see if he had the shop key with him, he cursed. It was in his overalls. Toying with the idea of kicking the door in, he was distracted by a car pulling up. It was Leo.

'You're early, Johnnie. Couldn't you sleep?' Leo got out of his car.

'We've got problems here! Sandy phoned me. Her basement's flooding!'

'So where is she?'

'I don't know.' He pressed the bell again. 'Unlock your shop, Leo. I'll go through the garden.'

'The basement . . .?' he murmured worriedly as he pushed his door open. 'I can't believe it. Why should it flood?'

Johnnie wasted no time. He rushed into the shop and through to the back door. 'Come on, Leo! Move yourself. Let's 'ave the key.'

'You don't need a key. Aren't three bolts enough?'

Slamming back the iron bolts, Johnnie stepped into the garden, through a gap in the fence and into Sandy's back doorway. When he saw her sitting on the stairs with her head between her knees his heart sank. She had had more than her fair share of misfortune, and by the look of her wet clothes and hair and the despair on her face, she was obviously shattered.

'You all right, babe?' He placed an arm around her shoulder.

'See to the pipe, Johnnie. I'll be OK. I fell and hit my arm and then, I don't know . . . I must have passed out. I'll be fine.'

'Well stay there, right? Don't get up.' He tiptoed furtively through the water and turned off the stopcock, looking to see where the leak was coming from. The pipe was underwater now, so it was difficult to tell.

'It's there!' Sandy pointed a finger at the pipe. 'Directly under the bracket under that shelf. There!' She leaned forward again, resting her head on her bent arm.

Cursing himself for leaving his tool bag outside in his van, he turned, ready to go and fetch it.

'Here. See what you can find.' Leo had arrived carrying a box of tools. 'I don't know what's in there. They belong to Albert. I borrowed them one day to bang a nail in the wall. That was a year ago.'

'Good old Albert.' There was everything there he needed. 'What's he doing with plumbing tools?'

'He was a hairdresser, wasn't he? What would you expect?'

'Hairdriers?'

'Sure, but what is the bane of a hairdresser's life? Plumbing! Blocked sinks. It's all the hair and lacquer and permanents . . . I should know. I had to put up with all the problems *after* we had the sinks removed. The pipes were clogged with hair, so the plumber said.'

'You'd best go and check your basement to see—'

'I have, when I went down to get the toolbox. The wall is wet but not much is seeping through. You know what I think?' He pushed his face closer to Johnnie's and lowered his voice. 'Sabotage.'

'Oh yeah?' Johnnie chuckled.

'The cement between the bricks has been scraped away. Once this water has been pumped out, you'll see for yourself.'

'It would take days to scrape it away, Leo. It's rock-hard.'

'I'm telling you. It wasn't like that yesterday. I would have seen. There a bloody gap between the brick – and there's a chip on one of the bricks and it's fresh. I know who did this. The new owner. Her sister.'

'Go away, Leo. Her sister doesn't own next door.'

'I'm telling you she does. And she wants to own this one too. Come and see me once you've sorted this out. It's quite a story.'

Pushing a makeshift cap on to the end of the sawn pipe, Johnnie looked Leo in the eye. 'If you're serious about this, keep it to yourself, OK?'

'I wasn't thinking of calling the papers. Why?'

'Would you like to be told that your own sister had done something like this to you?'

Leo shook his head. 'No I wouldn't.' Splashing through the water towards the garden door Leo felt even more animosity towards Ms Brown. If he was right, he had her to thank for soaking wet shoes and turn-ups. He would have to

116

rely on the sun drying out his socks, too.

'There is a drain just outside that door, ain't there, Leo?' Johnnie asked.

'Yes! The water's going down it, so you can relax!'

In water up to his ankles, a broken pipe to repair, Sandy on the stairs looking like death – he could *relax*? 'Wouldn't mind a cup of tea, babe.'

Sandy slowly raised her head, her glassy eyes peering at him as if he was something the dog had dragged in. 'I can't. I've had it.'

Placing one arm under her tiny waist, Johnnie lifted her over his shoulder and carried her upstairs, her limp, soaking wet body drenching his shirt.

'I was gonna ask if you wanted me to put you to bed . . .' he joked.

'Yes please. But take my wet clothes off first. Down to my underwear.'

He laughed at her sense of humour and then realized that she actually meant it. She was seeing him as a father figure, and it hurt. Pushing open her bedroom door with one foot, he carefully lowered her on to the bed and helped her take off her wet T-shirt and soaking jeans. Guilty that he should feel aroused at seeing her in her brief black knickers and touching her soft skin, he felt himself blush.

'I'll make some tea while you take off . . .' He waved a hand at her wet underwear. 'Tea or coffee?'

'Tea,' she murmured. 'Thanks.'

Once in the kitchen, he leaned against the unit and slowly shook his head. 'Jesus Christ. She must think I'm made of stone.' He switched on the kettle, his mind full of her naked body lying between those sheets. 'Forget it, Johnnie – she sees you as a soulmate and nothing more.' There was a strange feeling in his chest, one he didn't recognize, almost as if there was a hole inside which needed to be filled with something. What it was, he wasn't quite sure.

'Will all the water run out of the doorway into the drain?' Sandy was standing in the kitchen now, with a sheet wrapped around her Egyptian-style.

'No. I'll go down and sweep as much out as I can. Then I'll get my mate Billy to fetch his pump round.' He busied himself with cups, spoons, tea bags . . . keeping his eyes off her.

'But there's no real urgency now? Nothing terrible will happen?'

'I think it already has,' he murmured, keeping his thoughts to himself. He could feel her presence and smell her perfume.

'So you'll have a hot drink with me then?'

'Yep.'

'Good. I feel really shaken, Johnnie.' She moved closer and gave him a hug. 'Thanks for coming round. You're a brick.'

'Don't do that, Sandy,' he said, pulling away. 'Unlike a brick, I've got feelings.'

She stepped back, embarrassed. 'Sorry. Wasn't thinking.'

'Why should you have been? I'm your dad's mate and older than you. You're just a kid. I'm like an uncle.'

'Don't be stupid – an uncle! You're not that much older.'

'OK, fair enough. I'm your friend. Your soulmate.'

''Course you are. I like you a lot, Johnnie.'

'Well that's good because –' he winked at her as he carried

their tea through to the sitting room – 'I like you as well.'

Gazing after him, she warned herself to be careful, not to say too much. Keep a tight reign on her feelings. It was too soon after Roy to put herself in a position to get hurt again. And Johnnie was, after all, a very desirable and available man, with, no doubt, many women after him. Attractive women, with experience.

She went into her bedroom and replaced the makeshift robe with her long sensible dressing gown. Better to keep Johnnie as a friend than frighten him away altogether. He had just made his position very clear. He saw her as a kid, as a niece. Well, fine.

Having returned from his mission, Dave stood by the bed holding two mugs of coffee. 'And I thought you'd be pacing the floor, worried. Don't open your eyes, or anything so polite, will you, my darling Ruth? I mean . . . I've only broken the law for you, that's all.'

Pulling the duvet over her head, Ruth mumbled sleepily, 'Put it on the chair. I'm not awake properly.'

'It's half past seven.'

'OK! Just leave me for five minutes.'

He sipped his coffee and slowly shook his head. 'Don't you want to know how it went?'

'Later.'

He sat on the edge of the bed and sighed deliberately. 'I can't believe this. Couldn't thank me enough when I finally gave in to your pleading. Now you can't even be bothered to say thank you.'

'Fuck off, Dave. Go and get breakfast started. I fancy

eggs and bacon.' She curled into a ball under the covers.

'I had visions of you lying naked on the bed, waiting for me. Where have all the promises gone?' He pulled the duvet back and grinned at her. 'Don't I even get a kiss?'

'I said – fuck off.' She kicked him and yanked the cover back over her. 'I'm not an object.'

'No? How disappointing. I saw you as my toy. Something I could play with whenever I wanted. Something I could break if I chose. Now you're telling me you're human.'

Slowly drawing herself up into a sitting position, Ruth threw him a filthy look and reached for her coffee. 'Don't bother with breakfast. Pack your bags instead.'

'That sounds like an order. Is that an order?'

'Yes. Don't take your keys – I'll only get the locks changed if you do. I'll parcel up your stereo and the rest of your stuff and send it on to your mother's.'

'If I didn't think you were a bitch I'd think you were a comedian. Why all this hostility? I did what you wanted, didn't I?'

'What was that?' She was wearing a bored expression. 'I don't know what you're talking about.'

By the look of his face she knew that he was finally taking it in. He looked angry and suspicious. 'What's that supposed to mean?'

'What you heard is what it meant. Have you been at the whisky already?'

He stood up, stared out of the window and kept his back to her. 'So I didn't get up in the night and drive through the backstreets like a thief for you. I didn't break a water pipe and flood your sister's basement. I dreamt all that, did I?'

'I should hope so,' she smirked. 'I would hate to see you in prison. Handsome guy like you – they'd crucify you. You shouldn't even be thinking a thing like that. If I thought you wanted to sabotage my own sister's shop I'd turn you in.'

Furious, he spun round. 'That's far enough. It's not funny. Your stupid games are becoming a cliché!'

'Good. You won't mind leaving then, will you? And it's not a game. If you don't get out of my life without a whimper . . . And if I hear that there has been sabotage at number eleven, I'll grass. Goodbye Dave.' He raised a hand ready to swipe her. 'I wouldn't if I were you. You must have seen that I've already let Shadow in. All I have to do is call and she'll be at your throat.' She placed her cup on the chair, hugged her knees and avoided his eyes.

'Look – it's over. I would have asked you to go yesterday but I needed you to . . . well, we won't go into that. We've finished. It's over. I don't want you here any more. Our personal *and* our business partnership has come to an end, that's all. Simple. You'll get your money with interest . . . in about four months. I've got a deal in the pipeline which will give me an excellent return.' She raised her eyes to his. 'Go back to Helen. She's bound to take you back. Miss Mouse is still nuts about you.'

'You fucking cow.' He stared at her in disbelief.

'Spare me all of that, Dave. It's so negative. Just go quietly and put it down to . . . poor judgement of character. But remember: you give me any grief and I'll go to the police.'

Standing by the door he looked fit to kill. 'You set me up.'

'Yep. Set you up and put my sister down. Two birds with

one stone, or what?' Ruth smiled broadly, very pleased with herself. 'You'll look back and laugh at this one day. You'll dine out on it for years.'

He pointed a finger at her smug face. 'You need to see someone.' He tapped his temple. 'Crazy . . . mental.'

'Bye-bye, big boy. Thanks for the ride.'

The bedroom door slamming loudly behind him was perfect. A perfect end to a bad relationship – all brawn and no brain was Dave. He had been useful in ferreting out simple-minded people with an older property to sell, and he had proved an excellent liar when it came to giving them what he had called a fair price. But to agree to have Ruth's name on the deeds and documents? If that wasn't crazy and mental she didn't know what was. When she had said that it would be safer to keep his name off the contracts in case their game was discovered, he had actually commended her for smart thinking!

'And blondes are supposed to be dumb?' She leaned back on her plumped pillows, relishing her success. 'When will they ever learn – we just pretend to be dim.'

She opened the drawer of her bedside table, withdrew a small hand mirror and looked at herself. 'You are beautiful. You are bright. You've got everything.' She kissed her reflection. 'And you are worthy of any man, but you don't need him. And there's the rub. You – don't – need – them! They're the pits.'

Hugging the mirror to her breasts she thought about Sandy, if she had discovered her flooded basement yet. Soon she would move in with an offer to buy her out. Soon. But plans two and three had to be put into operation first. She looked at herself in the mirror again. 'It's her own fault, Ruth. She knew you wanted that property and that's why she put in a higher bid.' She reached for her cigarettes, wondering just how much Sandy had paid for number eleven. It wouldn't take long to find out. The painted lady would tell her. If not, she would find another way.

The estate agent, Freda Goldstein, was no more than a tarted-up, frustrated old bitch. A Jew who lived for money and who could no doubt be bought if the price was right. But money would not pass between them. Goldstein owed her one, and she would repay her debt.

'Shadow! Come here, girl!'

Obeying, the cross-breed ran into her room and leaped on her bed, licking her face and neck. Laughing, she squeezed and hugged her. 'Enough girl. Rest!'

The Dobermann-Labrador's reflexes were instant. She lay her head down and was as still as the bronze replica of her that stood in the corner of the bedroom. 'Good girl,' Ruth whispered, 'good girl.'

Chapter Five

Sitting on the garden steps in the shade enjoying cheese and pickle poppy-seed rolls, Johnnie fancied a beer. He and his mate Billy had pumped the water from the basement and installed two dehumidifiers, ready to draw moisture from the air overnight once the door and window were shut. With the midday sun burning down at eighty degrees and the window and door open, he reckoned the girls could resume working down there the following day.

The only real damage was to the satin fabric that was now drying in the sun. 'She putting on a front, or what?' Billy the skinny fifty-year-old plumber asked. 'Smile looked genuine enough.' He popped the remaining piece of roll into his mouth and licked his lips. 'I enjoyed that.'

'She's a survivor. Has to be. Twenty-six and a widow? It don't get worse than that. Poor little cow.'

Billy shook his head. 'What 'appened?'

'Car crash. She was in the passenger seat.'

'Tch. Terrible. Still, good-looking woman like that – she won't be on 'er own for long. They'll be after 'er like bees round the 'oney pot. Got a lovely smile. How long she 'ad this shop, then? I've only ever known it as the optician's.

Goes back donkey's years. My old grandad came 'ere when he was a boy. Always goin' on about the wonders of science, he was. Shocking eyesight. Reckoned he never knew there were leaves on trees till he was ten, when he was brought in 'ere. Had an old photo of himself as a kid wearing the bloomin' things.' He started to laugh. 'No wonder they used to call 'em four-eyes. That's just what he looked like in the picture. As if he had two pairs of orbs.'

'I could murder a pint, Billy.'

'Yeah?' He looked at his watch. 'I'll 'ave a quick one. This 'as put me back a bit.'

'Sorry about that. You're the only one I know with a pump. I'll make it up to yer.' He stood up and brushed his trousers down. 'I'll see you over the road in five minutes.' He pulled out his wallet and gave Billy a twenty-pound note. 'That cover it?'

'Plenty.'

'And here's another fiver. Beer money. Get me a pint in.'

Once Billy had gone and he was alone in the basement, Johnnie went over to look at the fractured pipe. He knew his work was sound but there was something else he wanted to check. Something he hadn't noticed when he'd first cleaned the brick floor and sealed it two months previously. To one side of the damaged pipe there were four bricks which were raised slightly higher than the rest, had no mortar packed between them and had been loosened by the water.

A builder since he left school, Johnnie had come across hiding places in the past – two of them. One had contained a sweet tin full of old white five-pound notes, and the other an important will and other documents which had caused a lot of trouble within the family he had been working for at the time.

He had been in hundreds of old houses and seen many cellars, but for some strange reason he had a strong feeling about Sandy's basement and those bricks.

Carefully easing one out, he scraped away the sludge and tapped with his fingernail, hitting metal. Cursing himself as he remembered arranging to have a drink with Billy, he replaced the brick. He would come back later and check further. Standing up and stretching his back, he started to laugh.

'Something's in there,' he murmured. 'I know it.'

'I'm just gonna put the kettle on, Johnnie! Do you want a cup of tea?' It was Maggie, Sandy's mother, there to help Sandy sort herself out.

'No thanks!' He pulled his mind away from hidden treasure and went upstairs.

'That looks OK. Should be dry enough to work in by tomorrow.'

'What about tonight?' Sandy asked.

'What about tonight?'

'Will it be dry enough for the girls to work down there? If I put in an extra heater—'

'You can't do that, babe! Give 'em a break. Poor cows — working through the night?' He thought he was seeing a different side to Sandy.

Laughing, she told him to go upstairs to her living room and take a look inside.

'Why?'

'Just go and listen outside the door if you don't want

to join in.' She was still smiling.

'I promised Billy I'd go over for a drink. He's only got fifteen minutes. Go on then, spit it out. What's going on up there?'

'Six machinists drinking tea. I said I'd pay them for the day. Told them to go away and sunbathe. They've offered to go home and sleep until tonight and then come back. They've seen the orders and they're just as pleased as I am.'

'Fair enough. Yeah, it should be all right down there; bit damp, but if you've got the heaters on . . .' He shrugged and walked out.

'Johnnie! Thanks.'

'See you in fifteen minutes. I wanna check the basement before I go. The cheese rolls were great.'

'He's such a nice man,' Maggie murmured. 'If I wasn't married to your father . . .'

'Bit young for you, isn't he?'

'Cheeky cow. What's ten years?'

'Have you got six red boob tubes?' A teenager stood in the doorway looking worried. 'We're in a show tonight and we've been let down with our costumes.'

'You're lucky. The girls have been making them up since eight this morning.' The last thing Sandy wanted was for people to know she'd had a disaster already. 'I'll just nip down and get them.'

'You have got six! Great!' The girl looked as if she would burst with happiness. 'Be back in fifteen minutes. Don't sell them!' She went out as quickly as she'd come in.

'Sandy . . . if this goes on you're not going to be able to keep up.'

'You wanna bet? There's always your conservatory, don't forget.' She opened the door to the basement. 'Dad did offer it!'

Clasping her hands together and closing her eyes, Maggie thanked God that things were going so well for her daughter. She couldn't believe how Sandy had taken the flood in her stride.

'Hello, Mum. Got a new job then? Or are you just helping your favourite child out?'

Turning slowly, Maggie was speechless. She hadn't seen Ruth for over four months and there she stood, as if nothing had happened, a spiteful look on her face. 'I've never favoured either of you. You know that.' She held out her hands, believing Ruth would take them.

'I'm not stopping. I just thought I'd let Sandy know that should she fail –' she glanced at the clothes on the rail – 'and I have a feeling she might . . . then I would still like to buy the property that *I* was promised first refusal of. If she makes me pay over the odds, then so be it. I need this space, as I'm sure you know. Tell her not to leave it too long. Property prices are predicted to fall. Come on, Shadow.' She turned on her heels, her obedient dog close by.

Stunned, Maggie felt a surge of anger. Surely Sandy hadn't pulled such a trick on her sister? She felt like shouting for her to come up from the basement but sat down instead. She had to think. Had things been going on behind her back? Was Sandy keeping things from her? It seemed obvious that Ruth had been visiting the shop. Why hadn't Sandy said she had seen her? Sandy knew how much she was fretting and missing Ruth.

'Six boob tubes and still four left!' Sandy looked at Maggie and waited for her reaction. Maggie knew as well as Sandy that it would have been bad for business if she couldn't meet the request. 'Mum? You OK?'

'Why didn't you tell me Ruth was back, Sandy?'

'What?'

'She's been in. Well, in the doorway, anyway.'

Angry with Ruth for sneaking around, Sandy dropped the garments into an empty cardboard box. 'It wouldn't have made you any happier if I *had* told you. If you knew *how* she made her appearance yesterday.'

Tearful, Maggie looked at her. 'Yesterday? You mean you hadn't seen her before then?'

'Of course not! D'you really think I would keep something like that from you?' She pulled up a chair and sat down. 'Yesterday, when I was out the back, just before the guests arrived, a big black dog came rushing out of next door. I was terrified. I had my eyes shut tight. When I opened them, standing next to the dog at the bottom of the garden was Ruth. I'll never forget the look on her face.' Sandy swallowed and covered her face with both hands. 'It was horrible, Mum. Really, really horrible. It was as if she was my enemy and not my own flesh and blood. What did I do? What did I do to make her hate me so much?'

'She came in the back way? Through next door?'

'Yes. She owns it. I only found out yesterday, from Freda. She had no idea we were sisters. Ruth wanted this shop as well.'

'But next door is a tobacconist's. Leo owns it, doesn't he?'

'No, he rents it. According to Freda, Ruth's forcing him out. Pushing up the rent or the lease . . . I don't know. Anyway, she's my next-door neighbour. I s'pose she's gone in there today because of the burst pipe. Their basement probably got wet too.' She laid her hand on Maggie's. 'I was gonna phone you last night to tell you, but, well, Johnnie came round and then Freda and we got talking and the time slipped away. I can't say I was looking forward to telling you, that she'd brought a *big black dog* with her!'

Try as she might, Sandy couldn't stop herself from crying. 'How could she do that, Mum? How could she! You know how terrified I am of dogs. I still have nightmares. The one she had with her was just like the one I've always dreamed about! She *knew* that! I even drew a picture of one once, remember? She knew and she went out and bought one and she brought it here!'

'She wasn't thinking . . .'

'Yes she was! She knew exactly what she was doing. If you saw the way she stood there with it—'

'All right, love, all right. We'll get to the bottom of this. I'll get Father to talk to her . . .'

Wiping her eyes, Sandy shook her head. 'I don't know what's going on.' She looked at Maggie. 'What's happening to us? We used to be a proper family, didn't we? Me and Ruth were all right when we were little . . .'

'You were all right together for longer than that. It was Ruthie who changed. When she was in her late teens.'

'But *why*? What did we do?'

'I don't know. She went from being an ordinary rebellious teenager to someone very bitter. I must have missed something along the way. I've racked my brains enough in the past wondering what could have gone wrong. Was she unhappy and I missed it? Was I so full of my job at John Lewis's that I couldn't see what was under my nose?'

'Flying visit.' Johnnie strode into the shop and straight through to the basement door. He could see that the women were talking privately and shedding tears. 'Just check the pipe and I'll be off,' he said, making himself scarce.

'Can you think of anything?' Maggie was searching for an answer but Sandy couldn't give her one. Didn't dare give one. Yes, there had been some incidents in the past that neither parent knew about, and there seemed little point in dragging it all up now. Sandy wasn't one for dwelling on history or worrying about the future. She lived for the here and now, one day at a time. Get that right, and the future would take care of itself and the past would stay in the past.

'No, Mum. We had a good childhood – you and Dad have been great. We couldn't have done better. Stop blaming yourself. We both love you.'

'If only I could be sure of that. It's the way she looks at me sometimes . . . as if there's something she wants to say. As if she's harbouring something. Something she blames me for.'

'No. It's your imagination.' Standing, she moved her chair to one side and glanced at a customer who was holding a satin dress to her. 'What size are you?' she asked, trying to clear her mind of other things.

'Depends really . . . on the cut. If it's true to size, then a fourteen should fit.' She lowered her head to one side and checked her appearance in the full-length mirror. 'I don't usually wear red. My cheeks flush so easily . . .'

'So do mine. Have you tried green foundation?'

The woman looked at her as if she were taking the rise. 'Not lately.'

'I'm serious. You can buy it in the chemist's. It tones down your red. It's good. I've got a tube I haven't used if you'd like. You only need a touch.'

'Yeah, OK. I would like to. Thanks. I'll just try this on.'

Smiling to herself, Maggie commended her daughter for her good business manner. She had brought her mood round and managed to look natural, as if she hadn't just been having a heart-to-heart talk.

Placing the four loose bricks one on top of the other, Johnnie carefully lifted an old tin box from its hiding place. He felt a surge of excitement. Telling himself not to be stupid, that it was probably a load of old junk, he freed the lid. The box, twelve inches by twelve inches, was crammed full. On top of some old, neatly folded documents there was a collection of jewellery. A gold pocket watch and chain, some jewelled rings, a couple of brooches, a heavy, ornate gold locket and some necklaces. None of it was modern: it all looked as if it might be early Victorian.

Collecting himself, he replaced the lid and lowered the box back in, covered the secret place with the bricks and then scanned the basement. What other secrets might it hold, and how long had the treasure trove been there? Would old man Cohen have known about it and then forgotten it in his old age? He doubted it.

'See you tonight for the palm-reading,' he whispered into Sandy's ear on his way out.

'Don't be late. I'm making shepherd's pie. My speciality.'

'No need for that. We can eat before we come.' He didn't want her to feel under any obligation.

'For the Chinese.' She didn't want to be in his debt.

'Fair enough. I'll bring a bottle of wine.' He nodded at Maggie and went out whistling.

Passing Leo's, he resisted the temptation to go in and find out more about this business of Sandy's sister and the sabotage. If Leo had got his facts right and she did own number ten, Sandy would tell him about it in her own good time. Meanwhile he would keep quiet about the pipe having been damaged deliberately.

Crossing over Roman Road, like other men in the market he couldn't take his eyes off the tanned leggy blonde with hair down to her waist. *Must be ugly*, he told himself, stepping up his pace to come level with her. A side glance proved him wrong. Her blue-green almond-shaped eyes, small, straight nose, full lips and cleavage were enough to raise a wilting tulip.

'Nice dog.' He smiled, making contact. 'What's his name?'

'Her name is Shadow. What's yours?'

'Johnnie.' He admired her front.

'Why the overalls, Johnnie?'

'I'm working. Builder and decorator. Is she friendly?'

'If I tell her to be. Cheap, are you?'

'Depends.'

'On?'

'The job. Got something you want looking at?'

'Give me your card and I'll let you know.' She smiled seductively, showing off perfect white teeth. 'I'll ask around. See how good you are.'

'I'll write my number down,' he said, ignoring her last remark. 'I'm out of cards. I've got a notebook in here somewhere,' he said, searching through his overall pockets. 'Ah, here it is.' He scribbled his telephone number and added his name. 'My reputation stands me in good stead, as you'll no doubt find out. What do you want doing?'

'I'll tell you when I call. We should meet up to discuss the work. You'll be on my premises for a few months, so I want to be sure we can get on. I can't stand bad feelings, can you?'

'No, Shadow's mum, I can't.' He felt as if they'd met before.

Ruth glanced at the slip of paper, at his name. 'Married, Johnnie?'

'Divorced.'

'That helps. I hate it when people break off from work because of domestic problems. I prefer to get the job done once it's started. Prepared to work late, are you?'

'Keep me supplied with tea and biscuits and there's no saying what favours I'll do.'

'Keep your price down and I might surprise you too.' She tugged at Shadow's lead and walked away, teasing him with her arse.

Feeling lucky, Johnnie went into the betting shop, unaware that he was being watched. Freda had seen the little tête-à-tête, and didn't like the way he had drooled over Ms Brown. She had known Johnnie for years and was wise to his womanizing, and hoped she had seen a change in him since Sandy came on the scene. He had treated her with respect, and Freda had been full of admiration. She liked him a lot, and had overlooked his flirting in the past; if women were attracted to him and he was unattached, who could blame him? But with Sandy it was different. She was still grieving, and in her vulnerable state could easily be hurt.

It seemed obvious to Freda that Sandy was becoming fond of Johnnie and she was now wondering if she should perhaps have a quiet word in his ear.

Before going into Nova to see her friend, Freda caught sight of a young lady wearing a red sequinned miniskirt, a dark green T-shirt which had been ripped in three places and was held together with large safety pins. Her cropped hair had been dyed black with bleached white streaks running through it. Her face was heavily made-up with thick black lines around her eyes and white lipstick. On her feet were Doc Martens; on her legs, thin black tights with ladders.

Bemused by the sight, Freda had to admit that though bizarre, the look worked. *Who would have thought it – a glitzy evening skirt with rags and clodhoppers.* Grinning, she went into the shop to tell Sandy that she had seen three people in her clothes already. Soon the entire Roman Road would be full of ladies in red.

Meeting Maggie, who was just leaving, she was ready to tell her about the young girl with the safety pins when she saw the look on her face. 'What's wrong, Maggie? You look as if you've lost a shilling and found a copper.'

'What a nightmare.' She moved closer and whispered in her ear. 'A burst pipe. The basement was flooded. It's drying out. She doesn't want the customers to know.'

'Stock?'

'Just one roll damaged. It could have been a disaster. But what a shock! Listen, I must go, I'm supposed to be at work. I'll catch up with you.'

Seeing to three customers at once, Sandy signalled to Freda to put the kettle on for coffee. Freda signalled back that she would take a look downstairs first.

Pleased that things were not as bad as Maggie had had her believe, she went into the garden and saw the red satin drying on a chair under the piercing sun. The watermark running through the fabric created a pattern. She moved closer and examined it, and decided there and then to get Sandy to run up a frock for her.

Taking it back inside for safe keeping, she placed it on some tissue paper on a shelf and imagined herself in a creation of her own design.

'It's a bloody scandal.' Leo had seen her go into Nova and knew she would have to check on the damage. 'Sabotage. It's a disgrace.'

'I wish you wouldn't do that, Leo. You're like a ghost wrapped in flesh the way you appear from nowhere! What are you talking about, sabotage?'

'There you go, using the same tone as Johnnie. I told him, but I don't think he wanted to know either.' He flicked the air with his hand and turned away.

'Stop sulking! Come here and say what you've got to say. Go on, I'm listening.'

'That pipe didn't break by itself. And the cement around the bricks on my side of the wall has been deliberately

137

knocked out. Someone managed to push through and burst that pipe. We all know who that someone could be. Take a look for yourself.' He showed her the section of pipe which had been replaced.

'Interesting.' She peered at the bricks, and it did look as if Leo could be right. 'But Johnnie didn't agree with you?'

'Ah . . . he was non-committal. Said that even if it were true, we shouldn't say anything upstairs. Thought that Sandy would be shattered if she knew her sister—'

'He's right, we shouldn't say anything. At least the damage is minor.'

'What about the cost? She'll get a bill from Johnnie, from Billy the plumber; not to mention the price of hiring the dehumidifiers.'

'Insurance. Didn't Albert hear anything?'

'Do me a favour – Albert? The man's almost completely deaf. But never mind that. My point is this: what might this sister do next? Maybe I'm gonna get some of her treatment. She wants me out before the end of the month, before my lease runs out. She wants us all out of the way! She's bloody ruthless.'

'Leave it be for now. She's got us to contend with if she—'

'You mean let's bury our heads in the sand? Meanwhile she plots behind our backs and we all go down the pan.'

'You're overreacting.'

'Am I? Did you ever imagine I would be out of business in a couple of weeks?'

She had to admit that he was right. The futures of three people were being jeopardized by one person: Leo's, Albert's and Sandy's. Yet to look at Ms Brown, butter wouldn't melt in her mouth. There was little point in confronting her; of course she would deny everything. The only course to take, as far as she could tell, was to keep one step ahead of her.

Now that Ms Brown knew who had successfully purchased number eleven, no doubt she would make it her business to find out how much Sandy had paid. She would find Cohen's nephew soon enough and could stir up trouble for Freda, adding her to the hit list. Her young assistant Barbara had been right in advising her not to underprice for the sake of her feelings. There really was no place for those in business. Young Cohen could report her and she could lose her licence.

'I think I'll befriend her. See how that works,' said Freda aloud.

'Don't bother. She's made of iron. I tried being nice – she saw through me. If you had seen the bloody smirk on her face . . .'

'OK, Leo. What do you suggest?'

'Simple. Tell Sandy she should go to the police. Say that someone got into my basement and sabotaged the pipe – that Ms Brown sabotaged the pipe. They can take fingerprints.' He shrugged. 'Why make life difficult? Go to the police.' He brushed the air twice with his hand.

'It's not that easy.' She turned from him and stared out into the garden. 'I let Sandy have the shop for a thousand pounds less than what Brown offered. I told young Cohen that Brown had pulled out. I advised him to take ten thousand.' She turned slowly and looked him in the eye. 'I lied.'

'You think I don't know that? How long have we known each other? Thirty years? More?'

'What if Cohen finds out?'

'I'll say I was there when Ms Brown told you she was withdrawing her offer. I'm not adverse to white lies occasionally. I'll tell him how lucky he was that another contender was there and that you were right to take a drop and make a quick sale.' He sniffed and smiled. 'Next?'

'Why don't we offer to buy *her* out? Next door is useless to her if she can't have this place. In fact, I bet she's already thinking that way – Plan B. Plan A is to drive Sandy out and if that fails, I'll bet my bottom dollar that she'll sell.'

'Freda, you're getting carried away. Keep it simple: police.' He flicked the air and went out through the garden door.

'Leo!'

'What now?'

'When exactly are you going to wind up the business?'

'Depends.'

'On?'

'On whether my cousin's son offers me a decent price for my stock. He's just taken over a small shop in Stratford. He's gonna see the bank manager today for a loan. If he can, he'll buy me out lock, stock and barrel and I shall put my hands together.

'She's doing me a favour. It was forced on me, but now . . . I quite like the idea of not having to get up and travel in from Chingford every bloody morning through the traffic. I've been up at five o'clock since I don't know when! I'm ready to retire. Sixty-two next birthday. Ha! I feel more like eighty! A month in the Canaries, that's what I need – and that is what I shall have. Find myself a nice dolly-bird over there.'

Smiling, Freda waved him away. He had a point: keep it simple. Brown wouldn't be able to hold on to that building without letting the shop. She had taken out a loan for the full amount, that much Freda did know. So she must have a mortgage on another property – probably the one she lived in. Ms Brown wasn't quite as clever in business as she liked to make out. She had lost herself a good reliable rent from Leo. It was a good thing he was ready to get out. All that she had to do was sit tight and wait. She had nothing to lose now that Leo had said he would lie for her.

Having fed Shadow, Ruth settled her in her basket in the living room and went upstairs to check in the wardrobe to see if Dave's clothes were still there. As predicted, he had returned while she was out and packed his case. No doubt he would be back for his stereo and other things soon, so she would have to act quickly if she was to keep them.

She picked up the telephone and called a locksmith, asking him to come immediately. Lying through her back teeth, with as much charm as she could muster, she told him that she had disturbed a burglar who had let himself in with a key – probably one of the many lodgers who had lived there before she moved in. The man bought the story and promised to be there within the hour.

Once she had him change the lock, she would drive to the factory where Sandy used to work, to Johnson's, and buy as many remnants as she could from their tiny retail outlet shop

141

where they usually sold waste at rock-bottom prices to the Petticoat Lane market traders. Remnants, scraps and seconds was what she was after. Plan B would soon be put into operation. Leo had told her he planned to be out as soon as possible and that suited her down to the ground. His little speech, intended to prick her conscience, had achieved the very opposite. Telling her she was a heartless person who would never have any friends had only fuelled her desire, her determination to see the back of him.

Standing in front of her full-length mirror Ruth decided that she was bored with her looks. Johnnie the builder had liked them, but she had a feeling he might prefer it if she looked a little more mature. A bit more wifey-looking. He was the type who screwed tarts for pleasure, but was really on the lookout for someone who would put on his slippers and have his tea ready when he came home.

She drew her fingers through her long silky hair. She would have it cut short. A soft perm to make her look warm and cuddly. Maybe a pastel twinset from Marks and Spencer's and a pair of slacks to match. Nothing too old-fashioned; an outfit for the slightly older woman. It would be amusing to dress like a thirty-five-year-old instead of twenty-three. It would be the first time she had aged up instead of down and Ruth loved *first times*.

Once she had perfected the new image, she would visit her parents to show them what a lovely lady she had turned out to be. She would need her dad to rewire number ten, once Leo had left and Albert had kicked the bucket. The shock of a ferocious dog snarling in his face could easily prove fatal.

Yes, Ruthie . . . it's time for a new look. At work and on the home front. She would adopt the part of a mature estate agent – pleasant and charming as she showed boring people around boring properties. She might even charm her boss into giving her a rise.

Now that Dave was out of her life she would need to supplement her salary in some other way. Builders had enjoyed a boom since the sixties. Johnnie had the confidence of someone with a very healthy bank balance. She would phone and invite him round for a meal to discuss the work which she would eventually screw him for.

'One bottle of wine, box of Milk Tray, and this.' Johnnie handed Sandy a small, flat paper bag. 'What time's Freda coming?'

'Not till half past eight. She's got a property to look at.' Sandy pulled the slim grey book from the bag and looked puzzled. '*English Silver and Gold Hallmarks*?'

'It goes with the other present,' he grinned, hardly able to contain himself. 'What time are the girls getting 'ere?'

'They're not. We decided against it in the end. They're coming in at five in the morning. So I can't be up late tonight, Johnnie . . .' Sandy narrowed her eyes, a serious look on her face. 'What other present?'

'Come on. Basement.' He stood up, desperately trying to keep a straight face.

'What's going on?'

'Come *on*.' He walked out of the sitting room with Sandy following, firing questions which he wouldn't answer. Down in the basement, Johnnie pointed to the four bricks. 'Use this to prise 'em up.' He handed her a small lever.

'What *is* this?' Now she was smiling. 'You're not telling me there's something under there?'

'Have a look!'

Getting down on her knees, she cursed him as she broke a fingernail lifting the first brick. Seeing the tin box, she giggled. '*You* put it there, you sod.'

'Don't be a silly girl. I wouldn't do a thing like that. The water caused the brick to rise a bit. I saw it earlier when I was checking the pipe.'

'Have you looked inside?' she was chuckling now, her eyes shining. '*Have* you?'

'Just a peep.'

'I bet!'

'I'm telling you! A quick shufti, than I put the lid back on. It's your treasure.'

She pulled the lid off and put a hand to her mouth. 'Jesus,' was all she could say.

'Come on! I want to see what's underneath all the junk jewellery!'

'This isn't junk, Johnnie. This is *not* junk.'

'Take it out then. It's the papers I'm interested in.'

She carefully lifted the ornate gold pocket watch and chain. 'Bloody hell – feel the weight of that.' She passed it over and then picked up a beautiful platinum butterfly brooch which was encrusted with small diamonds and rubies. She turned it over and sure enough, there was a hallmark. 'Do you think it's silver?'

'How am I s'posed to know that?' He peered at it and then took it from her, turning it in his hand. 'That's not silver, babe – that's white gold and diamonds if I'm not mistaken.'

She looked at Johnnie. 'It's a hoard!'

'Yep.'

'I can't believe it!' She opened her arms and he pulled her close. Resting her head on his shoulder, his warm, soft body against hers and his masculine smell – a mixture of himself and aftershave – reminded her briefly of Roy. There was that same comfortable, trusting feeling between two people that she missed so much. He kissed her lightly on the neck and then looked into her eyes, smiling. 'Congratulations, babe.'

'Can I really keep it? I mean, it's not mine. What if it belonged to Mr Cohen? It should go to his nephew, surely?'

Letting her go, embarrassed by his instant arousal, he shook his head. 'No . . . I reckon that box 'asn't been disturbed in over a hundred years. Let's 'ave a look at the papers underneath. That should throw some light on it.'

'We'll take it upstairs,' she said, rising. 'You wait till Freda sees this.'

A look of concern passed across his face. 'I think you should wait, babe. Let's check it first, eh? If it's as old and valuable as I think it is, you'll 'ave to report it to the local coroner, through the police.'

'Johnnie! They'll keep it!'

'Not necessarily. The treasure-trove laws are just as beneficial to the finder as they are to the Crown. If they do declare it the property of the Crown you'll get a reward – full current value. You can't lose.'

'I want to *keep* it!'

'All right, all right! You might well do. It depends. Come on, this is driving me mad. I want to have a butcher's at them documents.'

Settled in the sitting room with a glass of wine and a cigarette to calm her excitement, Sandy examined each piece, giving out small gasps of disbelief every now and then, while Johnnie read in silence.

'Well . . . we can wipe out the theory of it belonging to Cohen's nephew. These receipts are in the name of a Reverend Montgomery, and dated between 1789 and 1816.'

'Where does that leave me?'

He shrugged. 'Treasure trove. Financially you're on to a winner but you can't keep anything.'

'Not even the brooch? Or one of these rings?'

'Nope.'

'Oh, come on! What's with all this honesty? Why should the bloody Crown have it and not us?' She picked up the pocket watch and stroked it teasingly with her thumb. 'Don't tell me you wouldn't love to have this in your waistcoat pocket.'

''Course I would. But someone else might 'ave the same idea. The burst pipe didn't 'appen on its own.'

'What's that supposed to mean?'

He leaned back in the armchair and sipped his wine. 'What if someone else noticed them bricks when they were viewing? I'm sure Freda showed quite a few people round. What if they had access to next door; began drilling through and burst a pipe?'

'Drilling . . .' Sandy said thoughtfully. *Drilling*. Maybe it hadn't just been her imagination. Maybe she *had* heard it.

146

'But who would have a key to next door other than Leo, Freda and old Albert?'

'Dunno; but the point is, someone else might 'ave known that little lot was under there, and that someone could get you into a lot of trouble if you don't declare the find. *All* of the find.'

Sandy pressed her lips together thoughtfully. 'I'll take that risk, hide this somewhere else – up there right by me – and wait. If anyone does blab then I'll put it back. Nothing lost.'

'Why? You could use the cash, couldn't you?'

She looked again at the beautiful pieces in the box. 'I don't think I could part with any of it. I want it. It's a girl's dream to find a box of treasure. I mean look at it, for Christ's sake! It's jewellery! *Jewels*!'

'So you don't need the cash?'

'I won't starve.'

The sound of the doorbell interrupted them. 'Freda. Put it away and we'll talk about it later, once she's gone.'

'Can't we show it to her, Johnnie? I don't want to put it away. I want to get every piece out *and* I want to read those old papers and things . . .'

'Put it *away*!' he said urgently. 'Till you've had time to take it in. Wait till you've decided what you're gonna do.'

'I know what I'm gonna do. I'm keeping it.' She stood up to answer the door. 'And what's more, I'm showing it to her!'

Women. Impatient and impulsive. Johnnie picked up the tin and the papers and hid them behind an armchair in a corner of the room. It could be anyone ringing that bell.

Settling himself down again, another mood overtook him, another thought filled his mind. Why was he so concerned for Sandy's welfare? Why was it that after just a short time knowing each other, they seemed so close? *Gonna 'ave to pull back a bit, Johnnie.* He had been hurt more than he could describe when his Shirley had left him for another man. *Wise men never fall in love*, he told himself. The song 'Fools Rush In', ran through his brain. He felt a warmth as he remembered the way she had held out her arms. Snapping himself out of it, he reminded himself that he could get laid whenever he pleased. There were plenty of women out there who wanted it. Why should Sandy be any different?

'What's all this about buried treasure?' Freda said, disbelieving but hopeful. 'She's like a cat with double cream.'

'It's behind the armchair.' He nodded to the corner and then looked up at Sandy, mildly disapproving. When she winked back at him flirtatiously, he hid his smile.

'I'm just gonna throw the vegetables into hot water – won't be a sec. Wait for me, Freda – I want to show you what's inside. You wait,' she chuckled, 'you're in for a shock.'

Once Sandy was in the kitchen, Freda sat down very close to Johnnie, leaned forward and looked him in the eye. 'Don't mess with her emotions.'

'Leave off, Freda! Bloody cheek. What d'yer take me for?'

'Just warning you, that's all.' She stood up. 'She's a nice girl. Who was the tall blonde I saw you ogling earlier?' As if she didn't know. She was testing his integrity.

'Don't miss a trick, do you?'

'No. Friend of yours, is she?'

'Only just met 'er. Asked me if I'd like her to 'old me

willy. I said I'd think about it. All right?' He shrugged. 'Don't even remember 'er name.' And neither could he. She hadn't meant that much; although now that Freda mentioned her, he had to admit that she was a little cracker and seemed to be up for grabs. He might give her a tinkle the next day. He couldn't remember if he'd taken her number. Or rather, if she had given it to him. He had a feeling she hadn't. Clever little cow, teasing him like that.

'Right!' Arriving, Sandy rubbed her hands together and then wiggled her fingers over the tin. 'Ready?'

'Oh, just open the bloody thing and get it over with.' Freda tried to sound bored; in truth she couldn't wait to see what was inside.

Johnnie sat back and watched Sandy behaving like a child, her face lighting up when she held the jewels in her hand. He tried to imagine her as a little girl with her bead box. She had told him about her collection of different coloured beads, some cut glass, which she had thought were diamonds at the time, and which an older girl had stolen from her. Fuck it. He crossed his legs and rapped his fingers on the arm of the chair. If he wasn't careful he would go and fall in love.

Time to get out, he told himself. Time to run.

Preoccupied, the women's laughter as they tried on the jewellery went over his head. He thought about Sandy's dad, and what he might say if he, Johnnie, started courting his girl. After all, the nine-year gap was almost a decade, and Terry might also be opposed to the idea of one of his own mates getting involved with Sandy. His own wife Shirley hadn't been one for having babies, so he couldn't relate to the way Terry might feel.

Johnnie's marriage hadn't been perfect, far from it. Sex had been more of a habit than an experience, and as for joint interests, he couldn't think of one. Shirley had liked a good time, while he preferred to relax in the evenings after grafting all day. So much for marrying your childhood sweetheart, he thought.

Nine years of marriage, eight years of pretence; lying not only to each other but to themselves. Keeping up appearances for the sake of it. In the big picture, did it matter? Did anyone give a damn whether he was happily married or not? Truth be known, most people liked to hear about a split; it made them feel smug and secure, the way he had been before Shirley had forced him to be honest and face up to the truth.

Johnnie had been brought up to believe that once married, you made it work. Only wimps threw in the towel. Maybe his parents had been exorcising their own disappointment through their offspring. He tried to remember a time when his mum and dad even looked as if they wanted to be in each other's company. He tried to stop thinking about it. In his mind's eye were their blank expressions: the boredom, the silences, the polite few words. All that changed when visitors came: then they'd be joking and laughing as if they were best of friends who enjoyed life between the sheets more than most married couples.

He wondered about love. Did it really exist? It if did, what did it mean? How were two people in love supposed to feel? Act? Live? He didn't lust after Sandy the way he did other women, but the feeling she inspired when he was close to her was different to anything he had experienced so far.

'What d'yer reckon, Johnnie?' Smiling, Sandy wiggled

her finger, showing off the diamond and emerald ring. He nodded thoughtfully; she had placed it on the third finger of her left hand, removing the gold band – her wedding ring.

'You're engaged to a ghost,' he said without thinking.

'Yeah . . .' Sandy slipped the ring off, the smile fading from her face. 'Still married to one too. I shouldn't have taken his ring off yet, should I?' She looked at Freda.

'Why not?' The familiar look of indifference was in her eyes. 'You plan to stay unmarried?'

'Maybe.'

'It's vegetable soup for dinner then, is it?' Johnnie changed the subject. 'Be cooked to a pulp by now.'

'See?' Freda shrugged. 'Men – they think only of their stomachs and their dicks.'

'Well there's not much between the two, is there?' Johnnie kept a straight face and spread out his finger and thumb. 'About that much,' he said.

Laughing, Sandy pushed the ring back on her finger and went into the kitchen to see to the meal.

'Not falling in love are you, Johnnie?' asked Freda.

'Why d'you ask?'

'The way you look at her.'

'Got eyes in the back of your 'ead, have you?'

'Yes; and in my kneecaps. You were bragging. A four-inch gap, more like.'

'Never. Want me to prove it?'

'No – not on an empty stomach.'

Entering with a steaming bowl of mixed vegetables, Sandy apologized for the overcooked courgettes.

'I do love courgettes.' Freda measured a nine-inch space

with her hands. 'They've got them *this* big in the market.' She eyed Johnnie – he was finding it difficult not to laugh at her vulgarity.

'I prefer smaller ones. They're sweeter. I'll fetch the shepherd's pie – it's done to a treat.' Sandy looked from Freda to Johnnie. 'What you laughing at?'

'Differences.'

'Oh right . . .' She eyed the dining table, checking that she hadn't forgotten anything.

'Get yourselves to the table then. Sit where you want.' Too involved with the meal to join in the joke, which didn't seem that funny to her, she flashed out of the room again.

'Not there, Freed –' he pointed to the end of the table – 'there. I want to sit opposite Sandy. Your kneecaps worry me.'

Returning with the shepherd's pie, Sandy found them laughing again. 'It can't be that funny.'

'It wasn't. Must 'ave been that glass of wine.' He took the steaming dish from Sandy and placed it on a heatproof table mat, enjoying the homely feeling that she had created.

The delicious smell that rose from the pie as she carefully scooped out a serving caused him to sigh inwardly. She could cook too.

One week later, as Leo and his cousin moved his things out of the shop, Ruth moved her boxes in: large cardboard boxes full of remnants. Not a word was said between them as they passed each other going in and out.

Shadow had been told to stay in the back garden and be quiet, and as usual she obeyed her mistress implicitly. Having taken a week of her holiday time to complete her plans and make more arrangements, Ruth was pleased that the sunny weather was still peaking. Once the shop had been cleared, she would lie in the garden for a while and top up her tan. She wondered if Sandy had seen Shadow from her upstairs window, trembling at the thought of him bounding into her backyard.

'You're very lucky, you know,' she said suddenly, keeping her back to Leo as he carried out the last of his things. 'If I'd raised the rent after you'd signed the new lease, you'd be in shit street now.'

'For small mercies . . .' he mumbled and walked out.

Not satisfied, Ruth strode to the door and called after him as he climbed into the passenger seat of his cousin's van. 'If you've forgotten anything, it's going out with the rubbish!'

Slamming the van door shut, Leo looked straight ahead so she would not have the pleasure of seeing his tears. Now that he was completely free of the place, and of her, he could go back whenever he liked – as a customer. She obviously intended to sell something there, and whether he wanted what she had to offer or not, he was going to go in and prove to be the most difficult customer ever likely to cross her threshold. After that, he would go up and see his friend Albert and the two of them would take tea in the garden. She could do nothing about that. Albert's lease gave him access, and it was watertight. If the dog was put out to bother them, he would welcome it. One tiny rip in his trousers, one faint scratch from those paws and he would have the monster put down. He could do it: like Albert's freedom to use the garden,

Leo had checked his rights about ferocious dogs too.

Bored once Leo was gone, Ruth scanned the shop. It looked dingy, dull and very dusty now that everything was out. The last thing she wanted was to start washing shelves and paintwork. She would get her mother to do that – Maggie always liked to feel needed, wanted even. Wanted. That was a joke. Ruth had stopped wanting either of her parents long ago. They hadn't been there when she needed them, so why should she fulfil her filial obligations.

She hadn't planned to go in to see Sandy quite so soon. Her first intention was to drive the old man upstairs into his grave, and she had planned to begin the execution that very day by taking Shadow up for an hour or so. But now that she was in the tobacconist's, feeling like a landlord, with just the wall between her and Sandy, the desire to go into the boutique was greater than sunbathing or tormenting the old man. She couldn't wait to see Sandy's face when she told her she was going to open up the next day selling remnants, so that customers could run up their own sequinned miniskirts and boob tubes for next to nothing.

Prising the large staples from one of the boxes, she was eager to inspect the goods inside. She had slipped fifty pounds into the young man's hand at Johnson's and told him to keep it for himself – she didn't want a receipt. Why shouldn't he have a bit of the family fortune?

The box open, she beheld a wondrous spectacle of sparkling colours as the sun shining through the window caught the sequins. Pulling out various fabrics, she smiled. The greasy, long-haired teenager had done her proud. The remnants were probably the best he had in stock. Some pieces

154

were six feet long, the smallest three feet – and all the fabric in the box was stretch. She felt like going back and showing the lad what his manhood was for. Maybe next time she would shock the life out of him and give the old come-on. Better to pay with her body and keep her bank account that bit healthier. The past began to come back.

Two shillings. That's how much *he* used to press into the palm of her hand and whisper . . . *for keeping our secret.* For that she could thank both her parents. For their faith in people; for seeing no evil, hearing no evil and suppressing Ruth into speaking no evil. The equilibrium was not to be disturbed. She stared ahead of her thoughtfully.

'Now that Leo's gone, what will you do with the shop?' Sandy said as she stood in the doorway.

Spinning around to face her sister, Ruth clenched both hands, her long nails digging painfully into her palms. She wanted to punch that smug, self-confident face, grab that ginger hair and drag her around the shop.

'I'm not sure, Sandy,' she said, controlling her voice. 'Poor Leo. I wish I could have kept the rent down for him. How's tricks?'

'I didn't know that you were the other interested party, Ruth. Not that it matters. You were only speculating.'

'And you're not?'

'No. Everything I've got is in there. It's my livelihood. I couldn't have just carried on working for Johnson's . . .'

'Why not? You always enjoyed it. At least that's the impression you gave off, with gusto.' Ruth glanced at Sandy's face and looked away. Those bloody freckles had always looked worse in the summer.

'Were you going to run the dry-cleaner's yourself, then? With your own delicate hands?'

'If it doesn't work out for you I'll take the property off your hands at the price you paid. What was it, by the way?'

'It'll work out. Has to.' Now it was Sandy who wanted to smack Ruth's self-assured face. 'I wouldn't sell it anyway. I'd let the shop and live upstairs. I love my flat; I love living in Roman Road. I've made some good friends.'

'Well . . . don't let your pride stop you from coming to me if things go wrong. We all have to do a bit of crawling before we turn to dust.' She cleared her throat, making it clear she wanted Sandy to go.

'You should go and see Mum and Dad. They're really cut up over you walking out of their lives like that.'

'That was the idea. *Don't know what you've got till it's gone,* and all that.' She grinned. 'I'm going round there tonight as it 'appens. Give 'em another chance. They might apologize – who knows?' She flicked the catch on the door, indicating that she was ready to lock up and leave.

'Apologize for what?'

'For disowning me years ago when I rebelled against society and they took it personally. When they threw all their attention at you, deliberately to upset me. Emotional cruelty.'

'That's bollocks and you know it!'

Ruth pushed her face up close to Sandy's. 'Is it? Sure about that, are you? Sure you didn't know what was going on and added to it by sucking up to them? You ginger-headed grovelling bitch. Mummy and Daddy's *firstborn*! Get your hair dyed and give us all a break!'

'Cut your wrists and give *us* one!'

Ruth moved in closer still. 'You'd love that, wouldn't you? Squeeze a bit more sympathy out of everyone; get them running round you. You really know 'ow to work people – using Roy's death to get sympathy – the poor young widow. You make me puke!'

The slap to her face was hard and knocked Ruth sideways. With her hand to her cheek, she narrowed her eyes and glared hatefully at her sister. Pulling back her fist, she launched it at Sandy's chin and sent her flying. Within seconds they were rolling around the floor, nails clawing, feet kicking, red and white hair flying as each of them pulled at the other's scalp. The screams were loud, the abuse and the swearing louder. Hate poured out as they punched, pulled, pinched and scratched.

It was a piercing scream that finally brought Maureen crashing through the doorway. Ruth had bitten into Sandy's arm just below the shoulder, her teeth sinking deeper and deeper.

Maureen and another machinist grabbed Ruth and yanked her off Sandy. As the sisters parted, Ruth's teeth ripped away flesh. The scream from Sandy sent shock waves through the girls.

Maureen looked from the bloody wound in Sandy's shoulder to Ruth's gaping mouth, and threw her hand forward and pressed the palm over the torn flesh.

'Someone phone for an ambulance!' screamed Maureen. Then, taking deep breaths, she willed herself not to faint as she pressed the flat of her hand against the injury and glared at Ruth, who was cowering back.

'They won't come.' Seema's soothing voice induced a

calmer mood. 'Not for that sort of injury. I'll call a cab.'

'My handbag, Seema . . .' said Sandy, laying her hand on Maureen's shoulder. 'My notebook. There's the number of a black taxi. The cabbie's called Siddy. I want him.'

'OK, I'll do my best and I'll get one of the others to bring a cold drink through and a couple of aspirins to help the pain.' Seema glided past Ruth, who had gone as white as a sheet.

'You all right?' Maureen murmured, stroking Sandy's hair off her clammy forehead.

'It hurts. It really hurts, Mo.'

'I know, I know.' She cradled her boss and rocked her. 'Aspirin's a good idea.' She raised her eyes to meet Ruth's, and baby-blue or not, she could see something in that gaze which sent a chill through her.

Lying on her bed and feeling very much alone, Ruth was crying. She was crying for her sister, for her parents, for her past. She wanted to turn back the clock to the day she was born and start all over again. Hearing herself sobbing in the silent house made her feel lonelier than ever.

'It wasn't *my* fault!' she screamed over and over again.

As her cries subsided, she covered her head with a pillow and drifted off to sleep, exhausted. Two hours later she awoke to the sound of the telephone ringing. It was Maggie, angry and upset. Sandy had had twelve stitches, and the doctor could not say whether the flesh would bond. If not, she would have to have skin grafted from her thigh on to her arm. She had all of this and more reported to her by her mother, in a sharp tone.

'What about *me*? Don't I count? My neck is scratched raw and my scalp's swollen where she pulled out my hair! *I'm* your daughter too! Don't I count?' she screamed furiously down the telephone, only to hear a click as Maggie replaced the receiver.

'Fucking bastards!' Ruth screamed, 'fucking, fucking bastards! I'll show you! I'll *show* you!' She stormed upstairs to the bathroom and bathed her face with cold water. The red scratches were sitting on raised weals and her eyes were swollen from crying. She stared at her reflection and cursed Sandy for spoiling her looks. 'I hope you *have* to have a skin graft! I'm only sorry that it's your shoulder and not your fucking face!'

Once she was curled up in an armchair with a mug of sweet tea, she picked up the phone and dialled Johnnie's number. She would begin the building work on number ten, and cause as much commotion and upheaval to number eleven as she possibly could. It would cost her. Walls would be knocked down where walls could be knocked down, and anything which required constant banging she would have the builder do. A bank loan would see to it. Blow the expense. It would be worth it to ruin Sandy's carefully made plans.

'Hi! Is that Johnnie the builder?' She tried to sound bright and cheerful.

'Who's that?'

'The girl with the black dog; we met in Roman Road. I want a lot of building work done. I said I would ring.'

'The lovely blonde with the legs that go up to her armpits?' She could tell he was smiling.

'Can you call in tomorrow evening to go through—'

'I'll come tonight if you like,' he joked.

'I've got a headache . . .' she purred seductively.

'Take some painkillers and get a good night's sleep. What's the address?'

Once she had given it and told him she was looking forward to discussing the details, she replaced the receiver feeling a hell of a lot better. Angry that she looked too much like a dog to invite him round that evening, she remembered her hair, which was still long. *Next time. On his second visit. He'll think I've done it for him.* She went to the bathroom to apply some antiseptic cream. She could have done with a visit – she felt like getting laid. A mature man would do her the world of good. She wondered if he was into flaying. She wanted to feel pain; a fiercer pain than the weal marks on her face were causing. She felt like commanding Shadow to sink her fangs in and give her a bite worse than the one she had given Sandy. One-upmanship. She thrived on it.

Instead she poured herself a large whisky, and played her favourite Rolling Stones record very loud; Mick Jagger was voicing her own feelings – *I want to paint it black.*

Siddy pressed his finger on the doorbell just as a cloud moved across the evening sun. It was just after nine o'clock, and he would have preferred to be anywhere other than at Sandy's door. The worst sort of passenger bitching at him would have been a better option than what he had let himself in for. Why was he playing saint? Why had he let that first shadow of guilt consume him? Why should he redress a stranger's grief? *Diversion from monotony*, he told himself, *and relief.*

'Siddy!' Her freckled face grinning at him cast out any doubts. She looked genuinely pleased to see him.

'Jump in.' He looked at his watch. 'Get your keys and we'll go.'

She tossed them in the air and caught them. 'I already did.' She pulled the door shut behind her. 'I saw your cab from the window.'

'So you weren't surprised to see me?' He threw her a sideways glance and got into the driver's seat.

'I was trying to sound pleased so you wouldn't change your mind.' She slammed the cab door and leaned back, looking at the bald patch at the back of his head surrounded by dark blonde curly hair. She felt like giving it an old-fashioned kiss. 'Why did you change your mind?'

'If you're not out of there in ten minutes, I'll go, right?'

'You don't 'ave to wait. Just come in with me—'

'Do what?' Laughing, he shook his head. 'No way. I've asked if they'll see yer. Be thankful.' He reached a hand behind and slid the glass partition shut.

Sandy slid it open. 'I am. And I do mean that. It's just that—'

'No more rabbiting, all right?' His tone was deliberate: he wanted to end the conversation. He pulled away, a stony look on his face.

'Fair enough.' She slowly slid the window closed again and settled herself to facing the family alone. In truth it was what she wanted, but the butterflies in her stomach were having a field day. She had never felt so nervous in her life. On the way to the hospital to get her arm stitched, Siddy had reluctantly answered a few more of her questions about the thirty-year-old who had been driving the Beetle. He had told her there was a younger brother who had taken his sister's death very badly; a father who, at the age of fifty, had suffered a heart attack but was recovering and out of hospital; a mother who still walked about in her own personal hell.

Sandy slid the window open again. 'What did you say their name was?'

'Armstrong.'

'First names?'

'Never you mind. Mister and Missus will suffice. The boy's name is Jac; he's at a funny age – fifteen. Don't go talking nineteen to the dozen.' He slid the window shut again. Sandy slid it open.

'What was her name?'

'Fuck me, don't you ever learn? I don't wanna talk about it!'

'Just her name, and I promise I'll shut up.'

Siddy sighed and paused. 'Kay.' Choked, he closed the window and swallowed the lump in his throat.

Turning into the council estate he tooted at a man and woman aged around seventy and waved. 'They're just back from bingo!' he called through the closed partition.

Pleased he was in a more talkative mood, Sandy slid the glass back, which was exactly what he expected her to do. 'Who are they?'

'My mum and dad. At least I know what I'm gonna look like in twenty years' time.' He was trying to lighten things up, because they were about to pull into the tarmacked grounds of the four-storey block of flats, and he knew that Laura and Jack Armstrong would be up there waiting to meet the girl whose husband had caused the death of their daughter.

Pulling up, he felt lighter inside. He felt he was doing the right thing for both injured parties – and it was nearly over; he could go about his business and push the redhead from his mind once and for all. 'Second floor – number twenty-one. Don't bother with the lift – it's not working.'

He turned to face Sandy. 'Well, go on then!'

'Come up with me.'

'I told yer. I'll wait down 'ere. You've got ten minutes.' This was one thing he wouldn't weaken on. Did she think he was completely without feelings? He looked at his watch and then eyed her. 'I've got a living to make.'

'OK.' She murmured and let herself out. Leaning on the closed taxi door she took a deep breath, feeling trapped. If she backed out now, Siddy would be angry and with good reason. After all, she was twenty-six, not a teenager. Acting like an adult had never been her forte. Playing boss over the girls at Nova had not been easy. More than once she had wished she could have been in the chorus line and not under the spotlight. Shy was not what most people believed she was. It wasn't coyness, it wasn't innocence: it was one of the worst afflictions, and learning to overcome it had probably been the most difficult thing in her life. Roy had helped, with his total lack of inhibitions. He had taught her to override the trembling inside. She wished his spirit was there now.

'They won't bite you! Go on!'

Nodding, Sandy turned and walked slowly towards the entrance into the 1940s brick building. She climbed the stairs, counting each step of the four flights. There were fifty-two.

She arrived at the freshly painted blue door and reached

for the knocker. Her hand was shaking. There was another voice in her head now, telling her to turn back. She leaned against the balcony wall staring at the door, caught between two worlds. When it opened, she felt instant panic.

'Come in.' It was Kay's mother, Laura Armstrong. Her face was drawn and her pale complexion looked wrong against her dark chestnut hair and green eyes. She looked as if she should be tanned; tanned and smiling. 'We saw you go by the window.'

'I'm sorry . . .'

Laura stood aside and waited. 'We've been looking forward to meeting you. Don't have to be nervous.'

With both hands clenched and every muscle taut, Sandy walked into the narrow passage and followed the woman into their living room. On the wall over the fireplace hung a collection of photographs of their daughter, from birth to death. Photographs of her with her brother; with her aunt Liz; with her parents and with her friend, Terry, taken on the hopfields years ago. In the centre was a specially enlarged picture of her aged twenty-three with her new husband, a very good-looking Romany.

Sandy stared at a portrait of Kay taken when she was twenty-one. She had long, silky blonde hair, blue eyes and a smile which Sandy recognized – the smile of a shy person hiding the tremors inside. 'Is that . . .?' She turned to Laura Armstrong, squeezing her lips together, willing herself to be as strong as the woman in front of her.

'Yeah. That's my Kay.' She smiled and pointed to a picture of her daughter as a baby. 'She came third in a bonny baby competition.'

The living-room door slowly opened. Jack Armstrong and his fifteen-year-old son Jac inched their way in, looking sheepishly at Sandy. 'She was always rushing about,' Jack said. 'Sit yourself down. My sister Liz is making a pot of tea.'

'Or would you prefer coffee?' asked Laura.

Sandy stopped breathing. She didn't move. She became a statue, a statue made of stone that couldn't feel or see or hear. More strained polite words were coming at her, but from way above her head. Her eyes felt dry, as if they had powder in them. She wanted to blink; but statues didn't blink.

The strong arm on her shoulder belonged to Jack. He gently but forcefully pushed her down on to the armchair. She wanted to scream that she was sorry. That it was her fault; but there was nothing there. Somehow the words had got lost on the journey from her brain to her mouth, and she was no longer trembling but shaking from head to toe.

Laura sat opposite her and leaned forward. 'This must be difficult for you, but it means a lot to us. Thanks for being brave.'

Sandy looked into her face. She meant it; she was being sincere. They *wanted* to see her. She had expected them to be angry, full of hate. Why weren't they accusing her? Laying on the blame with a trowel?

'I had to come.' She covered her face with her hands, composing herself.

'Would you like a drop of something?'

'A glass of water . . .' She could feel herself relaxing and lifted her face to look at Kay's brother. He half-smiled and lowered his eyes, shy. She wondered if his freckles bothered him the way Sandy's had when she was fifteen. His hair was ginger, too, but much lighter than Sandy's.

'That bloody kettle, Laura! Took an age to boil.' Jack's seventy-year-old sister Liz arrived carrying a tray. She looked at Sandy. 'You'll be all right, Mog, once you've got this tea inside yer.'

'It wasn't your niece's fault,' she said to Liz, surprising herself. 'Roy went through a red light. We were having a row.'

'Well, we'll let them battle it out in heaven, shall we? They *both* jumped the lights. Impatient as well, was he?' Liz sat on a high-backed chair and sipped her tea. 'Kay was like a streak of lightning. Always on the move. Be lucky if she stopped for a wee.'

Sandy chuckled quietly at her straightforward manner. 'Roy was impatient.'

'Fifty years early into the next world instead of ten minutes late in this one. You wait till I get up there – she'll get the sharp end of my tongue. They both will. She's left a lovely widower, Zacchi. He's a travel writer . . . which is a blessing. At least travelling the globe'll take his mind off it. Worshipped the ground she walked on, did Zacchi. He's a Romany. She met him down 'opping.'

'I don't suppose you're finding it none too easy, a widow at your age. You're still a baby.' Laura's voice floated above her.

'No. No, it's not all that easy, but then . . .' She looked from Laura to Jack. 'It must be just as bad for you.'

Jack, the father of the late Kay, turned his back and stared out of the balcony door. He felt like telling her that they were beginning to get used to swords coming in from nowhere and slicing another piece away. First his baby John; then Liz's husband, his best friend Bert; then Laura's dad, Billy; and now his only daughter, Kay.

'Did Kay have any children?' asked Sandy, regretting the words as soon as they were out. There was enough sadness in the room as it was.

'Yeah.' Laura smiled weakly. 'A boy and a girl; little Rosie and baby Zac. We're taking on a country pub in Kent, and they're coming to live with us . . . because of Zacchi's job. He'll have a room as well, though. He's one of the family.'

'Siddy was telling us you've opened a boutique in the Roman Road,' Liz said brightly, easing the conversation round.

Polite conversation again, thought Sandy. They had come full circle; it was time for her to go. If they invited her back she would stay longer the next time. 'Yes. I needed another . . .' she smiled bravely . . . 'beginning.'

''Course you did,' Liz said. 'Try and the world's with you; give up, and you're on your own,' she glanced at Laura. The quip was obviously meant for her.

Stepping out of the flats, Sandy was relieved to see that Siddy was still there. His black cab looked so familiar and welcoming. 'Wasn't too long, was I?'

'Jump in. Everything all right then?'

'Yeah. Everything's fine, thanks. I think it helped.'

He turned on his engine. 'Might not seem like it now, but in a couple of weeks you'll be pleased you did it.' He pulled slowly away, leaving the sliding window open.

'I hope so, Siddy. I hope so.'

Chapter Six

It was two o'clock in the morning when Johnnie walked out of Ruth's house feeling like the captain of the winning rugby team. With his sweatshirt on back to front, he got into his car and gave a short toot. Why the strange blonde had been all over him was a mystery. He checked his face in the mirror. 'You 'andsome bastard,' he grinned, and pulled away.

Once Ruth had learned from Johnnie that he had been working at number eleven Roman Road, she had changed her tactics and her story. She had lied to him, saying that the property she wanted him to refurbish was in Leytonstone, just by the railway. Having rushed through this inspired last-minute lie, she had cunningly set her trap, getting him to lay her and think it was all his idea.

When he had asked if she had been into Nova boutique and seen the way he had decorated it and fitted it out, she was taken aback. A few searching questions from her and she had deduced from his expression that he and Sandy were more than just business associates. Lady Luck had come over to her side again, giving her a prime no-lose position. She could let it slip to Sandy that her bit of rough had screwed her three times on the run, and smash any potential relationship with a few select words.

One of the things that niggled at Johnnie as he drove home was why it seemed the blonde hadn't even heard of Sandy's boutique. After all, Roman Road was narrow, and Ruth had been exactly opposite the shop when he first saw her. In fact, he could remember her glancing over towards Nova more than once.

'Sod it!' He slammed on his brakes and swerved to the left, pulling up sharply. Turning his engine off, he concentrated, tried to recall everything Ruth had said during the evening. He was searching for clues, because he had a feeling that she might be Sandy's dark sister. 'Little bitch!' He remembered her joking about being Cinderella, and having an ugly sister with ginger hair and freckles. That was *afterwards*, once he was dressing ready to leave. He remembered that smile, that fucking smile. It had disturbed him momentarily and then vanished when she coyly thanked him for being so loving and gentle with her.

Making a U-turn, his skidding tyres leaving a mark on the road, he drove off at speed, heading back to Mile End Place. If he didn't act now he might be sorry. Once the bitch reported back to Sandy, he doubted she would even want to see him again, let alone begin a proper courtship.

'Idiot! Fool!' He clenched his teeth and punched the steering wheel with one hand. 'You ageing teenager! You—'

The flashing blue light in his rear mirror caught his attention. He took his foot off the accelerator and allowed his speed to drop, hoping the patrol car would pass him by. But luck was not on his side. Slowly pulling alongside him, they beckoned for him to pull in.

'Going a bit fast, weren't you?' The police officer sported a supercilious expression.

'Sorry about that. Just had a row with my girlfriend.' He shrugged and tried to look repentant.

'Driving licence?'

'Come on . . . the road was clear. I wasn't doing more than—'

'And insurance.'

Gritting his teeth, he was thankful that at least he hadn't had much to drink. His tools were in the car though – no doubt they would take their time in checking every piece while firing questions at him, as if he only had half a brain.

He pulled his licence out of his top pocket and handed it over. This regime wasn't new to him. He drove a Jaguar saloon, four years old and immaculate. He loved his car and was proud of it. Envy was one of the passions he had to endure, police or otherwise.

'Step out of the car.'

'Sorry?' Try as he might, he couldn't resist undermining them. Sorry was an old trick. Make the bastard repeat himself – weaken his attack. 'I didn't catch that, officer.'

The officer, recognizing the old soldier act, leaned forward and spoke right into his face. 'Registration number?'

Sighing as if frustrated, he reeled off the number. Unfortunately it was the licence number of the van. *Shit*. He then excused his mistake and tried to remember the number of his Jag. He got it wrong three times.

'Out of the car, sir.'

Beginning to feel worried, Johnnie got out. He had upset

the jumped-up little twerp and would no doubt pay for it. He folded his arms submissively and waited.

'Open the boot, please.'

Johnnie sighed. 'Look, I'm a builder. My tools are in the back. I've been through this umpteen times—'

'Bit of an expensive car to drag on to a building site, isn't it?'

'I use a van for that. My girlfriend had a few things she wanted me to fix. You know how it is.'

'You can prove that, can you, sir?' The officer nodded to his mate to check the tools in the boot.

''Course I can.'

'Local, is she?'

'Mile End Place.'

'But you said you'd *been* to see her.' He frowned and narrowed his eyes.

'I told you, we had a row. I was on my way back to make up. You know what women are like. She's probably crying 'er eyes out.'

'Couldn't tell me her name, could you, sir?'

'I could, yeah.' He wasn't sure if he was bound to. The officer made it clear that he was waiting and that there would be trouble if Johnnie did not comply with his polite request.

A silence fell as Johnnie racked his brains. He could remember Ruth, but a surname? 'Ruth. Ruth Adams.' No sooner had he said it than he remembered Sandy's surname. 'Sorry – Brent.' Then he realized that that would be her married name and that the family name was Brown. He had known their parents long enough not to forget. 'No . . . wrong again. It's Brown. Ruth Brown.'

'Sure about that, are you?' He slowly walked to the back of the Jag and joined the other officer who was checking the tools.

'You won't mind coming down to the station, will you, sir? We'll want to check up on your girlfriend. Shouldn't take long.'

'Yes I would bloody mind! I'm tired, I've just bin laid. I've been working all day, long hours . . . and I want my bed. I've done nothing wrong—'

'You were speeding, sir.'

'All right! I'll appear at the station tomorrow with all my papers. That do?'

'No.' The young officer sneered. 'My colleague and I are not satisfied. Just follow us – we'll escort you. Harbour Square.'

Inside the interview room, Johnnie was questioned by a detective constable and his colleague. Apparently there had been a spate of break-ins during the past few weeks and small jewellery shops had been the latest target. To cap it all, a dark Jaguar had been seen speeding away from the scene of the crime. Dark green and not dark blue, but that, as far as the officer was concerned, could be the mistake of the witness.

'Why did you lie about your girlfriend's name?' DC Jackson looked Johnnie straight in the face.

'I told you. I couldn't remember it. And anyway, to me she's just Ruth,' he shrugged. 'Long tall Ruth.'

'But you said you went there to do a couple of jobs for her. That's why your tools were in the boot of the car. You must 'ave known her for a while to be on those terms, surely?'

'No. I met her the other day in Roman Road where I'd been working. She gave me the come-on. I think it was my overalls. She said she 'ad a lot of work needed doing. I gave her my number – she phoned me.'

Jackson leaned back in his chair and grinned. 'You said you didn't get there till early evening. Seven o'clock, wasn't it?'

'Thereabouts.'

'Sounds more like a date.'

'Come on! What's this got—'

'Answer the question.'

His irritating tone was getting to Johnnie. He sucked on his bottom lip – *don't lose it, John boy, don't lose it.* 'If you saw what she looked like . . .' He rubbed his chin and smiled.

'And which sort of screwing came first?'

Johnnie liked that. At least the bastard had a sense of humour. 'We only talked about work in the end. I'd got it wrong. She didn't want anything done to the place where she lives. She's a property dealer, wants a house refurbished in Leytonstone. We discussed that. Then we had a couple of drinks and . . . you can guess the rest.'

'So why the terrible row then? What brought that on?'

'I can't remember. I said something . . . I dunno . . . she took it the wrong way.'

'I think you're gonna have to come up with something better than that. Sure you don't want to call your solicitor?'

'Positive. I'm not chucking good money away.' He leaned forward. 'I haven't broken the law.'

'So tell us why you were heading west.'

'I did tell you. I was going back. I did a U-turn.'

'We know that. You were spotted by a patrol car. I'm asking *why*.'

Sighing, Johnnie ran a hand through his hair. 'You won't believe me if I tell you.'

'Try me.'

'I'm on the verge of a relationship. A good relationship. The blonde who seduced me—'

There was a burst of laughter from both officers. 'Oh yes? Go on.'

'She's the sister of my girlfriend. I didn't know it before I . . . the penny only dropped once I was on my way 'ome. She knew all right. She knew what she was doing. They don't see eye to eye. I was used. I wanted to make sure she would keep her mouth shut.'

The officer's tone and facial expression changed instantly. 'How did you propose doing that?'

'A warning, that's all.'

'Don't you mean a threat?'

'No, for God's sake! You know I 'aven't got a record! I'm in my mid-thirties. You think I'm gonna start knocking women about at my age? Or robbing jewellers, come to that?'

'Well, that's just the point. Whoever's been carrying out the crimes is very clever. Cunning. Might have been slipping our net for years for all we know. Doubt if he's got a record either.'

'Come on . . .'

'What's your girlfriend's name?'

'Do I have to?' He looked pleadingly into the hardened face.

'Name.'

175

'Sandy. Sandy Brent.' Johnnie squeezed his hands together. The last thing he wanted was to drag her into this.

'So the blonde . . . Ruth . . . well, she must be a Brent too. How come you didn't work that one out?'

'No.' He narrowed his eyes and stared DC Jackson out. 'Sandy's a widow. A young widow. Twenty-six. Her husband was killed in a car crash in Shoreditch.' He sighed and shook his head. 'Give us a break. She's a lovely girl. That's why I was going back. I didn't want the sister to hurt her. I was gonna tell her meself . . . in the morning.'

'Strange sort of behaviour, isn't it? Conning her sister's boyfriend into screwing her?'

Johnnie raised his eyes. 'She's a very strange girl. Not like anyone I've ever come across before.'

'But you enjoyed coming across her.'

'It was different.' He quietly chuckled. 'Very different.' He caught the officer's eye again. 'It was a fantastic . . . experience. No more than that. She frightens the life out of me.'

'Well, you can get over the shock of it all by yourself – in a cell for the night.'

'No way. You can't do that. I've done nothing wrong!'

DC Jackson knew that, but his time had been wasted. Wasted on emotional domestic affairs. A night in the cell would right this little mistake. Besides, he envied the lucky bastard. Fantastic is what he had called it. He should be so lucky; *and* he drove a Jaguar. He had to have a successful business or he was a fence. Builder and decorator – self-employed. Johnnie probably earned more than Jackson would ever take home on the force. More than the highest-ranking officer. Yes – a night in the cells would be good for this one.

As luck would have it, Johnnie fell asleep soon after his head touched down. At least it was cool in that small dark place. When he heard the clanking of keys in the lock he woke with a start, wondering where he was. It soon came flooding back.

Getting out of Harbour Square police station as soon as he could, he made his way to Mile End Place. It had just gone six-thirty by the time he drew up outside Ruth's small Victorian terrace. He would have to maintain a chummy mood, telling her he had popped in on his way to a job. The fact that it was so early would persuade her that she had made a very good impression. He hoped she wasn't feeling sexy, otherwise he might give the game away: his anger at what she had done was only just beneath the surface.

'Johnnie! What're you doing here at this godforsaken hour?' Ruth made it clear that he wasn't welcome; her face said it all.

'Just passing. Wanted to share the dawn with you.' He looked at his wristwatch. 'I'm a bit late for that but . . . at least we can have our first cup of tea together.'

'Get real.' She pushed the door closed, but his foot was already there. 'You're awake now. Come on, babe – I've got a little surprise for you.'

'If you mean a present – hand it over and go.'

'I haven't bought it yet. I want you to choose. You wasn't wearing earrings when I first saw you, nor last night. I think you should. Gold and blue to match your hair and eyes.'

'Blue?'

'Light sapphires. I know a man.' He grinned and winked at her.

'You are sweet, Johnnie.' She smiled demurely. 'Put the kettle on while I take a quick shower.'

'Coffee or tea?' he asked, going into the kitchen.

'Coffee! Laced with honey!'

He raised his eyebrows and mumbled the word arsenic. Catching sight of her dog in the garden, halfway out of its kennel and watching him, Johnnie shivered and wondered if she had a black cat, too.

Taking two mugs from a shelf, he noticed that her pottery dinner service and teaset were identical to Sandy's – the coffee, tea and sugar jars too. This girl had a problem. An identity crisis, perhaps? He felt distinctly uncomfortable and hoped she would be ready to leave soon. He wanted to get out of that house and into the fresh air.

'If you want breakfast you'll have to fry your own eggs and bacon. I don't like cooking first thing.' She appeared in the doorway dressed in a tight red catsuit, a towel wrapped around her head.

'Not me, babe. Tea and a cigarette is all I can manage at this hour.'

'Same here. This man you know – where's his jewellery shop?'

'We're not going to his shop. We're going to his house in Roman Road. The big Victorian one with the black railings.'

'Very nice too. I often wondered who lived there. How old is he?' Her mind was working overtime.

'Too old for you, babe. Too old and too involved with his

mistress.' He surprised himself at how easy it was to lie to this girl.

She blinked innocently. 'I wasn't fishing, Johnnie.' She couldn't wait to meet him. What a challenge. And a mistress to knock off the throne.

As they drove through the quiet market place towards Nova, Johnnie worked out his movements. He would park further down the road. He would hold Ruth's arm and walk her quickly along. When they arrived at Sandy's door he would grip her so tight she wouldn't be able to go anywhere.

'Out you get, then. We'll walk the rest of the way. He's funny about black market parking too near his 'ouse.'

Ruth's curiosity was aroused. This friend sounded like someone she would get on with very well. Someone she could relate to. She hoped he wasn't too old. She daren't ask a second time; Johnnie was obviously a jealous man, and by the way he had his hand around her arm, he seemed to be under the impression that she was his property. A pair of sapphire earrings? Hardly. It would take a hell of a lot more than that to gain ownership. Even then it would be short-lived. He tightened his grip and she began to feel something other than curiosity. Maybe they would do it in the Jag after the purchase. With Sandy's shop just a few yards ahead, she smiled inwardly. She would waltz in there later to show off her present.

'Why did you do that?'

Johnnie had stopped suddenly, his finger on Sandy's doorbell. 'What *is* this?' Ruth demanded.

'You'll see, babe.' He winked and blew her a kiss.

Intrigue won over suspicion. Whatever he was up to it was exciting her. She could feel her nipples tingling. Looking into his tanned face she remembered the night before. He was all right. Well stacked.

The look on Sandy's face when she opened the door made Ruth laugh. It was terrific. The usual composed expression was gone. She was shocked to see them both and it showed. It really showed.

'How's tricks?' Ruth said.

Sandy looked from her sister to Johnnie – speechless.

'Inside.' He was talking to Sandy.

'What?'

'Inside. And you!' He pushed Ruth into Sandy and closed the door behind all three of them. 'Upstairs. *Now!*'

Sheepish, confused and only half-awake, Sandy did as ordered with a bemused Ruth following closely behind. Once they were in the living room, he slyly pulled the key from the keyhole. 'Sit down. Both of you.'

Ruth stood defiant, smiling, eyebrows raised. He could order her about as much as he wanted in the bedroom, but here, with Sandy present, no way. She folded her arms and thrust out a hip. She stared into his face, smirking.

One firm shove from Johnnie and she was on the sofa. He turned to Sandy. 'Sit down, babe. I've got something to tell you.'

She nodded patiently and sat on the edge of the armchair.

'I didn't know this was your sister. I agreed to go round 'er place to work out an estimate of building work she wanted done. She came on really strong and I took it. It was sex and that's all. A one-nighter.'

'Now, I don't know what it is with you two, but life is too short for all this.' He pointed a finger at Ruth. 'You have only got one sister.' He pointed a finger at Sandy. 'So 'ave you!' He walked to the door. 'Enough shit'll come at you from out there without turning on each other.' He held up the door key. 'You're not coming out of here until you've talked. And I mean talked! You're like a pair of spoiled brats.'

He slammed the door shut and locked them in. Leaving the shop, he went into the Green Café opposite. Whether Sandy would talk to him again was a risk worth taking. If she felt half as much about him as he did her, she would come round. It would take time, he realized that, but as the old saying goes: something good is worth waiting for.

Gonna have to stop the womanizing, Johnnie, he told himself, as he settled down at a small corner table. *Time to settle down again.* And who better to rebuild a nest with than Sandy? If he was going to start a family he would have to get a move on. Thirty-six next month, and beginning to see the first signs of grey coming through his thick dark hair. *Time to start going down the gym again, do a bit of body-building before the muscles get slack.*

'You're looking thoughtful today, Johnnie.' The voice of Bridie, the young Irish waitress, floated across his thoughts. 'Full works, is it?'

He raised his eyes to meet hers. 'Do you ever smile, Bridie?'

'Of course I smile – when I've something to smile about. You should see me on the dance floor.'

'I 'ave. I was painting the church hall, wasn't I? Spanish dancing? I've never seen so many poker-faces at once.'

'Ah, but that was all part of the act. You should have watched us tap-dancing last night! Miles of smiles. The instructor insists on it.'

'Oh right, that accounts for the face-ache then. Two poached eggs on toast.' He winked at her and waited for a retort. There wasn't one. She raised an eyebrow and then zipped across the café in her usual manner, too busy for any more idle chit-chat. Passing the only other customer, a stallholder who was tucking into bacon, egg and beans, she managed to knock against his chair, causing a forkful to go flying.

Johnnie looked at his watch, a habit he could never shake. He automatically checked it every half-hour. It was approaching seven-thirty and the stallholders were setting up outside. The market would soon be in full swing. He would give the girls an hour to sort themselves out before he unlocked the door and disappeared.

His thoughts returned to Sandy. If she was genuinely hurt that he had slept with Ruth, surely that was a positive sign. Nothing like a bit of jealousy to keep them interested. On the other hand, Sandy might take the view that he had only been after *her* for what he could get, and refuse to have anything more to do with him. He was going to have to wait. Keep at arm's length for a while, perhaps write her a letter explaining exactly what had happened. No doubt Ruth, the minx, was giving a very different version of the story.

'Has Freda been in yet, Bridie?' he called out.

'It's too early! She usually comes in around nine if she's coming. Why?'

'None of your business.' He loved winding Bridie up;

she was an easy target. It was worth overcooked eggs to see the flash of anger in those Irish eyes. 'Where's the boss today?'

'If you mean Sam, he's at the wholesaler's. If you're referring to Eileen, she's not the boss. Just likes to think she is.' She arrived with his breakfast. The eggs were perfect. Sunny side up, and only just sealed by hot fat. 'She started a month before I did, that's all.'

'Thanks, Bridie – that looks lovely. I always thought you should be manageress and not Eileen,' he said, twisting the knife.

'She's *not* the manageress!' The lilting voice rose several pitches. 'All the acting in the world won't change matters.' She pushed her face closer to his. 'Give me a few more months, Johnnie – then we'll see who's boss.' She smiled properly and went to fetch him some bread and butter, head high, long curly hair flying behind her.

He dipped a piece of bacon into his egg yolk. Even Bridie, with her squeaky-clean appearance and fresh skin, managed to stir something. He had to admit that that kind of teasing and flirting was something he got a kick out of.

'All right, John?' Eileen called as she pulled her red and white slipover pinafore from her holdall. 'Plenty of work?'

'More'n plenty!' He pointed his fork at her. 'I'll soon be rich enough to get you where I want you.'

'You reckon?' She removed her glasses and wiped away the steam. 'So long as your bag's big enough for Bridie as well. Mustn't leave her out in the cold, eh, Bridie?'

'It's almost time for the rush and *your* tables need wiping!' Bridie snapped.

'So do a lot of things this early in the morning.'

'Do you have to be so coarse, Eileen?'

'This is a café, love – not a bloody convent. Chuck us the cloth.'

Johnnie shook his head and chuckled. He loved that kind of banter. He loved the Roman Road, always had. Now that Sandy was part of it, he couldn't think of anywhere he'd rather be, except perhaps on a desert island, with her to keep him company.

Leaving two five-pence pieces on the table, he winked at each of the women and left. They deserved more than that for the entertainment but it wasn't on to spoil things. The locals never left more than a five-pence tip.

Unlocking the door of the boutique, he decided to creep up the stairs to see how the girls were getting on. It was quiet in there. Very quiet. He would give them another fifteen minutes before going up. Sitting down on the shop floor, he stretched his legs and closed his eyes. No sooner had he made himself comfortable when the sound of banging came from above. One of them was thumping on the living-room door. He waited.

'I know you're down there, Johnnie! Open this fucking door!' It was Ruth.

No. Too early, he thought. They need a bit more time. 'Get it sorted!' he yelled back. That's when it really began. The yelling. The abuse. The tears of anger.

Ruth was standing, arms folded, chin stuck out. Sandy was on the sofa, legs curled under her, arms folded, staring at the floor.

'Yes I *do*! I blame you for it *all*!' Seething, Ruth began to pace the floor like a tiger trapped in a cage. 'You were older than me. You should have *known* what to do! You should have told me to tell!'

'I was twelve, that's hardly mature. You were such a clever little cow. Knew it all. Who was I to take the lead?'

'Oh, but you *did* take the lead. Remember?'

'No I don't. I don't, because I decided long ago not to harbour all that stuff. The past is the past.' She ripped open another packet of cigarettes.

'Well, that's where you're wrong. The past is never dead. It's like dog shit on the heel of your shoe – you drag it around with you. When you think it's worn away the smell creeps up on you again and makes you feel sick. The way *you* make me feel sick for telling me to get on with it!'

'I didn't tell you to get on with it!' Now it was Sandy's turn to yell. 'I told you not to tell! There's a difference! How was I to know he was still pestering you? You never mentioned him again. I presumed you had stopped going to his house!'

'How could I stop going without saying why, Sandy?' Her voice went quiet. She was looking for answers. Answers to questions she had wanted to ask all those years ago.

Sandy looked up, disturbed first by the pleading tone in her sister's voice, and then by her pitiful expression. 'I did, Ru. I stopped going after he came to his door with his flies open. I could only see his white pants showing but that was enough. Enough to confirm that he was someone to steer clear of.'

Ruth began to cry, quietly allowing the pent-up misery to escape. 'It was because you wouldn't go that I was sent more often with messages from Dad. Messages which were always a reply to one the perv had sent via me whenever he saw me in the street. Nothing messages. Anything to have me make a visit to his house. And every time our electricity meter ran low or went off altogether, I had to go and ask him for a separate shilling as well. The clever bastard made it known that he kept a cash bag full of shilling bits. I wasn't the only kid who was sent to him by their parents.

'When he first got me to slip my hand inside his fly and squeeze that bony thing, I was nearly sick. He said he wouldn't give me any coins for the meter if I didn't do it, and if I told Dad he would just say that I was a wicked little liar.

'Once I had kept my mouth shut after the first time when I was made to touch it, I didn't tell. He said Mum and Dad would think I liked doing it because I hadn't told them in the beginning.'

Dropping on to the cushioned sofa, she covered her face. 'It went from bad to worse instead of getting better. I kept telling myself that soon he would stop it and it would be all right again.' She held out her hand and flicked her fingers at the box of tissues.

Taking a small wad of them from her sister, Ruth mopped her face and took a few deep breaths. 'It was a nightmare when Mum left me with him and his crippled mother for a couple of hours. It was when Granny Brown was dying, remember?'

'Yes. I had to go. Mum thought you were too young to see death. Only two years older than you, but still I had to be there and watch Gran slip away.'

'Think yourself lucky. I had to spend two hours being stared at by that leering creep while his mother sat in the room, knitting. It was so silent. They didn't listen to the radio, never mind having a television set.' She shuddered and went cold. 'I can't bear to remember it. It sounds like a scene from a Hitchcock film. But it was real enough then. He used to talk to me as if I was a grown-up. How could Mum and Dad be friends with someone like that?'

'He taught Dad quite a bit about electrics, Ruth, when Dad was an apprentice. And they've always been there – the good neighbours – for donkey's years. Both families, ours and theirs, go back a few generations. Neighbours of old.'

Ruth suddenly began to chuckle and then to laugh. 'My God, what we had to put up with! Remember the vicar and Flying Angels at the Sunday club after Sunday school?'

Sandy found herself laughing too. 'The wheelbarrows he gave us were worse. I knew he was looking at my knickers.' She slowly shook her head. 'You would have thought one of us girls at the Sunday club would have said something. There were enough of us. Why didn't one of us tell our parents about the games vicars play?'

'Because we feared having our legs smacked for telling wicked lies,' said Ruth. 'Men! They're all the same.'

Sandy lit another cigarette. 'No, they're not. Stop being dramatic. They're not all bad. We just happened to brush up against two of the worst kind, that's all.'

'I've tested enough of 'em. Their dicks are a curse to them. They follow their penises around as if they're water diviners. Even your precious Roy. Sleeping with his wife's sister? I thought marriage was supposed to be all about trust.'

Ready to defend Roy, Sandy's sudden anger was halted by a rat-a-tat on the door. When it flew open and Johnnie stood there grinning, she glanced at Ruth. In her present mood she could easily have flown at him.

'Talking yet?'

Quick to her feet, Sandy ushered him out. 'Leave it for a while. I'll phone you once I've . . . once I've got over this.' She had no intention of calling him, and by the expression on his face she could tell that he knew it.

'Listen, babe . . .'

'Please, Johnnie.' She took him outside and spoke in a whisper. 'You don't owe me an explanation or an apology. You and I were just good friends. What you do is your business, OK? At least you've got me and Ruth talking again, and that's more important than anything.'

'Fair enough.' He pressed his lips together and breathed slowly through his nose. 'Take care.' He stroked her long hair and left.

With a feeling of regret, Sandy said a silent goodbye to the only man she had ever really felt close to. Even she and Roy hadn't enjoyed that kind of intimacy, when two people are so relaxed with each other that they can say whatever is on their minds.

Returning to the living room, Sandy dropped into an armchair, wishing it could be different. Wishing that Johnnie hadn't slept with Ruth. Wishing he would be calling on her that evening.

'*He's* not worth the shoes he stands in, either. Should have seen the way he came on to me,' said Ruth, gesturing after Johnnie.

'I would rather not think about that. Why don't we forget about men and talk about us and our future?' Sandy decided there and then, on impulse, to put the past behind her and renew her bond with Ruth. 'Maybe we could work together. As partners.'

'You're asking me to come in with you? After all that's happened?'

'Roy was weak when it came to a pretty face, I knew that. The future is what counts. What are you up to next door?'

Ruth shrugged. 'Investing, I s'pose. I bought it jointly with Dave.'

'Dave?'

'You remember Helen . . . my flatmate?'

'Of course I do.' The penny dropped. '*That* Dave? Helen's boyfriend? Surely not.' She wondered if her sister had any sense of loyalty.

Ruth held up both hands defensively. 'A business deal – no more. I'm ready to buy him out, as it happens. He's not very bright. No wonder Helen gave him the push,' she lied.

'Helen gave him the push? But she worshipped him!'

'True, but . . .' Ruth had to think quickly. 'He's actually bi-sexual.' She shrugged again. 'And a secret transvestite.' The thought of Dave in a frock made her smile. 'Helen caught him entertaining a man . . . dressed up in one of her long skirts and frilly blouses. Kinky or what?' She was beginning to believe her own fantasies.

'Jesus . . .' Sandy sighed. 'Where have I been?'

'Cloud-cuckoo-land?'

'Do people really behave that way?'

'Oh come on, Sandy! This is the seventies! Everyone's

189

into everything. Now then, about this partnership. What's on your mind?'

Shaking herself out of mild shock, she shrugged. 'Come in with me. We could knock through to next door. I need more space.' She poured them both a whisky and soda. 'This business is gonna go. I'm gonna have to run with it. You should see the orders already.'

'You'd have to buy Dave out, unless . . .' Ruth's mind was working overtime. 'Tell you what – I'll take care of that side of things. We'll keep it straightforward. You own this one, I'll own next door. We'll go fifty-fifty with the expense of knocking the shop into one and I'll let you use my space rent-free.'

'If we can get permission?'

'Sure.' Ruth emptied her glass and considered her timing. Now would be as good a time as any. 'I don't wanna put you down, Sand, but . . . sequins, satin and lace? What are we talking . . . two, three years if you're lucky? I've seen other boutiques going down like dead flies. You can't compete with the chains . . . C and A, Dorothy Perkins . . .'

'I don't aim to. My main interest is designing my own clothes. With a bit of luck I'll be selling to the chains.' Her morale sinking, Sandy asked Ruth what she had in mind. While Ruth slowly got into her repertoire, she poured her another whisky, herself a dry ginger. It was almost time for the machinists to arrive and she should really have been downstairs herself, cutting. Drinking at that time of the morning was the last thing she'd imagined herself doing.

'People will always want their clothes dry-cleaned, Sand. My idea is to offer a laundry service, with ironing an optional extra. We'd only 'ave to invest in three industrial machines – one dry-cleaning, two laundry. We could undercut the other laundries in the area. They all send theirs out so they have to charge more than we would. We could get really cheap labour. Probably wouldn't have to do much ourselves. In fact I wouldn't want to. I'd keep my job on at Burns and keep an eye out for cheap premises.'

'How would you raise the money?'

'Sell the house I'm in, at a decent profit, and live above my shop. That flat's enormous.'

'What about the old boy?' She avoided calling him by name to keep Ruth talking. If she thought that Sandy was sympathetic towards him for any reason, she would shut up.

'Exactly. Old boy. What is he – eighty? He's a danger to 'imself living alone. Should be in a home. You should see the state of his kitchen!' Freda had seen it many times and had mentioned how fussy Albert was about keeping everything bleachy-clean. 'So you think we could get rid of him?'

'One way or another.' Ruth raised an eyebrow and smirked. 'You can leave that to me. So – what d'yer think?'

'The laundry idea sounds great, but it's not for me. I'll stick to what I know and enjoy. At least we'll be next-door neighbours, Ru. I'm really pleased we've made up.'

'Anyway . . .' said Ruth, rising, 'I'll think about your offer of me coming in with you. Maybe you should think about opening another shop somewhere else. Get someone to manage it for you.'

'Maybe.' That was exactly what Sandy had in mind, but she would keep it under wraps before disclosing any new plans. She wasn't sure yet about Ruth, not entirely; her state of mind was still a cause for concern. She loved her and was pleased to have her back, and would do her level best to make up for the past when she should have been looking out for her younger sister.

'Do you know . . .' said Sandy, showing Ruth out of the shop, 'I can't even remember that guy's name. The perv.'

'Lucky you. It's etched across my brain. Don't ask me to tell you, I would throw up. I don't want to think about him. See you later,' she said, 'I've got to rush. Shadow's on her own again.' Ruth suddenly stopped and turned to face Sandy. 'I'm really sorry I bit you.' There was a genuine look of regret on her face.

'So am I,' laughed Sandy.

'I s'pose there'll be a scar?'

'Probably.' She didn't want to think about it.

'Well . . . we all have scars of one kind or another, don't we?' Ruth's sincerity seemed to waver. Sandy thought she saw a fading smile.

As Ruth left, Maureen and a couple of the girls arrived, bringing a lighter atmosphere into the shop.

'Go on down, girls, I'll be with you in a minute.' There was a sparkle in Maureen's eyes and her cheeks were flushed. She turned to Sandy and grinned. 'Can I have a quick word?'

'So long as it is quick, Maureen. I'm a bit behind, to say the least. It's been one hell of a morning.' She tried to sound hurried, but in truth what she really wanted to do was sit down and have a coffee with her machinist. A coffee, a cigarette and a sit-down.

'Last night I went to a reunion,' said Maureen,

'schoolfriends, girls I grew up with, that kind of stuff. One of the girls – an arty-farty type, all cheesecloth and Indian beads – is goin' to Delhi. Chucking everything up, buying a camper van and reckons she won't be back—'

'Maureen . . .' Sandy glanced at the wall clock.

'There's another three years to run on 'er lease and she's looking for someone to take it over – cheap. She's 'ad no luck so far.' Maureen broke into a beaming smile. 'It sounds perfect. The floor space is just under a thousand square feet. There's only a tiny showroom, but –' she waved her hands – 'that's all we'd need.'

'Where is it?'

'Well, there's the rub.' She held a hand against her breast, still grinning. 'For you, that is, not me. I'd work there at the drop of a hat. Jump on a tube and be there in no time. Ladbroke Grove from Farringdon? Twenty minutes. And this place is close to Notting Hill Gate – Central line.'

'Maureen, I don't know that part of London. I'd be a fish out of water. Where is it exactly?'

'Portobello Road! It'll be brilliant, Sand. I've only bin there a couple of times but I tell you – it's buzzing! It's where all the—'

'I know! I went there once. I know what it's like. And I *did* feel like a river fish out to sea. I'd never fit in.'

'You would! Anyway, I'm not talking about a shop, but what we need now and what we'll be desperate for soon – more working space. You could slice off a corner for yourself and cut the patterns in your own bit, and the girls'd 'ave a bit more elbow room to work in.'

'All right . . . I'll give it some thought.'

'Go *today*. I'll look after the shop,' Maureen insisted. 'One of the other women was showing a lot of interest. She's run out of space as well. Imports Spanish shoes and leather bags, and going a bomb! If you let this break slip through your fingers you'll be sorry. This woman's into Eastern religion – she'll be happy to pay half the full-term lease to go off to find herself.'

'What if we get busy?'

Maureen folded her arms, eyebrows raised. 'I can't cut patterns, Sandy, but I can sell, as you well know.'

'Maybe I should give her a ring . . .?'

'No need. She's there today giving her last sessions of yoga and meditation. I told 'er you'd drop in.'

'Bit presumptuous, wasn't it?'

'Are you gonna go?'

'Yes.'

'Well then, it wasn't, was it?' Maureen winked at her boss and made for the basement. 'I'll let the girls know I'll be up here today. Get your skates on!'

Get her skates on? Sandy felt as if they'd been on since dawn. She wondered what else could happen in one day. Finding out that Johnnie had slept with Ruth was bad enough, not to mention the confirmation that her sister had suffered abuse as a child – and now this. *Portobello Road?* She didn't have a clue how to get there by car, and if she drove to Bethnal Green underground there would be nowhere to park. *Notting Hill Gate* – it sounded like another world. She had only ever lived and worked in the East End, apart from the couple of years she'd spent in Woodford.

Wearing a black miniskirt and white skinny-rib top, her

red hair flowing down her back, straight as a die, she went outside and hailed a taxi. There had been no time to eat breakfast, take care over her make-up or put heated rollers in her hair. If she was to go, she wanted to be back in the shop by early afternoon.

Once on the tube she wondered why she had let herself be talked into this rendezvous. Maureen was a slight girl and not very tall, but she had will-power. If she wanted to do something, she did it. Sandy wished she could be the same. She had come a long way since Roy first began to reject her, and during the last months she had gained enough self-confidence to be her own person. But still that need, that hunger for someone to talk things over with, was as strong as ever.

Roy used to be her best friend – or so she had thought. His favourite singer came to mind – Don Williams. Whenever they had had a few cross words he would play 'You're My Friend' and win her round. Disjointed lines from the song came flooding back.

Feeling herself sink, she remembered Maureen and her cheeky feminist attitude. She had told Sandy that she had been dumped on the rubbish heap three times before she learned how to treat men. *Single 'nice' girls get respect – married 'nice' women get treated with contempt.* Those had been her enlightening words, and having listened to Freda and a couple of other women whose men had gone off and left them, Sandy had to admit that there was something to be said for Maureen's cynicism. *If you want to keep a man, keep him on his toes. Make him jealous, make him believe he could lose you – but most of all, make yourself indispensable. If he thinks he can't make it without you, you're safe. Stay in the driving seat, but let him change the gears.*

Sandy covered her mouth to hide her smile. Maureen's face when she had given that little speech had been hilarious. Her pointed chin stuck out, upper lip curled, eyes wide. Her comical sneer had made not only Sandy laugh but the other machinists too. She had become the light which the girls couldn't help going towards. For all her swearing and coarse talk, she was great to have around.

Turning out of Westbourne Grove into Portobello Road was like entering another world. The atmosphere was buzzing, Maureen was right. Saturday was obviously *the* day. Apart from the daily fruit and vegetable trade, there was everything and anything on sale from old wirelesses to a stall full of buttons, every shape, size and colour. Buttons and belts were the speciality of a very tall, ageing student with short dark hair, wearing an enormous pair of red glasses, big black boots, jeans and a t-shirt. She was moving in time to the music coming out of some speakers on a van. The singer had an electric piano aboard and was singing 'Stay Lady Stay'. Every time the button-seller felt passionate about a line of the lyrics, which obviously reminded her of a lover, she joined in with her own unique rendition. 'Lay across my big brass bed,' seemed to be her favourite line.

There were other musicians scattered throughout Portobello Road, mostly buskers. One young man with very long dark wavy hair, sporting a red American civil war uniform with gold frogging, was playing the hurdy-gurdy, 'My Old Man Said Follow the Van'. On the other side of the road a busker sang 'Streets of London'. Here, anything went. It was like a festival.

Sandy's initial concern at seeing the women dressed mostly in Indian prints and cheesecloth soon changed to optimism. If the men could look good in period uniforms, then why not design something similar for the women, in red satin? Johnson's had just about every trimming imaginable. Plaited gold braid was just one of them. She could feel the old creativity drive again, and couldn't wait to get back to the drawing board.

Resisting the urge to stop at a collector's stall, she remained blinkered; old silver spoons and salt cellars were items she had always wanted to collect. There would be other days and many of them. She was ready for this part of London – it made quite a contrast to the Roman Road.

One familiar woman, an actress whom Sandy had seen on television but whose name she could not remember, was striding along as if she had a purpose, as if she had no time to spare. Her long purple satin cape blowing in the warm breeze, she made her entrance into Julie's, the French restaurant. Sandy felt like following her in, but she was on a mission and would not be sidetracked.

Once she had found the building and the woman she was to see, she felt more relaxed. The place looked as if it would be just right for what she had in mind. Maureen, as usual, had been spot on.

'Mo told me about your awful accident. You must be feeling pretty low.' The yoga expert, dressed in a mauve and gold sari, spoke with a compassionate smile. 'Feeling like shit, I expect?'

How could Sandy tell her that in actual fact she was elated, thrilled by her surroundings and by the spacious ground floor of the converted Regency building? 'I'm getting over it,' she said, hoping the matter would be dropped.

'You're very brave. Have you thought about meditation?'

'Ye-es . . .' said Sandy, not wishing to offend. 'I have often thought about it. I . . . er . . . plan to take it up one day, when I've a bit more time to myself; for myself,' she quickly added. 'It's difficult right now, starting a business. Still, I expect you know all about that.'

Poonam showed Sandy into the reception area, which was separated from the meditation area by a dark red curtain. Squatting on a large Indian gold-embroidered cushion, she gestured that Sandy follow suit and sit on one of the others. Taking a ready-made joint from her tobacco tin, she reached out for a bottle of home-made red wine and filled two cracked Rockingham teacups.

'Spiced wine,' she smiled, 'courtesy of Thane. His is the fried green banana stand. Have you tried fried green bananas, Sandy? They are an experience.'

'No . . . I can't say I have.'

'He serves them in small wooden bowls with rice and peas . . . or beans. Are you carnivorous?'

'I never have been,' Sandy fibbed, wishing to keep on good terms with Poonam. 'Apparently . . .' she said, remembering a childhood experience that she could elaborate on, 'when I was very young, I saw cows for the first time in a field on a trip out into the countryside, and my dad told me they were Sunday dinner. I refused to eat any kind of meat after that.' *Nice one, Sandy. Keep 'em flowing.*

Poonam almost choked on her drink. 'You mean I'm sharing . . .' she held out her joint to Sandy . . . 'I'm sharing the best grass ever with practically a natural-born vegetarian?' She showed her approval by holding up two fingers on each hand.

'My parents brought me up to believe that meat was part of our natural diet. Can you believe that? You were so lucky to have parents who were ahead of their time.'

Sandy turned down the offer of a drag on the reefer. 'Nicotine during the day. I only smoke grass after I've closed the door on the world.'

'You'll learn.' She smiled and sucked on her drug as if she were kissing a long-lost lover. 'Do you have a garden, Sandy?'

'A tiny one.'

'Grow your own?'

'Er . . . no, I . . . um—'

'I know. Good seeds are hard to find. Not here though. Portobello is like heaven – overcrowded with untroubled spirits. They make the best friends, do you know that? In this market we all love each other. Even the greedy and very-expensive-antiques profiteers. Love one – love all.'

Sandy lit a Rothman's and narrowed her eyes. 'Your accent, Poonam . . . I can't quite place it.'

'Labels –' she smiled and shrugged – 'we rip them off.'

'It sounds a bit like a mixture of Welsh, Birmingham and the West country. Yet you look as if you've just come over from India with your dark skin and black hair.' She couldn't bring herself to mention the red spot on her forehead.

'A previous life?' Poonam looked up, smiled, drew on

her smoke and closed her eyes. 'Or from a present one. We each live many lives at once, Saffron. Sometimes we are just a passer-by in someone else's dream.' She opened her eyes. 'Saffron shall be your Portobello name.'

Time to get on to money. 'How much is the ground rent?' Sandy risked giving offence but time was running on. She couldn't imagine Poonam liked to talk about such vulgarities, but there it was.

'Cheque or cash?' Still smiling and casting closed eyes to heaven, Poonam said, 'Lucre is not filthy. It protects us from bureaucracy.'

And paying tax, thought Sandy. 'Cash.'

'Three years – make it one and a half grand and it's yours.'

'One and a quarter and you've got a deal.'

Poonam offered her hand as if it were a wilting leaf. Sandy took it, not quite knowing whether she was meant to give it a shake or kiss it. She settled for the brushing of fingers. Opening her big sleepy brown eyes, the south Londoner dropped into another strange regional accent and asked if she could have the readies as soon as possible. She wanted to secure a ticket on a bargain flight to India. 'Five days and the bargain offer closes.' She was referring to both deals.

Passing two debs who were selling expensive memorabilia to American tourists, Sandy smiled. They were obviously there for fun, and not for the revenue. She stopped to examine an early Victorian plaque advertising Colman's mustard. Posing as an interested customer she observed every bit of their designer-label clothing. If she could sketch something that wealthy posh people thought of as fun clothes, she would be on to a winner. She would come up with something outrageously working-class and sexy – something they could refer to as cheap and cheerful but would secretly adore. *Cheap and cheerful* – that was it! That's what she would call the Portobello Road shop.

'I wouldn't buy anything off this pair!' A tall, dark-haired and very attractive thirty-year-old gave Sandy a welcome smile. 'Far too expensive.'

'Thank you, Derick.' Amanda the deb narrowed her eyes and looked daggers at him. 'I shouldn't trust him for one moment. Anything halfway decent on *his* stall will have been bought from our second-rate box and sold on at four times the price he paid us.'

Sandy looked from the deb to the dark blue eyes of the sexy stranger. 'Where's your stall then?' She used her strongest cockney accent.

'On the sunny side of the road . . .' Derick said, changing his expression to one of intrigue. 'Outside one of the best cafés in the world. You should try their coffee and croissants.'

'Should I?' Sandy handed the plaque to one of the girls and asked the price.

'Four pounds if you don't go to the coffee shop with *him*.'

'And if I do?'

'Twenty. It's for your own good. He's a rogue – trust me.'

Taking Sandy by the arm and smiling benignly at the debs, Derick led her away. 'I want to know all about you.'

His deep, quiet voice was having an effect. She felt the sunshine move in and light up her small gloomy corners. 'Coffee and croissants first. You might not bother to treat me otherwise.'

'That dull?'

'Might be.'

'I don't think so. What's your name?'

'Saffron.'

'No way.'

'Sandy . . .?'

'More like it. So, Sandy . . . where do you get it from? The air of confidence? You stroll along as if you belong.' He pushed open the green-and-red-painted door of the café.

'Wherever my feet touch down –' she shrugged – 'I belong, man.'

'Nice philosophy if you can pull it off.'

She sat down at a green-and-red-painted table for two by a green-and-red-painted window. 'You saying I don't?'

'I'm saying you do.' He sat down and raised his eyes to meet hers. 'I'm asking how. Where does it come from? I've been around here a long time. When I saw you walking by earlier it was for the first time. Sarah's and Amanda's stall was the second time. Yet you act as if this is your habitat.' With an elbow on the round table and a hand under his chin, he gazed into her face and waited.

She copied his pose and grinned. 'If you've lived in one market, you've lived in 'em all.'

'And overdoing your cockney accent?'

'You ask too many questions, Derick – hardly give a girl the chance to answer any.'

'Go on then.' He turned in his chair and called to one of the two effeminate waiters. 'Richie! You look *fantastic* in red! Two coffees – two croissants!'

Throwing him a sideways smirk, the waiter shook his head. Derick was jumping the queue again and using his charm to do it. 'Café au lait, café noir, Turkish, espresso, cappuccino, Blue Mountain . . .'

Derick looked questioningly at Sandy.

'Camp?'

Derick burst out laughing. She didn't think it was that funny.

'Two cappuccinos!'

He looked at Sandy again. 'Sense of humour as well. What is it they say about you cockneys – salt of the earth?'

'Mmm . . . and it don't half sting the eye, salt. Take the piss once too often . . .' She leaned back in her chair and gave him one of her stony looks. 'Your accent's not so great.'

'At least I don't exaggerate it.'

'Where you from anyway – not that I'm interested?'

'Chester.'

'Lester from Chester.' She raised an eyebrow and grinned. 'Did you ever watch *Gunsmoke*? It was a western—'

'Yes, I've heard the joke before.' He leaned forward again. 'Now then – are we gonna sup with a long spoon for much longer, or are we going to talk properly?'

'Sup with a long spoon? Arm's length? I've never heard it put that way before. Coffee's coming.'

'Don't believe a word he says, love.' The waiter placed their refreshments on the table and swanned off, swaying his hips.

'You seem to have a reputation. Been taking advantage of your cool looks?' asked Sandy.

'So why are you in this neck of the woods?'

She spooned brown sugar crystals into her coffee. 'I've been to look at some premises. I'm taking over a lease.

Ladies' fashion. Hope to be in by the end of next week. The meditation centre is soon to be a sweatshop. I'll be looking for machinists. Know any?'

'Expanding?'

'Uh-huh.' She bit carefully into her croissant. It wouldn't do to have crumbs on her chin while she was play-acting. 'My premises in the Roman Road, Old Ford, are too small. We need more space.'

'Why here?'

'It came up.' She shrugged. 'I won't spend that much time over this side. Once I've set it up I'll find someone to manage it. It'll be more like a little factory than a shop. We'll have a small showroom though. Show off the goods.'

'What kind of clothes?'

'Wait and see.' She looked at him over the edge of her handmade pottery mug and winked.

'What's the shop in Roman Road called?'

'Nova boutique.'

He looked impressed. 'Just you?'

'Yep. I'm a widow.'

He was taken aback and it showed. 'I'm sorry to hear that.' He offered her a French cigarette. 'Can I run you back?'

'What about your stall?'

'My mother's looking after it. She loves selling. It would make her day if I disappeared and left her in charge.'

'Mother?' She didn't believe him.

'Yes.' He read her mind. 'I'm not married. Lived with someone for six years. She ran off with the insurance man,' he joked. 'And I'm very happy living on my own.'

'If you do run me back I won't have time to sit around and chat.'

'We'll save that for later. Once I've spied out the junk shops and you've closed for the day. We can go for a meal. Mother'll pack up the stall for me.'

'Dutch?'

'Suits me.'

'No strings?'

'What about straps?'

Smiling at his cheek, she tilted her head to one side, her expression thoughtful. 'Nah . . . it's not me.'

'Can't have everything.' He checked she had finished her coffee and went to pay. 'Come on.' He spoke as if he'd known her for ages and she liked it. She liked it a lot. With his black t-shirt and blue jeans he looked positively gorgeous. Scarlet woman or not, she wanted him. Live for today was becoming her thought for the day. *Long may it last.* She followed him out, feeling like a leading lady in some *cinéma vérité*.

'You didn't tell me your sister owns next door,' Maureen said as soon as Sandy stepped into the shop.

'No customers?'

'No, thank God. She looked a bit upset. I 'ad a shopful so I couldn't really do much. She's coming back later.'

'You have been busy then.'

'I 'aven't stopped, Sandy! Till now.' Leaning back in her chair, Maureen stretched her legs. 'I could do with another cup of tea. How'd you get on?'

'So it's been good then?'

Maureen laughed. ''Course it's bin good. It's bin brilliant. I just had a count-up. We took two 'undred and sixty pound. You should see the order book. Four of 'em are coming back later, special orders. One wants long sleeves added. One wants a different neckline and the other wants a long evening dress made up in black sequin.'

'Honest?'

'Before you put the kettle on, tell me what 'appened.'

'You were right. The place was buzzing. I've taken it.'

'*Yes*!' Maureen leaped up, threw her arms out and grabbed Sandy's hands. Together they skipped round in a circle like two girls in the school playground, laughing and shrieking.

'I'm glad someone's happy.' It was Ruth, looking as if her world had collapsed around her.

Sandy let go of Maureen's hand and grabbed Ruth's. Maureen grabbed her other one, and between them they forced her to join in. They were singing now, 'Who Wants to be a Millionaire'. With tears streaming down her cheeks, smiling and crying, Ruth managed the chorus. Round and round they went, while two teenagers stood in the doorway.

'Don't mind us,' Sandy said, breathless. 'We've just had a bit of good news. Do you want any help or are you just here to browse?'

'These are *my* customers, thank you very much. Got the rest of the dosh, girls?' Maureen gently pushed Sandy and Ruth towards the stairs.

'Yeah. Me mum lent it to us,' said the thirteen-year-old. 'She's coming up 'erself later on, once I go back and watch the stall for 'er. She wants a little red dress for Saturday night. Big darts match – she's in the finals. Wants to put the men in the other teams off their game.'

'Good for 'er! We'll make it low and short, then.'

With an arm around her sister, Sandy couldn't help smiling at Maureen and the way she seemed to get on with the customers. She wasn't so sure about Portobello Road, though. The women swore – she had heard them in passing – but there was a difference. *What a load of bollocks* is what she had heard more than once from the posh girls, and somehow it didn't sound like swearing coming from them. Maureen's version of it would be simply *bollocks!* There was a world of difference.

Easing Ruth on to the sofa, she held her hand. 'I thought you got over this morning's outburst a bit quick. We both need more time to adjust. You've been harbouring that pain for how many years – fourteen? It only took a few minutes to blurt it out. I don't think it's really sunk in with me yet.'

'It's not that.' Ruth wiped away her tears, blew her nose and took a deep breath. 'I've done all my crying over that.'

'Well what then?'

'I've been given the push – thanks to dear old Dave. He put the knife in. They won't say what, just asked me not to go back.' She snapped her fingers. 'Just like that. Out you go.'

'They can't do that!'

'At least they paid me to the end of the month. Three weeks' pay for nothing. Small mercies.' She remembered Leo from next door saying the same thing.

'They have to give a reason. And they have to give you a letter of warning first. Two, in fact. Believe me – I've read up on it. Forewarned is forearmed.'

207

'Dave's found a buyer for the house, or so he says. Unless I can find a better offer within a month, he's got the right to sell. By the time we've paid solicitor's fees, we'll come out with not one penny more than we paid.'

'Well you have only just bought it. There's hardly been time for it to go up in value.'

'It was worth more than we paid, much more. It was one of his little finds. A gem. I know what he's up to and there's nothing I can do about it. Except run him down one dark night.' The matter-of-fact way in which Ruth made that statement should have been followed by a smile, but her face remained earnest.

Sandy felt herself shiver. 'Nothing lost, nothing gained, then? You expected to move in next door anyway. You'll have to shack up with me while Albert's still there . . . or until you find a flat.'

'I might move back in with Mum and Dad.' She spoke as if she hadn't heard the offer from Sandy. 'They owe me. I'll soon find another job. I'm good at what I do.'

'But do you like what you do?'

'I hate it. You'd be surprised at what I 'ave to take from toffee-nosed sods who begrudge paying commission.'

'This could be fate, you know.'

'Fate! Come on, Sandy. This is the real world. Fate doesn't rule – money does.'

'I'm renting more premises. I'll need someone to manage them for me.'

Ruth threw her a sidelong glance. 'You want me to work for you?'

'Why not?'

She could think of a million reasons why not, but now was not the time to voice her contempt, which would no doubt be seen as jealousy. Ruth's dream of being the richer sister was fading too fast for her liking. 'Where is it?'

'Portobello Road.'

'Living space?'

'No.'

'You expect me to schlep backwards and forwards up there every day? Why can't I manage this shop?'

'Because I do.'

'Thanks for the offer, but no thanks. I'm not exactly unemployable.'

'I know that. I need someone I can trust. You'd have fifteen machinists to keep your eye on, and a small showroom to manage.'

'Salary?'

'I'll match what you get now.'

'You know I'm on commission. My salary's not brilliant.'

'It's the best I can do. You can be on commission. The machinists are. I'll give you a percentage.'

'Sounds more like it. When would I start?'

'Monday. The back bedroom's my office. You can work from there for now. Order the sewing machines, advertise for machinists in that area, go over there and interview them, see the machines in. Organize a cleaning company to scrub the place down. The sooner all that's done the better.'

Ruth stared. 'Why're you doing this, Sandy? After all I've put you through?' She looked at the injured part of her arm which was covered by the sleeve of her skinny-rib top.

'Because you're my sister.'

Ruth closed her eyes tight and screwed up her face. Pushing her hands through her blonde hair she began to cry again. 'What's happening to me?'

Sandy pulled her to her chest and kissed the top of her head. 'It's all right, Ru. No one's gonna hurt you again. We'll be together just like old times. Sandy and Ruth. We had our differences, but we were close; went everywhere together, once.' She stroked her back. 'We'll be the way we were. We used to giggle all the time, remember? Dad used to get really angry. The more he told us to stop it, the more we giggled. They'll be so pleased you're back in the fold. They've missed you something rotten. Me too.'

Sandy's patronizing speech ruffled Ruth's feathers. She would have loved to hit back with her own speech and send her reeling, but now was not the time. She would have to get back on her feet first and feel on top of things. Until then, she would take everything her family was ready to offer. Let them try to clear their guilty consciences. Well, they could try. She smiled at the thought of it.

'That's more like it. The old Ruthie toothy smile. I'll put the kettle on.'

Ruth hid her face in a cushion to smother her laughter. Nothing like a good old cup of tea to make everything come right! What an armpit Sandy was. She had quite forgotten the wimp side of her.

Chapter Seven

By the end of September, the site at Portobello Road was in operation. Ruth had proved herself to be an excellent organizer, and number ten Roman Road had been sold. Once Terry had managed to get his daughter to sit down and show him exactly what she had been getting up to, he had hit the roof.

'You're worth as much as you can borrow,' Ruth had told him, and that had been the last straw. For over two hours he had explained the pros and cons of borrowing. She was in so deep that had he not intervened when he did, she would certainly have ended up in the finance courts. At least she had come out breaking even.

Back home now, with her mother doing her cooking, washing and ironing, Ruth was in her element. With low outgoings she could afford to run a small car and keep a good wardrobe. She had every intention of getting back into property once she was on her feet: there was no way she was going to remain the poor relative. *True character shows with success* was something she had heard and never forgotten.

Acting like a saint, assuming the pose of angelic daughter

and receiving a salary from Sandy was OK for now, but her role-playing didn't usually last for more than six months. She got her kicks from stepping out of one mode and into another, and shocking everyone with her extreme changes of appearance and behaviour.

She couldn't wait to be on top and flaunt her true nature. It wasn't only riches she was after but power. Money was easy to come by. There were plenty of wealthy men on the lookout for a mistress with Ruth's looks. She could rise to any occasion; dress and behave like royalty if called upon to do so.

Sandy and her parents were eating out of her hand. Shadow had helped with the bonding. She had told her family that one of her reasons for keeping her was to help Sandy get over her fear, and that once she had learned to love Shadow, maybe she would lose her terror of dogs.

Terry, Maggie and Sandy had swallowed that fabrication, and the look of remorse on their faces was the best response she could have asked for.

But Sandy's new friend Derick was proving to be a problem. She saw him as the male version of herself. Out to enjoy life come what may, and yet he had shown no interest in Ruth whatever, no matter how hard she tried. Even wearing her black leather gear she couldn't imagine winning him over. There was something about him she didn't like. There wasn't a man yet who had not succumbed to her charms. It was as if Derick put up an invisible shield of steel when Ruth was around. His polite smile conveyed nothing sexual and he was beginning to annoy her. Maybe Sandy had finally found a man who was impervious to Ruth's beauty.

'I think we'd better install some electric heaters in there soon.' Maureen was being her usual polite self with Ruth.

'Because a couple of clouds went over? Give me a break, Maureen.' Ruth was in the small Portobello Road showroom, flicking through *Vogue*.

'The nights are drawing in and the temperature's dropping. Autumn'll be over before we know it.'

'Autumn? It's September – late summer! We'll heat the place when it gets cold. Whose turn is it to get the sandwiches?'

'I'll just see what the girls want.' Leaving Ruth to herself, Maureen went into the workroom. The natural light was better there than the basement at Roman Road, and there was far more space and plenty of shelving, and enough machinists to cope with the workload. She loved the area, the buzz, the people. The only snag was Ruth. One solitary person was dampening her world. With her naturally forthright manner, Maureen should have been able to ignore the bitchiness and enjoy the good things about working in Portobello Road – but she couldn't and it was getting her down. She wanted to go back to Roman Road, but to do so would be like giving in. What she didn't want to do was leave, but she was beginning to see that that might be her fate.

More interested in her fashion magazine than the two guys who had strolled in and who now stood quietly in front of her, Ruth asked what they wanted without taking her eyes off the article she was skimming through.

'Hello, I'm Ian.'

'And I'm John.'

'Selling or buying?' she said, deadpan.

'We are here to share. To share what we consider to be the answer to all people's problems.'

Ruth raised her eyes to the boyish young men wearing clean-cut suits and pretty flowery ties with pale pastel shirts to match. 'Is it free?'

'TM is not just a personal relief for the world's worriers. It is also worth money to business concerns.'

'TM makes people more relaxed and happier; it makes them more efficient and keeps their minds clear.' They spoke one after the other, leaving their listener no space to get a word in.

'It is invaluable to commercial concerns expecting maximum output and efficiency.'

'Worriers stop worrying, ulcers stop growing, blood pressure is reduced, reactions are better.'

'Decisions are made quicker, memory is improved.'

Ruth swept her long hair off her face and smiled. 'TM? Ah! Tia Maria. I keep a bottle by the bed. Are you a couple?' She quite fancied partying. One at a time, though.

'We are disciples of the Yogi. He can't teach everyone in the world transcendental meditation on his own. It would take too long. We charge a fee for our teaching, but this isn't our primary purpose.'

'So you are a couple then?'

'Close friends.' John's smile reminded her of the vicar who wore nothing under his cassock.

'The World Plan has seven goals. To develop the full potential of the individual.'

'To improve government achievements.'

'To realize the highest ideal of education.'

214

'To solve crime and all behaviour that brings unhappiness to the family of man.'

'To maximize the intelligent use of the environment.'

'To bring fulfilment to the economic aspirations of individuals and society.'

'To achieve the spiritual goals of mankind . . .'

'. . . in this generation.'

'We are not asking you to completely wash out your brain,' said John, getting carried away and speaking for Ian. It was unusual for them to be allowed to get this far with their repertoire.

'Now I know who you remind me of – Paul McCartney and John Lennon, in the early sixties. The Beatles went on a pilgrimage to see the Maharishi Mahesh Yogi, didn't they? Came back and spent a couple of months meditating. I don't think they went much on it, do you?'

'I didn't know that.'

'Neither did I.'

She went back to her fashion journal, leaving them standing, waiting to be dismissed.

'My brain needs putting through a washing machine.' Maureen was in the doorway. 'And I want to take up smoking again but I 'aven't got the will-power to do it by myself. Will TM help the likes of me?'

'I'm sure it will . . .?'

'Maureen. But you can call me Mo. Tell you what. You let me 'ave some of your pamphlets and I'll have a butchers while you're up the sandwich shop. Here's the list and here's the money. It's our lunch break, so while we're filling our tummies you can fill our minds. Tell us all about it. The

215

girls'll love it. The sandwich shop's three doors down.'

'I'm happy with that.'

'It's refreshing to find someone so trusting.' Pleased with themselves, they walked out side by side, one mission being much like another.

'Well done, Maureen. Now we'll never get rid of them!'

'The girls need a bit of light relief now and then. You should try it.' She grinned and went to the machine room.

Once the machinists had eaten their lunch and listened to the disciples, they struck a deal. One trial session at a special rate in the machine room. The lads seemed happy with that too.

'You expect me to stay behind for an extra hour while you play silly buggers? Take a powder!' Ruth was having none of it.

'I'll lock up. Keys?'

'And how am I supposed to get in tomorrow morning?'

'I'll open up. Keys.'

The thought of a lie-in was attractive. 'Be it on your own head. Sandy will throw a wobbler, but there you go. You know best, Maureen. You know what the girls need.' Ruth took the keys from the desk drawer and dropped them into her open palm. 'Now if you'll cover for me, I would like some lunch. My name wasn't included on your sandwich list.'

'I'm sure that Derick'll be pleased to see you . . . as long as you don't outstay your welcome.' Maureen pushed her face forward. 'He's not interested, babe.'

'We *are* a plucky little cow all of a sudden!'

'It's the effect those disciples had on me. I'm so relaxed,' she said, lifting her arms and flopping them down again. 'My mind is at peace.' She laid a hand on Ruth's arm. 'I'm full of love. I even love you, Ruth.'

'Fuck off!' She pushed her hand away and stormed out of the showroom into the busy street; and the sound of the hurdy gurdy playing 'Pack Up Your Troubles in Your Old Kit Bag' floated into the room.

'Maybe it's not so bad here,' Maureen murmured. She felt she had just won her very first round with Ruth.

'Maureen has got to go!' Ruth wasted no time in bending Sandy's ear. No sooner was she home than on the phone. 'She's stirring the girls up, whispering about forming their own union, asking for a pay rise, demanding better working conditions. And she's been slipping into your cutting room to have a crafty smoke – and taking the other smokers with her!'

'Maureen doesn't smoke.'

'No?'

'No.'

'That goes to show how much you're in touch these days. Coming over here two days a week to cut isn't enough. You should be here three days! I don't know why you're so stubborn about it. What's the problem? I'm more than happy to manage Nova for you. I'll do Nova on Tuesdays, Thursdays and Fridays; Cheap and Cheerful on Mondays and Wednesdays.' She had chosen the three days Derick was in the East End, hunting and buying collectors' items.

'Maureen likes to do one day a week here, you know that.'

'Maureen is taking fucking liberties! She's running rings

217

round you, and you're so bloody grateful for her *friendship*. She's taking advantage of the fact that you're a widow and don't have any friends. She knows you're only using her until you start socializing again. You'd never choose the likes of her as a friend, you know you wouldn't. She's as common as muck! I'm telling you – either get rid of her now or downgrade her.'

'Ruth . . . this is all a bit sudden, and I've got customers in—'

'It's gone six o'clock! What *is* it with you?' She changed her tone in order to patronize Sandy. 'Don't get greedy, Sandy . . .' There was a click and then the dialling tone.

'She put the phone down on me!' Ruth gazed across at her mother who had just come into the front room. 'I was offering more help and she hangs up.' She slowly shook her head. 'I don't think she took Roy's death quite as well as she pretended. I think she should see a counsellor, Mum. Get some help.' She stared miserably at the floor.

With an arm around Ruth's shoulders, Maggie sighed. 'She's got you back, love. That's the most important thing. She was really cut up about . . . well . . . least said—'

'About me and Roy?'

Maggie shrugged. 'Of course. It cut her deep. She thinks the world of you, Ruth. Always has done.'

Forcing back feelings of regret, Ruth clenched her teeth and counted to five. She daren't weaken. She daren't cry. She daren't open up again. Once to Sandy was enough. 'I'll drive up Nova's and see her. Maybe she needs someone to moan at.' This time she meant what she said, and she wanted to see Sandy. It wasn't the first time she had felt a fleeting desire to be with her. The trouble was, once she was there it seemed to disappear. She could never quite hold on to the feeling. Although it was slowly changing: she had stopped wanting to get out of her company as soon as she was in it.

With Maureen out of the way, she felt sure that she and her sister could become close friends again – in time. It hurt, seeing the way Sandy and that common tart joked and talked. The pain inside was a strange one, more like an ache. An ache for something lost. She sometimes wished that Maureen would just disappear. Die, even. Maybe then the sisters would have a chance to get close again, without any interference from an outsider.

Closing Nova's, Sandy caught sight of Derick looking very pleased with himself. He gave her a thumbs-up sign and winked.

'What have you found now?'

'A corner shop, would you believe. It's a dealer's paradise. No wonder it's been kept quiet. Came across it by accident in the back and beyond of Shoreditch.'

Touched by his boyish grin, she took his hand and led him upstairs. 'First things first. I want a very large glass of wine and a ciggy. It's been a long day.'

'Busy?'

'Very.'

Once they were settled in the living room, Derick began to unpack his small cardboard box. 'I wasn't even in the mood for buying.' He shrugged. 'Always the way. When you're not looking. Bit like us when we met down Portobello Road.' He carefully peeled the brown paper from one of his purchases. It was an engraved pinchbeck fob watch with matching albert.

'Mid-Victorian, I should think.' He held it by the chain and smiled, a look of triumph on his face. 'How much?'

'What would I want with a pocket watch?' She sipped her wine and silently compared his find to hers. She hadn't looked in her tin for a month or so.

'You know what I mean. How much did I give for it?'

'A fiver?'

'Don't be funny. Thirty quid. Worth three times as much.' He admired it again. 'If I sell it.'

'Why was it so cheap then?'

'The old girl hasn't kept up with inflation,' he smiled. 'Probably got a store of goodies tucked away. I don't s'pose she paid much for it either.'

'But when she bought it, she thought she had paid through the nose?'

'Not necessarily. She's a canny lady.'

'But not as canny as you and the other dealers.'

Derick unwrapped another small parcel. 'If you had seen the look on her face when I counted out two hundred pounds, you wouldn't be fighting her case. She was happy, I'm happy. It's all part of the game. What goes around, comes around. Don't knock it.'

'Sorry. Didn't mean to sound preachy.'

'People outside the trade don't understand. Stick to what you know. You're making a fair profit, aren't you?'

'I said I was sorry.' She topped up his glass. 'Don't be so touchy.'

He removed a brooch from the brown paper, placed it on

220

the palm of his hand and offered it to her. 'Art nouveau. Silver enamel.'

'Derick! That is *gorgeous*!' She took it from him. The elegant peacock was enamelled in rich colours, the plumage on its fanned tail sprinkled with marcasite. 'How much did this set you back?'

'Never you mind. It's a present.' He took it from her and carefully pinned it to her deep blue shift dress.

Leaping up, she admired it in the mirror. 'It's lovely.' She turned to him. 'Is it really for me?'

'You like it then?' he said, pleased with himself.

'I love it.' She held out her arms and he was quick to accept the invitation. Feeling his warm body against hers, she felt safe and secure. They had been spending quite a bit of time together, and he had helped to take her mind off Johnnie, whom she hadn't seen since the day he told her he'd slept with Ruth.

'I'll show you the rest. There's no more jewellery, just bric-a-brac and memorabilia . . . which includes a small piece of Rockingham.'

'Before you go on, there's something *I* want to show *you*. Sit down; you're in for a bit of a surprise.' Flicking her long hair off her face, she raised her eyebrows and left the room. Johnnie came to mind, his words of warning flooding back. *Show no one.* Pushing a tiny doubt to the back of her thoughts, she decided there should be no secrets between them. Besides which, she was longing to see his reaction.

Determined to hide her excitement she returned with the tin, keeping a straight face. 'Just a few bits and pieces,' she said, sitting beside him on the sofa. He had uncovered his piece of Rockingham: delicate hand-painted flowers in a basket.

Slowly easing the lid off the black metal box, she glanced sideways at his face and smiled inwardly at his cool exterior. 'Close your eyes,' she said.

'No.'

'I won't open it then.'

'Suits me.' He reached out for his piece of china, turned it upside down and studied the marks.

'You're a tormenting bastard at times.'

'And you're not?'

She left him to his Rockingham and picked up the diamond and ruby brooch as the first piece to gloat over. 'This is my favourite find,' she murmured casually.

He looked from the piece to her face. 'Now you're gonna tell me you were a dealer once.'

'No. I don't like ripping people off.'

'No? How much do you make on one of those scanty boob tubes then?'

She held the brooch in the palm of her hand. 'It's so delicate.'

'Is it real?'

'Yep. Platinum.'

'You called it a find. So it can't be a family heirloom.'

'Nope.'

'All right, I'm impressed. Where'd you get it?'

'It was in this tin, with the rest of the hoard.' She replaced the brooch and slowly withdrew the gold watch and chain. 'This is nice, but it's not my favourite. Second to the brooch –' she took out a diamond ring – 'is this.' She took out a ring set with sapphires. 'And this.'

He crossed his legs and sat back nonchalantly. 'And where did you find the tin?'

'Hidden under the floor in the basement.' She slipped a ring on her finger and admired it. 'The documents are a good read. Most of the receipts for this little find are there. Dating back to the early nineteenth century, if my memory serves me right.'

'Is this a wind-up?'

She slowly shook her head and smiled. 'No. Stop sodding about and take a look at what's in here. You'll 'ave more idea than me as to what it's worth.'

His casual act over, he leaped on the tin and spread out the contents on her small coffee table. 'You honestly found this in the cellar?'

'Basement. What do you think the brooch is worth?'

'Out of my league. This is first-division. I could find out though. But then, so could you.'

'I wouldn't know who to approach and besides, the less people know about this the better. It's not really mine to keep.'

'Why not? Found it on your premises, didn't you?'

'Exactly. But someone said it belonged to the Crown.'

'And the Pope's as pure as bottled holy water.' He peered at the hallmarks. 'You're right. This is platinum. Which means these must be diamonds.'

'My friend told me I should declare it . . .'

'That's a load of bollocks, Sandy—'

She found herself laughing at him. At his Portobello market affectedness. 'That's one way of putting it.'

'Who is this friend, anyway?'

'No one special.' She instantly reprimanded herself. Johnnie was special, but it wasn't what Derick would want to hear. 'A very old lady who used to babysit me. She died two months ago, in her sleep. She was ninety-four. Can you imagine living to that age? Her brain was as sharp as a razor though.' She thought it best to kill off her fictitious character almost as soon as she'd brought her into being.

'Who else knows about this?' He was beginning to sound like Johnnie, almost.

'You, me and . . . whoever put it there.'

'If you want, I'll take you to an honest dealer who'll give you two prices. One for insurance and a real one. He'll know what this would fetch on the market or at auction.'

'Why do I have to come with you?'

He slowly turned his head and looked into her face. 'I would have thought you'd want to.'

'You think I don't trust you?'

He held the brooch between his finger and thumb. 'We're not talking about a fairground trinket. This could be worth thousands.'

'If the situation was reversed, would you trust me?'

'Yes, but I haven't just accused you of ripping off an old lady.'

'Come on! I was joking, for Christ's sake.'

'Those kind of jokes hurt.'

She slipped down on to her knees, placed her hands together and pleaded with him to forgive her. Wrapping his long legs around her waist, he squeezed. 'Seductress.'

'Is that a request?'

He placed the brooch back in the tin and pulled her on to the sofa. 'I thought you'd never ask.' His dark blue eyes bore into hers. 'Who's going to take off your clothes – you or me?'

'Neither. It's Freda's evening for popping in. It could be embarrassing.'

'She knocks first, doesn't she?'

'Yeah, but . . . rushing around pulling our clothes on? Bit . . . ignoble?'

'For my little cockney?'

'Derick . . .'

'My East End strumpet . . .' His hand was already halfway up her leg. 'My harlot . . .' He smiled his sexy smile, slowly pushed his hand under her knickers and gently massaged. 'If you keep your legs crossed she won't know whether these are on or not, will she.' His breath was hot on her neck, his voice deeper by the second as he slipped a finger inside her.

'OK . . .' She tried to control her sudden erratic breathing. 'Pull them down, then.'

'I'm hardly going to pull them up,' he chuckled, squeezing her.

'You know what I mean . . . don't rip them off this time. They're my best ones.' She opened her legs a fraction more and jiggled her hips. 'You've got magic fingers, did you know that?'

'What's so special about these knickers, then?'

'They're new . . . expensive . . . soft lace and silk . . . French . . .'

'Uh-huh.' He slipped his hand from inside her knickers, eased her short dress up above her waist and admired, half-

225

impressed. 'Very nice, but I would rather see what's underneath.' He inched them down slowly, not taking his eyes off her thighs and flame-coloured bush.

Tossing the silk knickers over his shoulder and kneeling before her, he gently eased her legs apart and looked from the lips of her fleshy, moist crevice up to her face, gazing into those big hazel eyes.

Cursing her bad timing, Ruth did her best to look sympathetic as Freda tried to stop herself from trembling. Leaning on her car and gazing into the tear-stained face, she thought that Freda looked as if she had pushed her face into her make-up bag and jerked it around a bit. Mascara, green eyeshadow and eyebrow pencil were smudged together giving the impression of two heavily bruised black eyes, and her tears had streaked the panstick and face powder. Her lips were in there somewhere, behind the smeared red lipstick.

'He was such a lovely man. To go like that, with no one there. I should have known, I should have sensed it. He was depressed, sure —' Freda shrugged mournfully — 'who isn't these days?'

'He's better off out of it. How old was he – gone eighty? Think of it as a favourite old plant that's come to the end of its life.' Ruth was more annoyed because he had pegged out *after* she had been forced into selling number ten. 'The new owner won't burst a pipe over it.'

Freda felt herself go cold. What a cold-hearted bitch this young woman was. Ruth's words struck her. *Burst a pipe.* Why was she even breathing the same air as this person?

Shaken by her insensitivity, she turned away and rang Sandy's bell. When the door finally opened she threw her hands in the air. 'Albert took an overdose!' She fell into Sandy's arms as Ruth squeezed past them and up the stairs.

'He left a note. The police are up there now. Said he'd had enough of this world and wanted to be with his friends and family on the other side. How can anyone be that unhappy?'

Sandy held her close and gently rubbed her back. 'He might not have been unhappy, Freda. You can't blame someone his age and living alone for wanting to go to sleep for ever. That's probably how he saw it, eternal sleep. It was attractive to me once . . .'

'No, don't say that. Life is a gift . . .' She started to cry again.

'Come on. You need a bit of privacy and a double whisky.'

Meeting Ruth and Derick on the stairs took Sandy by surprise. The last thing she expected was for him to go home. They had only just made love.

'I think Freda should have you to herself for half an hour, Sand. Me and Derick are goin' across the road for a drink. Come and join us once she's gone.' Ruth tossed back her blonde hair and continued down the stairs.

'Derick?' Sandy looked him straight in the eye.

'That's OK, isn't it?' He flashed his eyes in Freda's direction. 'She needs a shoulder, doesn't she?'

'Go up, Freed.' Sandy barred Derick's way and waited until they were alone. 'You sure that's the only reason?'

'Come on, Sandy! She's your sister!'

'Exactly.'

'What's that supposed to mean?'

'Forget it. I'll see you later – if you can drag yourself away.' She pulled back her arm as he reached out for her. 'Did you put the tin away?'

'In the pine cupboard, where you told me to put it. And don't worry – everything's there!'

'Did you put it away before Ruth saw it?'

He looked at her as if he was seeing her for the first time. 'As it happens, yes. You don't have much faith in her, do you?'

'No, Derick, and with good reason. Take care.'

'I'm only going to be gone half an hour at the most. What do you think's going to happen during that short time?'

She tapped her temple with one finger. 'Stay sharp.'

Mystified, he shrugged and left her feeling as if she were the one in the wrong. She watched him leave and resisted the urge to call him back. It would take more than a few minutes to explain her fear and trepidation about her sister's pattern of behaviour when it came to other people's men. Helen, Ruth's sensitive and quiet flatmate, had been her last victim, and she had moved in on the couple very soon after Roy's death, by all accounts. It seemed that Ruth was hell-bent on shattering relationships.

Burdened by the worry that she was about to lose Derick, she joined Freda in the sitting room and managed a weak smile. 'Dare I say he's better off?' She remembered when Louise at Johnson's had said the same thing to her about Roy – but Sandy truly believed that Albert had had enough. Two weeks previously he had ventured outside to the market, only to be laughed at by a small gang of youths who had flicked off his toupee and called him a dirty old queer. When she found him trying to get his key in the lock he was trembling from head to toe.

'You're probably right, Sandy, but what must he have gone through during those last minutes?'

Sandy joined Freda on the sofa and thought about it. 'I bet he was relieved. Relieved that he had the freedom to do with his life whatever he wanted.' She stared ahead, thinking about the time when she had contemplated her own end. Realizing how cruel that would have been for her parents had pulled her away from such thoughts. But Albert hadn't had anyone to feel guilty over. There hadn't been any family coming to visit him.

'He did look at peace . . . his head resting on his pillow, his blue silk eiderdown up to his chin.' She raised her eyes to meet Sandy's. 'I swear to God there was a faint smile on his face.'

'Well there you are then. What else did the note say?'

'*Goodbye cruel world, I'm off to join the circus.*'

'You are joking?'

Freda slowly shook her head and laughed. 'No I'm not. He had a dry sense of humour, did Albert. There was a postscript. He thanked all of us for making his last years . . . more bearable.'

'Why was he so unhappy? He had a nice flat. Didn't look short of a few bob . . .'

'Bobby died. Simple as that. They had lived together above that shop for over thirty years. He was a hairdresser too. They were like an old married couple. Everyone knew they were queer and no one cared. They were loved, the pair of them. Always had time for a chat. Very caring. I shall miss him. All I've got left of a very good friend and neighbour is an empty space. An empty flat.' She wiped her eyes and sighed. 'Do you think I should move in there?'

'No . . . no, I don't, Freda . . .' Now it was Sandy's turn to choke back the tears. She had visions of Freda, old and lonely, staring out of the window just like Albert had. 'Your little house is lovely. You're your own boss. Can you imagine, someone like you having to pay rent to some property magnate? Don't even think about it.'

'I wouldn't have to pay rent. I own the place. I . . . I am the private buyer who wished to be nameless. Albert was the only one who knew. You should have seen the look on his face when I told him. The look of relief.'

'You old fox.' Sandy beamed. It was the best news yet. Freda was her neighbour. 'Don't tell me – you're gonna open a shoe shop.'

Freda looked into Sandy's face. 'Unless you want to expand?'

'No. Definitely not. I've got enough on my plate. I love the Portobello Road site and I've got no regrets; but what with being over there half the week and here the other half . . .'

'You should slow down a bit.'

'I will, I will. But not yet. I can't. I've got to run with it while we're this busy. Once things slow down a bit I'll delegate.'

'Well if that's not arse about face I don't know what is. You should delegate now, to relieve the pressure.'

'Sure, but where am I s'posed to find the time to look for

another pattern-cutter? A good pattern-cutter? One I can trust to follow my designs?'

'Well, just . . . don't do too much, that's all.' Freda lay her head back and closed her eyes. 'So what do you think? Shall I sell my back-to-back and move in next door?'

'No, I don't want you as a neighbour. In and out every five minutes asking for a cup of sugar; playing loud music till the early hours; entertaining men all the time . . .'

'That's settled then. I'll phone Johnnie today and book him to do the place up better than he did yours. I quite fancy some of that William Morris wallpaper with curtains to match.'

Sandy went quiet. William Morris. Honeysuckle. That had been the design she had picked for hers and Roy's cottage. 'I'll come with you if you like, to Sanderson's . . . to help you choose.' *And lay a ghost*, she told herself.

'It'll be nice seeing Johnnie's smiling face again.'

'Yes, Freda, it will.'

'You gonna tell me what happened? Why you finished it?'

'No, Freda, I'm not.'

'Fair enough. I'll ask him.'

'I don't think he'll tell you.' She felt herself sink again. Ruth had caused the rift between them, and as likely as not she was doing the same thing at that very moment with Derick. She stood up and went to the window. 'There's an ambulance outside.'

'I don't want to see. I've said goodbye.'

'And Leo's just arrived.'

'That was quick! I only phoned him half an hour ago.

He'll get done for speeding one of these days. Go and get him, Sandy. I expect he'll be breaking his heart.'

Sandy opened the window and called out to him. 'Leo! Freda's up here. I'll come down and open the door!'

'Is he in tears?' asked Freda.

'Sobbing his heart out.'

'I guessed as much. It's all changing. Old neighbours going ... new people coming in. And there's nothing we can do to stop it. Old Ford will be a different place in a few years — you see if I'm wrong.'

Sandy left Freda to herself and went to let Leo in. She didn't need to be reminded of change. This time last year she had a husband she loved and trusted, a dream cottage and a good career without all the pressures of running a business. If she could turn back the clock she would do so without hesitation.

'What did he bloody well go and do a thing like that for?' Tears were dropping off the end of Leo's over-large nose. 'He could have come with me to the Canaries next year. We'd have been all right. A dolly-bird for me and a boy for Albert. The place is brimming with young people looking for a sugar daddy.'

'Go on up, Leo. Freda's in the sitting room. Get her to make you both a cup of tea or pour yourselves a drink. I've got to pop over the road to see someone.'

'Life doesn't begin at forty, it begins much later. The old fool.' Still crying, he slowly climbed the stairs.

Anger eating away at her, Sandy made her way towards the pub, unsure as to who was causing her turmoil, Ruth or Derick, or both. She rehearsed her first cutting remark; she would not behave like a jealous lover and give Ruth the satisfaction – she would act as if she couldn't have cared less that Derick had walked out when she needed a bit of moral support, trailing behind her sister as if she were a goddess.

As she entered the saloon bar her heart sank. People were talking, laughing and enjoying the atmosphere, and the record playing on the jukebox was 'Lola' by the Kinks; but Derick and Ruth were nowhere to be seen. Slightly embarrassed at being on her own, she walked slowly to the bar and ordered herself a gin and tonic, ignoring the turning heads of three men who were ready with their chat-up lines, if only to impress one another.

Taking her drink to a small round table away from the crowd, she sat down and lit a cigarette, wondering if they had gone on to another pub and if so, why? Surely Derick was more sensitive than that? He must have considered the possibility that she might have gone in there sooner than they had suggested . . . taken Freda in to cheer her up, even? She began to have doubts about this new relationship. It had all happened so quickly she hadn't had time to think straight. Maybe Derick saw her as a pushover, a young widow with her own business. She cursed herself for behaving like a teenager. Of course he would be attracted to Ruth. What man wouldn't?

'Hello babe – all right?' It was Johnnie.

Surprised at just how pleased she was to see him, she smiled and found herself laughing. It was as if the two months since she'd last seen him hadn't happened. 'Not so bad, Johnnie. You gonna sit down, or what?'

'Yeah, of course. Shame about poor old Albert. Sad bastard.' He sat opposite her and sighed. 'Makes you feel bad, don't it? All them days and nights on his own. Still – there you go.' He downed the remains of his beer.

'I didn't see you when I came in.' She quickly scanned the bar. Maybe Derick was there too. 'Tucked away in a dark corner, were you?'

'I was in the public. What you drinking?'

She looked at her glass and was mildly taken aback to see it almost empty. 'Gin and tonic.'

'Your sister's in there if you're looking for 'er; playing at playing bar billiards with your boyfriend.' He collected her glass and stood up.

'What makes you think he's my boyfriend?'

'Stretched over the table, arse in the air – she's going all-out. Teasing the life out of the blokes watching, but getting nowhere with her prey.' He leaned forward expressing his regret. 'I wasn't as sharp, was I? You've found a wary bloke there.' He went to the bar, leaving her to ponder his meaning. Johnnie had introduced yet another doubt into her mind. Was Derick playing games, playing the innocent? After all, this was Sandy's local, and if he showed no interest in Ruth, or otherwise, it was fairly certain that word would get back to her – as indeed it had. She watched Johnnie flirting with the barmaid, who was all over him. He could have been winding her up with his barbed comments: after all he did have a vested interest. Men of his stature would find rejection a challenge and Sandy had, whichever way she looked at it, given him the boot. Seeing how attractive Derick was had perhaps reactivated Johnnie's passion for the chase. Better to travel than to arrive, maybe? This was cynicism at its worst, but it was working – the adrenaline was pumping again. She would play her own little game, and bollocks to the pair of them.

'Do you know what I think we should do?' she said on his return. 'I think we should get in some drinks, go back to my flat with Ruth and Derick and have a wake for Albert.'

'Your sister *without* drink inside 'er is more than I can handle.'

'Don't be an arsehole,' she said, going all-out to shock him.

He glanced sideways at her and grinned. 'Nice people you've been mixing with, Sandy. Savoury lot, the west London crowd – all fart and no art.' He managed to drink his beer and chuckle at the same time. 'What does your boyfriend do?'

'Me, amongst other women.'

'And you're happy with that, are yer?'

'Share and share alike is what I say, don't you?' Now it was her turn to smile. 'Ruth looks well, doesn't she?'

Johnnie leaned back in his chair and looked thoughtful. 'I reckon he's one of these blokes who buys second-hand furniture dead cheap, and chucks it in a bath of acid, hoses it down with varnish and sells it on as an antique – once he's screwed a few old brass handles and knobs on.'

'Why don't you ask him?' She looked over Johnnie's shoulder and flashed a smile.

'I didn't know you were in here.' Derick looked from Sandy to her drinking partner and waited.

'This is an old mate of mine and Ruth's – Johnnie the

builder. Johnnie, this is Derick – Derick the collector.'

'Dealer,' Derick corrected, a touch displeased. 'Memorabilia, collectors' items . . . that kind of thing.' He looked at Sandy. 'You OK?'

'Who won?' She smiled first at Derick and then at Ruth. 'How was your game, hot?'

'First time I've played.' Ruth placed both hands on Johnnie's broad shoulders and lightly kissed the top of his head. 'Where have you been hiding yourself?'

'Anywhere that was safe from you.' Johnnie stood up. 'What's your poison?'

'Forgotten already?' She stroked his face with the back of her hand. 'Vodka and tonic – remember?'

He pulled his face away and turned to Derick. 'What's it to be?'

'Not for me, thanks. We're just leaving.' He looked at Sandy and creased his brow. 'Ready?'

'Yep. Thanks for the drink, Johnnie. Come over when you're ready, say hello to Freda and Leo. They should have done all their crying and reminiscing by then.'

'I might just take you up on that, babe. See you, Derick.'

Walking away, Derick showed Johnnie a hand. 'Thanks for the game, Ruth.'

'Thanks for the lesson!' she called brightly, and then lowered her voice, speaking out of the side of her mouth. 'Get me a drink, Johnnie. I need it. Talk about hard work.'

Roaring with laughter, he shook his head. 'You're a strange girl, Ruth.' He thought she was admitting her part in trying to win Derick over. 'Underpants like iron, eh – even you couldn't drill your way through. Unlike Sandy's mains pipe.'

'Ah . . . clever Johnnie, put two and two together. Actually, it wasn't me, it was Dave, my ex. He needs to be taught a lesson. I threw him out once I learned what he'd done.'

'I'm sure.' He pointed a finger in her face. 'I'll buy you a drink, Ruth, I'll put up with your play-acting . . . but don't underestimate . . .' He tapped the side of his head. 'Don't give me any of your old fanny 'cos I won't buy it. All right?'

'I'm pleased to hear it. I'm quite attached to my old fanny.'

Wincing, he turned away, unable to stop himself smiling at her vulgarity. 'Do you want a bag of crisps?'

'Yes, please. Salt and vinegar.'

Before going into the flat above Nova, Derick insisted on knowing what was bothering Sandy. He realized that she was upset at the old boy committing suicide, but there was something else. Something which was causing her to be hostile towards him. Pinning her against the wall, he told her she was going nowhere until she told him what was wrong.

'I didn't expect you to go off with Ruth, that's all. Let's leave it at that. I was being . . .' She folded her arms and gazed thoughtfully at the sky. 'I was being . . .' She couldn't think of the right word. It wasn't jealous; it wasn't selfish; it wasn't possessive – or was it? 'I don't know what I was being. But you were heartless.'

'Because I agreed to take your sister for a drink, when I would have been happier to nip into your bedroom and take a catnap while you comforted your friend? I was up at five

237

o'clock this morning, don't forget. I had to pick up my mother, help her set up the stall and then drive through the rush hour to hunt for my living.' He pursed his lips and shrugged. 'If that's selfish, Sandy, then yes, I'm your man.'

'So it was her suggestion?'

'No . . . I couldn't wait to get her into that pub!'

Sandy lowered her eyes, confused and feeling somewhat pathetic. 'I'm sorry. It's just that . . . oh, forget it. Come on, let's go up.'

'No.'

'I will explain but not now. It's too complex. I was jealous, OK? You wouldn't have been the first man I had lost to Ruth. Now can we go up?'

He put his arm around her and pulled her close. 'In a minute. Once you're OK.'

'I am OK!'

'No you're not. Your cheeks are glowing – and it's not from the gin and tonic.' He kissed her lightly on the neck. 'Pinched one of your boyfriends, did she?' He brushed a few strands of hair out of her eyes. 'Old freckle-face lost out to the Barbie doll?'

'She stole my husband.' Sandy pushed her fingertips into the corners of her eyes to stop the tears.

'Honestly?'

She nodded, unable to speak.

'Was it serious?'

She nodded again. 'Very.'

'He didn't leave you for her?'

'Was going to.' She pushed the toe of her shoe into a section of broken paving stone. 'But he was killed before he could, minutes after he told me.'

'Jesus,' he whispered, and held her tight. 'I'm sorry, I shouldn't have pushed it.'

Derick was more than sorry, he was floored. His devious plan, conjured up the moment he set eyes on her hoard, might have to be delayed or even dropped. He had seen her as a fairly flush, resourceful young lady destined for the high life, affluent and successful. She had already cut a fine dash with the Portobello set. Cheap and Cheerful was now the place to applaud, and Sandy Brent a designer with fresh and plucky ideas. Now he was seeing her as a poor cow instead of rich pickings.

'I haven't told you much about my past because the one thing I didn't want was sympathy. I wanted you to want me for myself, silly grin, freckles and all.'

He cursed himself for insisting on honesty. This wasn't what he wanted. He should have ignored her mood and won her round later when they were alone. Somehow he would have to call a halt to all this.

Placing a finger under her chin, he lifted her face. 'I hope you remembered to put your knickers on before you went into that pub.'

Her hand flew to her mouth. 'Jesus . . . I completely forgot.' She pulled away from him and started to laugh. 'Can you imagine . . . if some dirty old sod had put his hand up my skirt – he would have thought it was Christmas!'

He hugged her again. 'Listen . . . I'll have to go soon. Pack up the stall. In fact, unless you want me to, I would rather not come up. I think it would be an intrusion anyway.'

'To tell you the truth, I would rather you didn't. But there

is something I want you to do for me. The diamond brooch.
Will you get it valued? Just out of interest.'

He considered the offer and nodded, thinking fast. Maybe
this would be the compromise, take the brooch and run. His
mind went to the gold watch and chain. If he could manage
to secure that as well, he might come out with enough to
make his exit worthwhile. He had been running the stall down
for a few months now, with every intention of getting out.
Buying bits and pieces was a cover for those in the market
whose debt he was already in. With Sandy's treasures and
the bits he had picked up that morning, he would have more
than enough to begin again in France, where Monique would
be waiting for him.

'OK. I'll go in and see Solly on my way back and call you
tonight. I'll get him to value the things I bought today while
I'm at it. The watch and chain might give us an idea of how
much yours is worth.'

'Listen, this is silly. Why not take the tin? Get him to
value each piece. But *don't* leave it there.'

'It'd be a damn sight safer in his lock-up than it is in your
cupboard.'

'You could be right there. You do trust him?'

'No.'

She gave him an affectionate punch on the shoulder.
'Tormenting sod.'

'Go on then. I'll wait down here. Fetch the brooch on its
own or a couple more pieces or the lot – I don't mind. Solly
will charge for each piece though, I warn you. A pound a
piece.'

'I think I can stretch to that. Won't be a sec.' She left him leaning on the wall enjoying a cigarette.

Thinking of France, of red wine, French bread, brie and tomatoes, pastries and coffee, he had no room for guilt. Easy come, easy go. She found it and now she was about to lose it. It was time his luck changed. That it should come out of the blue like this was a miracle. He would have to act fast – double quick. Once he had dropped off his mother, he would throw some clothes into a suitcase, drive to Dover and be on the first cross-channel ferry to Calais.

'Here we are then.' She handed Derick a carrier bag. 'The works. Don't have an accident or get killed or anything.'

'I'll try not to. What am I on – ten per cent, or staying a whole night instead of being thrown out in the early hours?'

'Five per cent if I sell it. I'm not ready for slippers under the bed or sharing my eggs and bacon with you.'

'When will you be?'

'Soon, Derick. Don't rush me. It's not that long since Roy . . .'

He kissed her on the mouth and looked earnestly into her face. 'What about your slippers under my bed? One night – that's all I'm asking. I want to see your freckles on my pillow.'

'Maybe . . . maybe.' She became pensive. 'Yeah . . . I think that might be the thing to do. OK: a week today. How's that?'

'I'll think about it. Don't rush me.' He grabbed her hair playfully and told her not to flirt with Johnnie, that he had seen the way he looked at her.

Watching his car drive away, she saw Johnnie and Ruth coming out of the pub, arms linked and laughing. The pang of jealousy which caught her stomach disturbed her. Ruth had every right to play up to him; he wasn't Sandy's property and never had been. One spur-of-the-moment lovemaking session hardly made Ruth and Johnnie an item.

'Boyfriend gone then,' Johnnie said, freeing himself from Ruth's hold.

'Looks like it. Coming up?'

'If the offer's still on. The wake?'

'Definitely.' She took Ruth's hand and squeezed it. 'It's time we got merry together.'

Returning Sandy's smile, her sister appeared both surprised and moved. She leaned forward and whispered in her ear, 'Thanks, babe.' For the first time in a very long while they hugged, each of them making up for lost time.

'Right, I'll pop down the off-licence then.' Johnnie walked away, leaving the sisters to themselves. Touched by the brief emotional scene though he was, still the gut feeling that Sandy was being a bit too trusting was playing on his mind. He had met characters like Ruth before and in his experience, self-centred people were just that: blinkered and only able to focus on their own goals. Nevertheless, he had to admit their sisterly embrace looked genuine enough. He hoped he had been wrong, and that the girls had sorted out their differences – albeit at his expense. He smiled at the irony. His loss was Ruth's gain.

'Coincidence or what?' he murmured to himself before going into the off-licence. Getting laid by Ruth was probably the worst mistake of his life. All he could expect from Sandy now was friendship. That one impulsive night of passion would stand between them like a dinosaur now that she and Ruth were reunited. The sixties song 'Running Bear' came to mind, and he found himself wishing that Ruth would disappear into the woods. Go back to where she came from, or move on to pastures new. If something was going on between Ruth and Derick, so much the better. If they were to go off and build a nest together, that would be the killing of two birds with one stone. He cursed himself for allowing his emotions to place him in such a vulnerable position. When Shirley left him he had vowed never to fall in love again.

'What can I get you?' the young smiling assistant asked in her practised sing-song voice, as he approached the counter in the off-licence.

'A new brain?'

'Sorry?' Her smile fading, she looked at him, concerned.

'A bottle of Johnnie Walker, a bottle of vodka, some tonic and ginger ale.'

'Sounds like someone's gonna have a good time,' she said, reaching for a bottle of whisky.

'We're gonna drown our sorrows. Celebrate Albert the hairdresser's life.'

'Albert the queer?'

'The *hairdresser*! There was nothing queer about him.'

'I was thinking about that flat, as it happens; wondering 'ow much it is a week. Me and my fella are looking for somewhere to live.' She wrapped tissue paper around the bottles of drink.

Peeling a five-pound note from a small wad, he shook his head. Not five minutes out of his body and the vultures were moving in to pick off the bones. He could hear someone saying the same thing about his own two-up, two-down, and made a mental note to do something about his personal letters and family photographs. The thought of a stranger going through his things chilled him.

Walking slowly back to Nova, he thought about Sandy's treasure box and what the owner might have thought if he could have seen them poring over his things. He decided that the look of childlike pleasure on Sandy's face would have melted a ghost's heart too.

Later, relaxed and listening to a Randy Crawford LP, Sandy ran the evening through her mind. It had been great. Watching Freda and Leo slowly getting drunk had been very funny, their repertoire even funnier. The jokes might not have seemed quite so hilarious had they all been sober, and Leo's singing voice not quite so well-tuned. His rendition of Hava Negillah had been so moving that they were all tearful as they joined in the chorus.

Ruth seemed different, too, happy to be part of the crowd, all signs of the compulsive flirt gone. She had given old Leo just as much attention as Johnnie, and it had made his night. Everyone, it seemed, was in a forgiving mood – even Freda. Her attitude towards Ruth was almost friendly – almost. Albert, in his absence, had given Sandy one of the best evenings of her life. The only missing element had been Derick. She glanced at the clock again: it was now eleven-thirty, and still no word from him. It seemed far too late for her to call: he had after all been up since five, and likely his mother had too. They were probably both fast asleep.

Wide awake herself, she wished the others hadn't left. Freda, not quite as drunk as Leo, had insisted she drive him to her house and that he sleep there overnight, and Johnnie had driven the inebriated Ruth back to her parents'. He had joked about his best mate Terry tearing him limb from limb if he let his daughter drive her drunken self home. Sandy had seen this as an excuse; that he imagined she would be hurt to think that he and her sister were getting it together. What he couldn't know, because she had no intention of showing her true feelings, was that she had completely fallen for Derick. It was his face which was often the last thing in her mind at night, and sometimes he was the first person in her thoughts when she woke up.

Everything about Derick aroused her: his smell, his deep blue eyes, the way his dark hair curled around his neck and, last but not least, his lean muscular body and strong arms. She glanced from the clock to the phone and toyed with the idea of asking him to come over there and then and stay the night. Tell him that she *was* ready for slippers under the bed after all, and that she was also in a sexy mood.

Believing her imagination to be playing tricks, Sandy raised her head and listened as Freda and Leo sang in the street below. She leaped up and opened the window. Her appearance encouraged them to sing even louder . . .

'Abie, Abie, Abie my boy, what are you waiting for now? You promised to marry me one day in June . . . it's never too late and it's never too soon.
All the family, keep on asking me, vhich day, vhat day, I don't know vhat to say . . .
Abie, Abie, Abie my boy, what are you waiting for now . . . owwww . . .'

Laughing, she just managed to ask what was going on. Freda spread her hands, Leo flicked the air and repeated: 'Vhich day, vhat day, I don't know vhat to say . . .'

Freda followed with: 'He's promised to marry me one day in June . . . it's never too late and it's never too soon . . .'

'You're both mad! Go home and sleep it off!'

'So you don't think we should, then?' Freda shouted.

'Should what?'

The drunken pair looked at each other, linked arms and tumbled into Freda's car singing, 'Vhich day, vhat day, I don't know *vhat* to say!'

'Freda! Maybe you shouldn't –' the car doors slammed shut – 'drive,' she murmured, watching them zoom off along the almost deserted Roman Road.

Bemused by the scenario, she poured herself another drink and turned the LP over. Now she really was wide awake. She stared at the phone again, puzzled as to why Derick hadn't called as soon as he got home. Surely he would be just as excited about the worth of her treasure.

She walked slowly up and down, more doubtful with each passing moment, telling herself not to be so untrusting . . . suspicious. The sudden ring of the doorbell made her jump. 'Derick!' Excited, she ran out of the room and skipped down the stairs.

'I saw your light was on . . . I s'pose there's no chance of a cup of coffee?'

She stood aside and nodded towards the stairs, still too worried to say anything. Seeing the look of concern in Johnnie's eyes, she lowered her head and cleared her throat.

'It's always a bit of a downer when you've had a great

time,' he said, taking the stairs two at a time. 'I just passed Freda and Leo bombing down the road like a couple of young punks on a joyride. Just shows what a few drinks can do.' He went into the living room and waited before sitting down. He wasn't sure if he was welcome or not.

'Do you want coffee or something stronger?' Sandy's voice was flat. 'Personally, I'm happy to keep on drinking.'

'Coffee. I'm driving, don't forget.'

'Well sit down then, Johnnie. Anyone'd think you were a stranger.'

Women. He couldn't puzzle them. When he had left she was on top of the world, happy as a sandboy. He wondered if she was disappointed that it was the older-man-Johnnie on the doorstep and not her boyfriend. Not that Derick was that much younger than himself. He had placed him around thirty-one-ish, which made him only five years younger.

'I could be wrong . . .' Sandy said, arriving with the coffee, 'but I think that Leo has asked Freda to name the day.'

Johnnie started to laugh. 'Don't be silly – those two? They're more like brother and sister . . .'

'Bit like us, then?'

'Oh, right . . . that's what we are, is it?'

'Well we can't really be anything else, Johnnie, can we? Not really.' She sat on the armchair and shrugged. 'Not now . . . not since . . .'

'Yeah, all right. Don't talk that to death.' He sipped his coffee. 'So what's bugging yer?'

'Nothing's bugging me.'

'Not much.'

'I'm being silly . . .' She lowered her eyes.

'Go on then.'

'What did you think of Derick?' Her tone conveyed her worry and he picked up on it.

'Good-looking chap. Sharp as a razor.'

'What makes you say that?'

'He's got you running rings round 'im.'

'You reckon?'

''Course he has. Didn't he turn up then?'

Irritated that he could read her like a book, she stood up and turned her back on him, pretending to be interested in what was outside. She wiped a smudge off the window. 'Actually, I'm a bit concerned about his integrity.' There was a pregnant pause.

'Don't tell me. Please don't tell me.' He clapped a hand to his forehead. 'You've told him about the tin.'

'I've done more than that, Johnnie. I've given it to him to get the pieces valued.' She turned and looked directly into his face. 'This afternoon. I was hoping he'd phone and give me the news . . . good or otherwise.'

'And he hasn't,' he said, all-knowing.

'No.'

'But he said he would.'

'Uh-huh.'

'Great. Where does he live?' He frowned and narrowed his eyes. 'Sandy . . . you do know where he lives?'

'Holland Park.'

'Address?'

'Don't know.'

He leaned back in his chair, stretched his legs and smiled

wryly. 'Well, we can say goodbye to the diamond brooch...'

'I might have *known* you'd say that! I was hoping you might ease my worry!'

'Do you happen to know anyone who might know his address?' He spoke slowly, as if she was a dimwit.

'Probably.'

'Oh, for Christ's sake! Do you or don't you?'

'Yes.'

'Well what are we waiting for, then?'

'No. No, no, no! You're overreacting!'

'Get your coat on.' He stood up, seething.

'No, Johnnie. What's he gonna think? Checking up on him as if he's a criminal. He only took the stuff today! He's been up since five this morning, working non-stop. He probably fell asleep as soon as he got home.'

Johnnie smiled a different smile. 'Coat.'

'Why? Why should we do this? Give me a good sound reason. Please, Johnnie, I'm being serious. I need a reason!'

'You've already got one.' He jabbed a finger into her chest. 'In there. Your instincts. They're screaming at you, babe, and you know it.'

Her bottom lip curled under and her face became distorted.

'Don't you *dare* cry!'

'I can't help it.'

'Yes you can. That bastard has got your treasure and if we don't get our skates on now, you won't see it again. Got it? He's probably on the motorway now, to Land's End or Scotland or any one of the places in between! *Coat!*'

* * *

Crawling along Holland Park Avenue, Johnnie arrived at the entrance to Abbotsbury Road. 'Is this it?' His temper was slightly frayed, but that was to be expected. It was the second time he had asked, the third time he had driven along that particular stretch of the road.

'No. Keep going, but creep. I'm sure it's along here somewhere. We're nearly there, I can sense it.'

'Pity you couldn't sense it the first time round.'

Craning her neck to peer down each turning they approached, Sandy suddenly emitted a piercing screech. 'That's it! That's the one!'

Gritting his teeth, he did a sharp left as the driver behind blasted his horn. 'You're sure this is it?'

'Yes. Just along here, flat three . . . it's at the top. A penthouse.'

'Well it would be, wouldn't it? Couldn't be a run-of-the-mill top-floor flat with a bit of roof space. Not in Holland Park.'

'Stop bitching. They've got a proper balcony with chairs and tubs full of flowers. This is it!' She opened her window and studied the large stucco-fronted terraced house. 'I think . . .'

'If it's not, you're gonna look a bit silly. Knocking someone up at this hour.' He looked at his watch. 'Just gone one.'

'*I'm* going to knock someone up? Does this mean you're staying in the car?'

'Till you find the right flat, yeah.' He turned off the engine and pulled on the brake. 'Good luck.'

She glared at him, too angry for words. It was his idea

that they make this journey, and he'd done nothing but complain since they hit Holland Park. 'I've only been here once and it's dark! I've got us this far by memory; the least you can do is give me a bit of support. What if some rich cow opens the door and rants on at me?'

'Run.'

'Thanks.'

'Go on then . . . get out.' He opened the driver's door and slammed it behind him. 'You should write people's addresses down!'

'I did. It's in the address book at Cheap and Cheerful. I thought I would remember once I was here. Anyway, I'm sure this is it.'

Johnnie looked up at the top flat. It was in darkness. 'This is gonna be fun.' He pressed the bell.

'They won't mind. I'm surprised they're in bed. I thought their set burned the midnight oil, smoking joints and that.'

'You've been watching too many bad TV films.' He rang the bell again.

'If I'd 'ave known you were gonna be in a foul mood, I wouldn't have come.'

'Life's not always a bowl of cherries.'

'Mine is,' she snapped, wanting to punch him.

'Who the fuck are you?' Amanda, the deb who shared an antiques stall with her sister in Portobello Road and was now one of Sandy's best customers at Cheap and Cheerful, sounded angry to say the least, her voice booming through the entryphone.

'Amanda, it's me, Sandy, from Cheap and Cheerful. I need to speak to you. It'll only take a couple of minutes.'

'Go on then.' She sounded far from pleased.

'Do you have Derick's address?'

'Derick? Derick who?'

'You know . . . Derick . . . from Portobello Road. He's got a stall.'

'Oh him. Hammersmith.' She replaced the handset.

Seething inside, Johnnie rang the bell again.

'That's all I know, darling,' said Amanda, coming back on the entryphone. 'Somewhere in Hammersmith. He lives with his mother in some seedy block of flats. Rumour has it he's done a bunk. I presume he owes you some pound notes too?'

'He couldn't have done a bunk, Amanda. I only saw him this afternoon, after I closed Nova. He left just after six.'

'He left his poor mother in tears, darling. Left her and poor Harry to cart everything home on a wheelbarrow. I should think he's on his way to Calais by now.'

'Calais? France?'

'Bye, sweetie.' There was more than a touch of derision in her voice.

'Which port?' Johnnie quickly asked before she cut off.

'Dover, I would have thought. That's the route he usually takes, when visiting the lovely Monique. But then who can tell, with Derick? Oh and Sandy – don't say we didn't warn you. We told you not to buy anything from him. He's a shark, sweetie, a bastard.' With a sharp click, she was gone.

'Come on.' Johnnie was in no mood to waste precious time. He strode towards the car, with Sandy close behind.

Fastening her seat belt, she looked sideways at him. 'You're not really going to drive to Dover.'

'Things I do for you,' he said, pulling away.

'Johnnie . . . this is mad. It'll take hours. What if he's gone to Folkestone?'

'We'll cross that barrier when we come to it. Who's Monique?'

'I don't know.' She gazed out of her window and went quiet.

Johnnie now had two reasons for making the long trip. To retrieve Sandy's treasures, and smack the gigolo in the face. If Sandy wasn't with him, he would ruin the bastard's love life for good. 'There's a knob on the left side of your seat; turn it clockwise till it's as far back as you want. You might as well get some shut-eye.'

'I'm OK.'

'Once we hit the motorway you'll see why I've got a Jaguar.' He turned on the radio and tuned it in to a station playing ballads. Nat King Cole's voice filled the car with 'Unforgettable'.

'Why are we *doing* this?' Sandy adjusted her seat so that she was only just reclining.

'To get your tin of beads back.'

Quietly laughing, she closed her eyes. 'Thanks, Johnnie; you're a true friend.'

'I've known your dad a long time.' He could bounce the truth about when he wanted. Let her think that she wasn't the only reason he was behaving like a saint. 'He took me fishing for the first time when I was ten. I was so 'appy I nearly wet meself – and I caught a fish. He was engaged to your mother at the time, but when he was about seventeen he used to go out with my sister. I used to go swimming over the lido with 'em. Victoria Park. I was a cute little thing then, of course.'

Her eyes closed, Sandy was beginning to feel relaxed. She put it down to the music. 'You're still cute – grown man or not. I'm surprised you've not been snapped up by now.'

'Once was bad enough. I'm happy as I am. Footloose, fancy-free – and what's mine is my own. This car, for instance. If I was married I wouldn't be running around in this.'

'What about Shirley? Did she marry again?'

'Yep.'

'Children?'

'Nope. Hasn't got maternal instincts . . . unlike me.'

'Johnnie . . . you old softie! You wanna be a dad.' She gazed at his profile. 'Yeah . . . you've got a dad sort of face. Warm, loving . . . but strict.'

'Like a teddy bear.'

She leaned back again and closed her eyes. 'Just like a teddy bear. I feel like hugging you.'

'Save it for your boyfriend,' he said, testing her.

'Maybe, maybe.'

The very thought of it infuriated him. Seeing her with Derick had cut him to the quick, and he didn't like it. He didn't like it one bit. If they were meant to be together, then it would happen. Let the river flow, was his new motto. As long as he could spend some time alone with her, that was enough. At least lover boy might be out of the picture after tonight.

'You and Ruth are OK now, then?'

'Yeah, we're fine, Johnnie. We should have had a barney long ago. Clear the air. Long before Roy came on the scene.

Our problem goes way back to when we were small.'

'Oh yeah?'

'You don't want to know, Johnnie. I don't think it's the sort of thing men can handle.

'Once we're on the motorway,' she said, changing the subject, 'would you mind if I did float off for ten minutes? This car is a dream . . . and what with that music . . .' Now it was John Lennon and 'Imagine'.

'It's a misconception, you know. That men can't handle emotional stuff. It's OK when it's someone else's problem. It's our own we can't hack.'

'Wasn't emotional – well not in the sense you mean. Child abuse. Not me, Ruth. I turned ostrich – buried my head in the sand.'

Johnnie fell silent. He prayed she wasn't going to elaborate. She was right – he didn't want to hear it. 'Shouldn't be long now before I can really put my foot down.'

'It was a neighbour. Dad's friend. I knew what he was like, but I honestly thought that Ruth had suffered no more than I had: the leering looks, the brushing against you . . . that sort of thing. If I had thought he was so much as touching her at the time I would have told Dad, make no mistake!

'I should have been looking after her, but I was too interested in going out to the youth club, jiving with one of the best rockers in the Bethnal Green gang.'

'Poor kid.' He fell silent for a second time. What he would like to have found out was who the pervert was, but if she wanted him to know she would tell him in her own time. He slowly shook his head. 'No wonder she's the way she is.'

'Ah, but she isn't the way she was. She's changing. Now

that we've talked about it and she knows she can bring it up whenever she wants, she seems to be more . . . I don't know . . . relaxed? Not so spiteful. We're gonna pay him a visit soon. Well, not so much a visit . . . just stare at him from afar. See if we can exorcise the bastard once and for all.'

'He's local, then?'

'Forget it, Johnnie. This is our fight.' She closed her eyes, lay back and waited for the motorway so that she could go to sleep. Seeing her like that, Johnnie wondered if he would ever see her head on a pillow next to him. She looked so young and innocent, like a baby. His hand moved from the steering wheel to her head, but just before it brushed against her hair he pulled it away. If he couldn't touch her when she was awake, he wouldn't go near her when she was asleep – it seemed wrong.

As he cruised along he thought of what he would like to do to the bastard who had stolen her treasure. The worst kind of men were those who preyed on women who, for one reason or another, were going it alone. He wondered if the creep had already sold her possessions. If so, there was no telling how this little drama would end.

His stomach rumbled, and he realized that he hadn't eaten since lunch time. Even then it had been no more than a quick cheese roll and a mug of tea. He would stop at an all-nighter once he had broken the back of the journey, somewhere around Maidstone would be about right.

He glanced at Sandy, and listened to her breathing. She was in a deep sleep, and he tried to imagine her dreaming of him.

* * *

The trek to Dover had proved to be a pleasure rather than a chore; Johnnie had had plenty to think about, and the Music Through the Night programme had played some of his favourite songs. Sandy had slept up until the moment he pulled in at the all-nighter just past Maidstone, and they had enjoyed an early breakfast – or late supper, depending on which way you looked at it. Eggs, crispy bacon, grilled tomatoes, beans and fried mushrooms with fresh bread and butter.

The journey from then on had been fun. Johnnie had gone through his 'hardships' repertoire, revealed what he had got up to as a kid and a teenager, and Sandy had talked more about herself, her aims and ambitions, her past life. He was touched by the intimacy, and very pleased to hear that her main desire was to be settled in a cottage in the country, growing flowers in front and vegetables at the back. She had changed her mind a couple of times about how many children she wanted, going from six down to three.

'We'll pull in at the car park and then check the times of the ferries which 'ave left,' Johnnie said as they drove down to the port. 'He had a good four-hour start, but from your description of his van I reckon we've knocked off two hours. I doubt he would 'ave got on a boat straight away, so with a bit of luck . . .'

'He'll be waiting for the next ferry?'

'If luck's on our side, and I've got a feeling it is. Don't ask me why.'

'Why?' She repeated Freda's quip, and was pleased that Johnnie remembered it too. They both chuckled at the memory of the evening he had treated them to a Chinese takeaway.

'Trouble is . . .' Johnnie said thoughtfully, 'there are gonna be quite a few dark blue vans parked up . . .'

'I would recognize his anywhere.'

Shaking his head and smiling, he wondered if she was being funny or whether she was so smitten with him that she could recall everything in detail, every scratch and bump on his motor. 'Have you thought about what you're gonna say?'

'No. I've tried not to think about it.' Her voice gave nothing away. She was angry, hurt, humiliated – but that she would keep to herself.

'Keep it simple then.' He pulled into the car park and took the first space.

'It's so dark . . .'

'That's OK – I've got a powerful torch in the boot.' He switched off the engine and turned to face her. 'Ready?'

'As I'll ever be,' she murmured.

'Just remember what that girl said . . .'

'Amanda.' She nodded emphatically. 'She's known him for a long time. She should know.' Hating the situation she had been forced into, she cursed inwardly. 'I just can't believe he would do something like this.' She stared out at the blackness. 'What if we're wrong? What if he left the tin with Solly for safe keeping? What if he had a call from France – a business deal too good to miss? For all we know—'

'And Monique?' Johnnie said, a touch exasperated. There was no response. She became poker-faced and silent. 'All you have to do is ask for your jewellery. Tell him we all went to the pub after he left and got drunk, and you shot your mouth off about your find. Say the guy you told happened to be a copper, off-duty . . . tell him you've had a visit from the boys in blue. Say—'

'Johnnie, that's *brilliant*. You're sodding amazing. What a brain!' He forgave her for swearing – the look of sheer happiness on her face would have him pardon her anything. 'What are we waiting for?'

'Sandy, listen . . .' His expression became serious and his voice fatherly. 'He might well have gone already, OK? Don't get your hopes up too high.'

'No, he's here. He's somewhere in this port. I know it. I can feel it. Feel his presence.' She looked earnestly at him. 'And as sure as I'm sitting here with you, in the middle of the night, I know that he's not doing a runner. My treasure *will* be in Solly's safe, you see if I'm wrong.' She gazed out of the window again. 'I can't wait to see him. I feel as if I want to hug him to death. But I mustn't, must I? I mustn't let on that I was suspicious and small-minded.'

She had no idea how much that little speech hurt. Every word went in like a silver dart scoring the highest marks, the last line hitting a bull's-eye. Whether she had meant to or not, she had just blamed him for causing her to be suspicious and faithless. And she was tarring him with that same imprecatory brush.

'I'll get the torch,' he said flatly, getting out of the Jag.

Standing next to him and pulling her coat around her, she shivered. 'Winter's on its way,' she said, throwing him another insult by offering polite chit-chat.

He closed the boot and locked the car. 'Right, let's get this over with.' He silently cursed himself for being an old fool. She was still seeing him as nothing more than a mate.

So far he had spent one night in a cell because of her, driven through another, and was about to creep around a car park like someone out of a comic strip. If the blokes he knew and worked with could see him now, he would lose all credibility.

'Don't move.' She became rigid, staring across the car park, at a point beyond two rows of parked vehicles. 'It's Derick. Over there outside the café, talking to those men.'

'Thank Christ for that. Go on then – do your bit. I'll wait in the car. Oh and Sandy, whether you want to or not, we're booking into that small motel we passed on the way in to Dover. I'm not driving back without a kip. Don't be long.' He got back into the driving seat and slammed the door shut, cursing all females. 'All as hard as nails. Callous bitches – every one of them.' He watched from the corner of his eye as she walked slowly away, not giving him a second glance.

'At least she's got something right,' he murmured as he saw the toad greet her. It was him. Giving the men a thumbs-up sign, Derick took Sandy to one side, hugging her as if she was the best thing since sliced bread. He perceived what he could from their body language. Derick's head was cocked to one side as he listened to Sandy. When he pulled her close, Johnnie looked away. Reduced to the ranks of peeping Tom, he closed his eyes, his anger at Sandy rising by the second. She had made a complete fool of him, and he had made a worse fool of himself.

When she finally climbed into the passenger seat, he half expected her to say she was going on the ferry with him. 'Well?'

'I didn't notice a motel on the way in.' She spoke as if nothing had happened since he mentioned it.

'Everything's all right then – hunky-dory?'

'Yep.' She looked more than pleased with herself. 'You're a genius. He swallowed the story hook, line and sinker. Let's go. I need a strong drink.'

'The glass beads are safe and sound, then?'

'Yep.'

While waiting for her he had realized there had been a hole in the spur-of-the-moment yarn he had told her to relate. All Derick had to say was that the jewellery was in Solly's safe. In her frame of mind, wanting to believe him, she would have swallowed it without question. He wondered whether to question it, but decided not to. He had had enough.

'That's good. They're tucked up nice and safe in the safe, eh? Now we can get a good sleep.' He turned on the ignition and reversed out of the parking space.

'I wish you'd been there to see his face when he saw me,' she beamed. 'That kind of thing only happens once in a lifetime. He was shocked – and I do mean shocked. It was great – and all thanks to you for driving all this way. You wait till I tell Dad. I don't think he realizes what a mate he's got in you.'

'Yeah, all right, Sandy. You've said your thanks, let's leave it at that.' He pulled out of the car park and caught a glimpse of Derick in his rear mirror. He was leaning against the café wall, smoking a cigarette. 'You look happy enough anyway. What did he do, propose? Tell you how clever you were to catch him?'

'Something like that.' Her voice was full of pride, and he could feel his respect for her slipping away.

'And I s'pose you told him how smart he was, having them safely locked away?'

'No.'

'Oh right . . . it was more romantic than that. Silly me. You called him sweetheart and told him to have a safe crossing.'

'No. I called him a fucking bastard and said I hoped he slipped overboard.' She reached into her pocket, pulled out a dark blue linen cash bag and gently shook it. 'I'm not as green as you think . . . sweetheart,' she chuckled.

Knocked sideways, he was speechless. He couldn't begin to fathom it. He shook his head to clear his brain. Lack of sleep could have had an effect . . .

'I wanted my treasure back, Johnnie, I really did. But more importantly, I didn't want Derick to get a hiding from you and I had a strong feeling that that was on your mind. I've caused you enough trouble as it is, and I didn't want him to hurt you. Not that he would have done, I'm sure,' she added quickly, to protect his pride.

'I'd have knocked the coward from here to—'

'Exactly. And I would have to spend my time visiting you in prison.' She stared out of the window. 'I couldn't bear the thought of someone like you being locked up over that gibbering idiot. You should have heard him trying to worm his way out of it. His good looks and charm vanished in an instant. He's made me feel like a fool. What did I ever see in him, Johnnie? And why didn't you or Freda step in?'

'I only met him tonight, Sandy. Give me a break.'

'I walked straight into it, didn't I? The biggest cliché

ever. Rich widow, relatively speaking, and gigolo shark. I never loved him, you know.'

Relieved and confused, he could think of nothing to say.

'When you took over the way you did, coming out at this time of night to help me get my beads back . . . I wanted to cry. Not quite as much as when I found out about you and Ruth, though. I was crazy about you, you know. Scared to show it though, in case you weren't interested. And I was right, wasn't I?'

Conscious of the sudden embarrassing silence, she quickly changed the subject. 'I used your story and held out my hand. You should have seen his face. I know how to look someone in the eye and defy them to lie. I'm not as soft as you think. And I wasn't husband-hunting.' She splayed the fingers on her left hand and studied them. 'My hand does look naked without a gold band. And I am in love. But does he love me – that's the question?'

Johnnie was hearing her, but this time he was not going to assume that she was referring to him. Knowing Sandy, she could easily come out with the news that there was another man in her life.

'Sandy, listen . . .'

'It's all right. You don't have to say anything.'

'Shut up for five minutes and listen! I've been in love with you for. . . I don't know . . . since that night when you cried over Roy and we had the Chinese takeaway, I s'pose. Anyway . . . anyway, now I've said it, so there we are. It's out of the bag.'

'You took your bloody time telling me. I don't think we should spend the night together . . .'

'Christ, is that all you can say? Is that what you think I want, a quickie in a motel? You think that's why I said I loved you?'

'In fact . . . I think we should go on as we are for a while. My emotions are a little mixed up at the moment, and I don't mean Derick. I want to spend time with Ruth without you being there encouraging her to get up to her old tricks—'

'Sandy . . .'

'No. Let me ramble on, Johnnie, it helps. I need to do it, all right? Please?'

Sighing, he slowly shook his head. 'Go on then.'

'Let's keep everyone thinking we're soulmates . . . until Ruth finds someone. Someone who'll love her the way you love me – and I love you.'

'Sandy please!' Johnnie swallowed against the lump in his throat, but with both hands on the steering wheel he could do nothing about the tears welling behind his eyes. 'I'm not made of stone.'

'I know that.' She looked into his face and smiled. 'I love you, Johnnie. And on the way down here, when you thought I was sleeping, I wasn't. I was thinking about all you'd done for me and running some of the veiled messages through my mind. I had a feeling we both felt the same, but misunderstandings kept us apart. Now tell me I'm wrong.'

'You are. I was hoping to dump you off with the gigolo. That's why I dragged you down 'ere. Let France 'ave you for a while.'

Laughing, she placed her hand on his shoulder. 'I'm sorry I had to get my own back by ignoring you – but you making love to Ruth really hurt. *Really* hurt.'

'I didn't make love to Ruth. We had sex. There's a big difference.'

'You'd better believe it,' she teased, and switched on the radio hoping for an appropriate love song, but all she got was Elvis singing 'Old Shep'.

Chapter Eight

On one of the best October mornings, Sandy drove Ruth to Petticoat Lane to buy some remnants and help her sister choose a winter coat. At least that was the reason given. Sandy had an ulterior motive – to put a ghost to rest.

After discarding remnants and purchasing some good-quality satin lining for one of her latest designs, and the trying-on of several coats in various shops and at different stalls, both Sandy and Ruth were dog-tired and ready for a cup of coffee and a cigarette. Having planned their route with precision, they conveniently ended up close to a coffee bar which Sandy had singled out weeks before.

Settled at a table for two by the window they kicked off their shoes, joking as to whose feet would smell the most. 'Think I'll have a sausage sandwich,' said Ruth as she leaned back in the chair and closed her eyes. 'We must have walked miles.'

'You don't have to tell me. I've never known anyone so indecisive as you. I bet we end up back at the first shop, and you buy the first coat you tried on.'

'Not the first one. I might go for that light grey suede coat though, if I can bait her down.'

'It looked good on you,' Sandy murmured, looking out of the window at the milling crowd. 'In fact it looked terrific. If you don't buy it, I might.'

'What are you looking at?' asked Ruth.

'Nothing.'

'There we are, girls – two strong coffees as requested,' the ageing waiter smiled at them.

'Couldn't do me a sausage sandwich, could you?' Ruth asked.

''Course. Do you want sauce, or are you saucy enough?'

'French mustard?'

'Oh, oui oui, madame!' He turned away laughing. 'Be asking for frogs' legs next!'

Sipping her coffee, Sandy raised her eyes and gazed at her sister, wondering if this was the right time to broach the subject uppermost in her mind. Aware that there might never be a right time and that Ruth could act unfavourably, still she was ready to take the plunge. Nothing ventured, nothing gained.

'Can you see that stall directly opposite? The biscuit stall,' said Sandy casually.

'Just. Why?'

'That's where he used to have his stall. The leering perv.'

Staring back at her sister, Ruth became rigid. 'And what makes you think I would want to be anywhere *near* where that slob's been?' She jerked her head, tossing her hair back. 'It might not mean that much to you – you never felt his hand go up your skirt!'

'It's why we're here. I hate him for spoiling your childhood. His fat, smarmy face keeps coming into my dreams, turning them into the worst kind of nightmare.'

'Well it's your fight then, not mine. I've put it behind me. I thought you knew that.' There was a slight tremble to Ruth's voice. 'I don't want to think about him, talk about him – and I definitely don't want to look at that face again, ever.'

'You won't have to. I've been doing some detective work which led me here, and then on to the news I didn't want to hear. I wanted him to be out there, where we could see him, confront him, stare at him, torment him. Tip up his stall and cover him with tar and feathers.'

'Here you are then, mademoiselle – one sausage sandwich with French mustard!' The waiter placed Ruth's snack in front of her. 'Anything else, girls? You name it, I'll get it. Been running this little café for forty-two years. That's shocked you, innit?' He grew with pride. 'Used to own it once upon a time. Me and me brother. I sold my 'alf to 'im in the finish. He's a go-getter, and I'm a give-us-it-if-you-want.'

Stretching and looking thoughtful, he narrowed his eyes. 'He must 'ave, what, five little cafés now? Five cafés and a bloody great ulcer. Whereas me –' he shrugged – 'I've got no worries about who to leave my money to, 'cos I ain't got none!' He tapped the side of his nose and turned away laughing. 'Or so I lead him to believe,' he said over his shoulder.

'Help me out with this sandwich, Sand. My appetite's suddenly gone,' said Ruth. 'We'll get a running commentary on these being the best sausages in the world if I leave it.'

Quick to oblige, Sandy took half, pleased that Ruth had

not walked out on her and that the risky set-up was paying off.

'I'm going to buy that suede coat, I've just decided,' Ruth suddenly announced. 'Blow the expense.'

'And the long suede boots?'

'Yep – them as well. I'll be the lady in off-white suede. And next week it'll be your turn to buy something. All you ever think about, or talk about, is your business. It's a wonder you don't see sequins at night instead of stars. So why did you bring me here, Sandy – what are you trying to prove?'

'That you can lay a ghost. Just imagine him serving on that stall, selling his bits of electrical equipment. Grown men buying off him. Imagine what they would do to him if they knew what he did to you and other kids. I doubt we were the only ones he was after.'

'What did you mean – you had hoped he would be out there?' Ruth looked straight into Sandy's eyes. 'Where is he?'

'In a secure unit in a mental hospital. I couldn't find out why or where exactly he is, but it was enough to know that he won't be coming out and that he's non compos mentis, reliant on drugs. They tell me he was always considered to be subnormal.'

'Who are *they* when they're at home?' Ruth sipped her coffee and waited.

'Anyone I spoke to around Petticoat Lane. I didn't tell them why I was interested in him, before you ask.' Knowing she was on delicate ground, Sandy chose her words carefully and the tone she used, to keep Ruth in this easy-listening mood.

'So in a way, it was a child's mind in a man's body . . . he must have seen us kids as his equals.'

'Mmm.' Ruth stared out, caught up in her own thoughts. 'That makes sense. So we've not only got to forgive but to sympathize, is that what you're telling me?'

Sandy put up her hands defensively. 'No, babe; I'm not telling you to do that, no way. I'm just trying to understand it myself. Understand why . . . why it happens. And Jesus, doesn't it happen? I dread to think what I'll be like when I've got kids. How can you let them play in Victoria Park, for instance, and feel good about it? Kids are just not safe out there on their own. But everyone blames the press for scaremongering . . .'

'Just as well,' said Ruth with honesty. 'Maybe if the press made more of it, parents might get their priorities right. Children first, possessions second.'

'The possessions were meant to make our lives more comfortable, Ruth. Don't be too hard on Mum and Dad.'

'OK – one question and then I'll drop it.' Ruth leaned back in her chair and paused. 'What would you have preferred: to have Mum there when we came home from school, or a nice big feather-cushioned sofa to curl up on when we watched that great big telly?'

'Mum, of course. But that's not to say I blame them. They thought they were doing right by us, doing their best. At least we can learn from it when we're parents.'

'But will we, Sandy? Or will the temptation of owning a better car or maybe living in a bigger house draw us into the same old trap?'

'Probably.' Sandy lit a cigarette and became thoughtful.

'OK. Let's make a pact. If you see me going down that road, give me a good bollocking – and I'll do the same for you.'

Ruth laughed at the thought of it. 'And you think we'll take that from each other?'

'You can lead a horse to water,' Sandy smiled, repeating something her schoolteacher had said many times, 'but you can't make it drink!'

Ruth pointed a finger at her. 'Right. That'll be the line we'll chuck at each other when the time comes. If it comes.'

'You're on,' said Sandy. 'Now . . . about this lovely soft grey suede coat . . .'

'You buy it – I'll borrow it. You've got more money than me.'

Shaking her head and laughing, Sandy agreed. 'I'll share my clothes with you, Ruth, but leave my men alone.' The message, delivered in a light-hearted tone, carried weight.

Avoiding her sister's eyes, Ruth lowered her face. 'I'm sorry about Roy. I don't know why I did it. We didn't love each other; I don't think we even liked each other that much. We were feeding our egos – at your expense.' She looked up, swallowed, pressed her lips together, and said, 'I'm sorry.'

'It's gonna take some time for it to go away, Ruth. Go completely, that is. You'll have to bear with me sometimes when I spit venom. When I'm in a wicked mood.'

'It's all gonna take time, babe. All of it. I ain't gonna change overnight, that's for sure. We'll just have to bear with each other when others want to wring our necks.'

'But you will leave my men alone?'

Ruth chuckled quietly. 'I'll try.'

'And I'll say this just one time and then I promise to

leave it alone. If you want to talk about what happened when we were kids, I'm here and ready to listen; to reason it out, whatever you want. OK?'

'OK. But in my time, Sandy, right? But you've got to promise that no matter what you're doing at the time, when I come to you you'll drop it. Because if you don't, babe, you'll destroy me.'

Knocked back by Ruth's sincerity, she nodded slowly. 'You have my word on it.'

For Sandy the sudden downpour was refreshing. Having enjoyed a relaxing soak in the bath, she was curled up on her sofa, which she had pulled closer to the fire. It was the first time she had lit a fire since moving in to number eleven, and she was pleased now that Johnnie had insisted, back in June, she have the chimney swept before he started decorating. The warm glow from the orange-red coals created a homely atmosphere, and she had never felt more comfortable since first moving in.

Sipping her mug of Horlicks, she looked from the flickering flames to the rain-dashed window and watched as the wind blew the raindrops across the pane, making patterns on the glass. Treasuring the moment, the solitude and the quiet, she allowed her thoughts to wander. She and Johnnie had picked up their relationship where it had left off after the risky admission that he had slept with her sister. In so far as others were concerned they were still just good friends, seeing as much of each other as they had previously. It hadn't been easy turning him out with the others after card-game sessions, but since she had managed to persuade Ruth to join the small circle, she felt it wise for them to keep a low profile. Strangely enough it had had the right effect on Ruth, who no longer bothered to tease Johnnie. His friendly arm's-length response seemed to work a treat too, the banter between them becoming more like the dry humour he enjoyed with Freda.

There were nine of them in the singles group, Rubber Souls as it had been christened, each one widowed, divorced, or, as Johnnie had put it, too bloody shrewd to get caught in the first place.

Ruth still seemed only interested in men who weren't easy pushovers, and if they were already in a relationship, it seemed to fire her instinct for challenge. For some reason which Sandy couldn't fathom, her sister thrived on the chase; she was a power seeker. She had a constant hunger for something that couldn't be satisfied. Until she had nourished her needs by meeting someone she could love and who would love her in return, Sandy and Johnnie would remain, on the surface, good friends and soulmates only.

Carried away by her thoughts of finding the right man for Ruth, and pushing the pervert from her mind, Sandy ignored the sounds coming from number ten's back garden: entertaining just a fleeting supposition that it was Freda moving a few of her things in, she allowed her mind to wander. She imagined Ruth in a bride's dress, herself walking slowly behind holding a white satin train, following her sister down the aisle – a fantasy which could surely become real.

When the shrill, bad-tempered cry of a child pierced the late Sunday afternoon quiet Sandy began to pay attention. The voice of a scolding mother and the cries of a baby motivated her to go into the back room and peer out of the window. The sight below sent shock waves through her. It didn't need a genius to work out what was happening. There in Freda's garden were three scruffy young adults dressed like hippies, three grubby children and one baby, in the arms of one of the women.

Outside the back door of number ten were numerous overflowing cardboard boxes and carrier bags. Without thinking, Sandy opened her window. 'What d'you think you're doing!' she yelled.

There was no retort from the unkempt group, just a flurry of activity as the adults manoeuvred the young around the baggage and in through the back door. With uncharacteristic speed they proceeded to throw all their belongings inside without giving Sandy a second glance. The reality of the situation hit her. 'Squatters!' Panic-stricken, she rushed to the telephone and dialled Freda's number. Receiving no reply, she wondered if the next best thing would be to call the police. There had been quite a bit of publicity about people setting up house in unoccupied premises, and she could remember reading that unless violence was used or threatened, and providing no damage was caused, it was not in fact a crime, and that it could take months to get them out if the squatters knew how to work the system. It was patently clear from their passive reaction to her demand as to what they were up to, that they were mindful of the correct way in which to take over someone else's property. She quickly dialled her parents' number and when Ruth answered, she wasted no time in asking for her father.

'What's up?' Ruth asked in her annoying, leisurely

manner. 'Is it a drama or a crisis?'

'Stop messing about, Ruth, and get Dad! Squatters have moved into next door.' Her tone defied her sister to play games.

'They've gone out for a drink with some friends. Doing a pub crawl. They could be in the Sun . . . the Artichoke . . . the Golden Eagle . . .' She remained unhurried, as if she'd automatically gone into a low gear because Sandy was racing. 'Phone Johnnie. He'll know what to do.'

'*I'm* sure! He'll bring a couple of his mates and kick the door in if I know him.'

'I know. What a laugh, eh?' There was a smile in her voice.

'It's not funny, Ruth! Freda was planning to move in next week!'

'Has she found a buyer for her little house then?'

'You know full well she hasn't!' She felt like slapping her sister's smug face.

'It's not as if she hasn't got anywhere to live, Sand. Not like the poor bastards who've gone in. Are there any kids?'

Sandy drew breath. 'What difference does that make? They're trespassing! That's Freda's flat! Next thing we know they'll let their friends in and start selling things in the shop!'

'Get off your soapbox. Freda's not short of somewhere to live or a few bob. Let it ride. She'll get them out – eventually.'

'You've not been reading the papers, obviously! Once they lock themselves in, you can't get them out!'

'We're talking about human beings, Sandy, not rodents. And I thought you were a humanitarian.'

'I s'pose you'd be this calm if it was still your property?'

'If it was my property I'd be living there and the problem wouldn't arise. If I wasn't living there . . . I'd light rockets and shove them through the letter box, then I'd kick the door down and go in with a few of my beefy pals and chuck them out. But as you say, it's not my property, is it? It's Freda's. Good old salt-of-the-earth, golden-arse Freda.' She started to laugh. 'God, I would love to see her face when she finds out. Let me come and watch.'

Sandy slammed down the receiver and called Johnnie, whose reaction was much the same as Ruth's – shoulder-shrugging. He told her to leave it until the morning and that nothing could be done straight away. He said this kind of thing was happening all the time, and there was a proper way of going about sorting it. He asked whether they had broken in or used a key.

'They went in through the back door and no, they didn't kick it in. I would have heard. They looked confident, as if they were pros. I suppose they've got one of those master keys.'

'Not necessarily. You-know-who might be getting her own back on Freda. There's no love lost between those two, is there?'

'Ruth wouldn't do a thing like that!'

'No?'

'No! What kind of a person do you think my sister is? She *is* my sister, in case you'd forgotten.'

'Come on, babe . . .' he said chidingly, 'you're letting family bonds rule your head. It's Ruth we're talking about. She's not exactly an angel now, is she?'

'All right. Fair enough.' She ignored his condemnation

of her sister and returned to her original reason for calling him. 'You don't seem disturbed for Freda, so I won't be. Maybe I'll pop next door and ask if they need a cup of sugar or milk for the baby. They seem quite nice, as it happens. And after all, they are homeless. Yeah . . . thanks Johnnie, you've made me see the light.' She slammed the phone down. Furious that he was ever ready to have a dig at Ruth when he knew they were beginning to get close again, she vowed not to let him or Freda stand between them. If she had to choose between her friends and her family, she might stand firmly on the side of Ruth. Blood being thicker than water.

The ringing of her doorbell took her by surprise. Surely someone hadn't told Freda about the intrusion already?

'I'm sorry if we frightened you.' The young woman who had been holding the baby stood on the doorstep, looking sheepish. 'We won't be any trouble, and we won't be there for long. A couple of months or so until the housing finds us somewhere to live.'

Open-mouthed, Sandy gazed at the pale, drawn face. 'That's OK . . .' She had been caught off guard, and wasn't sure how to react. 'Will you be all right? I mean . . . the electricity's been cut off and—'

'We've got a roof over our 'eads. We've got a small Primus stove so we can boil a kettle and cook lentils and that. 'Course, it is getting colder now that the nights 'ave drawn in and winter's on its way, but . . .'

Consumed by guilt, comparing her comforts to theirs, Sandy tried to think of a way to balance things. 'I've got a couple of oil heaters that were in the shed when I bought the place . . . I know they work . . . I used 'em when we had it rewired, before the heatwave.'

'Great; it all helps. Thanks. Shall I come through?'

'No, that's OK, I'll pass them over the back fence. They're in the shed.'

'Lights are gonna be the problem. We've got candles, but the children play with 'em when we're not looking . . .' There was a pause while Sandy waited to hear the worst. She knew what was coming.

'We've got an extension lead. If you could plug it in to just one of your points, that would make things a lot safer . . . for the kids. We could go from our window to yours. We'd pay for the power a light bulb takes.'

'Let me think about that. It's a bit awkward . . . I know the owner, she's a good friend of mine, and—'

'She wouldn't 'ave to know. All you'd 'ave to do is whip out the plug and give us a yell. We'd soon pull the lead in. A coloured woman gave us the idea when we was squatting in south London. She insisted we didn't go without lighting, 'cos of the baby. My friend's baby. The two little 'uns are mine. Their dad was killed in an accident at work. Didn't see a penny for it, neither. He wasn't on the books, see.' She shrugged.

Lying through her back teeth or not, Sandy was between the devil and the deep blue sea. If a candle was knocked over and there was a fire next door, she would never forgive herself. 'What if it starts to rain again . . .?'

'Micky's got a special outside lead and you'd only 'ave to 'ave your window open that much.' She measured a tiny gap with her finger and thumb.

'Let me think about it. Go round the back and I'll pass the oil heaters over.'

'You don't 'ave to look so worried. Neighbours always rally round. We've never caused 'em any problems. In fact one woman got some good publicity out of it. She lived above a shop as well. The press are on our side, you see. We give 'em ammunition to knock the government.'

'I'll think about it.' Irritated that she was being placed in the position of being seen as a traitor in Freda's eyes, she smiled and closed the door. Racking her brains for an answer, she decided on a compromise. She would let them have access to her electricity but only for that night. She would keep trying to get Freda on the phone and explain why she had made the decision, putting forward the argument that it was in both parties' interests to avoid any possibility of damage to the property.

Once the lead had been passed from the back doorway of number ten into her basement, all doubts of right and wrong ebbed away. The two children, who looked to be no more than three or four years old, had been firing questions at Sandy, weakening her emotional resilience. It was as much as she could do to stop herself from giving them blankets, pillows and food. If Freda was as casual about their intrusion as Johnnie and Ruth had been, she would go all-out to make their short stay comfortable.

'Is Sandy your proper name?' the scraggly, long-haired girl asked, while wolfing down a thick slice of bread and marmite.

'It's Sandra really,' Sandy said, smiling down at the two white-blonde waifs as they stood in the back doorway.

'That's wot my mum said it must be. 'Cos my name's Sandra and once someone called me Bandy Sandy and my mum went bonkers.'

'She is bandy, though,' the three-year-old boy added.

'No I'm bleedin' not!'

'You are.'

'I ain't!' She slapped his arm as if she were his mother. 'Now shut up!'

Seeing his bottom lip curl under was the last straw. If Sandy didn't call a halt to this, her maternal instincts would have her proposing to Johnnie. 'Off you go then. I want to lock up.' She gently guided them towards the gap in the fence.

'Your garden's better than ours,' Sandra pouted. 'Can we play on your side? It's full of stinging nettles over there.'

'No, Sandra, you can't. We're going to have to have some rules and one of them is that you don't come through the gap unless you know I'm in, and only on a Sunday. OK? I'm running a business, and I don't want you two in and out, disturbing the women who work for me.'

'Are you the boss then?' Sandra wrinkled her nose, instantly bringing a comical expression to her grubby face.

'Yes. And I can be very bossy – so behave yourselves!'

They raised their eyebrows at each other and, grimacing, they backed away and disappeared through the gap in the fence.

Hearing her doorbell, Sandy went upstairs to open the door and was pleased to see the smiling face of Johnnie. 'I knew you'd have to poke your nose in,' she chuckled.

'I've come to see you, not them. Did you get hold of

Freda?' He kissed her lightly on the mouth and pushed the door shut with his foot. 'You smell lovely.'

'So do you.' She wrapped her arms around him and kissed him properly.

'This is the best welcome so far.' He cupped her face and kissed the tip of her nose. 'Feeling romantic, are we?'

'A bit. You?'

'First things first.' He allowed her to lead him up the stairs. 'A cup of tea, a butcher's next door to see what they're up to and then . . . you can use my body.'

'There's no need to go next door,' she said casually while filling the kettle. 'I've already had a word. They won't be any trouble and they don't reckon on staying long. Just until they're rehoused. You should see the two skinny kids.' She smiled and shook her head. 'I could squeeze 'em to death.'

'That was a bit rapid, wasn't it? They've not bin in there five minutes and you're eating your heart out.'

'Poor sods.' She spooned sugar into two mugs. 'Can you imagine what it must feel like to be homeless?'

'Like the other thousands out there who think the world owes 'em a living. Lazy sods who've never seen a dawn. Thoughtless buggers who take from anyone daft enough to give, and anyone who isn't. I'll give Freda a buzz now, shall I?'

'No . . . not yet. I want ten minutes on my own with you. Not too much to ask, is it?'

'Depends.' He took his mug of tea and went into the sitting room, making himself comfortable on the sofa, legs up and head back. 'What do you want?'

'I don't want anything. Just to talk, that's all. Move over.'

She eased herself on to the feather-cushioned sofa, careful not to have him spill his tea. 'Did you miss me today?'

'No,' he sniffed nonchalantly, 'should I 'ave done?'

Pushing a finger through a gap between his shirt buttons, she twirled a few hairs on his chest. 'I just thought, what with the rain and it being Sunday and me being here with a fire glowing in the hearth, you might have . . .' She raised her eyes to meet his and smiled seductively.

'I came round 'cos I fancied a game of cards. Thought you could get on the blower and invite the Rubber Souls round.' He sipped his tea. 'I feel lucky.'

Laying her head on his chest, she inhaled sleepily. 'No. I just want to lie here with you and listen to the fire hissing. I'll put a record on in a minute. Your favourite – Nat King Cole.'

'I'd prefer the Rolling Stones. A good head-crasher, nice and loud. That was a nice cup of tea.'

She sat up and glared at him. 'You mean you'd like another one?'

'If it's no trouble. Couldn't make me a cheese sandwich with thick slices of Spanish onion as well, could yer? Or pickled onions – I'm easy.'

'Some lover you are!' She swung her legs off the sofa.

'Silly cow – come 'ere.' He grabbed her round the waist. 'I was getting one up on your teasing act.' Undoing her silk blouse buttons he gazed into her eyes. 'You didn't really think I came for a game of cards, did you?'

'I was beginning to wonder.'

Just as their lips were about to meet Sandy heard her name being called by both children. They were out the front, below her window. 'That's them – the kids I was telling you about.' She slipped her leg from his hand.

'Where are you going?' His voice was deep, his breath hot on her neck as he smothered her with kisses.

'See what they want.' She began to wriggle out of his hold. 'I don't know if Freda turned the water off. They might be thirsty.'

Gripping her shoulders, he held her down. 'They're pros, remember; you said so yourself. They'll know all about stopcocks. Ignore 'em.' He buried his head in her thick, long red hair. 'It's your hair that smells so lovely. Can't just be shampoo.'

'Conditioner.' She relaxed again, lifted her long leg and gripped him.

'*Sandy!*' they called her name in unison. '*Sand-y!*'

'I'd best see what they want, John—'

'Sodding kids! Go on then, but don't blame me if I go off the boil.' He released her and lay back, sulking.

'You? Go off the boil?' She smoothed her skirt and opened the window. 'What do you want?'

'Mummy said 'ave you got any spare milk – for the baby?'

Sighing, she closed the window. 'I'm gonna have to have a word with their mother.'

'*After* you've given 'em a pint of milk, I s'pose?'

'Yeah. That's all right, isn't it? It's not as if they're asking for the earth.'

'What else 'ave you given 'em?' He joined her at the window and eyed the two urchins. 'Well?'

'Nothing.'

'No?' He turned and looked her in the eye. 'Why are you blushing then?'

'I'm *not* blushing!'

'Yes you are.' He folded his arms and waited.

'All right. Yeah. I'm helping them out . . . but only for tonight, until I have a word with Freda. If she doesn't like it I'll pull the plug out.'

'Pull the plug out? Bit life and death, innit? I was thinking more along the lines of groceries, tea, sugar . . .' He narrowed his eyes and peered at her face. 'What's going on?'

'Freda had the electricity cut off, so I've let them use their extension lead for a bit of light, that's all. It's plugged into the basement.'

'Bloody hell! What is it with you? You let people walk all over you!'

'One light bulb, for Christ's sake! That's not gonna break the bank, is it?'

'That's not the point! You're *assisting* them! Condoning what they're doing! How do you think Freda'll feel when she finds out? You're supposed to be friends!'

'I told you, if she's not *happy*, I'll *pull* the *plug* out!' she emphasized each word to annoy him.

'Grow up, Sandy. If she's not happy! Of course she won't be happy! They're squatters! They're in *her* property! They broke in!'

'You don't *know* that. She might feel the same as me – sorry for them. What right have you got to speak for Freda?'

He picked up the telephone receiver. 'Shall I call and ask, or will you?'

Folding her arms defiantly, Sandy felt like telling him to

put her phone down. 'Be my guest.'

Johnnie turned his back on her and dialled. 'If she's not back yet then I'll go next door and check 'em out for myself. Freda! Good, you're there. Don't talk – just listen. Because I said so. Happy? I'm furious! Listen. You've got problems next door, squatters . . .'

Sandy stepped forward and pulled the receiver from his hand. 'It's a small family, Freda, two little kids, a baby and a mother . . . another couple. They must have had a master key to the back door because—' She looked from the receiver to Johnnie. 'She put the phone down.'

'Well, what did you expect? A long drawn-out discussion on their family tree? Of course she put the phone down. Give it five minutes and you'll hear her car screeching to a halt.'

'When I phoned you, *you* said I was to leave it and not worry! *You* said that we'd get it sorted in the morning. That this sort of thing happens all the time! I was the one who wanted to have them thrown out tonight! *You* told me to leave it! I thought you were in sympathy with *them*!' She clenched her fists, stamped her foot and swore, furious that once again she was the one in tears. 'And don't think that I'm crying because I'm unhappy! I'm *angry*!'

He pointed a finger at her. 'No, it's because you're in the wrong and you won't admit it. I've never known anyone so obstinate!'

'I'm not wrong! What if there was an accident next door and those kids were hurt? What then?'

'You're talking out the back of your 'ead. I'm going downstairs to wait for Freda.'

'Wait!'

He turned in the doorway and hoped she had seen sense. 'What now?'

'If you're going, you can take the pint of milk down for me.'

He raised an eyebrow, inhaled slowly and left.

When Sandy awoke the next morning to the sound of rain pounding on the window, her heart sank. She had hoped that the long hot summer signified a warm dry autumn and mild winter. Already behind with her new designs for Christmas meant that she had had little time to sketch a casual winter collection, as planned. Cursing herself for wasting too much time chasing around after other people, she got out of bed and pulled on her warm blue dressing gown. Six o'clock on a Monday morning was not the best of times to sit in bed sipping coffee, smoking cigarettes and roughing out quick, simple day dresses.

Once she was settled back on top of her bed, pillows propped behind her, she pushed all thoughts of the squatters and Freda from her mind. The fact that she had not come up the evening before was a sure sign that Sandy was out of favour, to say the least. Johnnie, delivering the message that they were going off to speak to someone who had suffered a similar nightmare with squatters, who sounded nothing like the two families next door, had given her a peck on the cheek before he had rushed back down to Freda. But try as he might, he hadn't been able to hide the vibes he had given out: he was clearly annoyed with her. Even so, she had remained resolute in her thinking that she was right to supply some electricity to next door, and having slept on it, was no less

287

certain of her gut feeling. Once they had had time to get used to the families' plight, she felt sure that both he and Freda would soften, and especially once they had seen the baby and the two children.

Sandy's main objective now was to attend to her business, making up for lost time. At least she had had the foresight to buy up a stock of lightweight stretch-jersey fabric during the summer months, and was pleased with her choice of colours. Soft warm tones of rust, burgundy, French navy and charcoal were ideal for the styles she had in mind: plain, close-fitting, long-sleeved dresses with the skirt cut on the bias to create a feminine twist movement below the hips.

With her sketch pad on her lap and her pencils sharpened, she scribbled in the top right-hand corner, *Twist Dress*. With her softest pencil poised, her hand flew across the clean white cartridge paper. She was on form, and could feel the creative energy flow through her arm into her hand and fingers. She would draw until the very last minute before opening up for the machinists. She would phone Maureen at eight o'clock and tell her she would be looking after the shop, while she herself was in the basement working on the new pattern.

'Maureen,' she murmured, gazing up at the ceiling. There lay another problem she had shelved. Her most prized employee had asked if she could be moved back to the Roman Road shop, and three weeks had slipped by without her doing anything about it. If Maureen upped and left Sandy would be in deep trouble: she had, without trying, become indispensable. Her mind flew to Ruth, the cause of Maureen's disgruntlement. They were too alike for their own good, and constantly rubbed each other up the wrong way. To keep them apart was by far the best thing to do. Ruth should be top dog at Cheap and Cheerful, with Maureen resuming her role as manageress at Nova.

Sandy laid down her sketch pencil and picked up an HB and a notepad. Scribbling her notes for the day, she underlined Maureen's name and the words *pay rise*.

'Trouble is . . .' she murmured, chewing on the end of her pencil, 'if Ruth gets to hear, she'll go bananas.' But Maureen was worth more than Ruth; she was Sandy's number one and she knew it. Her sister was OK at running the Portobello Road branch, but only just OK. In truth, one of the other women, Rita, would make an excellent manageress. She was efficient, reliable and the girls liked her. She was also an excellent seamstress, whereas Ruth had made it clear from the beginning that sitting in front of a sewing machine was beneath her.

'You'll have to keep your mouth shut, Maureen, difficult though that may be . . .' She knew that announcing the pay rise to Ruth would have meant as much to Maureen as the extra cash.

Smiling to herself, Sandy continued to sketch, feeling contented. All in all her new project was a success, and Nova was going a bomb. She had no regrets now about leaving Johnson's, as much as she had enjoyed working there; but working for herself was incomparable. A tiny feeling of guilt crept in as Michael Johnson's warm face came to mind. She hadn't yet paid him for the fabric which had started her off on the road to success. She scribbled another note, reminding herself to go and see him and explain, the best way she knew how, that she was now buying her sequined fabric from

Korea. He would feel hurt, betrayed even, but she was in no position to use top-quality fabric like the top designers and department stores. She was, after all, a market trader, and although her sights were set high, achieving a reputation among the top designers was a touch out of her league.

Turning her attention back to her sketch pad, Sandy was surprised at how close to her original vision she was. The final drawing, apart from the neckline, was exactly what she had had in mind; simple and elegant, something that would suit the slim and the fuller figure, the young and the older woman.

Allowing her mind to wander, she tried to imagine the various customers who came into Nova and Cheap and Cheerful. She found herself shrugging at the obvious: any of the colours would suit any of her customers. The important thing now was to work on the pattern.

Pulling on her dark green jogging pants and top, she made her way to the basement, fired up and impatient to get her hands on her big, friendly cutting scissors.

Chapter Nine

Some time had passed since the squatters had moved in at number ten, and Sandy hadn't seen or heard from Freda in that time. Johnnie had telephoned once, but only to find out if she was still supplying next door with electricity. His conversation – if conversation it could be called – had been brief and to the point. Once she had told him that she was still lending a hand, attempting to persuade him that the squatters were only trying to get by in life, he had switched off, politely saying that he would see her sometime.

Johnnie's staying away hadn't worried her too much because she had been busier than ever, sometimes cutting fabric into the small hours. But now that she was up to date and working a normal day, she realized how much she missed him, and wondered if he and Freda were teaching her a lesson or if they really had turned against her.

Locking the shop after a busy market day, she felt a strong compulsion to call Johnnie and ask him to come over so that they could talk properly, one-to-one. Thinking about it, she realized that while their strong difference of opinion over the squatters stood between them, they would find it difficult to talk about anything.

What she was coming to understand during Johnnie's absence, usually just before she switched off her bedside light at night, was that she loved him deeply. She had also thought about Derick, and could now see that with them it had been chemistry, and no more than that. When she brought his looks to mind, his dark hair and deep blue eyes, his sinewy body and the way he dressed, she had regrets about their brief love affair. It had been sex and nothing else. She was relieved to think she would not see him again to remind her of how cheap he must have thought her. How easy she had been to bed.

His reason for taking her jewels to France – to get a better price – was an obvious shenanigan, but even that didn't arouse any hatred towards him. She simply felt nothing. Whereas with Johnnie the relationship had gone through the love-hate routine and still the bond was there, probably stronger than ever. She knew, like it or not, that he was part of her life, part of her, and the thought of his not being there left an empty, raw feeling inside.

After relaxing in her sitting room with a vodka and tonic, she called Ruth on the phone, inviting her round for a fish and chip supper that would be her treat, if Ruth was prepared to pick them up on the way. At first Ruth said that she would rather stay at home and tuck into grilled pork chops cooked by her mother, but when Sandy said she wanted her advice, she agreed without hesitation. Ruth could not resist an opportunity to be in the dominant position. It was what she thrived on, and Sandy was beginning to see why. Her sister was slowly rebuilding her self-esteem.

Once the girls were seated by the television, sprinkling

salt and vinegar on their supper, Sandy opened up.

'I'm in Freda's bad books and Johnnie's gone cold on me,' she said, popping a chip into her mouth.

'Big deal.'

'They're my friends – or so I thought. It's all over one light bulb, can you believe?'

'That doesn't surprise me – we are talking about Freda –' Ruth pointed her fork – 'and Johnnie's in her pocket. Perhaps they've got something going. Maybe he likes his women old. He had the chance of you and me, and what did he do? Blank us. The man's got a problem.'

Ignoring her warped way of thinking, Sandy got to the point. 'I let the squatters plug into my basement socket so they wouldn't have to rely on candles.'

Ruth slowly raised her eyes to meet her sister's. 'You are joking?'

'There are two small children and a baby in there, for God's sake!'

'You're siding with Freda's enemies?' She shook her head, smiling. 'Rather you than me.'

'You don't think I should have done it, then?'

'As it happens, no. I'm not saying I'd join in the fight to get 'em out, but helping them to stay? No way. Put yourself in Freda's place. How would you feel?'

Surprised by Ruth's attitude, she felt herself sink. If Ruth could side with someone she had no time for . . . maybe Sandy had been a bit unthinking. 'You saying I should pull the plug out?'

'Definitely. Freda's not my kind of person, but you seem to get on well with her. Why spoil it?' She drank some of her

293

wine and eyed Sandy again. 'A proper friendship isn't easy to come by. I should know. You're the only real friend I've got.'

'Well, you've only yourself to blame for that, Ruth.'

'I know, but it's not always my fault. People don't understand me.' She stared thoughtfully into space. 'Don't make a mistake you'll regret. Hang on to Freda for dear life. Johnnie I'm not so sure about.'

Changing the subject, and seeing an opportunity to be more intimate, Sandy touched on the past. 'I suppose, in a way, that's why you and me drifted apart. I let you down. I should have realized that he was pestering you and done something about it.'

'Maybe. Let's leave it for now.'

A brief silence followed while they ate their meal and slipped into their own private thoughts. 'I don't want to think that you're bottling it up, all that resentment. The more we talk about it the better, surely.'

'As the Father said to the confessor.'

'Very funny,' Sandy chuckled, 'but I take your point. I won't bring it up again.'

'You're wrong, anyway,' said Ruth. 'I haven't bottled it up – not entirely. I took the first step towards coming to terms with it years ago, when I was seventeen. I wrote to a woman's magazine advising mothers to look out for the warning signs, in case their little girls were being abused by a neighbour.' She looked thoughtful. 'When I'm ready, I'll put myself forward as a speaker at the appropriate meetings. If I can stop some poor little cow from having to endure all of *that*... then at least it won't have been for nothing, will it?'

Stunned by Ruth's words, Sandy gazed at her. This was a side she had not seen before. 'Did they print your letter?'

'Yep. Edited, of course. All the swear words removed; but they did get the point across. I even had a few fan letters passed on. The editor asked if I could write an in-depth article about my trauma.'

'And?'

'I cried for two days, hiding away in my room. Then I tore her letter up and promised myself that I would do more when I was ready, once I was sure I could handle it. It was all too fresh then, I suppose. It still is, in a way.

'Now then,' she said brightly, changing the subject, 'what are you gonna do about next door?'

Pleased for the diversion, Sandy sighed. 'I don't know. My head tells me one thing, but my heart is saying something else.'

'You always was a soft touch. Guilt: trying to make amends the best way you know how.'

'What's that supposed to mean?'

'I think you knew something was going on and chose to ignore it, hoping it would go away.' Back to the pervert. 'Not that I blame you, not now; I did then, when you ignored the hints I threw out.'

'No. You're wrong. I didn't know. How can you even think that, Ruth? It's horrible. I just knew he was someone to avoid and you were a smart kid, so I thought you would have done just that – avoided him.'

'I couldn't! I had to run messages to him for Dad. What was I supposed to do? Tell Dad I was terrified of his friend? Look, I'm not blaming you. You were a kid too. Mum and

Dad led a Persil-white life, don't forget. We were protected from anything that had the slightest taint to it. If *they* thought he was OK, what were *we* supposed to think? I even thought it was my imagination! I thought I had an evil, sick mind! Can you believe that? We just didn't understand – that's all.'

'Let's change the subject, Ruth. I don't think I can take any more of this.'

Ruth smiled benignly. 'No, I don't suppose you can. I'll make the coffee then, since you're not moving.'

'Please,' Sandy murmured. Left alone with her guilt and her conscience, Sandy became more determined. 'Sorry Freda,' she whispered, 'but I'm not going to place those kids next door in danger of any kind. Right or wrong, I'm leaving the power switched on.'

'Where *is* the coffee?' Ruth was in the doorway. 'The kitchen's so tidy I can't find a thing.'

'Cupboard left of the sink, top shelf. Ruth – would you be happier if Maureen stayed at Nova and you ran Cheap and Cheerful?'

Ruth gave a thumbs-up sign. 'Now you're thinking straight. That cow gets on my tits.'

'She shouldn't do, you're like two peas in a pod. You'll probably end up best friends once you're separated.'

'Don't bet on it.'

While Ruth busied herself in the kitchen, Sandy stared at the glowing coals, wondering why her feelings about next door clashed so with those of the three people who were closest to her. Either she was wrong or they were misguided, because none of them had actually met the squatters.

'I found your choccy biscuits in the cupboard, chocolate Bath Olivers no less. Spoil yourself on the quiet, don't you?' Ruth placed the tray on the coffee table. 'Help yourself to milk and sugar. I'm not into playing mum.'

'Do you fancy popping next door with me, say hello to my temporary neighbours?'

'No.' Ruth curled her legs under her and snuggled into the armchair. 'Why would I want to do that?'

'Just an idea.'

'To get me on your side?'

'Yep.'

'Not me, I'm not getting involved. I really couldn't care less whether they stay or go. Playing social worker is not my idea of fun. I s'pose they're hippies?'

'No. Just ordinary people who dress in clothes from the Oxfam shop because they can't afford anything else.'

'Bullshit. It's a uniform. They're followers of fashion. If you had said they were wearing dated C and A clothes bought at jumble sales, then I *would* be impressed.'

Slowly shaking her head, Sandy sighed. 'You're a cynical bitch at times.'

'Long may it last. At least I don't let scroungers take advantage. You always were a bit of a missionary. Should join the Salvation Army. These biscuits are nice.'

'You still think I should pull the plug out?'

'I'm not really thinking about it, Sandy. Do what you want. It's hardly major, is it? Now then, more importantly, Cheap and Cheerful. I've got some ideas.' She looked sideways at her sister and waited.

'Go on then.' Sandy bit on a chocolate Oliver.

'First and foremost, we've got to put a stop to this weekly meditation session with Bill and Ben the holy men.'

'Why? It's in the girls' own time, and if it keeps 'em happy, what's the problem?'

'They're a joke, that's the problem. I've never seen such a pair of smug, conceited arseholes in my life. I feel like punching their angelic, glossy faces. How working-class girls can fall for all that crap is beyond me. And as for Maureen, she sucks up to 'em as if they're God's gift. Hasn't even clocked that they're queers.'

'She knows they're gay, Ruth. She's taking the piss.' Sandy spoke slowly, emphasizing her words. 'It's a couple of hours of light relief, that's all. It helps with the monotony of the daily routine. You should try it.'

'Bollocks to that!'

'So what are the other ideas?' Sandy wanted to move on before an argument broke out and spoiled their evening.

'*And* they smoke pot after a session. The workroom reeks of it the next morning.'

Sandy burst out laughing and almost choked on her coffee. 'You lying cow! You'd try anything . . .' Now she was coughing and laughing at the same time. '. . . Maureen, sharing a joint?' She became hysterical with laughter.

'Why not? She came in the other day wearing a bloody kaftan, rows of wooden beads and braids in 'er 'air!'

'You liar!' Sandy doubled up on the sofa. 'You bloody fibber!'

Now Ruth was laughing too. 'I'm telling the truth! She's started hanging round with left-wingers in the West Indian café when she's not in the Rising Sun with the poets, painters and poofs. All spouting bullshit with a cut-glass accent or a Liverpool twang. I asked her to get me a bag of crisps the other lunch time; she came back with a bag of fucking Bombay mix. And that's another thing . . . she's started to eat garlic bread for lunch instead of cheese sandwiches!'

Screaming with laughter, both girls were oblivious to the short ring on the doorbell. 'She eats fried green bananas, sitting in the lotus position!' She wiped her eyes and began to chuckle again. 'She'll be sitting on one of the artists' balconies soon, drinking Earl Grey tea before going off to the Electric cinema to see a French film.'

The doorbell went again. 'That's probably Maureen now, fetching her new friends over to look at some cockneys and write a song.'

'You're mad, Ruth. Potty.' Laughing, Sandy left the room.

Opening the door to Freda and Johnnie, she tried to wipe the smile from her face. 'Slumming?'

'Well?' Freda pursed her red lips and gave her her half-asleep look. 'Are you still feeding the enemy?'

'Yeah, but only with leftovers. I was just going to take my spare bed in there for the three- and four-year-olds. You can give me a hand.'

Johnnie sighed heavily and turned his back on her. 'Come on, Freda – there's no point.'

'It's going to cost me to get them out, you do realize?'

'Leave them alone. They're only staying until—'

'Until I can get a possession order! And I can't get that until I know their names.'

'Go and ask them then. They won't bite.'

'Goodbye, Sandy. Good luck.' Choked, Freda lowered

her head and slipped her arm through Johnnie's, murmuring, 'Take me home, Johnnie.'

'At least you've *got* a home to go to, Freda.' Ignoring her, they walked away.

Closing the door and leaning on it, Sandy closed her eyes, consumed by that old invisible pain which lived somewhere inside and struck when she least expected it to. If she could stop loving Johnnie and never fall in love again, maybe then the ache would go away.

'What did they want?' Ruth was standing by the window.

'To know if I was still on the side of the squatters, I s'pose.' She returned her sister's look of concern. 'I think I've just lost two friends.'

Ruth drew on her cigarette and blew out a perfect smoke ring. 'Stop being melodramatic. They'll be back once the squatters are out, if not before.'

'I don't think so.' She lowered herself on to the sofa, preoccupied.

'The whole point of being a friend is that you recognize each other's failings. Unless a friendship can cope with rifts, then you have to ask yourself whether it was true friendship in the first place.'

'That's true . . .' She looked at Ruth. 'Yeah . . .' She nodded thoughtfully. 'That sounds as if it comes out of experience.'

'I have had a life or two, you know.' Ruth turned away and gazed out of the window. 'Someone I once loved said the same thing – before he turned his back on me.'

'You never mentioned anyone special before?'

'No. And I shan't again. History, and all that.' She

squashed her cigarette out in the ashtray. 'Time I was going. The other thing I was going to suggest re Cheap and Cheerful is expansion. Why don't we expand the showroom by a few feet and turn it into a proper shop? People are in and out all the time wanting to browse and buy. What do you think?'

'Can the machine room afford to lose a bit of space?'

'Easily. And it wouldn't cost much to push the partition back.'

'OK –' Sandy shrugged – 'nothing to lose, is there?'

'You can only gain by it. More sales.'

'Will you organize the restructuring or do you want me to—'

'I think I can cope,' Ruth cut in. 'I'll give Johnnie a bell tomorrow.'

Surprised that she should say that, Sandy narrowed her eyes suspiciously. 'Why Johnnie? I should think there'll be plenty of handymen around Portobello Road without having to drag him halfway across London.'

'The devil you know, and all that.' She kissed her sister on the cheek and left Sandy wondering. She went into rewind, remembering the card games and any incriminating innuendoes she might have passed over as banter at the time. 'Everything and nothing,' she murmured, too tired to rack her brains.

'Sandy, this collection is the best yet! And they're not just day dresses either. A plain gold necklace, a gold pendant ... you're fucking amazing, my life.' Maureen stepped back and admired the rail of colour coordinated wraps which had been made up in matching fabric. 'If those weren't a flash of genius, I don't know what.'

'You know what I'd really love to see? A row of court shoes in soft leather, just a shade deeper than the dresses.' Sandy sighed and slowly shook her head. 'I wish Freda would stop sulking and talk to me again. We could work together. She could get shoes made up in Hackney to match my collections. Can you imagine how that would go down? In one shop and out the other.'

'Brilliant! Handbags as well.'

'Leather belts.'

'Kid boots up to the knee. Suede . . .'

'To match my winter coats.'

Maureen laughed. 'To what?'

'You heard. Not this year but next. Dead plain, mid-calf, softly fitted to the body with a slight swing to the skirt. Peter Pan collar in black velvet . . . jet buttons . . . small belt at the back.'

'Fitted, soft black leather boots,' Maureen added, a glazed look to her eyes. 'Tiny leather buttons running up the side.'

'Neat felt hats to match the coats . . .'

'. . . with black velvet trim.' Maureen looked at Sandy and beamed. 'Fucking brilliant!' She grabbed Sandy and the pair of them danced around Nova like kids at school.

'Don't you think we should open the shop?' Seema, smiling, stood in the basement doorway. 'You have a customer waiting to come in.'

'Look at 'em, Seema! Now that they're pressed and on the rail. You wouldn't see better than that in Harrods.'

'I know,' Seema said thoughtfully, 'but . . .'

'But what?' The smile drained from Sandy's face. She

valued her girls' advice and she could tell that Seema was worried.

'Maybe something . . . a small black appliqué . . . perhaps beaded or sequined . . . ' She splayed her hands. 'I'm not sure . . . they want *something*. They're so plain.'

'A belt in the same fabric with a fancy buckle?' said Maureen.

'Maybe a sequined belt, even,' offered Seema.

'I know what you're saying, girls, but I don't agree,' said Sandy thoughtfully. 'They are plain, it's true . . . but everyone's got different taste when it comes to adornments and jewellery.' She looked from Seema to Maureen. 'Let's leave them and see what the reaction is. Give it a couple of days, until Saturday afternoon. That should be a good enough guide.' She admired the row of dresses again. 'If I was a customer I'd prefer them plain.' She imagined her diamond and ruby brooch on the charcoal.

'Actually, Sandy, to be honest, so would I. I've got some lovely necklaces which don't seem to go with anything . . .'

'Exactly, Seema! That's my point: every woman has. We buy something we love with no thought to what it might go with.'

'I don't,' Maureen said. 'Everything I buy has a purpose.'

Sandy eyed her outfit, pink and blue floral flares with a matching top. Remembering what Ruth had said Maureen had been wearing at Cheap and Cheerful, she smiled inwardly at her sister's sense of humour. Maureen was hardly a trendsetter.

'I'll tell you what – why don't we each wear one in a different colour, with different necklines?'

'Like a uniform, you mean?' Seema liked the idea. 'I would love to try the sweetheart neck.'

'I'll go for the V-shape in soft rust,' Maureen said.

'With my colour hair I think I'd better stick to French navy.' Sandy hoped they would tell her that the burgundy would suit her, but they both nodded in agreement.

'Not today though.' Maureen looked at her platform shoes. 'I've got some plain black stilettos. I'd rather wear them.'

'OK. Let's do it on Saturday. The three of us'll serve in the shop and make a killing.'

'Five-foot nothing and she's got me modelling.' Maureen grinned. 'I've not been back a week and I'm promoted. Can't be bad.'

'You will be staying then, Maureen?' Seema asked hopefully.

'Definitely. Me, Portobello Road and Ruth wasn't a good cocktail.' She nodded towards the shop door. 'We've got visitors.' There were two police officers peering in the shop window.

'Oh God . . . the squatters! Back me, girls; tell them they've been no trouble.'

'They haven't! We love them kids to death,' Maureen blurted indignantly.

Unlocking the door, Sandy apologized to the two customers who had been waiting for her to open up, and then smiled at the police. 'You're just in time to see our new collection.'

Not a glimmer of a smile crossed their faces. 'Sandra Brent?' the policewoman spoke in a quiet, caring voice.

'That's me,' Sandy chirped, ignoring the sudden heaviness

inside. 'You want to talk to me about the squatters. Come in.'

Removing his helmet, the policeman asked if they could go somewhere private. The expression on his face confirmed Sandy's gut feeling that something was wrong. Her parents came to mind. Her parents and car crashes. Car crashes and Roy. She turned to the customers and asked if they minded waiting just a few minutes more. They too had picked up on the gravity of the visit.

'That's all right, love, we'll come back in half an hour.'

Once the officers were inside, Sandy locked the shop. 'We can talk here. I would rather my friends stayed, if that's OK.'

Seema squeezed Sandy's arm. 'I think that we should go downstairs, Sandy.'

'No! Don't leave me.' Turning to the police officers, she whispered, 'Is it one of my parents?'

'No.' The policewoman looked to her colleague for approval to go on. 'We've just had a call from Kensington. I believe you're the owner of Cheap and Cheerful?'

Relieved that her parents were OK, Sandy sighed and shook her head. 'God, you had me worried. Yeah, that's my other shop. Why?'

'I'm afraid there's been an accident; a fire.'

'On my premises?'

'The fire service is still there. We understand it's under control now but—'

'You are sure it's *my* shop?'

'I'm very sorry . . .' He lowered his eyes, embarrassed.

Sandy instinctively checked her watch; it was five minutes to ten. The machinists would have arrived there at eight-thirty, Ruth at nine. 'What time did it start?'

'The fire brigade was called at nine-fifteen. They managed to get everyone out unharmed . . . except one.'

The female officer stepped in. 'Why don't you sit down, Mrs Brent? This can't be easy for you.'

'Someone's trapped in there?'

'No. She's out now, but they weren't in time. I'm afraid she was overcome by the fumes. She was in the ladies'—'

'Are you telling me . . . are you saying that . . . that one of my staff is dead?'

'I'm very sorry, Mrs Brent,' the policeman's voice cut through her. 'We understand that Ruth Brown was your sister?'

'*No*! You've got it wrong! It must be someone else! It *can't* have been Ruth!'

'Strong sweet tea,' the policeman addressed himself to Maureen.

'You bastard. You fucking *bastard*!' She clenched her fist, pulled back her arm and began to pummel him. 'Don't you dare say that! Don't you *dare*!'

Grabbing Sandy and screaming at the officers to go, Maureen caught a blow on her face. 'Help me, Seema! Don't just stand there!'

Between them, Maureen and Seema managed to restrain Sandy's flailing arms. 'It's *not* Ruth!' she screamed. 'My sister's *alive*! She's got long blonde hair! She's tall and beautiful! You've made a rotten *mistake*!' She pulled away from the girls and pushed her face up close to the policeman's: 'You *stupid* bastard!'

Her legs turned to jelly, her head filled with a white light and a faraway humming sound, and Sandy was consumed both with nausea and desperation to stay on her feet.

'Get a wet flannel for the back of her neck!'

Seema's distorted words drifted in from the sky, each one re-echoing as if she were floating somewhere above herself. 'Don't leave me, Seema.' Sandy hardly recognized her own sluggish voice.

Following instructions coming from everywhere, she pushed her head between her knees and waited for her body to go back to normal. 'What's happening?' she murmured, her head still drooping, heavier by the second.

'You'll be all right, babe,' Maureen said, holding the wet flannel against Sandy's forehead.

'There's been a fire, hasn't there?' Sandy raised her glazed eyes to meet Seema's.

'Yes, Sandy.'

'And the policeman said he thought Ruth was in the lavatory?'

'No. He said she *was* in there. She's out now . . . and not suffering. She's sleeping, Sandy. The way we'll all sleep one day, deep and undisturbed. Peaceful. No more struggling to survive.'

'She's dead? My sister is dead?' She waited for Seema to shake her head but she found her slowly nodding. 'My Ruth? My baby sister . . .? I won't hear her voice again?'

'No.' Seema slipped her hands into Sandy's. 'I'm sorry.'

'She won't ever come into the shop . . .' Sandy was talking to herself now, as if no one else was there. 'We won't sit on the settee drinking coffee and talking . . . laughing,' she was remembering the last time they were together, just the two of them. 'No more Ruth?'

'You have her memory, Sandy. You can relive your times together, over and over again. Memories live for ever.'

'I don't think . . .' Sandy stopped mid-sentence and gazed ahead of her. 'I don't think *I* will, then,' she said matter-of-factly. Looking up at the police officers, she shrugged. 'I'm not gonna live any more. Why should I? I've had enough.'

'Would you like us to take you to the site?' the male officer said.

'The site? Cheap and Cheerful?' She turned to Maureen. 'We'll all go. We'll get Siddy to take us. I'm sure they've made a mistake. The smoke probably made Ruth pass out, that's all.'

Maureen looked across at the police officers with that all-important question in her eyes. Their grave, slight shake of the head confirmed that the horror was real. Ruth was dead.

'What about your parents, Sandy?' Seema asked quietly. 'Wouldn't you rather go with them?'

Withdrawing from those around her, Sandy gazed at nothing and shrugged, as if words had no meaning, as if it were all a fiction in which she had no part, as if she were the onlooker and they the players.

'They haven't been informed yet.' The policeman looked at his watch. 'We called there first but there was no reply. I expect they're both out at work?' He got down on one knee and looked into Sandy's face. 'If you can just tell me where your parents work, we can contact them. They'll want to be with you.'

'John Lewis's,' she whispered.

'Would that be where your father works . . . or your mother?'

'John Lewis's,' she repeated, as if she were concentrating all her efforts on those two names.

'Her mum works there!' Maureen snapped, losing her patience. 'You don't have to interrogate her, for Christ's sake. *We* can tell you all you need to know. Her dad's an electrician and her mum works in the lighting department at John Lewis's. OK?'

Straightening, he threw her a hard-bitten look. 'This isn't easy for us, you know.' He turned to his female assistant. 'Get the number from Directory Enquiries and then phone from here.' He peered at Maureen. 'If that's all right – to use the phone?'

'You *are* joking?'

'No.' He looked questioningly at her.

'You're gonna tell her, on the phone, that her daughter is dead? What the fuck's wrong with you?'

He inhaled slowly and shook his head. 'Would you rather a policeman turned up at her workplace?'

'Yes, actually. Anyway, I know her . . . I'll get a cab there myself and—'

'We'll both go,' Sandy said, snapping back into reality. 'Seema, if you could tell the girls to go home and then lock up for me?'

'Of course.' Seema pursed her lips and began to cry. 'I'm sorry . . .' She turned away briskly and went down into the basement.

'Phone Siddy. His number's in the black address book in

the top drawer. He can take us on from there to . . . to Portobello Road.'

'We could take you,' the policewoman said, her own voice broken. 'We weren't trying to—'

'I know,' Sandy cut in, 'I know. But I would rather go in a taxi. I'll be all right. Thank you for coming.'

'You're sure there's nothing we—'

'No. Please. I'm not being . . . I just . . . it's your uniforms.' She swallowed and sucked on her bottom lip. 'Please . . . please go away.' She covered her face with her hands and wept. 'Just go.'

Catching a glimpse of Sandy and Maureen in his rear mirror, Siddy had to stop himself from choking up. Their arms were linked and they were holding hands and crying, each lost in their own world of sorrow. All that Maureen had told him was to take them to the West End store, wait while they collected Sandy's mother, and then drive them on to Portobello Road.

That another disaster had struck the family was patently clear. He wondered if Sandy's father had suddenly died and she was on the way to break the news to her mother. Whatever the tragedy, it was evidently close to the bone.

Siddy had taken Sandy to her new shop a couple of times when she was first setting it up, and had admired the way she had pulled her life together after it had been smashed to bits. He knew that her sister was working at Cheap and Cheerful, so guessed that was why that would be their next port of call – to give Ruth the devastating news. Easing his way through the heavy traffic and the back-doubles, he cursed the day he picked Sandy up for the first time, selfish though that was. He wasn't as tough as he liked to appear, and he would be the first to admit it right then.

Surprising him, Sandy pushed the sliding window open. 'My mum'll be in a state of shock, Siddy, so you will wait for us, won't you?' She could only just get her words out.

''Course I'll wait, silly. What's happened?'

'My shop's burned out. The fire brigade'll still be there. I want you to take us on to the hospital straight away, once we've seen it and they've told us where they've taken my sister.'

He exhaled slowly and shook his head. 'It never just rains, eh?' He dreaded to ask how bad she was. 'Try not to worry — she'll be all right.'

'I'm afraid not, Sid. She was trapped in there. In the ladies'. Overcome by fumes.'

'She'll be all right. Doctors can—'

'She's dead.'

'Stone me,' he muttered, swerving to avoid a car he should have seen. 'Don't do things by halves, does He?' He couldn't think what else to say. He was no different from anyone else who, on hearing tragic news, blamed God. It was the easiest way out.

Telling Siddy about it had helped, marginally, but that was all she needed to brace herself for the heartbreaking task ahead: that of facing her mother. Once again, she was going to have to be strong. March forward when all she wanted to do was crumble in a heap and have someone there, not touching her, not giving words of comfort, simply being there. She thought about Johnnie; yet when the going had been tough, at any time throughout that summer, Roy had been the one she had talked to during the long hours of the night when she couldn't sleep. Had anyone asked, she would have told them point-blank that his spirit was there, that he hadn't gone completely. Exactly when he had crossed over to the other side, she couldn't say. She only knew that when she woke up one morning feeling that things were finally going her way, she could no longer sense his presence.

'D'you want me to come in with you, Sand?' Maureen whispered in her ear.

'No, you wait in the taxi with Siddy. I've got to do this by myself.' She went quiet for a few moments and then added: 'If you could nip out and buy a half-bottle of brandy . . .'

'Good idea. I don't know about a half-bottle, though . . .'

Sandy managed a weak smile. 'True. I s'pose you could do with a strong drink as well.'

'Too right.'

'I hope you're not gonna get the guilts, Maureen. I know the two of you didn't see eye to eye, but in a way Ruth needed someone like you to rub up against.'

'You think I don't know that? I'm gonna give her a right telling-off when I go to church. She's done this on purpose. One-upmanship. What a bloody trump card to pull out, eh?'

Weeping and laughing at the same time, they couldn't help but notice that Siddy was doing the same. 'I wouldn't mind betting that life is a rehearsal, and she bloody well knew it,' Maureen said drily. 'She's probably in this taxi right now, sticking two fingers up at me and wishing she could boast about having risen to higher things.'

Sandy took a deep breath as the cab pulled up at the back

of John Lewis's department store. 'Don't forget the brandy, Mo.'

Maureen screwed up her face as a loud sob escaped. Pressing her fingers to her lips she began to bawl properly, the tears pouring out. 'I'm *sorry*! This shouldn't be happening to you! It's a bastard world!'

'I'll be all right.' Sandy gripped Maureen's pale, trembling hand. 'Don't you go all broken on me now. You're the well I draw strength from, you know that.'

Maureen nodded and sniffed. 'Gimme a hanky, for Christ's sake.' She started to cry again. Wiping her nose she said, 'You sure you don't want me to come in with you?'

'Positive.' Sandy smiled. 'Lot of bloody good you'd be. Don't let her drink all the brandy, Siddy!' She pushed open the cab door and got out before she herself broke down.

'Sandy!' Siddy called from his open window. 'You all right?'

'Yeah, I'm fine. Look after Mo.' She gave the thumbs-up and pushed open the glass swing door of the store and headed for the lighting department.

The moment Maggie set eyes on her daughter, the smile faded from her face. The flushed complexion, puffy eyes and tear-stained face was causing customers and assistants alike to stare at her.

'I'm sorry, Mum.' Sandy raised her arms and spread her hands hopelessly. 'Ruth's dead.' A ghostly hush spread around her as the shocking statement hit those within earshot. 'And the shop's burnt out.'

For a few moments no one moved or spoke, as if a photograph was being taken. Then came the hustle and bustle as they moved in to comfort mother and daughter . . . and life in the lighting department went on, the way buses had still run along the Whitechapel Road as Roy had taken his last breath.

With Sandy between her mother and father, gripping both their arms, the three of them walked slowly down the church aisle following the pall-bearers as they carried Ruth's coffin to her grave. Numbed with shock, yet stirred by the hymn that the congregation was softly singing, she wanted to cry out her sister's name. Her throat dry, she could not even manage to whisper it.

Glancing at the back pews she saw that all the girls had turned out, those from Cheap and Cheerful and from Nova. Standing at the end of the pew closest to her, she was pleased to see the warm and sympathetic smiles of Johnnie, Freda and Leo. On the opposite side of the aisle were the squatters, all in tears.

The burial over, Sandy, Maggie and Terry could not wait to get back into the funeral car and away from the cemetery, the flowers and the well-wishers. None of them wanted to accept that it was their Ruth who had just been lowered into the ground.

There was no funeral tea; those who had arrived at Terry and Maggie's house prior to the funeral had been plied with drinks and sandwiches prepared by a neighbour. The last thing they wanted was relatives and friends around them. All they needed right now was peace, quiet and each other.

'At least she didn't suffer burns,' Maggie said, sipping a

glass of Irish whiskey. 'I don't think I could have coped with the thought of her . . .'

'She wouldn't 'ave known much about it,' Terry said impatiently.

'I know, love, but . . . I wish I could be sure. The thought of her being trapped—'

'She *wasn't* trapped! She was found by the sink. She had been washing her hands. She saw the flames and instead of getting out she tried to fight it with the fire extinguisher. How many *more* times?'

'Mum just needs you to reassure her, Dad, that's all. I expect you'll have to go over it a few more times yet.' Curled up in an armchair, Sandy imagined her sister alive, trying to put the fire out.

The stockroom containing the fabrics, sequined or otherwise, backed on to the lavatory, and was where the fire had started. An electrical fault. Sandy thanked God it had not been an oversight of Terry's. Sandy had told him that the electrics looked fine, and that the place had been newly wired five years previously. She had not been wrong in her appraisal, but even so she secretly wished she had had him check it all over, even though she had been told by the fire services that the fault was a fluke occurrence.

'Will you look for new premises?' Terry asked, struggling to find something positive to talk about.

'No.' Sandy wished he would stay quiet and not feel under obligation to fill the silence. They were family, after all.

'Stick to the one shop? Yeah . . . I think that's for the best.'

She smiled and nodded, not yet ready to tell him of her

real plans to release herself from all commitments; that all she wanted was to sell up and go – maybe follow in Poonam's footsteps and make her way to India. She would tell her parents it was to be a short trip, three or four months; but in truth, if she could manage it, she would say goodbye to living in England. Goodbye to routine, to respectability and the stiff-upper-lip fraternity which she no longer wanted to be part of. She wanted to be where people could cry in public and go unnoticed. Where people believed that the body was no more than a vehicle for the soul, a house in which to propagate the human species, all part of a much wider picture. Where people actually might not be clinging to the notion that man is superior, and that nature produces for the sole purpose of *their* comforts and *their* needs.

'Better not spread yourself too far,' Terry said thoughtfully. 'A bird in the hand is worth two in the bush.'

'How's your business doing?' Sandy said, wishing to move the focus from herself to her dad.

'All right. Ticking along.' He stood up and refilled his glass, uncomfortable with the sudden change of form. His daughter talking to him as an equal? It wasn't on.

Standing by their patio doors, gazing out at the garden, Maggie spoke as if she were talking to herself instead of to Terry and Sandy. 'I suppose we should try to eat something.'

Terry shook his head. 'My stomach wouldn't thank me. Maybe later on, something hot.'

'Me neither.' Sandy stood up and stretched. 'I think I'll get back and catch up on some sleep. I've had it.'

'I'll give you a bell later on, make sure you're all right. OK?'

She kissed Terry on the cheek and thanked him. 'I know you're both longing to have a good cry. Once I've gone you can really let go. Sob your hearts out – it'll do you both good.'

'Be careful driving, Sandy. That drink was more like a treble than a single shot.' Maggie held out her arms and smiled.

Hugging her mother tight, she murmured, 'Don't worry about me, Mum, I'll take extra care. Whatever I do, wherever I go, I'll make sure you get me back in one piece.'

'What's that s'posed to mean?' Terry narrowed his red-rimmed eyes and peered at her.

'No more than what I said, Dad. Stop worrying – I'm not gonna emigrate . . . yet.' She winked at him. 'Maybe in a month or so. I might trip off to see a bit of the world.'

'Oh, a holiday,' he said, relieved.

'Yeah, sort of. A long holiday. Maybe. We'll see.'

By the time Sandy arrived back at Nova, her mind was made up. She would give the girls two weeks' notice, have a closing down sale and put the property on the market. Once it was sold, she would equip herself for her long and possibly permanent venture into another world. The thought of sunshine through the winter months lit her up. A typical Leo, Sandy loved the sunshine. Facing a bleak, cold winter in England with no Ruth and few friends, chilled her. Christmas would not be spent in this country – on that she was decided.

Later, having spoken with her parents on the phone, Sandy ensconced herself on the sofa by the cold ashes of yesterday's fire and sank lower than she could imagine possible. Planning to trek through the Far East now left her short of joy, and the dreadful realization that her sister was gone for ever made her feel like the loneliest human being in the world. Her flat had never seemed so quiet, so deserted.

Staring at the telephone, she willed it to ring. Johnnie and Freda had each given her warm, understanding looks at the funeral, so why hadn't they called to see if she was all right? She thought about the people she could phone; Maureen was the only one she could think of, but she wasn't just around the corner. She toyed with the idea of going to her parents, where relatives and friends had created an unwanted impromptu wake, each believing that they would be the only ones dropping in to comfort Maggie, Terry and themselves.

Settling for getting drunk in her own company, she carried in her pillows and eiderdown from her bedroom, deciding to snuggle down on the sofa for her night's sleep. She would watch television until the white spot appeared.

One hour later, she still hadn't switched on the TV. Behaving as if it was a normal day wasn't right, but it was beginning to feel as though it would never end. She wasn't ready to look at old photographs of her and Ruth, or to think about the times when they played together as children. She wasn't really ready to accept that she was gone. Having never given any thought to what it must be like to lose a sister, a one and only sister, she examined her feelings of utter frustration and anger. It was as if she had suddenly had an arm wrenched off; there one minute, gone the next. But more than that, her spirit was screaming out for Ruth's spirit, and there was nothing she could do. Ruth was gone – and for good. 'I feel like an orphan,' she murmured. 'I'm alone in the park with no one to play with or talk to.' She curled into a foetal position and cried. 'I want my sister back,' she sobbed over and over. '*I want her!*'

When the telephone finally rang she made no attempt to answer it. If she couldn't talk to Ruth, then she wouldn't speak to anyone. When it stopped ringing she cried even louder, screaming at whoever it was to call again.

Dropping her head down into the pillows, she realized that she was drunk as the room began to spin. Rushing to the bathroom she pressed her hand over her mouth, forcing herself not to throw up until her head was over the lavatory pan.

Seeing her reflection in the mirror above the bathroom sink did not help matters. She looked dreadful. Her usually large hazel eyes could only just be seen under her puffy red eyelids and her long red hair was in need of a good brushing. She was thankful that no one had called round. She wouldn't even want the children next door to see her like that, let alone Johnnie.

Johnnie again. Why was he always in the forefront of her mind? Whatever they had had between them was over – he had made that perfectly clear. He may have thought he loved her once, but now that he knew her better . . .

Pressing a cold wet flannel to her forehead and dampening her fringe, she felt better. Throwing up was the best thing. Maybe now she would get control of her emotions too. Hearing the doorbell caused her to freeze. She didn't want to see *anyone*.

Creeping into the sitting room, she switched off the lamps,

hoping that whoever it was hadn't looked up at the window. The doorbell went again. Slipping under her covers on the sofa, she lay quite still and waited for whoever it was to go away. But whoever it was was persistent – he or she would not take their finger off the buzzer.

'Bloody cheek! This is my *home*!' she yelled. 'I want a bit of *privacy*! Go away!' Getting off the sofa, she crawled towards the window, slowly raised her head above the sill and peered down. It was Freda, and she had positioned herself comfortably, leaning the fleshy part of her hand on the bell, making it clear that she could stay like that for a very long time.

Grabbing the shop keys from the side table, Sandy opened the window and threw them down, aiming to miss Freda but making it look as if her intention was otherwise. 'Open the door yourself! I'm not coming down!' She slammed the sash window shut and went back to her makeshift bed.

'Your mother was worried. She asked if I would check up on you.' Freda wore her usual bored expression.

'Don't tell fucking lies. She hasn't got your number.'

'Stop swearing. I'm not impressed, and it makes you sound like a fishwife.'

'Instead of a dead man's wife? Or both?'

'I guessed you'd be feeling sorry for yourself. That's why I came, otherwise I wouldn't have bothered. I'll help myself to a drink, then?'

'Sure. Ransack the cupboard for food, why don't you? I only live here.'

'It was a lovely service,' Freda said, pouring herself a large whisky.

'I don't want to talk about it.'

'We do things differently, of course. Bury the body within twenty-four hours if possible, and sit shiva—'

'You don't want to say that too quickly, Freda.'

Ignoring her ridicule – she had heard that one many times before – she continued, 'That way, by the time the seventh day is up, we've got used to the idea that they've gone.'

'What do you want, Freda?'

'I've come to tell you that Leo and I are going to live together. No point in getting married at our age. We're going to sell our houses and move in next door, now that *I've* got the borough to rehouse the squatters. Leo wants to run the tobacconist's again.'

'The squatters . . .' Sandy murmured, guilty that she hadn't thought about them since Ruth died.

'They're fine, Sandy. They'll be rehoused nearby. Stop worrying. Oh, and Johnny's going off to Canada for a year. Been offered a contract he could have refused, if he'd had anything to stay here for.'

'There's a sharp knife in the top drawer in the kitchen. Why don't you make a proper job of it?' She turned slightly, offering Freda her back.

'Carry on with this ridiculous feud and you'll lose a good man. It was none of your business in any case. That's my property, not yours; not Johnnie's.' She emptied her glass in one. 'Do you know what I think? I think the pair of you were using my predicament to test each other. And what have you done? You've created a bloody iron curtain between you.'

'You're miles out . . . well, half-wrong, anyway. Johnnie built the wall, not me. He wanted out. He probably knew about the Canadian contract, and the squatters popped up at just the right time to give him an excuse to go. He's probably got a woman lined up as well.'

'Well it wouldn't surprise me. He's a good-looking fella.'

'I'll be better off without him, won't I?'

'If you say so. Am I allowed another drink?'

'You're driving, not me.'

'No I'm not. I'm sleeping in your bed tonight. You look settled for the night. What are you drinking?'

'I'll have a scotch as well. How is the king of hearts, then?'

'Miserable. Drives me mad with his long face. I'll be glad when he's gone. Do you have any crisps?'

Sandy forced a sigh. 'In the kitchen, in the cupboard above the fridge where you'll find some fresh Cheddar. Cut it into small chunks. You'll find a jar of gherkins and some olives in the cupboard below the one where you'll find the crisps.'

'I don't suppose you fancy a Chinese?'

'You want me to go out looking like this?'

She handed Sandy her drink. 'No. Takeaway.'

Remembering their first meal together, the three of them, she glared at her friend. 'That's not funny.'

'Chinese takeaway?' Freda shrugged. 'Who said it was?'

'You know what I mean.'

'I do not.' Freda sucked her teeth and raised an eyebrow. 'Am I missing something?'

'That was the first time me and Johnnie . . . well . . . I suppose it was our first date. Stop pretending you don't remember.'

'There's been a few months in between.' She shrugged

and moved her head from side to side. 'I'm surprised you remember something like that, going by the way you've been treating him.'

'I haven't been treating him badly!'

'No? Ruth comes back into your life and hey presto, Johnnie must stay in the background – and then you slam the door in his face! No wonder he's running away to the other side of the world. He spent a night in a cell trying to hold on to you, you know.'

Sandy looked at her, bemused by her silly expression and her game-playing. 'Whatever are you talking about now?'

'Never mind. The point is, the man is in love with you. Properly in love. His face shows the pain in his heart. You've been very cold, Sandy. Uncaring.'

'Freda: if he felt the way you imagine he does, where is he now, in my greatest hour of need? With another woman, no doubt, making plans for their future in Canada!'

'I'll tell you where he is. He's over the road. In the pub. Waiting for you to join him. If you're not there within an hour and a half of my calling, he's going – and he won't be back. A man can only put so much of his pride in his pocket.'

Sandy held out her empty glass. 'Why didn't he come here instead of going into the pub, then?'

'Because he's afraid you'll reject him again!'

'I did *not* reject him! He turned his back on me!'

'If you want him, you've got to go over there. He's made the move – now it's up to you.'

'If that's all you came here for, I think you should go.'

'Go and wash your face, put on a bit of make-up and brush that bloody hair. It's like rats' tails!'

'He knows where I am. If he wants to he can come up. If he comes up I'll brush my hair.'

'If that's your final word . . .'

'It is!'

'Well I'm not going to let him sit there sweating. I'll deliver your message and leave the pair of you to it. I'll call in tomorrow to see how you are. Don't drink too much.'

'I thought you were staying?'

'I've changed my mind. With me out of the way, maybe the two of you can sort this out. I'll be round first thing. OK?' She held up the shop keys. 'I'll pop these through the letter box once I've let myself out.'

Sandy nodded slowly, a voice inside her screaming for Freda to ask if she wanted her to stay. The thought of sitting through the long night by herself was horrifying. 'See if you can get him to put himself in my shoes. See my side of it.'

Freda shrugged. 'I'll do my best. Don't expect him to ring on that doorbell because I think that's highly unlikely. He believes he's meeting you halfway already.'

'That's bollocks, Freda, and you should know it.'

Hearing the front door close, Sandy rushed to the bathroom and threw cold water on her face, brushed her hair and then peered despairingly into her make-up bag. Mascara was out of the question, so too was eyeliner. She would have to make do with foundation and lipstick.

Checking her appearance in the mirror, she was pleased that at least her chunky-knit sweater didn't clash with her flushed cheeks. She dabbed a little perfume behind her ears and prayed that Johnnie's love was stronger than his pride. But it was not to be.

Chapter Ten

One week after Ruth's funeral, Sandy called a meeting with her staff. A memo had been pinned to the small noticeboard in the basement, which read:

All work today will cease at 4 p.m. The shop will be closed at that time. A meeting to discuss the future of Nova will be held in the flat sitting room. Sandy.

Refusing to discuss it with Maureen first thing, Sandy told her not to stir up a hornets' nest and that all would be revealed later. She expected her friend to demand answers on the spot, but it was not so; her response was uncharacteristically subdued. Sandy presumed that Maureen had drawn her own conclusions, and understood why she could not go on running the shop as if nothing had happened. Sandy's sketch pad had not seen the light of day since the tragedy, and she had stopped talking her ideas through with the girls.

Terry had come up trumps in dealing with the insurance company, arguing her case. When it became obvious to him that although they were obliged to pay for building repairs to the shop, but the contents were not covered, he knew Sandy was to blame. When she had taken over the insurance of the premises, it hadn't occurred to her that she might not be covered for stock. Had she not been in such a hurry to open up, and had taken the time to consider everything, she would have realized that Poonam's requirements had been literally no more than floor space.

The losses were not colossal, but clearing the debts to suppliers, which she was obliged to do since she was the sole trader, was going to deplete her bank balance.

As far as Sandy was concerned, there was nothing that life could throw at her now to equal what she had had to endure over the past months. She had lost her husband, her sister, a large proportion of her funds and Johnnie had not come to her when she had hit rock bottom; his pride proving, in the end, to have overridden his feelings. All she had left was number eleven, and Freda had made it quite clear that the bottom was fast falling out of the property market. If she was lucky she would make £8,500 – if she could find a buyer. If not, she would have to stay put and get a job or let the premises. Letting was the option she intended to take. The deposit and advance rent, together with one thousand pounds in her account, would pay for her trip to India, and by her reckoning she could survive there, living simply, for at least a year. During that time the rent would accumulate and she would have something to come home to. All she had to do was find either a buyer or a tenant.

Staring at the rows of garments, she wondered how much she would have to reduce the prices in order to shift them quickly. It would break her heart to cut them by fifty per cent, but she had a feeling that was going to be her only option. If she were to hang on until Christmas, without adding to the stock and with no staff to pay, financially she would be better off. A clearance sale would not be necessary. But she didn't want to wait; each passing day was beginning to drag as her enthusiasm slowly drained away. Catching sight of her reflection in her full-length mirror, she toyed with the idea of bringing Maureen up from the basement to serve while she went upstairs and made an attempt to smarten herself. Her lank hair, dragged back into a ponytail, was in need of attention, and some make-up wouldn't go amiss. Lighting a cigarette, she decided she couldn't be bothered; customers came in to look at the goods, not her. Emptying the overflowing ashtray into a bin, she half-heartedly scolded herself for breaking the number-one rule – smoking in the shop. No doubt Freda would be in later, complaining about the smell. 'Well *fuck* her,' she murmured, and sipped her coffee, which was cold.

Seeing people she recognized going by her shop looking straight ahead, not daring to glance in, she cursed the human race. She was the one in mourning, yet they were acting as if it was their personal tragedy. 'They can't face you, love,' she mimicked her mother's cliché which she repeated over and over. 'Give them time, they'll be back.'

'Talking to yourself again?' Maureen was standing in the basement doorway.

'Maureen! Creeping about like a bloody ghost!'

'We've run out of French-navy yarn.'

'Oh have we? Well get the junior to run down to Woolworth's, then. The workshop is your department, not mine.'

'Junior?'

'That's right. I presume you do have one? It's usually the youngest or last in. If you've overlooked that little detail, you'd better go round asking their ages.'

'No, that's OK. I'll go myself.' She held out her hand for some money.

Gazing at her palm, Sandy drew on her cigarette. 'Freda's the fortune-teller, not me.'

'The petty cash tin's empty.'

'Christ, Maureen, how much is a reel of cotton?' She opened the till and flicked a fifty-pence piece across the counter. 'Get me a box of matches while you're at it. I've run out.'

'Gonna try and burn this place down as well, are yer?' She looked spitefully at her and left.

'Nice one, Mo,' Sandy said, turning the pages of a racing form. 'There you go; I wasn't there, but of course the fire had to be my fault. Everything's my fault. I'm an omen. Shave my head and you'll find three sixes.'

Aware that someone had entered the shop and was casually looking through the rail of dresses, she didn't look up. Why should she? If the woman wanted to try something on she would ask. As she picked up her pencil and marked one of the horses she fancied, a shadow fell across her.

'I'm sorry to hear about your sister.'

The voice, full of compassion, was not something she wanted to hear right then. Keeping her head down, she coolly thanked her and then added, 'That's life – or death, should I say.' She scribbled a pencil note next to her second fancy.

'I thought my loss was bad enough.'

Sandy slowly raised her eyes to meet Laura Armstrong's. 'Well, you certainly pick your time, don't you? Here to remind me of a third killing, are you?'

'No. Siddy told me what happened. I just felt I had to come.'

Sandy went back to her horses. 'You should have left it a couple of weeks. I'm having a closing-down sale.'

Laura sighed and placed a hand on Sandy's. 'If it's any consolation, I know what you're going through and yes, it does get less painful.'

Pulling her hand away, Sandy glared up at her. 'I'd like to help you, say something to make you feel good, but I can't. You go through your grieving, your way, and I'll go through mine. I'm sorry your daughter was killed, but there's nothing I can do about it. I still have nightmares – if *that's* any consolation.'

'You know where I live if you want to come round.' She offered Sandy a folded piece of paper. 'My phone number.'

Sandy took it and tore it into small pieces. 'Now will you accept that I'm a cold-hearted bitch who doesn't give a fuck about other people's misery? My husband's dead, your daughter's dead, my sister's dead, your husband might be in a year or two . . .' She shrugged. 'Ice cream melts in the sun.'

'Well . . . you know where I am.' Downcast, the woman turned away, wishing she had never come.

'Women and babies are dying by the thousands all over the world. What difference do two or three more make? Are we so special? My husband was a bastard, my sister a bitch; what was your Kay? A fucking *saint*?'

Laura Armstrong stood in the doorway and slowly turned to face her. 'She was my daughter and I loved her. I miss her.'

'Well what do you expect *me* to do!'

'Nothing.' She turned to leave.

'Don't you dare. Don't you *dare* walk away! *Don't you dare!*' She swept her arm across the counter, sending everything flying. Her eyes blazing, her arm rigid, she pointed a finger at Laura, trying to control her breathing and her temper. 'You get *right* back in this shop!' She stepped out from behind the counter, picked up a chair with one hand and slammed it down again. 'You fucking well sit down, you cow. You sit down and you tell me: what am I supposed to do!'

Thunderstruck, Laura froze. She had been aware that her visit might have gone down like a damp firework – but this? This was nothing short of a whole display.

'If you don't put your backside on this chair,' screamed Sandy, 'I'll smash it to pieces and then I'll rip every fucking dress in the shop!'

Sandy's sudden manic behaviour was proving too much for Laura. She pressed two fingers against her lips to stop herself from grinning. All she had to do was take a few paces and sit down, but she couldn't move. It was as if someone invisible was stopping her. She started to laugh. Someone was gripping her arm tight, willing her to stay where she was. That someone was Maureen.

'You're laughing at me, you hard-hearted cow! You wicked bitch!' She looked from Laura, who was trying but failing to keep a straight face, to Maureen, who was trying to smile.

'Say something,' Maureen murmured to Laura, 'say the worst thing you can think of.'

Laura was on to Sandy in a flash. 'Is that all you care about? Your precious glitzy dresses? And a *chair*? Smash it to bits, you selfish little bitch! No wonder your husband jumped the lights. Any man would do the same with a cow like you next to him. You *made* him crash! You made him smash into my Kay's car!'

Horrified, Maureen looked from Sandy to the strange woman. This lady was not acting. This was for real.

'Thirty years old! That's all she was! Driving through London to see her dad in hospital! Her dad who was on the danger list! She thought he might die but what happened? He pulled through and she's dead! How do you think that makes *him* feel?'

Taking one slow step at a time she moved in, her finger pointing at Sandy's face, her eyes full of anger and tears. 'You tell me that thousands are dying in Africa, as if that makes Kay's death all right. Well, selfish or not, my Kay meant everything to me. She meant more than a million people in Africa! I can't even *think* about the starving! *Pain*! That's all *I* know! The pain inside that won't go away! The pain that I have to smile through every day so that I won't depress everyone around me.' She pushed her face up close to Sandy's. 'We haven't got the right to do that, and *you* have no right to order me to sit down and tell you what you're supposed to do!' She poked her on the shoulder. 'You *know* what you've got to do. We all know what we've got to do. Be brave!'

Too stunned to speak, Sandy jerked a shoulder, threw her

head back and turned away, retreating to her flat.

'You don't mince your words, do you?' Maureen said bitterly.

'No, I don't.' Leaving the shop, Laura Armstrong felt better than she had in a long time. It was so good getting all that off her chest, and the ginger-headed brat had been a supreme target.

Turning the closed sign around and locking the door, Maureen went upstairs. There seemed little to lose now. She would extract from Sandy her intentions with regard to Nova. After all, it was Maureen's career, her future, which hung in the balance. She loved her work and could see that Nova, if it became a chain, was set for success. If Sandy didn't want to carry on, she did.

Without knocking, she pushed open the living-room door. 'I think it's time we had a chat, don't you?'

'Nothing to talk about.' Sandy was sitting on the edge of the sofa, puffing frantically at a cigarette. 'Go down and look after the shop.'

'I've closed the shop.'

'Well go and open it again. I take it you do want your wages this week?' she said, looking anywhere but at Maureen.

'I want my fucking wages *every* week! I've got a mother and kid brother to support, in case you've forgotten.'

'It's not the first thought that comes into my mind in the mornings.'

Suppressing her hurt, Maureen stiffened. 'If you're bent on running Nova down, I've got a suggestion to make. Let me take it over.'

Sandy smiled sarcastically. 'I'd love to, Maureen, but I

don't have the energy to train you.'

'I would hire a pattern-cutter. I know my limitations. Give me a month and I'll show you.'

'And what am I s'posed to do meanwhile – sit up here and twiddle my thumbs?'

'No. Do us all a favour and take a month's holiday, somewhere in the sun. You need a break and . . . you deserve it.' She sat down next to her friend. 'Stop running for five minutes, Sandy. You'll drive yourself into the ground. Everyone needs to stop now and then. Put yourself up as a victim and you'll be used.'

Used. Now there was a word that hit the mark. A furniture-maker who shared the premises in Portobello Road had done just that with an extortionate insurance claim against her!

'You could look after the shop for me today . . . I have to go somewhere.' Preoccupied, she gazed up at Maureen. 'A month in the sun would be heaven . . . but who am I supposed to go with, my mother?'

'No. That would defeat the object. Go on one of those singles holidays, you know, for the over-thirties.'

'I'm only twenty-seven, just.'

'You can lie, can't you?'

'I suppose I could go on a cruise.' She thought about her thousand pounds in the bank. 'Sail around the world for a month and . . . who knows? Some rich movie star might carry me off.'

'*Much* better. A cruise. Brilliant!'

'Get me off your back?'

Maureen rolled her eyes. 'The very thought of it!'

'And you really think that this shop would be better off

without me at the helm?' Her question was honest and sincere.

'You know I don't. But if you don't pull yourself together, *anywhere* would be better off without you. Look at the state you've let yourself get into! You've been wearing those jeans for a week.'

'I would love to take time to get a proper tan . . .'

'Well *do* it then!' Maureen jumped up. 'This is madness. The shop should be *open*!' She strode towards the door. 'And wash that bloody hair!'

'Mo?'

Maureen turned around. 'What now?'

'You didn't really think I'd let you get your hands on my shop, did you?' Sandy grinned.

''Course I did.' She left the room and closed the door behind her.

Heading for the bathroom, Sandy planned what she would wear for the visit she was about to make. 'Something that'll make me feel like the strong woman I'm supposed to be.' She smiled. 'Something that will bring out the male in me – to confront the insurance company.' She pulled off her unwashed clothes ready for a refreshing shower.

With her long, lustrous hair blowing in the breeze, wearing a black trouser suit, black suede cuban-heel shoes and her favourite red cashmere round-neck, Sandy walked purposefully along High Holborn towards the tall, imposing red-brick building, ready for battle. A letter had arrived two days previously informing her that not only were her contents not covered, but also that the landlord of the property had

had a clause written into his contract that any damage caused to a tenant's possessions by another tenant would be the responsibility of the party concerned. When the fire had caused water damage to the furniture-maker's on the second floor of the building in Portobello Road, the owner had wasted no time in fighting his corner and placing an outrageous claim.

Having made several phone calls and taken legal advice, Sandy was now ready to fight her case. She was not, as it turned out, liable for the furniture-maker's damage, and she had no intention of leaving the insurance company's offices until they accepted the fact. As it was, she had had to accept Cheap and Cheerful's financial losses, and she also faced having to lose Nova and everything she had worked so hard for.

It was with renewed energy that Sandy stepped into the company's elaborate reception area. She could feel that old adrenaline pumping once again: she was ready for anything.

Instead of making her way to the boutique after her demanding but successful ordeal, Sandy walked home, burning both physical and mental energy as she considered her future plans. She walked along Holborn Viaduct, down Cheapside to the City, past Liverpool Street station towards the East End. She had one visit to make before going to her shop. Johnnie had been doing some work for the record shop, a stone's throw from Nova. When she had passed that morning, glancing in the open doorway she had seen him fixing shelves back on to a wall which he had decorated.

It was precisely six days before he was due to go to

Canada, according to Freda, and Sandy was not going to let him go without offering to make up. She would wish him well, him and whoever he was going with, and she would thank him for all he had done for her. Without Johnnie, Freda, Maureen and now Laura Armstrong, Sandy wasn't sure which way she would have gone after Ruth's death.

Another port of call would be the florist's. She would send Mrs Armstrong a dozen red roses, together with a thank-you card. She would write her a letter of apology and ask to be excused for her outburst. She couldn't believe she had been so vicious. The woman had had every right to attack her the way she did. Whether she meant to or not, Laura Armstrong had somehow forced Sandy to see what she was turning into.

Johnnie was giving a screw in a metal bracket a forceful turn when she arrived at the record shop. Admiring him from behind, she was sorry that she had allowed them to drift apart – and all because of strangers, who were soon to be out of her life. He and Freda had been right in their approach to the squatters but so too had Sandy, in her opinion.

'Hello, Johnnie,' she said as she walked slowly towards him.

Tilting his head slightly to glance at her, he nodded. 'Sandy. How's it going?'

'Not so bad. I've just come from the insurance company. I'm not liable for the other tenant's losses at Portobello Road. I had to argue my case, though.'

'Good for you. How's your mum and dad?'

'As well as they can be. You should drop in to see them before you go. Dad thinks a great deal of you, you know.'

'Before I go where?' he said, dropping some of his tools into his bag.

'To Canada. That's why I've come in. Say goodbye, in case I missed you . . . before you left.' She was surprised at how choked she was feeling. His leaving to go across the world hadn't really sunk in until now. 'Thought maybe you'd let me buy you a beer . . .'

'Oh yeah?'

'Wish you well, and all that.'

'Uh-huh.' He wiped the perspiration from his forehead with a clean white handkerchief. 'I fancy a pint, as it happens.'

'The pubs won't be open yet, though.'

'No, but the off-licence will be. We'll get a couple of cans and sit in your backyard, enjoy the last of this year's sun. They reckon the Indian summer's about to end.'

'In the garden . . .' She gazed at him, surprised by his casual manner. He was acting as if nothing had changed since their dispute. Had their time apart meant so little to him? 'Johnnie—'

'Not now, Sandy. After a beer, or over one.'

She took a step closer. 'I only want to say I'm sorry. I don't know . . . I can't remember why I started to distrust you, but I shouldn't 'ave let it snowball.'

'What're you talking about, distrust?' He looked and sounded impatient.

'I thought you were seeing Ruth on the quiet. I was wrong, OK? You're seeing someone else now though, by all accounts. Canadian, is she?'

Pushing his handkerchief into his pocket, he slowly shook his head. 'You're a strange girl, Sandy. Come on, let's get out into the fresh air. I'm gasping for a drink.'

'Well, you are going to Canada for a year, and you're taking a woman with you. Is it so strange to imagine that she might be Canadian?'

'No, but what should you care? You're going to India to live.' He threw his screwdriver into his tool bag.

'No I'm not. I've changed my mind.' She followed him out of the shop. 'I'm gonna have to stay put for a while to sort out my affairs. I'll have to close Nova; let the shop and live above it until I can think of what else to do with my life. Maybe I'll open another Nova somewhere else . . . once my batteries are properly recharged.'

'Sounds all right, but don't call it Nova.' He glanced at her. 'I've always thought it was a daft name. You should call it something like . . . Now. A chain of shops called Now sounds much better than a chain called Nova.'

'Oh really? Well I don't agree.'

'Well, you wouldn't, would you?' She was walking by his side now, perfectly in step. 'I've never known anyone so unswayable.'

'I have. *You*.'

'I s'pose you're gonna insist on us getting married instead of keeping it simple. Living together would save all that expense and fuss.'

'If all you're looking for is a tart, look somewhere else. When I say yes it'll be in front of a registrar.'

At least he'd won on that score. Living in sin. No way. 'Try saying vicar instead and you might have me listening.'

'Vicar.' She smiled behind her straight face. She knew

how to handle Johnnie. A register office? Uh-uh. 'A nice white wedding.'

'No way.'

Another point scored. To wear a bride's dress was the last thing she wanted. Repeating history was out. 'Whatever you want, Johnnie, whatever you want. Who am I to argue?'

Spinning to face her, he grinned from ear to ear. 'So you do love me?'

'I suppose I must.' Still the straight face.

Laughing, he guided her into the off-licence and ordered a bottle of champagne. 'I suppose we'd better ask Freda to share the bubbly.'

'No. This one is for us and us alone. Tomorrow we'll buy another bottle and share that.'

'She'll probably suggest a double wedding.'

Sandy reflected for a moment, and then looked him straight in the face, and they both voiced the same word: 'No!'

Laughing, they left the off-licence. 'I thought I'd lost you, you know,' Johnnie said, taking her hand and locking fingers. 'You had me going for a while; till Freda said you were going to India. Then I knew it was all a game. You'd been testing me.'

'Maybe, maybe.' She squeezed his hand. 'I'm glad that Canada was a game too.'

'I didn't know anything about bloody Canada! But there you go, it worked, didn't it?'

'Yeah . . . it worked.' She slipped her arm around his waist. 'I suppose you'll want me to have babies?'

'I want *us* to have babies. You can't do that on your bloody own, can you? Miss Independent can't pull that off by herself,' he said, entering the shop.

'Where the bloody hell 'ave you been?' Maureen said. 'I've been run off me fucking feet!'

'Settling a few scores.' Sandy checked the time; it was almost five-thirty. 'You can lock up and go now.'

'Thanks. It would 'ave been nice to 'ave gone at five with the rest of the girls!'

'Are you really cross, Maureen, or acting?'

She grinned at Sandy. 'Acting. See you tomorrow. Oh, and I take it that we're out of the depression now?'

'Yes, Maureen, out of the depression and looking forward. Tomorrow I want to talk a few ideas through with you. My wedding outfit.'

Maureen looked thoughtful. 'Only if I'm gonna be maid of honour. Congratulations. It's about time you two sorted yourselves out.' She winked at Johnnie and gave first him a kiss and then Sandy. 'Here, you can lock up now.' She handed her the keys and left.

'If we can't agree over the name of a bloody shop, what's it gonna be like when it comes to naming our kids?' Johnnie said, following Sandy down the basement stairs.

'I quite like old-fashioned names . . . Sarah, Esther, Robin . . .'

'No way! No bloody way. We'll go for names like Karen, Jackie, Gary, Terry, Max, Craig, Jon, Emily, Joanne, Duncan . . .'

On went the banter until they were sitting on the swinging garden lounger, sipping champagne.

'All we have to do now,' Johnnie murmured, kissing her

neck, 'is break the news to your dad. I am nine years older than you and—'

'I know, but then life wouldn't be life, would it, with no battles to fight. Dad'll be easy when you consider the other fight on my hands, if I am to start up again in a year or two.'

'You won't 'ave to start up again, silly.'

'I'm not taking handouts, Johnnie. It's not my style.'

'I'm not offering . . . it's not *my* style. You'll be all right. The Crown won't let you down.'

'The jewels? I'm not sure if I had forgotten them or pushed them out of my mind. I wanted to keep them . . . but now . . . anyway, they won't be worth that much.'

'No? You mean four or five grand won't be enough?' he said, raising an eyebrow.

Choking on her champagne, Sandy began to giggle. 'Don't be daft. A thousand pound if I'm lucky.'

'I've checked. Done a little bit of homework. Asked around. What you've got there is worth a small fortune. And you're entitled to full market value. And . . . I was being conservative with the figures.'

Lying back, Sandy closed her eyes and smiled. 'I'm thinking of our honeymoon. A round-the-world cruise.'

'No way. Devon'll do me.'

'A round-the-world cruise, Johnnie – or nothing. We deserve to have something to remember. We both work hard, so why not?' She opened her eyes and looked into his handsome face. 'Why not, eh? Why not?'

'All right, babe. A world cruise it is.' He moved closer and put his arm around her shoulders. 'Did I ever tell you I love you?' he said, his face questioning. He was a good actor.

'No . . . no, I don't think so. No. I would definitely remember if you had.' But she remembered exactly when he had.

'Oh, right . . . that's OK then. Don't want you to get too big-headed, do we?'

'Oh no,' she said, moving her face close to his until they were nose-to-nose. 'We don't want that.'

Looking into her love-filled hazel eyes, he placed his lips on hers. 'I adore you, Sandy,' he murmured, and kissed her as she had never been kissed before.

With a lovely pink and orange sunset, champagne and a warm, gentle breeze, who could blame Johnnie for whispering . . . 'Can't we have a honeymoon before the wedding?'

The Farrans of Fellmonger Street

FROM THE BESTSELLING KING OF COCKNEY SAGAS

HARRY BOWLING

When widowed Ida Farran runs off with a bus
inspector in 1949, she leaves her five children to
fend for themselves. Preoccupied with the day-to-
day task of earning enough money to keep the
family together, eighteen-year-old Rose battles
bravely on, thankful for the mysterious benefactor
who pays the rent on their flat in Imperial Buildings
on Fellmonger Street, a little backwater off the
Tower Bridge Road.

Life isn't easy but between them Rose and her
younger brother Don just about manage to make
ends meet – though the welfare would soon put the
three young ones into foster homes if they believed
Rose couldn't cope. Recently, however, Don has
become rather too friendly with the Morgan boys.
Everyone knows the small-time Bermondsey
villains are a bad lot and Rose is desperately
worried Don might end up in trouble. But even this
concern pales into insignificance when Rose finds
herself pregnant. Now it'll need a miracle to keep
the Farrans of Fellmonger Street together.

FICTION / SAGA 0 7472 4795 1

More Enchanting Fiction from Headline

CARRIE OF CULVER ROAD

Dee Williams

As a little girl, brought up in an orphanage, Caroline
Parker had always been told that Dept Ford was the
place her disgraced mother had come from. So when
years later her husband dies, leaving her penniless and
with three young children to support, Caroline's first
thought is to head for the place she has envisaged as
home: Dept Ford. But to her horror, she arrives at her
local station to find that Dept Ford is not the country
village she'd imagined, but in the middle of London, a
huge, teeming city the likes of which she's never seen.

Luckily a kindly passer-by takes pity on her and her
weary children and puts them on the tram to a place
where she might find lodgings which, as it turns out, is
in Rotherhithe, not Deptford. And so it is Culver Road
that becomes her true home, where Carrie – as her
neighbours christen her – and her family, helped out by
the irrepressible Flo and her soft-hearted docker
husband Alf, find themselves battling through times
both good and bad: through strikes and street parties,
weddings and funerals, through the first war with
Kaiser Bill, and the tense build-up to the next. And it is
in Culver Road that Carrie meets Jim, the enigmatic
sailor who is to change her life . . .

FICTION / SAGA 0 7472 3607 0

A selection of bestsellers from Headline

LAND OF YOUR POSSESSION	Wendy Robertson	£5.99 ☐
DANGEROUS LADY	Martina Cole	£5.99 ☐
SEASONS OF HER LIFE	Fern Michaels	£5.99 ☐
GINGERBREAD AND GUILT	Peta Tayler	£5.99 ☐
HER HUNGRY HEART	Roberta Latow	£5.99 ☐
GOING TOO FAR	Catherine Alliott	£5.99 ☐
HANNAH OF HOPE STREET	Dee Williams	£4.99 ☐
THE WILLOW GIRLS	Pamela Evans	£5.99 ☐
A LITTLE BADNESS	Josephine Cox	£5.99 ☐
FOR MY DAUGHTERS	Barbara Delinsky	£4.99 ☐
SPLASH	Val Corbett, Joyce Hopkirk, Eve Pollard	£5.99 ☐
THEA'S PARROT	Marcia Willett	£5.99 ☐
QUEENIE	Harry Cole	£5.99 ☐
FARRANS OF FELLMONGER STREET	Harry Bowling	£5.99 ☐

All Headline books are available at your local bookshop or newsagent, or can be ordered direct from the publisher. Just tick the titles you want and fill in the form below. Prices and availability subject to change without notice.

Headline Book Publishing, Cash Sales Department, Bookpoint, 39 Milton Park, Abingdon, OXON, OX14 4TD, UK. If you have a credit card you may order by telephone – 01235 400400.

Please enclose a cheque or postal order made payable to Bookpoint Ltd to the value of the cover price and allow the following for postage and packing:

UK & BFPO: £1.00 for the first book, 50p for the second book and 30p for each additional book ordered up to a maximum charge of £3.00.
OVERSEAS & EIRE: £2.00 for the first book, £1.00 for the second book and 50p for each additional book.

Name ....

Address ....

....

....

If you would prefer to pay by credit card, please complete:
Please debit my Visa/Access/Diner's Card/American Express (delete as applicable) card no:

Signature .... Expiry Date...............